AN ERIN PRINCE THRILLER

Stacy Green

Killing Jane

ISBN: 978-1-944109-27-1

VESUVIAN BOOKS

Published by Vesuvian Books
www.vesuvianbooks.com

Printed in the United States of America

10 9 8 7 6 5 4 3 2 1

Other Books by Stacy Green

Killer Shorts: Murderers Among Us
(Non-Fiction Shorts ebook only)
Martha Beck
The Smiley Face Killer
Jane the Ripper
Mary Bell

Lucy Kendall Series
All Good Deeds
See Them Run
Gone to Die
All Fall Down

Stand Alone Novels
Into the Devil's Underground
Welcome to Las Vegas (short story)

Delta Crossroads Series
Tin God
Skeleton's Key
Ashes and Bone

Delta Detectives Series
Living Victim
Dead Wrong
Night Terror
Last Words
Shots Fired

Table of Contents

Chapter One

I am compelled to do this horrible thing. It is as if I am pulled by some larger force, a demon that will not rest. He whispers despicable things into my aggrieved mind. My heart knows I should not act, but my brain does not listen. I am no more than a slave to the blood I will yet spill tonight.

—JTR
31 August 1888

I drink in the words for the hundredth time. They make me feel out of breath, my lungs on fire like I just finished a morning run. Breathing harder, I bask in the sensation.

Jane Blackwood wrote those words over a century ago, when she roamed the dark London streets and terrorized the poor, stupid residents. The authorities—all men, of course—dismissed the chief inspector's idea that a woman, perhaps a midwife, committed the gruesome crimes. A fragile, innocent woman lurking in the London streets alone? Impossible.

Male chauvinists.

1

But I wish I could thank them. Jane escaped with her letters, and now they're mine.

I tiptoe through the attic. I don't want to screw up the big surprise.

Shoving my fist against my mouth, I imagine Bonnie's shocked face. She'll never see it coming. Not me—and not my beautiful knife.

A noise drifts up from downstairs: the bedroom door opening and closing followed by Bonnie's girly voice.

I slash the knife through the air, watching the steel glint in the afternoon sun.

Time for her punishment.

Chapter Two

Erin Prince needed to grow a pair. And she would, as soon as she yanked her nerves out of her throat. This one would be different—her first case as lead homicide investigator. And not some drug dealer gunned down in the street, but a young woman "torn all to hell," according to the sergeant.

Her fingers dug into the stitching on the steering wheel, and she took a deep breath. Just one more minute.

The blazing lights in the row house made it look like an anemic jack-o-lantern, its creep factor eclipsed only by the strange evening sky. Night had fallen more than an hour ago, but swollen clouds shrouded the harvest moon her nine-year-old daughter had waited all day to see. The resulting weird reddish hue made the sky look fantastically photogenic. A hefty crowd of people surrounded the perimeter and called out questions to beleaguered cops. A uniform who couldn't have been out of the academy more than a few months hid near a cruiser, his skin pale as a vampire's.

Erin checked her reflection in the rearview mirror. She'd actually done her makeup for the evening, choosing a lovely violet eye shadow to bring out her eyes and accentuate her dress. Her summer tan had faded, the foundation making her skin look almost porcelain save for the deep wrinkles between her eyes. The

3

expensive lipstick mother had given her for her last birthday still looked freshly applied. She spoke to her reflection, searching for the right tone of voice for the occasion: brisk, businesslike, controlled. "You clean up nice for being on the downhill slide to forty and never getting enough sleep. But the boy's club is going to love seeing you walk in all dolled up and living up to their stupid nickname."

Princess. Barely original. But tonight she fit the bill.

She sneered at the mirror. "Too bad you look like a wannabe beauty queen when you've got a homicide to handle."

No more time to waste. Erin stepped out of the car, heels scraping against the concrete. Smoke plumes from the nearby factory filled the air, their miasma blanketing the sewer fumes.

Fall wind sliced down the street and over Erin's bare legs. She tightened the belt of her dress coat. Tomorrow morning, she'd throw a change of clothes and a pair of tennis shoes in the trunk. Nothing worse than showing up to a scene looking like the centerpiece at a cocktail party. Not to mention the miserable shoes destined to snap Erin's ankles.

The crowd's mood changed at the click of her approaching heels, eyes and bodies of all shapes and races shifting toward her. Their heads bobbed up and down like hungry fish surfacing to snatch bugs. A girl chattered about being on television.

Erin's cheeks flamed. She yanked the badge out from beneath her coat, striding past the medico-legal death investigator's van.

The scent of backyard barbeque saturated the night air, mixed in with the stench of body odor. One of the younger men held tongs greased with dark red sauce. He absent-mindedly licked one of the ends, his beetle-like eyes taking in everything. Erin fixated on his pink tongue sliding around the tong's loop and back into his mouth. Some of the sauce ran down the handle and onto his fair skin. Their eyes locked. He blinked, buggy eyes opening and closing, and then slowly moved the tongs away.

Damn construction. It had taken over an hour to make the thirty-minute drive from her parent's house in McLean. Guilt slid into the pit of her stomach as she pictured her brother, Brad, sitting on the end of Abby's bed reading her a story as she drifted off to sleep. Storytime—the best part of the day, when all your cares could be pushed aside to enter a new world. She hated to miss those moments as much as she hated not being there to tuck Abby in.

She reached the yellow perimeter tape. The muted chatter beyond the line stopped. No turning back. Not with everyone watching. Hell if she'd give them a reason to spread fresh gossip.

A tall African-American man with graying hair and a slight limp made his way over to her. Detective Sergeant Vincent Clark needed to suck it up and succumb to knee surgery, but he refused to take the time away from the squad.

"Bout time, Prince." His tenor pitched lower than normal, worried and rushed. "We've got a new shooting in Anacostia and half the squad is working the Ted Moore murder."

The Ted Moore murder. Just yesterday she had cursed her luck at not getting the chance to work the case. Moore was the CEO of Endeavor Entertainment, a multimillion- dollar cable network, and the high profile case could make a homicide investigator's career and prove her worth. But Erin hadn't won the luck of the draw.

Bad mojo rippled from the row house, and every official milling in and out of the home looked sick to the gills.

Clark glanced at her attire, and his gray eyebrows raised at the sight of her high heels. "This is a new look for you."

She jammed her hands into the pockets of her Burberry and nodded at her boss. "Dinner with my parents. Jeans and hoodie not allowed." She scanned the crowd pressing against the crime scene tape like excess belly fat fighting for room against a too-small belt. "Who's questioning the locals? This is a busy area. Surely, someone saw something."

Clark jerked his head toward the tittering masses.

Countless sets of eyes stared back, demanding answers and a few juicy stories to share at work the next day.

"Two patrol units responded to the initial call. Most of the block was at a house party down the street. Officer went inside, saw the body, and immediately called for a full investigative unit and the medical guys."

"And you arrived then?"

What the hell was she thinking asking her boss a question like that? If she wanted to be respected as a homicide investigator, she needed to gain confidence. She normally appreciated Clark arriving at the scene with his investigators. He liked to do a walk-through and get the feel of the place, as he called it. He always let his people run the case. So he'd allow her the same privilege, wouldn't he?

Clark stroked his chin, his dark eyes worried. "The patrol officers had the scene secure when I arrived. We set up a command post." He pointed to the end of the cracked sidewalk where a lone officer stood with a clipboard and a pen. "We've set up a twelve-block perimeter, and I've got units looking. But this guy is long gone. She's going into rigor. The uniforms are still talking to people, but you and the new guy will need to follow up ASAP. He's already inside."

Pain darted to her temples; she'd been clenching her jaw again. Now wasn't the time for a TMJ headache. She wanted to start out on equal ground with the new guy, not tag along like a trained puppy. He might have more time on the job, but he'd yet to learn the fine art of navigating the convoluted mesh of D.C. crime and the always-attached political ramifications.

"His background's impressive."

Clark seemed to read her mind.

"But he's not interested in talking about it or showboating. He's just doing his job." Clark rubbed his smooth chin, looking at the crowd again. "Prick who did this probably knew about the party too. The victim's name is Bonnie Archer."

"Who found her?" Erin craned her neck to see whether anyone had been taken to one of the patrol cars.

"A boyfriend. Or as he put it, 'a friend who hangs out.'"

Erin got the gist. "He tell you anything about her?"

"She's a recovering drug addict getting her GED, works as a waitress part-time. I ran her through the system. She's got a couple of misdemeanors for drugs. He says she's been clean for months."

"Where is he?"

"We had a unit take him to the Old School. He's holding up, but we wanted to get him out of here."

Ugh. The nickname ruined the charm of the old building by bringing to mind the smell of sweaty gym socks. The Criminal Investigation Division and other specialized Metro divisions worked out of a converted school on M Street.

"Any sign he's our bad guy?"

"He's shook up," Clark said. "Asked for a victim's advocate. But that don't mean jack." He gazed over her head at the ever growing crowd. "Listen, I'm going to keep a lid on as many details as I can, but the friggin' media has a way of finding shit out. They've got eyes in every nook in the department—and in a few assholes, I think."

"Any sign of sexual assault?"

"Big time."

Bile burned the back of her throat. After the rape, she couldn't get out of sex crimes fast enough. What a bloody hypocrite, pushing women to testify against their attackers when she couldn't report her own. And now her first major homicide involved sexual assault. She deserved as much.

Clark reached into his pocket and then cursed. "Forgot I quit smoking last month."

His eyes bore into Erin's, their gravity igniting an icy wave of apprehension.

"Yeah, you caught a bad one, Prince. We've got to catch this guy quick—because when the details get out, people are going to panic."

Erin kept her expression neutral, but inside she spun like the teacup ride at Disney World. Nothing rattled Vincent Clark. What the hell was she about to walk into?

Before she could ask any more questions, headlights ricocheted off the house. Clark cursed under his breath at the sight of the Channel 4 news van. A bottle redhead slithered out and beelined for Clark.

"Speak of the miserable devils. I'll handle her. You go on inside."

Erin waved at the point officer charged with keeping the wrong people out of the crime scene. The man's hand trembled, his pen clenched in a death grip.

Her hands tightened on the slick yellow tape at the pallor of his ashen face. "You okay, Murray?"

He ran his hand over his cropped gray hair as if something had nested in it and he couldn't pry the bug loose. "I've been doing this job for twenty-five years. What I saw in there ..." His jaw grew taut. "Prepare yourself."

Erin's stomach soured. "Thanks for the warning." She glanced around once more, half searching for an excuse to put off going inside. Then she stepped over the yellow tape and made her way down the crumbling sidewalk.

The patrol cars' red and blue lights flashed off the building's peeling yellow paint, creating a dizzying disco ball effect.

Despite the sorry looking trio of front steps and bowed porch, Bonnie Archer's home seemed well taken care of. The small patch of grass in front of the duplex was neatly maintained, the ancient windows clean, and a pot of mums decorated the ugly stoop.

Bars rested over the lower window, and the deadbolt on the door offered some protection. Had Bonnie let her killer inside?

A lanky man she didn't recognize stepped out of the house. He had to be her new partner. Dressed professionally in a blue button-down dress shirt and black slacks, he had short brown hair cut precisely to code. He leaned against the house, his chest heaving as though he might vomit, and looked utterly awkward.

"Are you Todd Beckett?"

He had the plain face of an everyman, easily forgettable save for a ridiculous moustache. Strands of silver threaded the hair at his temples, but he was so unremarkable he could have been thirty or fifty.

"Erin Prince, I assume?"

She nodded and stretched out her hand. "I'm happy to be working with you." Not the entire truth, but having a partner again had its merits.

"You, as well," Beckett said. "Although I wish our first meeting wasn't under these circumstances." An undercurrent of nerves laced his soft tenor. "This is the worst thing I've ever seen."

Hopefully, he didn't notice the sweat beads sprouting on her forehead. Beckett's impressive file flashed through her head. Two different serial killer cases, each more gruesome than anything she'd experienced. "Worse than the Mary Weston case?"

Beckett's jaw flexed. "I didn't actually work that case. But I'm familiar with the crime scene photos. And yes. Far worse." He took another deep breath, still leaning against the weathered clapboards.

She had hit a nerve, but Erin wouldn't pick at it. Everyone had horror stories. "Uniforms are questioning the crowd and knocking on doors."

Beckett glanced over her head—an easy feat considering he had several inches on her five-foot-five-inch frame. "They likely won't get much. There was a party—"

"I heard." Erin cut him off with more force than she intended. The urge to get the worst over with beat at her chest. Thinking about how bad the scene might be gave the killer more power. A homicide cop couldn't be afraid of her job.

"Normally, we'd have a couple more detectives here, but the Ted Moore case and the gang shooting have us stretched thin. We'll have to follow up with most of these people ourselves." Good grief, why did she have to start babbling about manpower? "I don't know how you did it back in Philadelphia, but that's procedure here." Erin hadn't meant to sound condescending, but nerves prevailed over manners.

"Of course. I wanted to get initial impressions from everyone. Cases like this…" He shook his head. "I didn't want to wait. I hope that's not a problem."

His patient tone made it impossible for Erin to make it an issue.

A fresh wave of embarrassment flushed her cheeks. "Just wanted to clarify our usual procedure."

She cleared her throat, feeling like a student waiting for her teacher's permission to leave the classroom. "I suppose we should get to it. Sergeant Clark is dealing with the press."

She reached into a box sitting next to the pot of mums and retrieved a set of booties and a pair of gloves. The blue footwear slipped awkwardly onto her heels, the stilettos threatening to tear the fabric. Erin yanked the heels off, tucked them under her arm, and pulled the booties onto her bare feet. "I usually dress with common sense, but I had dinner with my parents tonight." *Really, Erin? Justifying your attire?*

Between the shoes and her sweating hands, she couldn't get the damned gloves on.

Beckett watched her without comment, and the back of Erin's neck heated. He had years of experience in homicide with bigger cases. Was he judging her already? The Philadelphia police had a reputation for harboring a grudge against anything perceived as a threat against the male status quo. Did he resent her being a woman? Indignation flashed through her, and she glared at him.

He smiled and held up his large hands. "Always clammy. I hate the gloves too."

Her irritation turned to shame. Her brother's words singsonged in her head. *You know what they say about assumptions. It makes an ass out of you not me.* She sat the heels a few feet away from the door, folding her coat over them.

Beckett disappeared into the narrow doorway as though he'd gone inside one of those creepy funhouses at the street carnivals Abby and her uncle loved so much.

A flash of vertigo forced Erin to lean against the doorframe. The house seemed to clench, blowing the foul stench of death in Erin's face. Her muscles tensed, pain shooting down her legs. The fear in Murray's eyes haunted her. *Get it together, Prince.*

"You coming?" Beckett waited a few feet away, watching her.

Erin gathered her composure and marched forward, the paper booties feeling strange against her bare feet. Immediately, the stench of dried blood and death bloomed in her nose and clung to her tongue like a moldy pasta sauce. Additional odors followed: the lingering hint of Chinese takeout, a musky perfume, the faintest tinge of bleach. The tiny entryway had less room than a sardine can. Erin breathed through her nose and found her voice. "Victim is Bonnie Archer, age twenty-six, right?"

"Right." Beckett's eyes focused somewhere over Erin's head. "The guy who's not a boyfriend discovered her about an hour ago. Rigor hasn't fully set in, so the death investigator estimates she's been dead about six hours. Maybe less."

A steep staircase hugged the wall to her right, a living room area to her left. The old floor beneath her paper-clad feet seemed uneven, bits and pieces of it settling over the years. She touched the shared wall, feeling its gritty plaster. "What about the house next door?"

"The responding officer reported no one answered," Todd said. "A neighbor two houses down said the woman works nights."

"Perfect," Erin said. "We'll have to get that confirmed, but it's sounding like my luck."

"Mine too," Todd said. "Add that to the big party, and I get the feeling we're screwed before we get started."

Erin almost smiled, but the cloying scent of blood, sweat, and bodily fluids threatened to dredge up her dinner. She moved into the living area, bracing for the horrible thing Clark and Murray warned her about. But the living room and the combined kitchen and dining area held nothing of interest. Someone had turned on the halogen lamp in the corner, the bulb casting a yellow tone over the home's worn furnishings.

Bonnie Archer appeared to be a tidy person; the crooked coffee table and cheap shelving were devoid of dust. Not a lot of personal touches scattered about, but she liked her tawdry romance novels. Her paperbacks appeared well-read, the spines heavily creased. One of the crime scene guys had already started collecting trace evidence.

"Prince?" A familiar female voice called from the narrow hallway.

Erin turned to see a tall woman wearing protective gear heading toward them. Built like a runway model with striking, exotic eyes, Marie Valari had been one of the first civilians to enter the Forensic Science Division at Metro P.D. Shortly after starting with the force, Erin watched the normally patient Marie skewer someone who made the mistake of assuming her excess of beauty also meant a lack of brains.

Marie pulled off her mask, breathing as if she'd been sprinting. "Jesus Christ, Erin. I had to walk away for a minute." Her olive skin had turned the color of flaxen melting wax. "Dan Mitchell's upstairs doing his thing. You should go ahead. Just brace yourself." Marie's voice trembled.

Those words yet again. Tension lodged in Erin's shoulders. Her fingers numbed. She struggled to maintain some sort of control over the anxiety threatening to cripple her. She had prepared for this moment, studying crime photos and reading the literature on how good cops coped. This wasn't her first dead body. And yet the chill emanating up her spine made her cold and electrified all at once. Erin's reflection in the mirror hanging crookedly in the pockmarked hall left no doubt her nerves shined for all to see. Her skin resembled gray ash, and her strained expression made her look like a Botox victim. What if she couldn't handle the horrific thing that rattled everyone else?

"Tell me our killer left us something we can use to find him. Name and address, preferably." Bad humor made working on a crime scene bearable, but her attempt at a joke came out crooked and pathetic.

Marie's gaze jerked to meet Erin's. "That's exactly what he did."

Chapter Three

Erin kept her hand against the wall for balance. The narrow wooden steps groaned as though they might collapse at any moment. The trio's footsteps clunked against the wood, each individual's pace different and yet still dragging in a slow march toward the inevitable. She spoke to break the pressure mounting in her skull. "This place is awfully big for a single girl working a part-time job and going to school. I don't know how Bonnie could afford to live alone."

The District—especially an emerging area like Columbia Heights—was expensive. Families struggled to afford a condo, let alone a house. Most single people, especially those without a full time job, needed a second or even a third source of income.

"Well, I'm new in town, but this area's not exactly high-end," Beckett said. "How much does rent cost?"

"High-end doesn't matter," Erin said. "I'd bet a place like this is at least $1800 a month."

Beckett whistled. "That's a lot, especially if she's just working part-time. Maybe her parents are helping out."

"That's why I live in Arlington, and I have a renter." She could always dig into her trust fund for a place closer to work, but she didn't want to live off her trust when she worked so hard to escape the family notoriety.

Upstairs, the smell of death intensified, trapped in the confines of the hallway. A yellow evidence placard sat to the side next to several large droplets of blood.

"So our killer missed something in his cleanup," she said. "If we're lucky, he cut himself, and he'll be in the system."

"That's not his blood." Marie looked at the ceiling as something dripped onto the floor.

"Holy shit." A metallic taste coated her mouth, and her lungs squashed inside her ribs. How much blood did a person need to lose for it to seep through the floorboards?

"Exactly." Marie led them past the second floor bedrooms. "We haven't found much downstairs or on this floor. Everything's up here." She took a deep breath and then disappeared up the attic stairs.

Anxiety burrowed into every synapse of Erin's brain. *Why did it have to be in the damned attic?*

The space narrowed further as though the house squished in on itself the higher they ascended.

Beckett's shoulders brushed the walls as he started up steps, which were barely deep enough to accommodate the average foot. He glanced down at her. "You coming?"

Her armpits heated. Her lightweight, fall dress was suddenly as heavy as a soldier's equipment pack. The man who raped her lived in an attic apartment. A year later and attics still terrified her.

Did Beckett notice the dampness on her forehead or the way her thick, wavy hair had gone limp from the sweat on her scalp? Once again, she wanted to cut and run, but Erin wasn't about to be victimized a second time.

The smell blistered her nostrils. Blood, urine, feces, already decaying flesh.

She climbed the dark stairs, the pressure in her head building by the second.

Evil.

An act borne of pure cruelty occurred in the attic and left behind a malicious energy that wound its way into every cell in Erin's body. The strange cone of light peering through the railing surrounding the attic's landing only heightened the sense of malice.

The light didn't come from the crime scene lights—their blue glow illuminated everything else, a garish gloom fit for a horror movie. She reached the top, dizzy with morbid anticipation. Everything came into hyper-focus.

First, the light source: a studio light typically used for photography had been knocked over, one of its muslin panels ripped. Its stream cast much of the attic in harsh shadows. The low-hanging beams seemed to float above them. Ghostly piles of discarded junk lurked in the corners.

Then the body.

Bile thickened in Erin's throat. The ghastly image imprinted on her consciousness. Some naïve part of her insisted it was a mannequin used for target practice.

Bonnie Archer lay in the middle of the attic surrounded by a river of blood cascading into the shadowy corner. Arms and legs stretched out in an X-pattern, her youthful, soft skin appeared waxen and almost lavender under the harsh glare of the Klieg lights. Blood loss had turned her hands and feet blue.

Erin catalogued each visible injury. Deep gouges on her breasts, the nipples sliced through the middle. Slashes on her snow-white arms and legs. A seven-inch kitchen cleaver protruding from her vagina.

She turned away, sucking in air and praying for composure. How could one human being inflict so much pain on another?

Erin's chest ached with the need to breathe deeply, but the combination of all things death and the musty stench of the attic wouldn't allow it.

"We wanted you to see her like this before we moved her." Dan Mitchell, lead medico-legal death investigator for the Office of the Chief Medical Examiner, looked mournfully at Erin.

His skeptical eyes and sagging cheeks always reminded her of Droopy the cartoon dog, and his perpetual need to shave didn't help the situation.

"All the necessary pictures have been taken, so as soon as you're done, we'd like to move the arm before rigor makes it impossible."

Erin focused on the mangled corpse. Bonnie Archer had most certainly felt pain. Her suffering was etched into her face—the only part of her relatively untouched. She'd died screaming, mouth stretched open and somehow frozen in place. Wide, terror-filled eyes the color of blue sky now lifeless. Her bloody left arm reached toward the steps; her slender, blue fingers curled and dug into the wood. A phone sat less than an inch way. The bright Klieg lights sitting next to the body added a final macabre touch worthy of the most gruesome horror films.

"How many times was she stabbed?" Erin's voice sounded as though she spoke through a tube. She needed to pull herself together. A female homicide investigator was still a rare gem in the District, and Erin would be damned if she broke down. Not after the way she'd busted her ass to get the position.

And her duty was to the woman lying prone on the attic floor. Bonnie Archer deserved justice.

Mitchell beckoned Erin to come closer. "Stabbed isn't the right word. Ripped is more like it." His gloved finger made a circling motion. "Come around to her right. The worst of the blood ran out of her left side from her carotid artery. Femoral too. But the throat came first."

Beckett stepped aside. "I've already been up close. Go ahead."

She didn't want a closer look. Four feet away seemed like more than enough. So much blood, with only paper booties to protect her feet. Erin imagined the blood soaking through and getting into some cut on her toe she didn't know she had. Why had she worn heels tonight?

Mitchell looked at her expectantly, and she skirted around to stand over Bonnie.

The gashes to her throat had nearly decapitated her. With most of the young woman's blood drained out of her body, the knife wounds gleamed purple-white, the edges of the skin serrated like a bad cut of meat. The coppery stench of dried blood made her still full stomach turn. God help her if she tossed up her mother's catered prime rib. Erin swallowed back her disgust and leaned closer for a better look.

Instead of the killer simply cutting her throat from side to side, he'd jabbed the knife straight into her throat, turning her larynx into shredded meat. Blood stained Bonnie's neck and shoulders—a cordlike, sinewy section of artery barely visible.

Mitchell spoke again. "He slashed her over and over again until he cut the carotid. I don't think he was in a hurry to kill her."

Erin squinted at the ruined flesh and tried not to think about the fact this girl had once been a human being. "Can you tell whether the knife entered from the front or behind?"

Mitchell pointed to the small strings of remaining skin. "Look at the wound pattern. The M.E. will confirm, but I say front. And given her position and the blood spatter on the downed portrait light, I'm guessing the killer used his right hand."

Erin followed his gaze. She hadn't noticed the haphazard dark red splotches on the thin muslin. The weird cone of brightness emitted by the photography light seemed to flow into nowhere, swallowed up by the dark corners of the attic. Erin snapped her arms around her chest and hoped no one noticed her trembling fingers.

Mitchell shined his light left and up onto the low beams, and more red streaks glowed in the dim light. "Pretty clear those are arterial spurt."

Fresh sickness swirled in Erin's stomach. "I hope he did that first, and she died quickly."

"I don't think so." Mitchell eased to his knees, his gloved hands hovering over Bonnie's bloody, naked body as though he was praying. "He cut her from pelvis to breastbone."

The gashes on Bonnie's thin stomach ran deep. Encrusted with drying blood, they resembled the red velvet cake Erin had for dessert.

"The first stab was to the stomach, right above her pelvis. She's a small girl, and it's fairly deep, although not life threatening in itself but enough to incapacitate. There's bruising on her cheek and above her eyebrows. He hit her early on, before she bled out." He pointed to Bonnie's open legs. "Those bruises on her knees are new. Definitely pre-mortem. And you can see lividity on the backs of her heels. We'll see more when we turn her over, but she bled out so much it won't be as significant as it could have been."

Lividity meant the blood pooling to the lowest part of the body. She narrowed her eyes, surveying Bonnie, trying to get a clearer picture, but Mitchell's words didn't quite make sense. Bruises of all colors dotted the upper part of her thighs not covered with blood. Another bruise decorated her thin upper arm.

"She lands on her back, and he starts in? The fighting came before? What about the bruises on her thighs and arm?"

"Those are yellowing around the edges," Mitchell said. "Look at her fingers, the bottom of her feet," Mitchell said. "Defense wounds and scrapes. She fought, but once she fell on her back, that was it."

"So." Beckett's soft voice made Erin jump.

She'd nearly forgotten about him.

"He surprises her up here, or he brings her up here. He hits her, and she fights back. She's stunned, likely in intense pain. He jabs the knife into her gut." He shifted his head to the side, lips pursed, his moustache nearly blocking his nostrils. "She falls to her knees?"

"And then is slammed to the floor." Mitchell cradled the back of Bonnie's head. "Big bump back here, nearly dead center. My guess is after she fell to her knees, he shoved her to the floor." He grimaced.

"And then he takes her clothes off?" Erin, the new girl on the team who'd never picked up a racquet, had fallen completely out of her element.

"Possibly. Or they were getting ready to have sex. She's

21

disrobed, doing half the job for him. She definitely expected the man who found her. Look at her makeup."

Smoky eyes, smeared red lipstick. Bright, straight teeth stained with blood from biting her tongue.

"And we checked the non-boyfriend for blood and trace?"

"I did it myself," Marie spoke again. "No blood on him. Some hairs, but that's normal. We've all got strays."

"But he came to see her. So was the door unlocked, or does he have a key?"

"Unlocked," Beckett supplied, edging closer. "So he told Sergeant Johnson. He went through every room. He wouldn't have gone into the attic, but he saw the blood leaking through the ceiling." He looked at Erin, his eyebrows slashed into a tight line. "And we've just gone over the first cuts. Right, Dan?"

Mitchell took over again. "It took several tries to get deep enough to slice all the way to her breastbone. The knife he used wasn't strong enough to do more than nick it."

"Pre or post-mortem?" Erin prayed for the latter, but Dan's sad eyes told her it wasn't the case.

"Definitely pre." Mitchell gently touched the gashes. "He cut through flesh and muscle, making her bleed profusely. If the arterial spurt happened prior to this cutting, the heart would have stopped, and there would be little to no bleeding from these wounds."

"He cut deep enough to make her bleed," Beckett said, "but not enough to get through the major organs."

"Correct," Mitchell said. "And my guess is that was intentional."

"To make sure she felt it." The blood and gore Erin could

handle. But the idea of any human being suffering something like this, feeling every minute of it …

"Until she passed out from the pain, yes," Mitchell said. "Like I said, severing her carotid is what killed her." He shifted to her lower extremities. "I think he hit the femoral artery next and probably very quickly. Thus the sea of red." He cleared his throat, hand poised over the knife sticking out of Bonnie. "It looks like he thrust this in several times. Pre-mortem, judging by the bloody tissue."

Everything outside seemed frozen in place while Erin's emotions ricocheted and dipped like a roller coaster. She knelt, Beckett hovering near her shoulder, the scent of his mint gum providing a welcome perfume to the smell of drying blood and decaying flesh. She tried not to think about the rancid odor of Bonnie's bowels.

Her hairless vagina was no more than a milky white slab of flesh, repeatedly sliced into like a block of cheese. The knife had been jammed to the hilt, tearing through her insides.

"It's a cleaver, right?" Erin's legs threatened to give out on her. She stood, unable to take the proximity any longer.

Mitchell nodded. "Likely the murder weapon."

A heady silence descended in the crowded attic between those living and the poor girl whose blood cascaded at their feet.

Beckett finally broke it. "Absolute rage. And he came here intending to kill her."

"How do you figure?" Erin asked.

"Look at the area around her." Beckett made a sweeping motion with his long right arm. "Notice what's missing?"

Dan Mitchell clucked in agreement.

Erin searched frantically, knowing the answer probably dangled in front of her. She only saw blood turning the wood into a muddy river.

"No tracks leading from the body," Beckett said softly. "And the killer had to have been covered in blood."

Erin's face flushed. "He had to take his clothes off and go down at least one floor to clean up."

"He likely used the upstairs bathroom," Marie said. "It reeks of bleach. So far no blood anywhere but right here. Not even on the steps." She shuddered. "Except for the leak."

Beckett stuffed his hands into the pockets of his pressed khakis. "He probably brought a trash bag or took one from Bonnie's. Stripped, put his clothes in, and then cleaned."

Erin rubbed her temples. "But there's no sign of breaking and entering. Either she knew him well enough to let him in, or he appeared completely nonthreatening."

"More than likely the former," Todd said. "Rage like this is usually personal."

Erin couldn't stop looking at Bonnie's ripped vagina. She had to compartmentalize, focus on the job at hand, and stop thinking of the body as a tortured woman. But this poor girl, with so much left to live for ... was she given the gift of unconsciousness before the worst of the cutting started, or did Bonnie endure until the near-end?

Erin cleared the clog of emotions in her throat. "There will be too much damage to tell whether he used anything but the knife. Maybe we'll get lucky, and the M.E. will find some bodily fluid."

"There's more." Mitchell's usually confident voice wavered.

Erin's throat dried up at the change. She tried to force spit into her mouth, but she only succeeded in making her throat burn.

Mitchell made eye contact with Marie, who stood on the opposite side in the dark corner Erin hadn't paid any attention to.

Marie turned on another light, illuminating the twin box bed in the corner. A rope was tied around one of the headboard's rails, the flimsy mattress hanging off the right side.

Panic swarmed Erin as she clung to rationality. The attic wasn't the same. It wasn't a living space. He wasn't there, beckoning Erin to sit with him on the loveseat. Yet for a minute, she catapulted to that moment a year ago, her date on top of her, threatening her, while she froze in shock and fear.

No. She wouldn't allow the memory to come back and unnerve her in front of everyone. If she could work with rape victims, she could handle this. "What the hell is this?" The scratchy voice belonged to her. Erin pointed to the metal objects scattered on the floor along with the studio light. Miniature pliers held together by a flimsy chain—nipple clamps. "Were those used on her during the assault?"

"It's possible," Mitchell said. "We haven't found any corresponding marks, but the M.E. might find some once the blood's all washed off.

Erin fought to hide her sweating fear. A silver set of handcuffs lay near Bonnie, along with a couple rolls of twine, a razor-thin black whip, and a dildo so thick Erin internally flinched.

"When was the last time anyone spoke to her?" Erin asked.

"The guy who found her," Beckett said. "Will Merritt. He talked to her earlier in the day. Said she was fine."

"So why is all this stuff up here? I get the killer brings stuff to torture her with, but he didn't exactly haul the bed with him."

Marie pointed to the other corner of the attic. "The studio light can be used for film or photography." She walked past Bonnie, her eyes flickering to the dead woman, to the pile of junk in the opposite corner. "The camera's been taken, but the tripod is still here. We've searched through everything and can't find it or the computer Bonnie used to upload online."

Marie held up an oblong black box. "This is a common wireless video transmitter and receiver. Picked up in any store that sells video equipment or online. You can use a digital camera to record and send video to a computer or whatever the transmitter is hooked up to. My guess is she filmed amateur porn, and someone didn't like it."

"He must be on the recording." Erin stated the obvious. "Maybe the guy didn't know about the recording and lost his shit. Or he finds out she's recorded him and put him on the Internet. That's enough to make someone snap this bad."

"There are two major hosting services allowing users to post their own videos," Beckett said. "They're both in the Netherlands. Although the chances of finding any of Bonnie's videos are about as slim as finding Atlantis. Thousands uploaded per day."

"She could also do a pay-per-view site of her own," Erin supplied. "Either way, both the domains and the financial information are going to bounce overseas unless God grants us a miracle." Which he won't.

She ran into the issue time and time again in sex crimes when trying to track down child pornography. The creeps ran hundreds of sites off servers in little foreign countries with no use—or reason to cooperate.

Marie had gone to kneel next to the bed, carefully sweeping

the messy bedding to be gathered for evidence aside. "Especially if he's keeping his interest in BDSM a secret. That's what all this looks like to me."

"It's certainly possible someone would want this kept a secret—especially if he's a married family man."

"What about the name and address?" Erin remembered Marie's earlier cryptic answer. "You said he left them."

"That's the annoying part. Beckett, I didn't get a chance to show this to you before." Marie angled her light toward the center of the attic, illuminating the beam directly over Bonnie's head.

Erin craned her neck to read. *Whore* had been scratched into the beam. Beneath that, *1888, Buck's Row* gouged in long, pointed, blood-stained letters.

"The killer had more than one knife then." Erin's dry throat longed for water. "The cleaver didn't make those marks."

"1888 brings up hundreds of addresses, so I searched by street name," Marie said. "There's no Buck's Row in the District or any of the surrounding suburbs. No street name, no suburb, no neighborhood slang names. Nothing." She stopped and huffed dramatically, a lock of black hair falling into her eyes. "I've got our forensic examiners searching, but I don't think they'll be able to find anything either."

"I don't think you're looking for a street." Beckett's flat tone sent a strange chill over Erin. He stood a few feet away from the rest of the group, staring up at the carving. His drawn, pale expression appeared far more tortured than it had been minutes ago.

"Then what am I looking for?" Marie's hands went to her hips. "A business name? Because I searched those terms too."

"Buck's Row was a street in an area of London in 1888." Fear ghosted in Beckett's eyes. "In Whitechapel. The city changed the name because of the unwanted attention after the murder of the first prostitute."

The floor suddenly turned liquid as Erin slowly looked down at Bonnie's eviscerated body. Her dry lips cracked as she forced them to move. "1888. Jack the Ripper."

"No way." Marie swallowed hard.

Her wide eyes mirrored the heady panic boiling through Erin.

"He murdered prostitutes in the streets. This can't be a Jack the Ripper copycat," Marie protested.

"Weren't all the victims' intestines taken out? Bonnie's are still intact." Erin never understood the infatuation with Jack the Ripper. She didn't consider him any worse than the sickos running around today. The police just didn't have the technology then to catch him. "And he didn't leave anything sticking in their crotches." The distinctions mattered. Because Erin simply wasn't ready for a case like this.

"He cut out some of the victims' entire abdominal cavities," Beckett said. "As well as their breasts. And he removed more than one uterus. This killer cut Bonnie deep enough he could have been trying to take her organs out. He either didn't have the fortitude or the right knife to get it done. Which means his planning wasn't as thorough as it could have been. That might work in our favor."

Beckett looked at Erin. "But you're right, there are a lot of discrepancies. Bonnie's throat was slashed vertically. As though the killer stood in front of her and hacked away at random. The first canonical victim's neck had a big circle cut into it. The Ripper cut through the tissue, clean to the vertebra."

He shrugged at Erin's stare. "I'm a history buff."

"All right, then." Her voice sounded far more confident than she felt. Clark's describing the case as bad barely touched the surface. More like layer upon layer of soul-sucking fear. What if some freak really did want to become a modern day Jack the Ripper, and Bonnie's murder was just the beginning? "Copycats obsess over minute details. All we've got here is a date and some mutilation. Probably trying to distract us from the real evidence." Her certainty grew as she spoke. "The Ripper innuendo is nothing but a smokescreen. Not to mention gaining media attention. If the reporters outside hear about this, they'll freak out the entire city."

"I agree," Beckett said. "At least for now." He took a long look around, his gaze lingering on the carved words.

Erin didn't like the way his mouth tightened, the cords in his neck straining. She had to keep talking, or she would start thinking about the implications of the name and date. She cleared her throat. "So going with the theory Bonnie knew her killer, are we dealing with a stalker? Someone she thought she could reason with?"

"Whoever did this is beyond reason." Mitchell said what everyone thought, his Droopy eyes so mournful Erin wanted to cry. "I'd like to start getting her ready for transport if you don't mind."

* * *

Erin and Beckett descended down two flights of stairs. Every step away from the attic eased the tension in Erin's lungs. She stood in the cramped entry with Beckett and Sergeant Clark while they gave him the gory details of the attic. He listened without reaction, his eyes on the stairs as though he expected the terrible energy in the house to materialize.

"Shit." He pulled on his coat and yanked up the zipper. "So our boy's got a Ripper fetish he wants us to know about."

"I don't think he's a real copycat," Beckett said. "But the inspiration is bad enough."

Clark glared out of the open door. The crowd seemed to have swelled, but so far, no additional press had showed up. Ted Moore's murder still held court. "Keep the Ripper message tight. Word gets out, Moore's murder will be old news, and we'll be up to our eyeballs in media. That reporter from Channel 4 is bad enough.

"You two need to talk to the boyfriend." Clark turned his back to the door, pitching his voice low. "He's down at the CID waiting for you. Tomorrow morning, I'll get our forensic examiners online and see if they can find any of Bonnie's videos. Maybe if we can get information from her bank and find some deposits from one of the big uploading sites, we'll have somewhere to start. But don't get your hopes up. That will take days, and even then, we don't have enough resources to go through all the content."

Beckett slouched in the low-ceilinged entry. "If you don't mind, I have a suggestion. What about asking NCMEC for help?" He pronounced the name as *nick-meck*, a nickname only privy to those within the organization and the agencies they intimately worked with. "They specialize in finding people, and they have techs who are skilled in searching the dark web."

"Nick-meck searches for missing kids," Sergeant Clark's tone listed toward impatience. "They aren't going to be interested in this."

"My girlfriend is a case manager there," Beckett said. "She'd help us, I'm sure."

Erin ran through the case managers at NCMEC. She'd worked with all of them, and she couldn't see Todd Beckett with any of them. Then again, looks didn't mean anything. Police work 101.

Clark shook his head. "Everything stays in house. I don't want anything other than the basics about this case getting out to the media. The Ripper angle is a reporter's wet dream. You guys head to the CID." He stepped onto the porch and started for the steps. "See if you can get anything from the boyfriend."

Chapter Four

The CID's M Street location meant relatively easy access to the interstate as well as a view of the Capitol building. It also meant the drive from Columbia Heights passed too quickly for Erin to collect her thoughts. Not to mention settle the turmoil the attic dredged up.

Her heart kicked into hyper-drive as the memories flooded back. As hard as she fought against it, the sensation of absolute terror and shock at her attack sometimes struck without warning.

Her handsome date had been a casual acquaintance of a colleague. On their third date, he asked her up to his apartment for a drink.

Sweat broke out over the bridge of her nose despite the cold gust of air cooling her skin. She breathed deeply and fought for control over the memory—his overpowering cologne, her body tearing as he forced his way inside of her.

When her date finished, he'd rolled over and smoked a cigarette while Erin lay in shock. How had this happened to her? Why hadn't she defended herself?

A horn honked somewhere on M Street, snapping her out of it. She pulled a pack of tissues out of her bag, dabbed at the sweat, and made sure her stupid mascara hadn't run.

She chickened out of reporting the rape despite Brad's pleading. But how could she hope to maintain any level of credibility in a world still dominated by men? She was a sex crimes investigator and one of only a few female investigators in the Violent Crimes Bureau. Reporting a rape would make her seem more like a woman and not an equal. Damned if she'd fail.

But the cost of keeping silent ate away at her. She'd jumped at the chance to test for the promotion to homicide, even if she'd be dealing with dead people. Erin hoped getting away from all the reminders of her mistake would allow her to put the past behind her.

The theory worked until tonight.

Shooting a gun was easy, quick, and decisive. But to cut someone up the way Bonnie had been, to make her suffer so horribly ... Erin couldn't understand the type of monster capable of such a thing.

He needed to be locked up before he killed again. A nagging voice in the back of her tumultuous mind worried she wasn't good enough to catch him. But she'd have to find a way. This killer couldn't be allowed to walk the streets. Or breathe the same air as decent society.

Her new partner had beaten her back to the CID just like he'd beaten her to the crime scene. She had no right to feel any hostility toward the guy, but his reputation preceded him and worked to his advantage. He'd walked into the crime scene as a brand new officer, and no one had batted an eye. He'd better not be interviewing the boyfriend, Will Merritt, without her.

Everyone accepted he knew how to do his job. Yet Erin being a rookie homicide investigator and a female meant she needed to prove herself on a daily basis.

Because I do, the voice insisted. How could she expect to find Bonnie's killer without assistance from everyone she could beg? She didn't have the experience. Maybe not the right instincts. Or the ability.

"All in your head," her twin brother, Brad, always told her.

The soundtrack of her life had been narrated by their half-sister, usually telling Erin she wasn't good enough. Telling herself the same thing came naturally as breathing.

Cold fall wind rustled through the well-lit parking lot as Erin headed into the Criminal Investigations Division offices. The late hour muted the usual sounds of the busy city, making the wind seem louder and somehow more ominous. Traffic and chaos comforted her. They were a sign of life and protection. Less chance of the Boogeyman jumping out of the shadows—or Jack the Ripper.

She shivered. This wasn't a copycat killer but a cruel bastard begging for attention. She wouldn't give him the satisfaction of letting his message shake her objective.

"Will Merritt," she muttered as she swiped her identification card. "Please give us something to find this madman."

* * *

When she'd first joined the CID, Erin hoped to be regaled with stories of finding old yearbooks with steamy, silly messages from friends who probably lost touch the moment they accepted their diplomas. Or maybe a ghost story or two, some desperate kid who hanged himself in the bathroom instead of failing his senior year.

But the juiciest story ended up being the school's decade-long vacancy before the city purchased it.

Erin first worked upstairs, stuck in the far corner of the sexual assault unit. Her promotion to investigator meant she had the privilege of sauntering into the first floor homicide unit. Thanks to her miserable heels, instead of sauntering, she limped across the finish line with as much grace as a used up racehorse.

Old coffee stunk up the squad room. Beckett stood near one of the desks rocking on the heels of his large, loafer-clad feet.

Nick Fowler, one of the senior homicide investigators on the squad who still enjoyed working the night shift, grinned. "Hey, Princess. I was just talkin' to your new partner. Sounds like you caught a crazy case."

Erin rolled her eyes at the nickname. Fowler didn't mean anything by it, and he remained one of the few old-school cops who were cool with women as equals. So she tolerated his teasing. "That's putting it lightly. The girl's ripped to shreds."

Fowler opened a bag of chocolates and popped a handful into his mouth. "Just cut up to brutalize her or more specific?" He chewed loudly, his chapped lips smacking together.

Erin had almost ripped Fowler's smacking lips right off him the nights they'd partnered during her training.

"He jammed the murder weapon up her crotch as a final send-off," Erin said. "What's that tell you?

Seasoned Fowler turned the shade of pond scum. "Jesus H. Christ."

"Dan Mitchell thinks he tried to take out some of her organs and wasn't able to get the job done."

"Call me if you need any help." Fowler offered Beckett the bag and then held it out to Erin.

They both shook their heads.

"I'll do what I can to catch this bastard."

"How's the Ted Moore case coming?" She had been jealous to miss out on working the high-profile case, but Fowler deserved it. He was a good cop: no-nonsense and dogged.

"It's looking like gang retribution for the documentary," Fowler said. "Moore had six months of death threats starting the night the thing aired."

Beckett looked between them, mild interest in his eyes. "Fill me in?"

"Big time cable producer," Fowler said. "Endeavor Network. Moore spent a year investigating the gangs of D.C. and then aired a tell-all documentary. Secretary found him the other day with his throat cut and his severed dick in his mouth." Fowler grinned with all the glee of the Cheshire cat. "Our gangs are moving up the brutality scale."

"People do terrible things to one another," Beckett said. "It's an awful world to live in."

"Welcome to Washington, D.C. Metropolitan, Beckett. At least you won't be bored. But after working a high-profile serial killer case, you'd probably welcome a little boredom." Fowler made a show of chewing and smiling, but the savvy cop wanted to twist up the new guy.

Erin enjoyed a brief whiff of satisfaction at someone doing the appropriate hazing.

Beckett's grim smile didn't extend to his eyes. His blazer hung from the chair in the corner, and his yellow dress shirt made his pale skin look slightly sallow. "Nope, I definitely won't be bored."

A chill tore through Erin as images of Bonnie played in the carousel of her mind, and a secret part of her envied Todd Beckett for the experience. The knowledge he must have gained from being anywhere near the high-profile case gave him a unique perspective. Not to mention her superiors' giddy excitement when Beckett requested a transfer.

Fowler grunted and took another handful of candy. "God's honest truth. This city's got enough depravity." Concern overrode his usual cocky grin. "You sure you're ready for this one? It's going to be different than a drug dealer. Every time you think you've hit on the answer, you're just going to peel back another layer of crazy. That kind of shit wears on a person."

She pursed her lips and tried to look unaffected. Fowler never treaded lightly when they rode together, and she respected him for it. "I can handle it."

"I have faith in you," he said. "Cases like these can worm into your head and mess you up. Don't let that happen. Not until you're at least five years on the job." He laughed at his own joke and then glanced up at Beckett, his tone sobering. "You know what I mean though, right?"

Beckett nodded. "I think she'll be fine. Ready to talk to Will Merritt?"

She snatched a chocolate out of Fowler's bag. "Absolutely."

Chapter Five

Erin's stupid heels clicked against the tile, reminding her of the way her sister always sounded when she arrived at their parents'. The clacking of Lisa's expensive, miserable-looking shoes always set Erin's teeth on edge—signaling Lisa would soon be insulting her. She should have worn flats tonight, but Lisa came to dinner too. And as usual, Erin fell victim to the urge to live up to her half-sister's expectations.

"Who's your girlfriend?"

Beckett laughed. "That's a bold question."

Erin turned to face him. "You mentioned she works at NCMEC. I used to be in sex crimes, and I've had several cases with them. I might know her."

"Lucy Kendall."

Erin managed to keep her mouth closed. Lucy Kendall was a knockout with auburn hair, green eyes, and the kind of curvy figure men loved. Beckett wasn't bad looking but still average. The randomness of attraction amazed her. "I worked a case with her. She's very good. Is that what brought you from Philadelphia?"

"I didn't want to work for Metro initially." Beckett said. "After the past couple of years, I wanted something less intense. I kept waiting for something else to open up. But it looked like my

38

only shot at moving out here. So I took it."

"What a ringing endorsement for us." They approached the interview room at the end of the hall.

"Sorry," Beckett said. "I didn't mean it like it sounded. Last year ... the Weston case—"

"Lucy Kendall was involved." Erin cut him off. "I remember reading about it."

Beckett's head jerked up and down. "The media reported mostly bunk, but we didn't want Lucy's name in the press. She planned to take the job at NCMEC and didn't want her ties to the Weston case to affect her new position. So I got stuck with credit for things she did. But keep that between us, all right? I don't care about myself, but I don't want Lucy to have to go through another media storm."

"No problem. I appreciate you trusting me." Erin stopped at the door of Interview Room A, the standard room used for witnesses and families and the only one not resembling the inside of a tomb.

Beckett skimmed his right hand over his mousey hair. "So the boyfriend—or whatever he is—is inside with the victim's advocate. Responding officers saw no sign of blood on him, including his shoes. But we're going to have to ask him to swab his hands for blood residue. After what he saw, he's going to love that."

"Assuming he isn't our killer." During her first weeks in homicide, Fowler pressed upon her that Occam's razor applied to most violent crimes: the most obvious answer was usually the right one, and more often than not, the assailant was someone the victim trusted.

Casual friend Will Merritt certainly fit the list. "He could have killed Bonnie, left to get rid of his clothes, and then came back to call in the scene. Although putting himself anywhere near her is pretty stupid."

"Thankfully, most criminals are stupid," Beckett said. "Let's hope our killer fits that bill instead of the alternative. We go in as his friends, let him think we're just crossing him off the list so we can get to the real killer."

"Do you want to question him first?" Watching Beckett question the witness might give Erin the chance to learn from his mistakes.

"Why don't you take the lead? Sometimes men will open up to a female cop more quickly."

At least Beckett wasn't coming in like the star player trying to save the season. Erin knocked and fresh butterflies attacked. She shouldn't be excited, but selfishness won out. This would be the first time she took lead in a homicide interview.

The victim's advocate answered the door. Heavy wrinkles around her eyes and a pug-like nose matched the air of authority that immediately sparked Erin's memories of every politician's wife who vied for her mother's attention. Big or small, women like this usually ran the show. But working as a victim's advocate had to be akin to picking up dog shit for a living, so Erin put her childhood chip aside.

The advocate glanced behind her. "He's ready to get out of here, as you can imagine." The woman raised her eyebrow and ducked her head, as if to warn Erin her witness was being a pain in the ass.

"Thanks for the heads-up."

The advocate stepped aside to allow Erin and Beckett to enter.

Unlike the other interrogation rooms, an attempt had been made to make this one slightly more comforting: padded chairs with only a few bits of oozing stuffing, blinds covering the windows, and a plant crying for moisture in the corner. A water cooler along with a table of cups and extra tissue boxes hid in the opposite corner.

The man sitting at the interview table jumped to his feet.

Erin quickly assessed him. He had trendy, over styled blond hair and wore perfectly distressed jeans, a shiny pair of Hermès shoes, and a designer casual jacket. Not exactly the standard apparel worn in Columbia Heights. His cologne—a cloying scent that sent Erin's olfactory glands running for cover—dominated the room. His fading summer tan barely gave his stricken face any color.

"Bonnie." His eyes flashed from Erin to Beckett. "Who did that to her?"

"That's what we're trying to find out." Erin kept her tone neutral. "What's your name?"

"Will Merritt." He took Erin's offered hand in a clammy grip and shook it once, decisively. "I knew Bonnie."

Erin motioned for Merritt to sit down. She took her time sitting down across from him, acutely aware of Merritt's nerves and Beckett's imposing figure leaning against the door. "You were her boyfriend?"

"Ah, no." Merritt's face flushed. "We hung out."

"Casual," Erin said. "No strings, right?"

Merritt nodded with the exuberance of a happy puppy. "Right."

"And that's why you came over tonight?"

"Bonnie called earlier today, asked me to come over." Merritt's hands rested on the table. He kept his nails clean and manicured. His fingers still shook. "This morning. Then she called back after lunch. Said to come as early as possible because she needed to talk to someone. I got there late. Traffic." The chair whined as Merritt rocked back and forth. "Maybe if I'd been there earlier …"

"That wouldn't have made a difference," Erin said. "She died a few hours before you arrived. Do you have any idea what she wanted to talk about?"

"No," Merritt said. "It surprised me because Bonnie didn't like to talk about feelings and things."

"She was upset?" Beckett asked.

"I don't remember. I was at the Capitol, so I let it go to voicemail." His chest puffed at the mention of the Capitol, his chin lifting a little higher. "I didn't pay attention to how she sounded, and I deleted it. I shouldn't have deleted it."

"Why were you at the Capitol?" Erin hoped this guy didn't turn out to be a protester. Last thing she needed was a bleeding heart with an agenda.

"My job," Merritt said. "I work for Baker-Allen as a lobbyist."

Her teeth clacked together. Her muscles turned to stone, and she willed herself to relax. "The defense contractor."

"We do more than that," Merritt said. "We provide several different consulting services to numerous clients. We also offer cutting-edge aerospace engineering." The standard company line.

"Your major client being the United States government. You specialize in military technology and equipment. Missile defense, biometrics, cybersecurity. And the list goes on." Erin needed to tread carefully, pick her battles. But she grew up surrounded by people like Will Merritt. People who approached life by way of socioeconomic class, who preached the value of their hard, white-collar work while usually riding the tailored coattails of family privilege.

But Merritt deserved the chance to prove her wrong.

"So you work for Baker-Allen. You're probably a frequent flyer on Capitol Hill. Right?"

Merritt nodded, chest puffing again. His eyes flickered to Beckett as if he wasn't sure why both cops weren't asking questions.

Erin regained his attention. "And Bonnie lived in Columbia Heights, getting her GED and back on her feet, as you said. Back on her feet from what?"

"Drugs." Merritt lost some of his swollen pride. "I told the officer that earlier." Sadness swept over him. "She had a rough life and worked her ass off to get clean."

A fresh pang of empathy hit Erin—for Bonnie, not for this pretty boy. "So is that the reason for the casual relationship? Bonnie wasn't up to your standards?"

Splotches broke out on Merritt's cheekbones, making him look like a teenaged girl with too much rouge. "No! We were at different places in our lives, and Bonnie—man, she had emotional issues." He tapped his chest. "I wasn't looking for someone who needed me to support them in any way. I just wanted to have some fun."

"And Bonnie knew this?" Beckett spoke for the first time, voice soft. A casual observer.

"Absolutely," Will said. "She told me she felt the same way. She didn't have time for a real relationship."

Erin watched his body language for some sign of deceit. He kept his arms open on the table, his large frame still slouched, and no trouble keeping eye contact. But some people came out of the womb as skilled liars. "How did the two of you meet? I can't see her in the Baker-Allen lobby, hanging out around the fountain." She caught her mistake too late, and any hope Merritt would miss it rapidly evaporated.

He cocked his head, narrowing his dark brown eyes. "I thought you looked familiar. You're Calvin Prince's youngest daughter. The cop. You look like your dad."

She refused to give him the upper hand. "Obviously."

Merritt looked at Beckett. "Is this a conflict of interest or something? Since I work for her family?"

To his credit, Beckett didn't hesitate. "Not unless you killed someone at Baker-Allen."

Merritt's eyes popped. "Uh. No."

"Then we're good," Beckett said.

Dead air filled the room. The sticky kind that coats people's skin and makes them crave a shower.

"So, Bonnie." Erin tried to get back on track. "Where did you two meet?"

Merritt shifted in the chair, hands going to his lap. "She waited tables at a restaurant near Capitol Hill. Daniel's."

Erin's father had taken her to lunch at the American steakhouse a few times during college, when he still hoped she'd join the family business, and he loved to wine and dine Republican senators there.

"You're sure she worked at Daniel's?" Erin pressed. "Washington's big boys make a lot of deals at those tables. The owners are careful about who they hire. Bonnie's got a couple of priors. Misdemeanors," she clarified. "But I find it hard to believe the owner would risk his business for wait staff."

"That's where we met." Merritt folded his arms on the table, his gaze listing to the right of Erin's.

Why had Merritt lied about where he met Bonnie? She raised an eyebrow. The light sheen of sweat on his forehead suggested he knew one phone call would confirm his lie, but he'd backed himself into a corner and wasn't ready to give up.

"When was the last time you saw her?" Erin asked. "Prior to today?"

"A couple of weeks ago."

"Had you spoken in the interim?"

"No," Merritt said. "Work kept me busy. She had school and her own job."

Erin wanted to be nice to this guy. She had no reason to think he was anything other than the poor soul who found Bonnie. But everything about him pissed her off. His nice clothes, the smug pride over Baker-Allen, his running his mouth about her family. She'd hoped for at least a few days before Beckett found out the real reason behind her nickname. Not to mention Merritt hadn't met Bonnie at Daniel's. One lie usually meant more lies, and Erin didn't have time for lies.

"Do you know Bonnie's neighborhood very well?" Beckett pushed off the wall and wandered to the opposite side of the room. He touched one of the dying plant leaves, still watching Merritt.

Merritt nodded. "I've been there a few times."

Erin wanted to ask whether it bothered him the girl he slept with lived alone in a questionable area, but she already knew the answer. Will never considered it. Men—and women—like him spent their days putting their own needs first.

"I assume you've been in every part of the house. We need your prints to compare and rule out, including the attic." She couldn't stop the harshness in her voice.

Will's eyes popped. "Am I a suspect?"

"Of course not." The victim's advocate stepped in. She'd melded into the background, only there in case Merritt asked for her or had some kind of breakdown. "They're just going through the standard routine."

Erin played nice. "We need to rule out as many known prints as possible if we're going to identify the killer's. What exactly did you touch in the attic?"

"I didn't go any farther than the top step. I didn't need to." He shuddered against the memory and then banded his arms across his chest. "Don't you need a warrant?"

"Not if you volunteer," Erin said. "Which an innocent person would do in order to not impede the investigation." She let the implication hang.

The advocate's eyes burned into Erin's skin, but she didn't acknowledge the woman's stare. One of the first rules of police work was to consider everyone a suspect until proven otherwise. Especially the casual sex partner who found the body.

"Right, right," Will said. "Whatever you need."

"Good. Because we need to swab your hands for any blood residue."

"Are you kidding me?" His voice pitched high. "I didn't do this."

"We know." Beckett again. Good guy, soft voice. Empathetic.

46

Apparently her role in their partnership was to be the bitch. Wonderful. "It's routine. Can you tell us about Bonnie's friends?"

Merritt glanced at Erin, his ears the color of ripe tomatoes. "We usually hung out at her place. We weren't serious at all," he insisted. "I met her parents. But Bonnie kind of sprung them on me."

"I bet you loved that." Erin said. "So maybe Bonnie wasn't as cool with your embarrassment about her as you thought."

Merritt's fist thudded against the table. "She didn't embarrass me. We had an understanding."

Erin wanted to believe the sadness in his eyes and the desperation in his voice. But something held her back. "So did you guys ever meet at your apartment? Which is in some über hip area like Logan Circle, right?"

Merritt flinched. "The DeSoto. And no. She didn't want to come over."

Beckett messed with his phone. "The reception in here sucks. Where exactly is The DeSoto? Sorry," he said to Merritt. "New guy in town."

"Posh." Erin filled Beckett in. "The DeSoto's on P Street, right in the heart of swank hipster city. There's a Whole Foods across the street, a Starbucks damned near next door, and a fitness center around the corner. What more could a young professional ask for?"

"It's a historic neighborhood near DuPont Circle," Merritt said.

"Northwest of Capitol Hill," Erin clarified. "Yet another gentrified area filling up with young, affluent people and driving out the old-time residents. Right?"

"You should talk," Merritt said. "You come from one of the wealthiest families in the District."

Erin dropped against the chair, folding her arms. "Back to Bonnie. She didn't want to come visit you at The DeSoto? My bet is you didn't want the neighbors to see you slumming."

"Investigator Prince." The advocate's harsh voice only made the tension thicker. "Will isn't on trial."

Erin turned an icy gaze on her. "I'm conducting an interview. My job is to serve Bonnie Archer. Not worry about anyone's feelings. And you're not his attorney." She snapped her head back to the man across the table. Let the woman go to Sergeant Clark.

Beckett watched in his unnerving silence.

Merritt's face turned several shades of red, making the roots of his hair appear almost white. "Hooking up with Bonnie was not slumming." His jaw muscles flexed. His eyes looked wet. "Why are you doing this? I'm the one who found Bonnie." His voice rattled, his head whipping from side to side as if to fend off the evil. "He stuck that thing inside of her! She was dead by then, right? Please tell me she didn't suffer."

"She lived for at least part of the attack. We don't know whether she was conscious." Erin didn't see the point in sugarcoating, and she wanted to see his reaction.

Will Merritt covered his face in an effort to hide his tears.

The advocate patted his shoulder.

"Were you aware Bonnie used the attic to film amateur porn?"

Merritt flinched, once again looking away. "She didn't."

"Surely you saw the bed in the corner. The rope. The toys." Erin's voice sounded sharper than she intended, but the dishonesty glistening in the sweat beading over his forehead fueled her

48

irritation. "Did you make the films with her?"

Merritt's cheeks flushed bright red. His head swiveled from side to side, but he still didn't meet Erin's eyes.

Erin glanced back at Beckett.

His impassive face finally flinched, revealing ... disappointment? Maybe she should not have allowed her personal experiences to cloud her line of questioning, but she'd taken the openings Merritt had given her. No way would she leave this room without some kind of information they could use.

"Look, Will. I grew up with guys like you. I know the drill. We're not supposed to mix with certain people, especially if we have political aspirations. Which you do, am I right?"

Merritt wiped his face and shrugged.

"So a relationship with Bonnie is not good for your career or social trajectory," Erin said. "But you like her, so you keep it secret. Maybe you like her adventurous side, so you agree to make the videos. No judgment there. But then she tricks you into meeting her parents, and you realize she is way more into you than you wanted. You're going to break it off, but Bonnie threatens to use the sex videos against you. You had to take care of her." A weak motive, but Erin needed the guy to tell the truth. He might be able to lead them to their killer.

Merritt jerked up straight, looking desperately at Beckett.

The advocate squawked, but Erin shushed her with the same look she gave her sister when she'd heard enough.

"No! The parents surprised me, especially since they got so excited. But Bonnie just wanted to get them off her back. She had to take bi-weekly drug tests to prove she was clean. She wanted to prove to them she had her life together. She worked really hard at school. Once she explained everything, we were cool again. And we didn't make any movies." Merritt's shock turned to anger. "You said I wasn't a suspect."

"I'm just giving you my theory."

"You're wrong. Bonnie's dead, and I found her. You think I want to have that image in my head?"

"Will, do you need to stop?" The advocate asked. "We can do this tomorrow."

"No, we can't." Erin kept her eyes locked on Merritt's sweating face. "We need to get as much information as possible."

Beckett sat down in between her and Merritt, leaning toward the nervous man. "You cared about Bonnie."

"As a friend, sure." Merritt relaxed some, shifting in the chair until he faced Beckett. Closing himself off to Erin and talking to his buddy Beckett. She ..." Merritt's voice caught. "Bonnie deserved better than this."

Beckett's face remained impassive as he made a note in his crumpled notebook. He leaned toward Merritt, half blocking Erin with his wide shoulders.

She gripped her pen until her fingers ached, but she kept her mouth shut.

"And Bonnie never talked about anyone else she might have been seeing? Since you two were casual?"

"No. She wasn't the type to have a boyfriend on the side."

Beckett nodded, looking as if contemplating some great life secret.

Erin's patience snapped. "Where were you this evening before you discovered Bonnie and called 9-1-1?"

The advocate sighed, but the defeat rang in her voice.

Hopefully, she'd stay quiet unless Merritt asked for her.

"At the office," Merritt said. "Working on a project I'm taking to the Senate next week."

Good for him. Little puppy trying to play with the old dogs. "I suppose Baker-Allen's state-of-the-art security system can confirm that?"

"I'm sure," Merritt snapped back. "As well as the front desk receptionist. I told her goodbye when I left."

Did he really think she didn't know Baker-Allen had multiple exits? Depending on his security access, he could have gone down to the parking garage and left at any time without the guards seeing him. But he should be on the film if he'd told the truth.

"We'll confirm your information, no problem." Buddy Beckett had returned, his hand on Merritt's arm. "Did Bonnie tell you about any problems she had with anyone? Maybe someone hanging around who scared her?"

Merritt's hands went to his head, his fingertips digging into his scalp. His legs bounced up and down. "I told your boss earlier, I don't know of anyone hanging around. But we never got too deep into personal things. You should talk to her cousin Sarah. They were close."

Beckett made another quick note. "You wouldn't happen to have her number?"

Merritt shook his head. "Do you have Bonnie's phone? I'm sure it's in her contacts."

"It's an iPhone," Erin said. "With a lock code. So it's going to take some time for our tech guys to break. Unless you can give us the code?"

"Bonnie never shared that sort of thing." A shadow crossed his tired face, and he reached for a tissue but didn't use it, instead tearing off sections and wadding them into balls.

"Did you buy her the phone?" Erin pressed. She couldn't quite believe Merritt had no idea how Bonnie made her money. "Did she ever ask for help with the rent?"

"No." Merritt's mouth curved into a tight smile. "Bonnie was determined to make it on her own."

"See, that's bugging me." Erin tapped her pen against her lip. "A single girl taking classes and working part-time renting a big house in Columbia Heights. The money doesn't add up—even if she sold amateur porn online. Is there anything you're not telling us? Because I think you're lying." She didn't intend for the words to pop out, but they shot across the table like daggers.

Merritt gnawed his lower lip, the apples of his cheeks pink. "I'm telling you everything. And I'm disgusted you think I'd hide anything from you after what I saw."

"It's my job to ask hard questions," she said. "And my gut tells me you're hiding something."

"No wonder your sister won't allow you to work for the family business. You're pretty damn dense."

Erin's temper flared, her mouth ready to chase after it.

A heavy hand pressed her shoulder, easing her back into her chair.

Her tongue burned from her teeth digging into it. "My sister tells a lot of lies. Work for her long enough, and you'll find out. Then again, you can probably spot your own kind." She leaned across the table, purposely invading his space. "Tell me what really happened. She blackmailed you over the videos. You snapped. Where's the knife?"

"I didn't kill her." Will Merritt stood, shoving his chair back. "And I don't have to sit here and listen to this."

The advocate rose as well, pulling her blouse over her belly. The look on her face told Erin she'd be having words with someone about her.

"You're absolutely right," Beckett said. "My partner's only doing her job. Please sit down, talk to me. I just have a few more questions."

Beckett hadn't exactly thrown her under the bus, but he'd definitely shoved her out the door. She kept silent as Beckett asked more routine questions, getting nothing from Will Merritt. Baker-Allen would make them get a subpoena for the security tapes.

Will took Beckett's card—a generic Metro P.D. card with Beckett's cell scribbled on the back. He hadn't been around long enough to get business cards, and he still made her feel like an ass.

The advocate wrapped a motherly arm around Merritt and led him out of the interview room, grabbing a handful of tissues as she left.

"You can't do that again." Beckett crossed his long arms. Patches of baby fine, dark hair covered the top of his hands. They matched his mustache.

She stalked out of the room, her shoes tapping an uneven beat on the old tile. She couldn't figure out exactly what pissed her off. Had Beckett naturally been playing off her bad cop? Or did he have something to say beyond his chastising look? Had she allowed old habits to come in and make her overly sensitive? He easily caught up with her.

She slowed, trying to gather some composure. "Do what?"

"Get combative with a guy before we have anything to use

against him. You alienated a potentially great witness."

"He's lying," Erin said. "I'll bet you anything he either willingly gave her money, or she blackmailed him. Which would account for her being able to live in a house that size alone. What else is he keeping from us?"

"He may not have known about the porn," Beckett said. "If he went upstairs and found her, chances are her body is all he saw. And we've got no physical evidence he did anything more. He agreed to the residue and fingerprinting. His alibi can be easily verified." He held up his hands, placating and gentle, as he'd been with Merritt. "You're not wrong about his lying. He knows a lot more than he's telling us. But we've got to earn his trust."

"I grew up surrounded by people like him. He's the kind of guy a girl from my social class is supposed to settle down with. I can tell you exactly how far they'll take their assumed privilege."

Erin had rebelled against the norm fairly early, much to the humiliation of her older half-sister. Their father humored Erin's choices, assuming she would eventually settle down with the right sort of man. When the right sort of man turned out to be a kleptomaniac with a juvenile record, her father hit the roof. Erin didn't listen. Her marriage ended up in flames, but she ended up with Abby. That made all the misery worth it.

She exhaled a raw breath. "But you're right. I need to stay objective."

"It's an acquired skill," Beckett said. "I'm sure the fact he works for your family worries you."

"It doesn't worry me," she said. "Only solidifies his type."

Beckett smiled, his eyes wary. "People are never who they seem."

"My point."

"You're making an assumption based on your own experiences. That's a dangerous thing to do in our line of work."

If she kept arguing, Erin would start spewing a bunch of unprofessional, hostile crap. And she didn't want to get into a major spat on their first night as partners, especially when they had a murder to solve. "So you know who I am. Do we have to go through the song and dance about how I earned my job, which has nothing to do with my family?"

Beckett shook his head. "I couldn't care less. Just do your job and have my back."

Erin's phone rang with Sergeant Clark's number. Her eyelids sagged as she put him on speaker.

Clark's urgent voice sent a tremor down Erin's spine. "Get back to the crime scene immediately. Marie found something else."

* * *

Some of the chaos had died down at Bonnie Archer's house. Most of the neighbors had retreated into their homes, although Erin caught a few peering out of their windows. The press had scattered. Their morbid curiosity ended when the detectives and the dead body left the house.

The house smelled far worse. Death imprints into the woodwork, leaving a specific smell behind. The various chemicals used by the technicians didn't help matters. A wicked energy still pervaded the air, pressing against Erin as she climbed the stairs to hell on earth.

The bloodstain on the attic floor resembled a baked river.

Good luck to the landlord on getting the blood completely out of the wood. Marie stood near the dormer window, on the phone. She held up her index finger, and Erin nodded.

She and Beckett stepped into the space, carefully avoiding the crusted area. Between the narrowness of the row house and the low hanging beams, the area was a minefield for a man his size.

Beckett scowled. "This place makes me feel like I'm losing my mind."

"Me too," Erin said. "I don't like confined spaces. But I guess that's partially my fault."

"Why?"

Erin had no idea why she felt compelled to share anything with him. But that's what partners did. And somehow through all the jokes and smack talk, you learned to trust each other. "My parents had a dinner party when my brother Brad and I were about six. Too young to attend, but our older half-sister did. She got to sit next to Nancy Reagan."

Beckett grinned. "Nancy Reagan? Cool. Is she as tiny in person as she looks on T.V.?"

Erin's muscles relaxed. "Yes. And I was so jealous of Lisa, because Nancy was an actress." *And because Nancy seemed so delicate and poised and soft spoken—all the things Erin wasn't and her sister said she should be.* "I didn't care about her being the First Lady. Anyway, my brother—we're fraternal twins if I didn't tell you— and I locked ourselves in the broom closet. We freaked out and got caught. My dad and the president laughed. My mother wasn't impressed."

Erin didn't remember her mother's punishment, but Nancy Reagan's bemused expression tattooed itself onto Erin's memory.

"See, that's a cool story." Beckett stepped onto the attic's threshold.

"Most people think I must have grown up like royalty," Erin said. "The perfect, sheltered life."

"There's no such thing, especially when you're growing up," Beckett said. "It's all varying degrees of shit." His tone deepened on the last word.

Before Erin could respond, he jumped back to the present task. "What exactly are we looking for up here?"

"I'm not sure."

Marie's crew had removed the drape covering the dormer window, but the reflection of the crime scene lights off the old glass only made the blood appear more garish. All of the bedding had been taken into evidence along with the sex paraphernalia.

Erin tried to ignore the sensation of the space closing in on her. "We've got to cast our online net wider. I wish the department had facial recognition software."

"Lucy has access to it," Beckett said. "She might be able to find Bonnie online a whole lot faster than us."

Clark would have their necks. Not exactly the way Erin wanted to start as lead on her first major homicide investigation. "We'd just have a person on a video. We need a location, a way to trace her."

"She can do that too." Beckett looked down at the floor. "Don't take this the wrong way. I realize I'm the new guy in town, but I've been a cop for more than fifteen years. Unless we get something viable quickly, a girl like Bonnie Archer is going to slip into the cold case files."

"Won't happen," Erin said. "But I'm not going against

Sergeant Clark. It's his show."

Marie finished her call. "So after you guys left, we found this over by the bed, wadded up and tossed in the corner." Marie held up a clear, plastic evidence bag containing a wrinkled piece of college-lined notebook paper with neat handwriting.

Erin read the words out loud.

I am compelled to do this horrible thing. It is if I am pulled by some larger force, a demon that will not rest. He whispers despicable things into my aggrieved mind. My heart knows I should not act, but my brain does not listen. I am no more than a slave to the blood I will yet spill tonight.

—JTR
31 August 1888

Erin squinted at the handwriting. The black ink looked generic, and the crisp paper showed no sign of yellowing from age. "This looks like a diary entry. Is this something found during the Ripper investigation?"

Beckett shook his head. "It's definitely not one of the letters he allegedly wrote."

"Since this guy seems to be picking and choosing from Jack's bag of cruelty, it makes sense he'd categorize Bonnie selling porn as a form of prostitution. But what's he playing at? Did he intend for us to find this? He didn't exactly leave it in plain sight like the message on the rafters." Erin glanced up at the beam where the bloody carving seemed to glow in the lousy lighting.

"We photographed it where we found it," Marie said. "But looks like he threw it away and forgot about it."

"I think it's all a game," Beckett said. "He's leaving these breadcrumbs to keep us off balance.

"Even if Will Merritt didn't know about the videos," Erin said, "I'd say finding out his girlfriend's playing prostitute on film would be humiliating and a good motive."

"Why the Ripper reference then?"

"There's more written on the back."

Something in Marie's tone made Erin's pulse stutter and sent butterflies through her system. Erin turned the paper over, and all of the blood in her body drained to her toes.

More words. This time emphatically scrawled. Written over and over again in an embellished flourish.

Abberline was right.
—Jane

Chapter Six

Beckett carefully took the paper and stared at it, his eyes roaming each letter of the signature. "Inspector Abberline was the lead investigator on the Jack the Ripper murders. He considered the possibility the Ripper could be a woman, possibly a midwife. He believed that might explain the Ripper's ability to escape the crime scenes covered in blood. But Abberline never had enough evidence to prove it."

Erin's lips numbed as she spoke. "What if our killer's a woman too?"

His gaze flashed to meet hers. "Because of this? If the killer actually wrote them, then the logical assumption is we're dealing with a Ripper fan who buys into Abberline's theory."

"But then why sign the name Jane?"

"He may not have meant for us to find this," Beckett said. "It's probably his notes and ramblings. Especially since Jill is the name used in the Ripper lore." He shook the evidence bag. "This is like crack to a reporter and keeping a lid on a high-profile murder investigation takes an act of God. It's not a stretch to think our killer is deliberately leaving these crumbs to muddy the case."

Jane the Ripper. The idea refused to leave Erin alone. "You do realize a lot of women are into true crime stories, right? Why couldn't our killer be one of those?"

Beckett's face had gone blank.

"She left us the note to make sure we knew. She practices the message she wanted to leave. Tosses it aside and forgets it. Or the paper falls out of her pocket while she's fighting with Bonnie."

Heat bloomed at the back of Erin's neck and then crept to her ears and cheeks. Self-doubt chiseled away at her confidence. Jumping to wild conclusions in a case like this usually meant disaster. "It's way too out there. Forget I said anything."

"No," Beckett said. "It's not out there. We keep the idea as a possibility and keep investigating. If this killer is a woman, the evidence will lead us there."

Chapter Seven

The demon speaks to me again. He basks in the furor stirred up by the slaying of the first woman and demands another. My stomach recoils at the thought of tearing another's flesh, and yet my mouth salivates at the prospect. What have I become?

—JTR
8 September 1888

This entry is my favorite. Jane is beginning to understand her own needs. Nine days after the first murder and no one in London had any clue who roamed the streets or the beautiful things yet to come. And poor Jane is still afraid to accept the demon, but with time, she learns.

Everything good comes in time.
The truth will be preserved.
My identity will be protected.
The world will be right again.

KILLING JANE

Mina's big, scared eyes always made Charlie feel like he'd been sucked under water. The little girl had been through so much unfairness in her short life. And yeah, maybe life wasn't fair. But little kids weren't supposed to know that. Kids Mina's age should still believe in Santa Claus and the Easter Bunny and their parents. She shouldn't be clinging to a confused teenager for protection.

But Charlie made a promise. He kept his promises.

He shoved his blond hair out of his face. It needed to be cut, but he couldn't spend the money. And he didn't want the argument from the others. They liked his hair long, and since Charlie believed in choosing his battles, he kept his mouth shut and dealt with the hair.

"Charlie." Mina whispered to him from her hiding spot. "Do you think the cops know about us?"

"No." He wasn't certain of anything, but he couldn't tell Mina. She already hung on by a frayed thread.

"But what about Bonnie?"

Charlie couldn't feel sorry for Bonnie—she didn't have the guts to do the right thing. And if she didn't want to tell the truth, then they wouldn't, either. He checked his bag to make sure the laptop and digital camera were still inside. "Stop worrying and help me find a place to hide these."

"But Charlie—"

"I'm not talking about it anymore." He hated losing his patience with the little girl. "Don't I always keep you safe? Don't I hide you from all the bad things?"

"Yes."

"Then you have to trust me, Mina. It's the only way we don't end up like Bonnie."

Mina sniffled. "Poor Bonnie."

"Yeah," Charlie said. "But she should have said something when she figured out the truth."

"You know what's going to happen."

"Hush." Charlie's hissed words cut through the quiet night. He searched in the darkness, hoping he and Mina hadn't been discovered. "You need to forget what we saw, or we'll end up like Bonnie. Is that what you want?"

"No, Charlie."

He settled back against the wall. "All right then. Let's get rid of this stuff and get out of here."

Chapter Eight

"Nice place." Erin met Beckett in front of the Archers' two-story, brick colonial in Forest Hills. Pine trees framed the quintessential family home, providing a nice natural privacy fence. Like every neighborhood except for the wealthy, the houses in Forest Hills sat too close together, every inch of available real estate used up. Growing up, Erin felt sorry for the "regular families," as her sister called them, who didn't have the luxury of sweeping, landscaped yards and large acreages. But those kids had something Erin didn't: a neighborhood to roam and friends across the street and down the block. She deliberately chose exactly that sort of neighborhood for her daughter to grow up in.

Beckett folded his long frame out of a small Toyota Prius and quietly shut his door. He'd donned a black windbreaker as nondescript as him. "Is this an expensive area?"

"Every place in D.C. is expensive compared to the rest of the country," Erin said. "This is average middle class." She hoped she didn't sound as snobby as it felt. She'd grown up in a house at least twice the size of the Archers', and her parents still held court in the mini-palace. "There are quite a few international embassies in the Forest Hills area, so it's a bit unique. Lots of cultural mix but still affordable for the most part." She spoke in low tones. It was after midnight, and every house on the street was dark.

Beckett leaned against the fender of her car. "So your nickname is Princess? Seems kind of obvious. You'd think the squad would come up with something better."

"I'm fine with the nickname, as long they back me up. So far, so good."

"From the way Merritt talked, your father must be a pretty significant political figure. He's a defense contractor?"

"Consulting is the magic word," Erin said. "And Baker-Allen provides that on all levels, but it's only a bonus to the defense contracts. My father plays politics to get what he wants. So did my grandfather. I'm sure there's a myriad of things they've been involved in I don't want to know about."

Beckett nodded. "And you never had any interest in their world?"

"No." Erin started down the quaint cobblestone path. Each stone was individually laid, well-worn from years of use. Dread settled into her shoulders.

They stepped onto the Archers' porch. A wooden swing hung at the far end, and two planters of yellow mums decorated the entrance.

Her legs became wooden and heavy. "How many of these notifications have you done?"

"More than I want to admit." Beckett cocked his head. "You?"

"A few." Truthfully, only one. "I haven't quite perfected the technique."

"I don't think anyone ever does," he said. "But if you want me to tell them, I can handle it."

His placid expression made Erin wonder how he'd perfected

the art of compartmentalizing. "Let's just do it together and be as compassionate as we can."

Beckett nodded. "I like the way you think."

Her stomach rolled with fresh nerves. The other death notification she'd made was to the mother of a gangbanger, and while the mother collapsed in silent tears, the woman wasn't shocked. She'd tried to get her son out of the life for years. But the Archers had witnessed their daughter descend into drugs and then pull herself back out. They must have had high hopes for her future. They certainly weren't expecting a visit like this in the middle of the night.

Erin took a deep breath and rang the doorbell.

An upstairs light flashed on. She breathed through her mouth, focusing on her breath.

The porch light came on. Erin knocked and held up her badge to the tiny peephole. "D.C. Police. We need to speak with Neil and Carmen Archer."

Slowly, the door opened, and a middle-aged man with rumpled pajamas and a balding head peered out. Suspicion filled his small eyes. "What's this about?"

Erin hoped the pity didn't show too strongly on her face. Surely the man had an inkling. He must be wondering about his only daughter living in a rough area. But his internal voice no doubt insisted this had to be something else, because this wasn't happening to them.

"Neil?" A sleepy sounding woman called from somewhere inside the house. "Why are the police here? Is it about Bonnie?"

Erin's heart dropped into her stomach. She refused to break; these people needed her to be strong. "I'm afraid so."

Neil Archer's sleepy face paled. "Is she in trouble? What's happened?"

"Mr. Archer." Beckett's smooth voice soothed Erin's nerves. "May we come in and speak to you and your wife?"

"Oh my God." Carmen Archer appeared beside her husband. Silver decorated the temples of her dark hair, mussed from sleep. The wrinkles between her eyes deepened. "Bonnie's dead, isn't she? That's the only reason you would be here at this time of night."

Putting the truth off another second felt cruel. "I'm so sorry," Erin said. "But Bonnie was murdered in her home tonight."

Carmen Archer clamped her hands over her mouth, her wedding rings glinting in the porch light. Wordlessly, she shook her head back and forth.

"You can't be right," Neil choked out. The smooth skin on his head flushed. His shaking hand rattled the doorknob. "Bonnie's doing good. She's smart. She wouldn't let someone in who would hurt her."

"Her friend Will Merritt found her," Beckett said. "It's Bonnie, and I'm so sorry."

Neil sagged against the doorframe as though his knees had turned liquid.

His wife closed her eyes, tears squeezing out of them, making the mascara she'd left on smear. Finally, she took a deep breath. "Who killed her?"

"We're doing everything we can to answer that question," Erin said. "I know this is a horrible time, but can we come in and ask a few questions?"

Carmen nodded, taking her husband's arm and guiding him out of the doorway. Erin and Beckett followed. The door closed with a click, the finality of the sound making Erin jump.

A tabby cat sitting on the arm of the couch stared at Erin with judgmental yellow eyes. "First, is there anyone we can call for you?"

Carmen shook her head, slightly rocking. She had the look of a woman who'd accepted the truth yet couldn't quite fathom the monumental change in her world. Erin couldn't blame her. A life without her daughter—a life where her daughter had been savagely taken from her—seemed unimaginable. "Where is Bonnie? We'll need to get her to the funeral home and make arrangements."

Erin's heart lurched at the woman's need for some kind of control over the situation.

"She's with the medical examiner." Beckett seemed the picture of compassion and calm. "Her autopsy is tomorrow, and we'll know more then. But the medical examiner will call you about releasing the body. It might be a few days."

"What happened to her?" Neil's raw voice sounded like his throat had been torn open. "Was she raped?"

"We don't know yet," Erin said. "Someone stabbed her." She swallowed, trying to gather her nerve. She didn't want to give them the horrific details. What good could it possibly do? But if the cops delivered this sort of news to her, Erin would demand every detail. "I'm going to be honest because I don't want you to hear this from the media. It was brutal."

Erin clamped her jaws tight as she watched the rest of the color drain from Carmen's face. Let the M.E. decide whether or not to give the specifics.

"Did she suffer?" Neil's broken voice cracked.

"The medical examiner will be able to tell you more," Beckett said, managing to defer the question without sounding dispassionate. "We're aware of her past, but can you tell us about her current life? Was she afraid of anyone? Worried about anything?"

"She took classes," Neil said. "She wanted to be a teacher, but she needed to get her GED first. She was doing great." He kept staring at them as though this should have been enough to keep some madman from murdering his child.

"Where did she attend classes?" Beckett asked.

"The Adult Learning Center in Edgewood," Carmen said. "She also worked part-time in the evenings as a server at a high-end restaurant in DuPont Circle. Daniel's. We've never had the chance to go. I don't like to drive into the area. But Bonnie said the place was black tie, great tips." Carmen reached for a tissue.

Erin kept silent. She'd have the information on Bonnie's employment at Daniel's in the morning, but she guessed Bonnie and Merritt had mutually agreed on the lie.

Erin made her voice as gentle as possible. "I hate to ask, but we have to address Bonnie's drug use. Is there a possibility she had started using again and upset a dealer? What drugs did she use in the past?"

Carmen Archer emphatically shook her head, her soft black hair dancing around her face. "Prescription pills. She had a talent for getting doctors to write her prescriptions, and then when that failed, she went to the streets. But there isn't a chance she was using again. Bonnie had bi-weekly drug tests. That's the only way we agreed to help her get on her feet."

A hint of guilt crept into her voice, and her pleading eyes made Erin feel worse by the minute.

"We knew her living here with us wouldn't help. She has our

support, but she needed—she wanted—to be on her own. And if she couldn't get clean without a babysitter, then she wouldn't stay clean." Carmen's voice broke, the guilt pouring into the crevice. "That's why she lived by herself."

"I think it's very brave of you to help her." Erin reached for the woman's hand, desperate to offer some kind of comfort. "And to stipulate the drug testing. Your support must have worked."

Carmen's cold fingers squeezed back. "It did. She also had to share her class information with us. We weren't going to help if she wasn't attending."

"Where was the drug testing done?" Beckett asked.

"At one of the Howard University Hospital clinics. Bonnie gave them permission to report to us."

"We'll need the contact information," Erin said. "And for you to let them know we have permission to access her records."

Carmen rubbed her cheeks, further smearing her mascara. "Of course. I'll call first thing in the morning."

"Can I ask if you helped her financially in any way?" Beckett said. "This is an expensive area for a single person to live on their own."

A hint of defense crept into Neil's posture. He folded his arms. "Occasional spending money, the first month's rent on the house. Her laptop for school. But she made great tips at Daniel's. She hasn't needed any help for several months."

"It's a high-end place," Carmen echoed the earlier conversation. "Good clientele."

But working part-time wouldn't cover everything. How could her parents not know this? Or had they played ignorant to make life easier? Bonnie's drug tests came back negative, and she went to school. Perhaps Carmen and Neil considered that more than enough.

Erin tried to frame her next question carefully, without giving too much away. But Beckett beat her to it.

"So Bonnie only took GED courses? Nothing recreational like film or photography?"

Carmen nodded. "The Adult Literacy Center has a college prep program as well. She planned on going through it so she could apply to schools. Once she passed the GED." Her small body seemed to shrink into the cushions as she realized someone snuffed out her daughter's dreams.

"What about her friends?" Erin asked.

"She didn't have a lot of friends," Carmen said. "Her old friends still did drugs, so she walked away. She left all of that behind."

"What about her cousin Sarah? Will Merritt said they were close. How do we get in touch with her?"

Carmen flinched as though Erin smacked her. Confusion overtook her grief. "That's not possible."

Neil Archer's face turned stormy. "Bonnie and Sarah haven't spoken since they were little. I don't know why he said that."

"Will found her?" Carmen still held Erin's hand. "He's a nice man. I'm glad he found her and not some stranger. She cared for him."

Erin glanced at Beckett. "How serious were they?"

"Bonnie focused on school. But he treated her really well, and she liked being with him," Carmen said. "I could tell when he came over to meet us. Did he tell you?"

"He did." Erin delicately picked at the scab they'd apparently pulled off. "But he seemed to be under the impression Bonnie and Sarah were close."

"My brother and I had a falling out years ago." Neil Archer's voice sounded like gravel. The grief on his face transformed to simmering anger. "We don't speak to them. We certainly don't hold it against Sarah, but after the argument, the girls didn't spend time together. It's been years since they saw each other."

"I'm just trying to piece together as much of Bonnie's life as possible."

If Bonnie had reconnected with her cousin, she hadn't told her parents. She was in her mid-twenties and probably far wiser than her years. She didn't have to tell them everything about her life. And judging from the hostility seeping through Neil, she wouldn't have told him about her cousin.

"Can you tell me about the falling out?"

He glared at Erin, big hands flexing. "It's a personal matter that happened years ago. There's no need to discuss it. I assure you it had nothing to do with what happened to my daughter."

Erin decided not to push the issue—for now.

"What about the drug use?" Beckett changed the subject. "How long did she use before getting clean?"

"She's been in and out of rehab since she was fifteen," Carmen said. "She was date raped. And she just couldn't handle the trauma."

Erin's insides turned cold. Her breath shortened, and the room suddenly blazed red.

Beckett glanced at her, a question in his eyes.

She ducked her head. *There's no time for this. And it's all in the past.*

Beckett turned back to the Archers. "Is there a possibility someone from her old life turned up and she tried to help them?

"I wouldn't be surprised," Neil Archer said. "Bonnie is— was—the kindest girl. She had so much compassion. She hated seeing anyone in pain, and she wanted to help people. That's why she wanted to be a teacher. She wanted to teach at-risk children. She's a helper." His voice broke again. He covered his face and unsuccessfully tried to mask his sobs.

Carmen released Erin's hand and wrapped her arms around her husband.

Erin bowed her head, and she and Beckett let them cry together. The grief became an entity, taking over the house with the strength of the meanest demon. It lodged in Erin's throat, her glands swelling as she fought off tears of her own. She needed to see her daughter.

"Can you give us names?" Beckett handed Carmen his notebook when she finally caught her breath and pulled away from her husband. "Write down anyone you can think of that Bonnie used to know. And anyone she's mentioned recently associating with. Any new friends at school."

Carmen's knuckles turned white from her tight grip on the pen.

Erin still believed the crime was about rage and passion and something else she had yet to figure out. She looked over Beckett's shoulder when Carmen handed back the notebook. Three names, none of them Jane.

"You're sure this is all of them? Bonnie never mentioned a friend named Jane?" She didn't look at Beckett, but she felt his eyes on her.

"After she finished rehab, Bonnie completely started over," Carmen said. "She kept her circle of people very tight. And she never told me much about the people in her past life. Those are the only names I know."

Beckett tucked the notebook into his pocket. "This is great, thank you."

Erin stood up, unable to sit any longer. The couple's grief made her legs twitch. She wanted to hold Abby, smell her sweet scent. Crawl into bed with her and never let go.

"Did Bonnie have any interest in history, specifically true crime?"

"No," Carmen said. "Why?"

Erin hated to say the words. The couple already knew their daughter's murder had been brutal. But mentioning Jack felt worse than showing them a crime scene photo.

"Bonnie never talked about studying Jack the Ripper, maybe for a school project?" Beckett asked.

Carmen Archer's face twisted into an expression barely resembling a human. "Oh my God. Was she cut up like that?"

"It's just a question." Beckett's mournful voice only made Carmen cry harder.

Neil stared as though he didn't quite believe the news yet.

Their pain made Erin feel helpless. Nothing she had to say would make Neil and Carmen feel any better. She sat her business card on the end table. "Please call me if you think of anything else."

Carmen continued to sob, so Erin directed her question at Neil. "Mr. Archer, did Bonnie have anything valuable other than her television and purse? Did she have jewelry or an expensive camera or anything someone could pawn?"

The man's glazed eyes shifted back to them.

Erin would never forget his stricken face.

"Her laptop. It was a cheap eleven-inch but vital to her. That's about it."

"Can you tell us the brand?" Beckett asked.

"Dell. But she had a Wonder Woman sticker over the logo." He covered his face with his hands, shoulders shaking.

"Thank you," Erin said. "We'll let ourselves out."

"Wait." Carmen Archer staggered to her feet like a drunk needing to find a bed. She went to the long table in the hall and dug around in a drawer. "Bonnie makes fun of me for still getting my pictures printed off. I like the feel of the pictures." She swayed a little and then handed the picture to Erin. "I want you to know what she looked like in life. This was taken a couple of weeks ago."

"Thank you." The picture fractured Erin's heart. Bonnie had been a beautiful, vibrant girl. Her cornflower eyes danced, her smile genuine. "We'll be in touch."

Chapter Nine

E rin shivered, the coldness unrelated to the crisp fall air. "Jesus."

"Yeah." Beckett fell into step next to her. "I know we're doing our job, but I always feel like a bastard when I talk to the family."

The sound of Carmen Archer's guttural crying reverberated in Erin's head. She doubted the memory would ever fade. "Thanks for being the one to mention the Ripper."

Beckett leaned against the bumper of Erin's car, expression contemplative. "So you've gone from thinking this killer may be a woman to believing her name is actually Jane?"

Erin wished she had an explanation for the acidic worry leeching into her nervous system. "I don't know what I think."

Beckett held up a slender finger. "Our killer likes Jack the Ripper. He's either not interested or not capable of copycatting Jack's crimes. But he carved the message into the rafter to pay homage to his inspiration."

"And then he got sloppy and left part of his research notes," Erin finished. "I'm reading too much into the name."

"Bonnie's killer planned her murder." Beckett's low voice matched the worry churning through Erin. "I have a hard time believing he was sloppy enough to accidentally leave that paper. He expected us to find it. But the question is whether or not he's telling us who he—or she—truly is or if he's leading us in circles."

Erin's pulse throbbed in the back of her skull, the sensation feeling in sync with the firing of her frayed nerves. "I can't get Jane out of my head."

"Don't." Beckett pushed away from the car and stretched. "Keep her as a possibility, because whoever did this has a taste for blood."

His unspoken words hung between them. If she and Beckett couldn't find the killer, another woman would end up as a victim. And another murder meant another message.

Beckett started walking toward his car but abruptly stopped. "What do you know about the BDSM scene around here?"

Erin couldn't resist. "You and Lucy looking to join?"

"Not quite." The tips of his ears turned pink.

"Honestly, not a lot," she said. "That's one of the few groups you don't see a lot of in sex crimes. Ironic, I guess."

"It's a culture where pushing boundaries is acceptable as long as both partners are willing. Probably a lot healthier attitude toward life and sex than the general population if you think about."

He made a good point, Erin conceded. "There are a few clubs, mostly nightclub types. My brother's not into BDSM, but he's an expert on the D.C. underground," she said, unlocking her car. "I'll see whether he has any idea where to start. But we'll probably have to show Bonnie's picture around. Which may or may not get us anywhere. I'll keep trying Sarah Archer. I hate to deliver bad news over the phone, but we might have to."

A yawn burst from her chest. "I'm calling uncle for tonight.

You know where the medical examiner's office is?"

Beckett nodded. "I'll meet you there in the morning. And maybe we'll get lucky and wake up to hear Bonnie's laptop has been found with our killer's picture front and center."

"Keep dreaming."

Chapter Ten

Erin quietly slipped through the back door of the Arlington house she shared with her brother and her daughter. Both of them slept like the dead—a gene Erin hadn't inherited. She normally tossed and turned, her noisy brain never ready to stop telling her a story.

East of the hub of the District and less than a ten-minute walk from historic Arlington National Cemetery and the Pentagon, Erin's modest home sat on a quarter-acre corner lot in the Aurora Highlands area. Built in the early 1900s, the little gray house resembled a carriage house, its location perfect for a young child. The Highlands felt more secluded than many of the other neighborhoods Erin and Brad looked into, almost like a little town hiding in a metropolitan city. Their sister—and their parents—didn't understand their desire to live within their own financial means rather than sucking off the trust funds. Erin gave up trying to explain the desire to be self-sufficient a long time ago. Living like a commoner—as her sister so eloquently called everyone who wasn't from a wealthy, politically connected family—made Erin happier than she'd ever been.

She moved silently through the cozy house. The heavenly aroma of Brad's homemade pasta sauce lingered. Erin breathed deeply and then whispered a curse when her stomach growled. She tiptoed up the stairs, careful to avoid the squeaky spots. Abby had the little bedroom to the far left. Anyone who broke into the house would have to encounter her and Brad before getting to her daughter.

As usual, Abby's covers rested in a ball around her long legs. A multitude of stuffed animals took up half the bed, the book she must have fallen asleep reading spread out over her small chest. Four American Girl dolls lay on the floor in various stages of undress, all watching Erin with their lifeless eyes. She shuddered and started for her daughter, longing to put her arms around her. But Abby sighed in her sleep, rolling over and knocking the book onto the floor.

Sudden tears broiled in Erin's eyes. She loved this little miracle more than she could articulate. What if something happened to her? What if someday, Erin became the broken parent clinging to a police officer after they told her Abby was dead?

She rubbed the tears away in a desperate effort to banish the idea, leaning down to gently kiss her daughter's temple, breathing in the scent of the vanilla cookie bath soap she loved. Erin picked up the book and set it on the nightstand and then quietly crept back downstairs to poach some of the leftover pasta.

There'd better be leftovers.

She settled down at the kitchen table with her pasta and her laptop and phone. Department-issued phones meant investigators could use them to take crime scene pictures, but the quality sucked. Dissecting the photos would likely have to wait until tomorrow when Maria emailed copies.

Erin bit into a spicy tomato, shamelessly moaning at its

goodness. She tried to focus on the meal, but her thoughts raced ahead to the morning and to Bonnie Archer's autopsy.

Erin had only attended one other postmortem. The victim died of a single gunshot wound to the chest, so the procedure was straightforward. She had little hope of the medical examiner finding anything useful in the mess of Bonnie's remains.

The floor above her head creaked, followed by the sound of steady footsteps. Erin listened as her brother descended the home's steep staircase and made his way into the kitchen.

Naturally, he turned on the light and blinded her.

"Why are you sitting here in the dark?"

Erin shielded her eyes. "Because it's 3:00 a.m."

Brad ran his fingers through his already wild blond hair. He was the older twin by nine minutes, and the physical similarities ended there. Erin had dark, curly hair she kept shoulder-length, and she walked a fine line between voluptuous and needing to lose a little weight. She might hit five-five with the right pair of shoes. With his blue eyes and toned figure, her twin brother resembled a Ken doll. The boys always liked him better than Erin.

"You look like shit." Brad snagged a penne noodle from her bowl. "How bad was it?"

"Really bad." Her throat suddenly closed. The evil energy from the attic suddenly pulsed through Erin as though some tiny bit had latched onto her during the crime scene investigation. "Brutal."

Brad made a face and put the noodle back in her bowl. "Please tell me you have a suspect."

"We have some leads but, so far, nothing concrete." She pushed the remaining pasta away, suddenly nauseated. "This guy cut her up while she was alive." She couldn't bring herself to tell him about the cleaver.

"Holy hell." He sat down next to her, and Erin leaned against his shoulder.

"Brad, whoever did this is a special kind of monster. This girl suffered, and he stood around and watched. Which means he'll do it again. Beckett and I need to find him before that happens."

"Beckett?"

"My new partner." Erin sat up straight and opened her laptop. She considered a web search for Beckett and the Weston case, but she didn't have the mental energy. And she didn't need her inexperience to shine brighter next to the guy. She quickly logged into Facebook and searched for Bonnie Archer. No profile. Will Merritt's was set to private, same as Sarah Archer's.

Her brother perked up. "What's he like? Is he single?"

"He's fine so far but hard to read. He's definitely competent." She shook her head. "He's taken and straight. And I thought you were seeing someone."

Brad picked at his manicured nails. "He's still not ready to own his sexuality, and I don't know whether I have the time or patience. The guy's thirty-five, and this is the age of gay rights. Own it and forget about it."

"It wasn't so long ago you were afraid to tell Mom and Dad," she reminded him. "So watch out because you sound like a hypocrite."

"Totally different. Dad saw me as a problem to his political connections and his business. Scott's parents are divorced, and he's bi-racial. It's not like they haven't had their share of prejudice. He's just not ready," Brad said. "And I can't change that. It's got to be his decision."

Erin's joints popped as she retrieved the picture of Bonnie from her bag and sat back down next to Brad. Prescription drugs didn't affect the teeth and skin like meth or heroine. And her straight teeth could be attributed to good dental care as a kid. But her bright smile obviously came from whitening products. Not a cheap grooming habit.

"Is that her?" Brad asked. "So pretty."

"Yeah." She prodded him in the ribs. "As for your guy, have some sympathy."

"I do," Brad said. "And don't act like I've got it easy. Dad still doesn't love the idea, and if it weren't for you, we probably wouldn't even be talking."

"Maybe." Erin couldn't believe their father would be so cold. When Brad came out as a young adult, Calvin Prince had been shocked and then worried about how his mostly Republican clients would take the news. But eventually, Erin and her mother convinced him to accept it, and Erin liked to think her father would have come around on his own.

Of course, their older half-sister patronized Brad, making a show of supporting him while talking out of the other side of her mouth about how it affected her social and political standing. Her two-faced attitude had been the cause of one of the first of many blowouts among the siblings. And Calvin stood up for Lisa, allowing his guilt to override his common sense. She was a selfish narcissist whose main interest in the family revolved around money. But Calvin would never see the truth.

"We notified her parents." Erin closed the laptop, suddenly exhausted again. "I thought getting out of sex crimes would be better, but after tonight, I'm not sure. Their pain was unlike anything I've ever experienced."

He wrapped his arm around her. "You had to get out. Dealing with rape victims ate you up inside."

Because she was a hypocrite. Laughable since she'd accused her brother of the same thing. But she hadn't wanted her family involved. The daughter of Calvin Prince as a rape victim? Her father's reputation and power as a major defense contractor for the United States extended around the world. He counted the last three Republican presidents as personal friends. The local media would have jumped on her story. Her peers who already begrudged her for being a Prince and a woman would have loved the story.

Brad stood up and yawned. "The best thing you can do right now is sleep. You can't kick ass without rest."

She rolled her eyes, but he was right. "How did Abby do? Did she pass out quickly?"

"Oh yeah." He locked the back door. "Grandma and Grandpa's gigantic mansion always wears the poor kid out."

Erin followed him down the hall. "Thanks so much for taking care of her. I'd be screwed without you."

"You need to get screwed. How long has it been?" Brad took the stairs two at a time.

"Oh my God, shut up." She shoved her brother across the second floor landing, dropping her voice to a hiss. "I can take her to school in the morning, but can you pick her up? I have no idea how my day is going to go."

"Sure," Brad said. He worked from home as a web designer. "Keep us posted about dinner. If you're not home, we're going out for pizza."

"Speaking of sex, do you know anyone into BDSM?"

Brad stopped shuffling and stared at her. "Wow. I said you needed to get laid, not spanked."

She rolled her eyes. "We think our victim made amateur BDSM videos and sold them online. Whoever killed her might be connected to the culture. So answer the question."

He yawned again. "The whole scene is very private, even with the new BDSM craze. I'd start with The Black Rose. It's the biggest club. Beyond that, I don't know. I'm not that kinky."

* * *

Erin sank into a deep sleep as soon as she closed her eyes. Bonnie's desecrated body floated through her dreams, illuminated by the gaudy glare of the cheap studio light. Sudden bursts of red splashed against the back of Erin's eyelids as though someone had thrown a bucket of blood into her dreams. Somewhere in the background, a woman screamed. Not a scream of pain, but animalistic and frenzied.

Jane the Ripper.

The dream changed. A cloaked female figure chased Erin, and the wild screaming grew louder. Erin clawed to the surface of her dreams, but fatigue kept her eyes pinched shut—until her cell phone rattled on the nightstand.

Erin flailed in the dusky darkness of her bedroom. A pink slice of dawn glimmered behind her curtains. Red digital numbers showed she hadn't slept two hours.

"Erin Prince." She sounded like a veteran smoker, although she'd never touched a cigarette.

"Is this the Princess?" A little girl's voice, soft and frightened.

Fuzzy-headed, Erin sat up. "Who is this?"

"Is this the Princess?" Demanding now, a petulant kid determined to get her way.

"This is Investigator Erin Prince. Who's this? How did you get this number?" She tried to keep her nerves at bay and focus on the scared child. "What's your name, sweetheart? Do you need help?"

Fast, frightened breathing. "Buck's Row was just the first one."

Ice formed in Erin's veins, turning her entire body frigid. "What's your name?"

The screen flashed, signaling the call ended.

Pain wracked Erin's chest as though she'd been hit by a hammer. Dozens of scenarios raced through her mind, none of them good. But the child's voice overrode them all. She checked the caller ID—blocked number. A blocked number whose owner had Erin's unlisted cell number. A bad feeling settled in the pit of her stomach.

Erin scrolled through her contacts and hit the green circle. Todd Beckett answered as groggily as she expected and listened in silence as Erin told him about the call.

"You're sure this was a child and not someone playing a joke?" He yawned, and a woman's husky voice rumbled in the background.

"Absolutely. I've got a nine-year-old daughter. I know a scared little girl when I hear one. And how did she know about Buck's Row unless she's with the killer? If she—" Erin could barely stomach the next thought. "She had to have witnessed the murder or, at least, the aftermath."

"Call your service provider and see if they can trace it. And make sure your doors are locked." Beckett ended the call.

Erin paced to the window. The sun rose, red-gold in the clear blue sky, making the frost on the brown grass and rooftops sparkle. Was Bonnie's killer watching the sunrise too?

And how long before another woman—or child—was found slaughtered?

Chapter Eleven

Tracking the call proved impossible. Erin confirmed with her service provider the call came from a pre-paid phone with its GPS turned off. She quickly showered and dressed and then tried to force down a bowl of cereal.

Beckett called back, this time more alert. "Lucy said the news mentioned your name, but their initial coverage didn't go into detail. I think someone used their kid to play a sick joke. I'm more concerned with how this person got your personal cell number. Do you give that out to work colleagues?"

"Only you and Clark. I always use my department cell for work. And I've made sure to keep my personal information as buried as possible. Every time my father makes the news, the press tries to find me. I don't have time for them."

"And your brother wouldn't give the number out, right?"

"Absolutely not." Brad had gone off the rails when she told him about the call this morning, going so far as to suggest she get a new phone number immediately. Erin refused. If the child called again, she might be able to help or trace the call.

"Buck's Row," Erin reminded Beckett as she washed out her bowl. "Only someone associated with the scene would know that, and if we had a leak, the press would have run with it."

"Unless they wanted to screw with you," Beckett said. "One of the crime scene people could have talked, maybe told a friend who turns it into a practical joke."

"That little girl wasn't joking. She was terrified, Beckett. She knows what happened. And she's trying to tell me another woman's going to die." Erin's pulse accelerated. If someone tracked down her number, they might find out where she lived, putting Brad and Abby at risk. She had to figure out a way to protect her daughter without scaring the hell out of her.

While Abby thundered around upstairs getting ready, Erin watched the Channel 4 morning news. The perky reporter's previously taped story ran front and center. Footage showed Clark, Erin, and Beckett talking on the steps, the crowd swelling and tittering, Bonnie's body brought out in a black bag and into the medical van.

So far, the worst of the details remained out of the public eye. But with descriptions like "mutilation" and "a sea of blood," Erin had little doubt someone had fed the reporter information. She gave it twenty-four hours before the bloodthirsty vultures reported everything, right down to the cleaver and Jack's message.

Jack or Jane? As Abby loaded what seemed like her entire life into her backpack, Erin familiarized herself with the Ripper's killing spree. Five known victims over the course of two and a half months, although there'd been a large gap between the fourth and fifth kills. Bonnie's murderer hadn't been nearly as vicious as the canonical five, as the Ripper experts called them, but definite similarities existed. Hysteria hampered the case from the start, along with the lack of the technological advances cops today took for granted. A main suspect list over thirty, with hundreds more speculated on over the years.

She clicked on the section titled "Jill the Ripper." The idea of a woman as a suspect surprised Erin. None of the females investigated panned out, however, and most experts believed Jack likely dressed as a woman to avoid attention.

Were the signed passages their killer's way of causing confusion? A modern-day Jack trying to be a Jane and putting his own flavor on the legend?

The Ripper's second known murder occurred nine days after the first. Erin prayed she had time to find the murderer before another woman—or worse, a child—was killed.

"Earth to Mom!" Abby's voice pulled her thoughts back to the present and the school carpool line. "Are you going to be home for dinner tonight?"

"Probably not. I just started a bad case." Guilt crept over Erin. When she worked sex crimes, her schedule had been more reliable.

"The woman who was murdered in Columbia Heights." Racing around doing her morning routine, chattering like a banshee, Abby missed nothing.

Erin nodded. "But I'll try to get home before you go to bed. I'm sorry." Sometimes she worried whether she should have kept swallowing the anxiety for an easier day for Abby. But at what cost? The daily, soul-crushing anxiety didn't exactly help her be a good mother.

Abby smiled, revealing the missing right molar she'd been so proud to lose last week. "I get it. Uncle Brad lets me watch bad TV with him anyway."

Erin pushed anxiety to the back of her mind and planted a kiss on her daughter's cheek before she could escape the car, breathing her in one last time for the day. She never got enough of Abby's scent. When Abby was a baby, Erin held her for hours to inhale the sweet goodness coming from her delicate head.

"Mom!" Abby looked out the window to see whether any of her friends had noticed. Her blue eyes shined with embarrassment. "You're not supposed to do that here."

"Why not? You're still a little girl."

Abby shouldered her backpack and flung the car door open. "I'm almost double digits."

Erin bit back a laugh at her serious expression. "Uncle Brad's picking you up from school. You don't leave with anyone but him. Right?"

"Right. See you!" Abby slammed the door too hard and raced to catch up with two little tow-headed girls whose names Erin couldn't remember.

She navigated the treacherous traffic with her hands tight against the wheel. Parents acted crazy in their morning rush. The medical examiner locked the doors to the autopsy suite during the procedure. Bonnie's started in thirty minutes.

Erin hit the gas.

Chapter Twelve

The surgical mask made Erin's face hot, but she appreciated the thin layer between her nose and the various chemicals in the autopsy suite. Bonnie Archer's body had been refrigerated before the worst of decomposition began, meaning the scent of chemicals overpowered everything else. Still, she appreciated the Mentholatum she'd rubbed beneath her nose when Deputy Medical Examiner Judy Temple unzipped the bag and began her initial examination.

She noted Bonnie Archer's height and weight, snapping photographs and dictating her findings. "The x-rays showed a broken wrist, probably from trying to break her fall. She also had a broken nose, most likely from the assailant's efforts to subdue her."

The woman's monotone voice made Erin want to run out of the room. Everything was cold and sterile, including the last person who would take care of Bonnie Archer. Her practical side accepted the detachment was necessary for the job, but Erin could hardly bear to listen.

In death, with the blood and torn flesh washed away, Bonnie looked more alien than human. Her once porcelain skin had taken on the gray pallor of dead flesh. With her carefully applied makeup removed, her face appeared even more childlike. Her luxurious eyelashes reminded Erin of Abby's.

She fought the urge to reach out and take Bonnie's hand.

"Did Sarah Archer return your calls?" Beckett's low voice drew Erin back to the immediate investigation.

"No," she said. "I left her another message this morning."

Beckett stood tall and motionless, eyes focused on the medical examiner. "If Will Merritt's telling the truth, why hasn't Sarah called? She should be one of the first in line demanding we find out who killed her cousin."

Dr. Temple removed the paper sheet, and Erin gasped. In the harsh light of the suite, Bonnie's nude body revealed the true scope of her suffering. Bruises ran all the way down her knees and shins. Her right wrist bent at a painful angle. A tattoo of angel wings on her hip had a superficial slash through it. The cleaver had been removed and bagged as evidence. Bonnie's vaginal area had been reduced to something resembling raw chicken.

Erin drew a shuddering breath to combat the swell of dizziness. "Maybe Merritt's lying."

"The bruises on her knees are pre-mortem and appear to be fresh." Temple glared over her recorder, thin lips pursed.

Beckett rubbed his temple. "You don't sound convinced."

Erin kept her eyes on Bonnie's face, partially out of respect and partially because she couldn't seem to draw her gaze away. She lowered her voice to a rasping whisper. "It's a dumb thing to lie about. And it makes sense for Bonnie to keep her reconciliation with her cousin from her parents. Whatever happened between the two families, Neil's clearly still pissed off."

"I thought so too. Which brings us back to my original

question. Why isn't Sarah Archer calling you back?"

Erin didn't have the answer, and she didn't like the worry percolating in her head. Did Sarah have something to hide?

"Dan Mitchell believed the first stab was to her stomach," Beckett said to the medical examiner as she brushed past him. "Did she fall after that?"

Temple's gray eyes met his. A renowned medical examiner and a veteran of the 9/11 death investigations, Temple resembled a bulldog in both demeanor and appearance. Fleshy and stout, she had wobbly cheeks and a burgeoning extra chin. She also took no shit off anyone in her autopsy suite. "Since you're new to us, I'll give you one pass, Investigator Beckett. I don't make guesses. And there's no definitive way to say, short of the entire thing being recorded. Mitchell's theory is sound, especially since lividity makes it clear she didn't get off her back once her killer got her into that position. Beyond that is speculation."

Beckett didn't seem fazed by the derisive tone. He nodded and waited for Temple to proceed.

Erin swayed as she watched the doctor inject the needle into Bonnie's right eye. Vitreous fluid was essential to chemical testing in an autopsy, but Erin hated anything to do with eyes.

She refused to do Bonnie the injustice of looking away. She and Beckett stayed silent while the medical examiner and her assistant continued to work.

"A series of bruises on her thighs and upper arms appear to be in various states of healing," Temple said, examining the yellowing blemishes Erin noticed last night.

"How old do you think those are?" Erin asked.

Temple sighed. "Everyone heals at different rates. The bruises on the arms are fading purple, while the upper thighs are clearly yellow, suggesting Bonnie received them at different times. My rough guess is between a few days and a couple of weeks—but that's a guess."

Erin murmured her appreciation and then turned to her partner. "One set of old bruises I could chalk up to an accident or being clumsy, but two? We need to chat with Will Merritt about those."

"He doesn't seem like the type to be abusive," Beckett said. "Of course, those guys are usually the meanest. By the way, I checked with the Archers this morning." Beckett turned to Erin, his soft voice barely audible behind the paper mask. "They thought I was crazy asking if they were sure they didn't have any grandchildren."

He paused then shook his head. "If they think she worked at Daniel's, I've got a feeling there's a lot about Bonnie's life her parents didn't know—including the fact Sarah had come back into it."

"You confirmed with Daniel's already?"

"Not yet, but I will." Restaurant owner and extreme cynic, John Daniel, ran in the same circles as her father. He didn't believe in any sort of second chance—unless it earned him something major in return.

Erin refocused her attention on the autopsy. "Dr. Temple, how long before we get tox results?"

"A couple of weeks."

"Any chance you could rush them?" Erin didn't shrink from Temple's sharp look. "We need to rule out this being drug related."

Temple grunted.

Erin couldn't hope for anything more.

"Did you try Sarah again?" Beckett never took his eyes off the procedure.

"Twice this morning and said I needed to discuss her cousin. She's probably not calling back because they're supposed to be on the down low, but surely I'll hear from her today. Clark released Bonnie's name this morning." If not, she'd have to hunt Sarah down.

The next few minutes passed in silence as Temple and the assistant made the Y-incision and pulled Bonnie's chest apart. Erin gritted her teeth as the doctor's incision tore open Bonnie's already ruptured abdomen.

"The killer nicked her spleen," Temple said. "She would have slowly bled out if he hadn't cut her carotid. His work in the abdominal area was fast and sloppy, and her organs are all still intact. He may not have had the stamina to finish the job, but there's been no serious effort made to remove them. "

"Was she still alive when he made those cuts?" Beckett asked the question they already knew the answer to.

"As I said," Temple's voice sharpened, "she would have bled out from the nicked spleen. But the coloration on the organs demonstrates blood flow. So yes, she was very much alive. I can't tell you if she was conscious, so don't ask."

"Have you narrowed down time of death yet?" Erin asked.

Temple continued to work as she answered, her eyes narrowed until her eyebrows touched. "Mitchell's original time line is correct. I'd say died at least six hours before Mitchell moved her."

Another round of silence, the only noise coming from Temple and her assistant.

"Did you ask your brother about the BDSM scene?" Beckett's whisper didn't faze Temple or her assistant.

"He said to start with The Black Rose. It's the biggest club. But we're facing the same thing we are with the online stuff: too many people to go through."

Beckett murmured his agreement. "We should split up and try to hit as many as we can."

"The cleaver sliced through her cervix," Temple said. "Her uterus is still here. Prince, did you say her boyfriend found her body?"

Erin's pulse accelerated at the interruption. Temple never spoke directly to the police during the autopsy unless she had something important.

"Yes," Erin said. "Why?"

"Because she was pregnant."

Chapter Thirteen

E rin's maternal instincts sent a flash of sorrow through her. She tucked the feeling away and focused on Judi Temple. "How far along?"

"From the size of the fetus, I'd say about ten weeks."

"Then she may not have known about the pregnancy," Erin said. "Especially if her cycle wasn't regular."

Temple waved her fingers at the assistant, who handed her what looked like a flattened Q-tip. "I'll do a buccal swab for fetal DNA, but the lab is backed up."

"Isn't this case pressing enough to rush?" Beckett sounded impatient for the first time.

Temple leveled another heated glare at him. "To you and to this family, of course. But what about those other families who are desperately waiting for results? Who am I to tell them this case is more important than their loved ones?"

"Because this is the type of violent crime that sparks more killing," Beckett fired back. "Rushing the results would be a preventive measure."

Temple shrugged. "I'll put in a request." She jerked her mask-covered face at Erin. "I'll put her name as requesting investigator. It might make the lab move faster."

"Go ahead." Most of the time, the Prince name was a hindrance. But every once in a while, it served a noble purpose.

Beckett leaned toward her. "Remember, Mary Kelly was pregnant."

His low whisper sent fresh fear over Erin.

They watched the rest of the autopsy in silence, the results mostly unsurprising. Temple confirmed the throat wound as the ultimate cause of death and believed the entire assault lasted less than thirty minutes.

Temple seemed to be in better humor once the procedure ended. "I'll tell the lab to rush the fetal DNA if at all possible. If we tell them it could help us stop a spree killing, they might be more inclined to listen."

"Thanks." Beckett left the suite.

Erin followed, desperate to shed her protective gear. She yanked it off and threw it into the bin marked toxic waste. "But Mary Kelly was the last Ripper victim." Erin addressed his earlier comment. "If this person's a fan of Jack's, he's picking and choosing."

Beckett folded his suit up before throwing it away. "Since Merritt works for your father, we shouldn't have any problem getting in to see him, right? If he knew about Bonnie's pregnancy and cared about his reputation as much as you think, he's got motive."

Erin scrubbed her hands with the antiseptic soap. "Definitely. I want to ask him about the girl too."

"We need to prioritize, so while we're waiting for Sergeant Clark to get the warrant, I think we should start contacting the BDSM clubs. We might get a lead on the child there too."

She hated to admit he was right. "It's barely eleven a.m. I doubt many will be open."

"Then we make phone calls. Email Bonnie's picture to them. Describe her, whatever it takes." Beckett held the door open, and they walked into the bright fall morning.

With the sun bright overhead and reflecting off the buildings, Erin's eyes watered. She fished for her sunglasses and noticed the message light blinking on her cell.

"Daniel's owner texted me back," she said, rolling her eyes. "Modern technology eroding the human experience. But we've got Will Merritt in a lie. Bonnie never worked there."

"She lied to her parents too," Beckett reminded her. "So he might have been protecting her."

"Why not help us find her killer?"

"That I don't have the answer to." Beckett donned his coat. "So let's find some BDSM and then go talk to Merritt again. You drive. Traffic here is worse than Philadelphia."

"Blame the tourists," Erin said.

* * *

Only four of the ten known BDSM clubs answered their phones. Erin dutifully emailed the cell phone picture she'd taken from the printed one Carmen gave her, asking whether the owners knew Bonnie. None recognized her, but all of them promised to pass the picture around.

Erin ended a call. "The guy from The Black Rose claims ninety-nine percent of the BDSM porn on the major sites is fake. Put out by studios trying to cash in on its popularity."

"Surprise, surprise," Beckett said. "He give you anything else?"

"He thinks she probably did pay-per-view, like I mentioned last night. Which means we need to go deep into the web to find her, and it's still a long shot. But get this," she turned to face Beckett reclining in her passenger seat. "He ran through a list of the standard BDSM equipment. We didn't see half of it in Bonnie's attic."

"Maybe she couldn't afford it," Beckett said.

"But it's the stuff people who watch that sort of porn expect to see. It's what they're paying for."

Beckett rubbed his temples. "Marie went through the entire house. We've got a list of everything she found." He opened his little notebook and started flipping through. "Handcuffs, rope, a whip, the nipple clamps. Condoms. The knife and gun."

"But no gag? No restraint? Any other BDSM stuff? Or a harness? Or a cock ring? What about any of the really painful stuff like spreaders?" Erin still shuddered at the idea.

"No," Beckett said. "Something's been bugging me about the attic scene. Maybe that's it. I assumed BDSM when I saw the items, but I could be wrong. Maybe she just filmed rough sex. Most people do what's familiar to them." He rubbed his temples. "I'm not making sense."

Erin's heart palpitated, a fine sheen of sweat misting over her lower lip. She turned the heat off and the air conditioner on full blast. "You're making perfect sense."

"What?" Beckett asked.

"You said most people do what's familiar." Erin's throat tasted like she'd inhaled a pound of sawdust. "Bonnie Archer was a victim of sexual assault. She kicked the drug habit, but we don't know whether she really made peace—if there is such a thing—with her attack. Rape porn is one of the web's dirty treasures. What if that's the kind of porn Bonnie filmed? Her healing bruises make a lot more sense."

Dizziness swarmed over her. She didn't want to search through the dark web looking at rape porn. Even if it was fake.

Beckett considered this. "You could be right. I'm no profiler, but the BDSM culture isn't about control or pain in the sense they want to hurt the other person. People enjoy the pain. And the goal isn't to humiliate or degrade. But rape porn?"

Erin's stomach lurched at the words. *Get a grip, Prince. Be cold and analytical.*

His thin upper lip disappeared into his mustache. "I've seen some, and it gets obscene. You're talking an entirely different type of participant."

"Who might lose his shit if he found out he'd gotten Bonnie pregnant?"

"We need to talk to the Archers again. Find out if Bonnie sought any kind of therapy," Beckett said. "If she believed she wasn't good enough, she might have been talked into filming by someone she thought was better than her. Someone who promised to give her a cut and help her get out of her current situation. Someone who had everything she wanted in life."

Erin put the car into gear. "Someone like Will Merritt. Let's head back to the CID and see whether Clark's got the warrant."

Chapter Fourteen

Erin kicked her chair, sending it rolling across the squad room floor and straight into Sergeant Clark's bad knee.

"Goddamn, Prince! Watch it!"

Heat crept through her.

Fowler, who'd been immersed in paperwork, snickered. His riding partner Max Ramirez, a barrel-shaped firecracker of a man, burst out laughing. Ramirez ducked behind his files at Erin's glare.

"I'm sorry," she said. "I can't get that little girl's voice out of my head. She reached out to me, and there's nothing I can do. This sick bastard must have put her up to it. She's in danger."

"I'd like to know how she knew to call you Princess," Beckett said. "It's not that original of a nickname, but it's not known outside of work, right?"

"It's strictly a Metro P.D. thing," Erin said. "I can't stand it. But it's stuck with me since I was on patrol."

"So how'd the little girl know your nickname and personal cell number?"

"Probably from the shitstain uniform who talked to Channel 4," Clark said. "So far the media has only the basics, but an "unnamed source" is quoted as saying the Metro's Princess is taking the lead. My guess is Beckett's right, and the same asshole told the little girl about Buck's Row. As for the cell, you're talking about cops with connections. Even if it's unlisted, it's not that hard for a cop to dig and find it. It's all a prank to get under your skin."

"Channel 4 referred to me as Princess?"

Fowler let a chuckle escape.

Erin wasn't sure whether crawling under a rock or beating the reporter's ass sounded like the better option.

Clark scowled. "We've got bigger issues. Have you heard back from Sarah Archer yet? If Merritt's telling the truth and she and Bonnie were close, we've got to assume Sarah may be at risk."

Erin already had Sarah on her list of people to worry about, for more reasons than one. "We've got two different stories on the cousins reconnecting. Sarah's lack of response might just mean Will Merritt's a liar. I left another message on the way here. Fowler, did you find out that information for me?"

Fowler stopped digging through the teetering mound of scattered notes on his desk. "Neil Archer works for one of the big insurance companies. Carmen's a teacher. Quiet lives, private people, according to their employers. Other than speeding tickets, both are clean."

As Erin expected, but she had to cross her t's and dot her i's. "And Neil's brother?"

"You know how hard it was to find the guy's name?" Fowler asked. "I had to go into the public records and search for birth records. Computers make it easier, but it still sucked. Screens give me a headache."

She made a rolling motion with her hand, signaling for him to get to the point.

"Simon Archer. He also happens to be the executive counsel

for the Republican Governors Association."

Erin threw up her hands and sank onto her desk. "Well, isn't that wonderful? Neil Archer will never tell us what the family fought over."

"Fill me in?" Beckett asked. "What's the Republican Governors Association?"

"It's a national organization," Clark said. "They work to elect Republican governors and help secure resources. Democrats have the same thing."

"Translation," Erin said. "They raise a fuck-ton of money in an effort to elect a Republican governor. And they put a lot into the presidential campaigns. Their legal counsel is probably the mother of all watchdogs. Fowler, you get an address?"

"Yeah. Chevy Chase. Richie-ville, second only to your neck of the woods." He smirked at her.

"I don't live in McLean," she snapped, not in the mood. "I only grew up there." She pushed off the desk, back aching from the awkward position. "No wonder Sarah isn't calling back. She probably has to clear it all with her father first. We'll visit her parents first thing in the morning if we don't hear from Sarah."

"I bet that'll go over well," Beckett said dryly. He made a face at his Styrofoam cup of thick coffee. "Sergeant, did you get the warrants?"

Clark sank into Erin's chair, rubbing his knee.

She'd have to buy him a decent cup of coffee as an apology.

Clark handed her a wad of paperwork. "The warrants for Merritt's DNA and Baker-Allen's security footage. I already sent a uniform to the drug clinic with the warrant. Her phone company emailed the last three months' records. They're in that pile too.

Pretty regular stuff. Calls to her parents, Merritt, her cousin. Her school. So far, looks like she lived as privately as everyone says. But," he pointed a long finger, "she's also got several incoming and outgoing calls to the same unknown number. Another drop phone, of course. Tech guys say they can't trace anything."

Erin's adrenaline rush watered down to a pathetic stream. "So we serve the warrant and get the DNA. Then what?" If Erin's next scene involved the body of a child destroyed like Bonnie Archer, how could she keep working? The kid's death would be on her hands.

"Merritt lied about meeting Bonnie at Daniel's," Beckett reminded him. "After the autopsy, we head to Baker-Allen and hit Merritt with that and the pregnancy. If he's innocent—and I think he is—he'll talk. He's hiding something."

"Go to the Adult Learning Center after you finish at Baker-Allen," Clark said. "Ferret out the administrator, teachers—anyone who knew her at all."

Erin compartmentalized the tasks, regrouping. "What about ViCAP? Did you get a hit?" The FBI's Violent Criminal Apprehension Program compiled information about major violent crimes across the country and was a useful tool in connecting similar crimes. But countless offenders still operated under the program's radar.

"Nothing that matched," Clark said. "Which is good, I guess. Nice to know there isn't someone else in another part of the country doing this shit."

"I'd rather he'd gone somewhere else." Erin checked to see her gun was loaded and slipped it into the holster on her hip. She checked her Taser, making sure it had a full charge and could be easily accessed from the outside pocket of her bag.

The freak had her phone number. Could he get her address?

"How secure is your house?" Clark read her mind. "I still think we're dealing with a prank, but you need to stay alert just in case."

"My father had a security system installed. It's military grade. A housewarming gift. I'm not on social media. But people can still find someone if they want to badly enough."

"Always be suspicious," Fowler said. "What about Abby?"

Erin's heart lurched at hearing her daughter's name, but she refused to consider the implication. "Brad is going to call her school and make it clear she's to be watched at all times and a teacher has to hand her off to one of us and no one else."

"Good," Clark said. "You guys see anything that makes you nervous or you get another call, I'll put a uniform on the house."

"Thank you." Erin put the warrant into her purse and motioned to Beckett. "Okay, Lurch. Let's go talk to Will Merritt. See whether he knows any kids."

"Merritt doesn't strike me as the type to involve a kid. Or to play mind games," Beckett said as Erin drove into McLean. "It's calculating. Devious. He looked wrecked. And why Lurch? I'm not freakishly tall."

"I'm five-five on a good day," Erin said. "To me, you're Lurch. And Merritt could be acting. Trying to throw us off."

Beckett considered it. "Maybe. The killer probably wore gloves. But if Merritt's involved in the porn, his prints should be in the attic."

"Motive," Erin said. "Along with Bonnie being pregnant. Merritt said himself he's not attached." The idea sounded better the more she thought about it. "Maybe she did tell him, and that was the final straw. He has a kid call me to fuck with me because I pissed him off and to send his own special little message." But another idea latched into her tired brain. "Then again, if some woman found out her man got Bonnie pregnant while he filmed with her, she might snap."

"And she's trying to tell us that by the Jane the Ripper passage?"

Erin shrugged. "Maybe a part of her wants credit for her work."

"There's no indication the killer knew about Bonnie's pregnancy," Beckett said. "Her uterus wasn't destroyed like Mary Kelly's. It may be a coincidence. Or a motive for murder. It's too soon to tell. And the kind of killer you're talking about is usually disorganized. There aren't usually signed notes left for the cops. None of this adds up, including the idea the killer is a woman obsessed with Jack being female."

"It doesn't have to add up for someone to become obsessed with it." Erin kept hearing the little girl's voice and interposing Abby's face into the nightmare.

Beckett sighed and stretched his long legs. "But nothing about this case makes sense."

"Murder is supposed to make sense?"

"No, but there are certain types of killers and certain types of kills. At first, I thought Bonnie's was about rage. Passion. Overkill."

"So?" She turned onto Prince Drive and hoped he didn't notice the namesake.

"So that kind of killer doesn't usually taunt. He either feels remorse or justifies it and goes on. He doesn't settle in for the long haul."

Erin parked at the back of the enormous parking lot, unwilling to use the company spot she had clearance for.

"This guy doesn't make sense. He's not the remorseful or justified type of killer. And that scares the hell out of me."

Erin ignored the rash of chills on her arms as they exited the car. She zipped up her coat—a black puffer style much less gaudy than the expensive Burberry from the night before—and they started the long walk across Baker-Allen's parking lot.

Clouds muted the sun completely, making the sky match the pavement and Erin's mood.

Baker-Allen's main office looked like something from the future, all sharp angles and glass. It also boasted adjacent buildings which held various testing areas as well as a fitness center and daycare. Her father was nothing if not cutting edge.

"How many locations are across the country?"

Erin gripped the signed warrant like a talisman. "Just this one. But they have offices in a dozen other countries."

"Do you and your father get along?"

The question took her by surprise, and she nearly tripped over her feet. "Yes. Why would you think we didn't?"

"He's obviously a powerful guy with a multimillion-dollar company. Instead of the family business, you're a cop. Don't get me wrong—I admire that. But since you didn't follow in his footsteps …"

"Billion-dollar company." Erin didn't add the *Washington Business Journal* had recently named her father as one of the most influential people in the District. "I had no interest. My father and I are fine. He's a bit old-school, but he's supported me."

He'd probably find out all about her half-sister before the day ended. Lisa knew everything that went on at Baker-Allen, and Erin had little chance of escaping without having to deal with her.

They walked into the Baker-Allen lobby. Everything about the space represented sleek, controlled technology. Too much steel and digital contraptions for Erin's taste. Some sort of sophisticated light display glowed on the wall instead of simple paint.

She stopped at the administration desk, which was larger than Abby's bedroom. "I need to speak with Will Merritt." With any luck, the lobbyist had gone to Capitol Hill. She'd rather wait outside the sessions to speak with him. The sooner she left Baker-Allen, the better.

"Do you have an appointment?" Margo Kepler stared at Erin with a blank expression.

Despite having worked the desk for more than a decade, Margo hadn't recognized Erin. Or had simply forgotten her. It wouldn't be the first time. Maybe this time it would work in her favor, and Lisa wouldn't know of her arrival.

"We need to speak with him about an ongoing case." She showed her badge, followed by the warrant. "And we need your security footage from yesterday—1:00 p.m. through 10:00 p.m." The judge had played it surprisingly safe with their timeline, and Erin wasn't complaining.

Margo called upstairs and requested Will Merritt to the lobby and then called the head of security to deal with the warrant. Erin could throw out her last name and simply walk in. But then she'd have to deal with Lisa. Only special people had full access to the top-level offices. People who appreciated the business. People who came from her father's first marriage and therefore counted as his real child.

"Before we deal with this guy," Erin turned to look up at Beckett, "how do you want to handle the pregnancy? I'm all for asking him point blank. It's motive."

"Agreed." Beckett nodded, his eyes focused on something behind Erin.

A built man who would have been right at home in an Ultimate Fighting ring glided toward them. The badge on his navy suit read *Head of Security*. "John Booker. How can I help you?"

Erin gave him the warrant and explained what they wanted. "We need the raw footage. Time-stamped."

Booker slowly perused the document. His gray hair shined like gossamer beneath the lobby's bright lights. "Seems everything's in order. Do you want to wait in your father's office while I get it for you, Investigator Prince?"

So much for no one putting it together. "No, we're interviewing Will Merritt."

"I'll make a copy and have it here at the front desk." Booker smiled pleasantly, but Erin hedged. What if he screwed with the footage? She glanced at Beckett, debating on asking whether he'd like to accompany Booker. Instead she asked about Will Merritt's security clearance.

"Low-level," Booker said smoothly. "His card only gets him in the main entrance."

Merritt trudged toward them looking far worse for wear than last night.

Booker excused himself, glancing sideways at Merritt on his way back to the security offices.

Will Merritt's puffy eyes and wrinkled clothes made Erin

wonder whether he'd slept at all. He hadn't shaved, his jaw spotty with wiry peach fuzz.

He pulled on his already loose tie and unbuttoned his tailored suit jacket. "I'm not sure what else I can tell you."

"Hello to you too." Erin said, feeling the receptionist's eyes on them. "Let's go into one of the downstairs conference rooms." She led the way down the east corridor and then waited for Will and Beckett to enter before closing the door.

Merritt pulled out a chair, its feet dragging across the sturdy Berber carpet. He didn't wait for Erin, instead falling into the chair with a dramatic sigh. "I didn't sleep. I keep seeing Bonnie lying there. All that blood."

"Now that some of the initial shock has worn off, I want to confirm you didn't go any farther than the top attic stair, did you?" Erin asked.

Merritt shook his head.

"But we'll find your fingerprints in the house because you've been inside before. Including the bedroom. On say, the headboard."

"I already told you," Merritt's defenses jacked up. "I'm sure you will."

"But you maintain you've never been in the attic?"

"I've never been in the attic." He spoke through gritted teeth. "Are we going to do this all over again?"

Erin sat down across from him. Beckett remained standing as usual. "So you didn't know Bonnie liked to make sex videos?"

Merritt focused on his lap. "She wasn't into that sort of thing."

Erin rested her elbows on the table and clasped her hands. "But she was, because we found evidence of recording equipment in the attic, plus some other fun sex stuff. Someone took the recording device and the videos. Probably her killer."

"So you think Bonnie filmed someone, and he got pissed off? He gutted her for that?" Once again, he directed his question to Beckett, either too irritated or too intimidated to speak directly to Erin.

He didn't strike her as the sexually dominant type. Then again, the man she went out with three times didn't strike her as a rapist, either.

"I think blackmail is a real possibility." Erin leaned across the table, closing in on Merritt's personal space. "There's no way Bonnie could afford the house on her own, waiting tables. I think her parents knew this too. They didn't want to think about it. So she had additional income."

Merritt continued to shake his head, rocking slightly. "I can't help you."

"Were you helping her out financially?" Beckett asked. "You cared for her. There's nothing wrong with someone in your financial position offering to help. But if you did, you need to tell us. Because if her financial records show big deposits in your name, you'll be hearing from us again."

"My financial position?" Merritt laughed. "I'm a second-year lobbyist. I can barely afford a lifestyle, let alone help someone else out." His eyes slid to Erin. "My name isn't Prince."

She smiled. "I can't help you there. And I'm not as tactful as my partner or as patient. Let's just get down to it—I had it right last night, didn't I? You got sick of the blackmail and killed her. Then you felt guilty and called it in."

"Are you serious?" The veins in Merritt's neck bulged. "I

would never ... she didn't film me. Or blackmail me. Bonnie was a nice girl!"

She believed him. But she wasn't leaving without Merritt telling them everything. "Fine, but you're lying about something. Bonnie didn't work at Daniel's. And you knew damn well I'd talk to the owner."

He glared at her with red eyes. He did look as if he hadn't slept. His skin had a grayness usually reserved for someone on his deathbed. Sorrow or guilt?

"We don't think you killed her." Beckett, the friend again. "But Investigator Prince is right. You're hiding something. And you lied about her cousin Sarah. Her parents say the two of them haven't spoken in years." His poker face could have won him millions.

Merritt's mouth formed an *O* and a deep crease formed between his eyes. "They're lying. They talked all the time."

"Why would grieving parents lie about something like that?" Was Merritt aware of the family estrangement? He claimed he and Bonnie didn't share deep thoughts. "Were there family issues?"

"I have no clue." He spread his arms wide across the table. "She talked about Sarah a lot. 'Sarah's so busy with school, Sarah's stressed. I need to call Sarah and check in on her.'"

"Did you know Bonnie was pregnant?" Erin's laser focus on Merritt's reaction sabotaged her attempt to soften her voice.

To his credit, Will Merritt was either innocent or one hell of an actor. The remaining color drained from his face. "I didn't." He stared ahead, not looking at Erin or Beckett. His chest jerked. "How far along?"

"Ten weeks," she said. "We'll need a DNA swab for

115

paternity."

Will Merritt immediately stiffened and straightened his tie. "It's awful, but the baby can't be mine. We used protection every time."

"Condoms break." Erin said. "And frankly, a baby is another motive for murder. I can't see you being too thrilled about knocking up someone like Bonnie."

"Stop talking about her like that," Merritt snapped. "You might think you know me because you come from all of this," he swept his arms around, "but I grew up barely above the poverty line. Both my parents worked two jobs. My uncle died from alcohol. My not being serious with Bonnie had zero to do with where she lived or her past. It had to do with what both of us wanted."

Erin refused to back down. "So you're saying she cheated on you?"

His face heated, but his gaze dropped down. "I told you we weren't exclusive." His lower lip trembled, and wetness brimmed in his eyes.

Will Merritt wasn't the one who didn't want a serious relationship. Erin reached into her bag and retrieved a tissue from the wrinkled packet. "All right, you cared about her. More than you want to admit. Fine. And maybe you think not telling us everything you know is protecting Bonnie's memory, but you're hurting our chances of finding out who did this."

Merritt's throat tightened, the veins in his forehead bulging with the effort not to cry. "I promised her I wouldn't tell anyone. Her parents would be devastated."

"They already are," Erin said. "Not getting closure will only make their lives worse." She glanced at Beckett out of the corner of her eye.

He nodded, and a foolish swell of pride rushed over Erin. Maybe she could do this job after all.

Merritt sagged down in the chair. "Bonnie was a stripper. Her parents don't know. She didn't want them to."

"Did you meet her at a strip club? When?" Beckett asked.

"At Sid's Gentleman's Club. A lot of men from Capitol Hill go there."

"For their nighttime meetings, right?" Erin asked dryly. "What would you call that? A power hard-on?"

Merritt ignored her. "It's strictly dancing. There's no hooking going on. Men paid Bonnie good money to dance. She never drank, never did drugs. She wasn't breaking her probation."

Erin jotted the name down. "Thank you. Did Bonnie tell you about being raped when she was fifteen?"

Merritt's chin dropped to his chest. "Yeah."

"Is that why she made the videos?"

Merritt's head shot up. "I didn't know about any videos at first. And when I found out, I couldn't believe ... I told her she deserved better. The things she did ... the way she saw herself. It broke my heart."

"How did Bonnie react when you tried to talk to her about it?" Beckett asked.

"She wouldn't listen," Merritt said. "She'd close up completely and then ask me to leave. So I kept my mouth shut." Regret colored his tone.

Erin wanted to say something encouraging, but she could think of nothing to make the man feel better. "Is that why she had so many bruises on her arms and legs?"

Merritt nodded. "She told her parents she was taking a self-defense class. I asked to have sex with the lights off—every time I saw the bruises, all I could think about was her allowing someone to treat her that way."

"Did Bonnie's having sex with other men bother you?" Erin asked.

"She only did it for the money," he said. "The way she saw herself bothered me. I thought things might get better ... and maybe she'd eventually change her mind." His chin wobbled, the big muscles in his neck straining.

Erin pressed on. "Do you think that's what she wanted to talk about when she called yesterday?"

"I have no idea," Merritt said. "I couldn't sleep last night, thinking about what she wanted to tell me. What if the killer were already there, and she needed my help?"

"I don't think so." The white lie wouldn't hurt. Erin had no idea whether Bonnie had called Will Merritt for help, but he needed to hear he couldn't have helped her. "Any idea who she made the videos with? Was her cousin Sarah involved?"

Merritt's lips curled, his cheeks reddening. "No, and she never said anything about Sarah being involved. You need to ask her yourself."

"We're working on it," Erin said. "Do you have any idea why Sarah wouldn't call us back?"

Merritt shook his head. "Bonnie mentioned Sarah being under a ton of stress with her thesis. Maybe she's not checking her voicemail."

Except the story broke on the news this morning, and most

people stayed glued to their phones these days. Erin kept the thought to herself and pulled the second warrant out of her bag. "I'm sorry to have to do this, but this is the warrant for us to take your DNA. You have twenty-four hours to go to the Criminal Investigations Division on M Street, and one of the forensics people will swab you." She'd debated bringing the kit here and doing it herself, but she didn't want any issue if things went to court.

Merritt's fair skin turned green, but he nodded.

What would he do if the baby was his? It certainly wouldn't help his case for innocence. "If the baby's yours—"

"I don't think it's mine. But I want to know."

His grief oozed out of every pore. Erin longed to give the young man his space, but she had one final question. "Were there any little girls in Bonnie's life—or yours?"

His eyebrows drew together, exhaustion etched into his handsome face. "What? No. Only child."

"What about anyone named Jane?" A long shot Erin had to take, but Merritt again shook his head no.

"Last question, I promise. Did Bonnie have any interest in history? Maybe criminal history? A lot of people like to read about serial killers and that sort of thing."

Deep lines etched into Merritt's forehead. "Not that I ever heard."

"Thank you for being honest. Please call me if you remember anything else."

The door swung open, and Erin's heart dropped all the way to her toes, yanking her confidence with it. Lisa stood there, looking perfectly chic as usual. The black business suit accentuating her runner's figure, cropped black hair framing her tanned face, and her bleached white teeth gleaming through a fake smile.

The daughter from Calvin Prince's previous marriage represented everything Erin never managed to achieve. Slim and tall, with a dazzling smile and dark eyes, Lisa's Italian heritage blessed her with the ability to tan, while Erin kept the sunscreen companies in business. Lisa embraced Calvin's conservative values, while Erin and Brad constantly questioned them. Erin hadn't been lying when she said she and her father got along. They did. But more like acquaintances. Lisa had taken everything else.

"I heard you were here interviewing one of my employees without my permission." Lisa glanced at Beckett. "Is this your new partner?"

"Yes." Erin refused to cower. "We're here on a case. Will Merritt is a witness to a murder. I don't need your permission to interview him."

"This is a private company," Lisa countered. "I have a right to know what's going on behind closed doors, especially when it could affect our reputation."

"There's no threat to anyone's reputation." Erin felt suddenly protective of Will Merritt, who had turned meek in Lisa's presence.

Lisa held up her smartphone. "He found his girlfriend gutted in Columbia Heights." She glanced at Merritt. "Interesting company you keep, Mr. Merritt. I'd say the association could affect us. Nice picture by the way."

Lisa held the phone out to Erin, but she refused to take it.

The salacious headline of Channel 4's web article said enough. *Slaughter on 16th Street.* A bad picture of Dan Mitchell bringing Bonnie out in a black bag accompanied the headline along with a shot of Erin and Beckett standing on the porch. At least she'd been dressed nicely. But the photographer had taken the shot of her looking up at Beckett, an almost green expression on her face. Beckett, in turn, appeared to be the picture of calm. A professor assuring his student.

"Detective Beckett," Lisa said. "Your résumé is quite impressive. I speak for the entire city when I say I hope your experience helps find this terrible person. Erin's still new at this, so she's certainly going to need your help."

Lisa's sweet smile made Erin want to punch her.

"It's Investigator," Beckett said. "And Erin's doing fine. I'm still learning the ropes here. I didn't get your name, however."

Lisa brushed by Erin. "Lisa Prince, Executive Vice President of Information Systems and Global Solutions."

She offered a beautifully manicured hand to Beckett. Lisa kept her fingernails impeccable. Erin didn't have the patience or the time to get hers done.

"I'm sorry your first case," she gave Erin a derisive look, "is such a nasty one. Mr. Merritt, I trust you're not a suspect in this terrible tragedy?"

White-faced, Merritt's head whipped back and forth like his neck muscles had become elastic. If Lisa saw him as a liability to Baker-Allen, she'd fire him without remorse.

"He's a material witness, and he's not required to tell you anything," Erin said. "This is a sensitive investigation. If any of it gets out, it could damage the case. So," Erin looked pointedly at Merritt, "the interview is confidential. Lisa, I'm sure you and Dad will understand."

Lisa caught the underlying threat, her mouth ticking up in a sneer. "No need to worry."

"Good." Erin walked out the door thinking she'd love to find a way to charge Lisa with interfering in an investigation if she ran her mouth. "Merritt, we'll see you later."

"Around six," Merritt said. He ducked his head and followed Erin out, mouthing a silent thank-you.

Her heart grew a tiny bit fond of him.

Beckett waited until Lisa sauntered ahead. "It was nice meeting you, but Erin and I need to get moving."

"Of course," Lisa said. "Erin, next time, call ahead. I'd love to catch up."

Erin grumbled and stalked ahead, marching through the lobby.

Booker waited at the administration desk with a smile on his round, pasty face. "Here are your copies, Ms. Prince. You'll see Will Merritt didn't leave the building until nearly eight thirty last night."

"Thank you." She shoved open the heavy glass door and breathed in the wet air. Rain fell in a delicate mist. Its coolness did nothing for the anger pulsing through her.

"Wow." Beckett turned up the collar of his coat. "You two really hate each other."

"Hate's a strong word." Erin walked so hard every stomp ricocheted up her legs. "And it was that obvious?"

"You seriously could have cut the tension with a knife." Beckett stood next to the passenger door of her car.

"I'm sorry," Erin said. "Lisa loves making everyone else feel uncomfortable."

"I noticed. But I admire you standing up for Merritt."

"I know what it's like to be helpless in her line of fire." She spat out her next words. "Do you feel the same way as Lisa?"

"About what?"

"My inexperience." Exhaustion and stress made her blunt. "You're working with a handicap on this case."

"Of course not. That article was ridiculous. The media's looking for the juiciest angle." He braced against the chill. "I'm lucky you got stuck with me."

Erin cleared her throat. "All right then. Let's go to the strip club."

Chapter Fifteen

"You know, I've only been to a strip club once." Beckett said as they parked across from Sid's Gentleman's Club on K Street. "Back during my vice days."

Erin raised her eyebrow. "Isn't going to a strip club some kind of rite of passage for men?"

He shrugged. "My dad never told me things like that."

Erin caught the disdainful tone but didn't push it.

"And strippers never interested me." He glanced around. "I can see the top of the White House from here."

"Because it's basically around the corner. Less than a ten-minute walk."

Sid's made no attempt to hide its identity. A large, burgundy umbrella guarded the entryway, the name of the club in bold white script. A sandwich shop sat right next door.

"Nice," Erin said as she opened the door to Sid's. "Get your fill of the girls dancing, get drunk, and go have a sub. Perfect single guy's night out."

She blinked, her eyes adjusting to the dim light. She hadn't been in one of these places since college, and Sid's was certainly nicer. A full bar with a large mirror took up most of the back wall, with the stage to the right. Sultry jazz music played over the speakers, but the stage stood empty. "I guess two in the afternoon is a slow time."

Beckett murmured in agreement as a curvy young woman dressed in black dress pants, a white shirt, and a red tie approached them. Her silken black hair hung around her face in thick waves, and her full lips were every man's fantasy. Her olive skin gleamed with the perfection of youth. Erin felt pasty, old, and chubby next to the young hostess.

"Can I help you?" The woman's husky voice bore a hint of an alluring Middle-Eastern accent, the lilt perfectly matching the mysteriousness of her green eyes.

But this girl looked barely legal enough to serve alcohol.

"I'd like to talk to the manager or owner. Both if possible."

The brunette cocked her head. "They usually only talk to people by appointment."

Erin unzipped her windbreaker to show her badge. "It's urgent."

The girl's eyes widened.

Erin envied her ability to use eyeliner without making a mess of it.

"I'll be right back with the owner."

Erin and Beckett stood awkwardly between the tables and the stage. Sid's appeared to be cleaner than any of the clubs she'd gone to, but she still didn't want to sit in one of the booths.

The waitress returned with a man Erin would have never imagined as a strip club owner. He wasn't much taller than Erin, but his presence demanded attention, his jet black hair cut in a trendy style made to look messy. Rich, olive-colored skin contrasted perfectly against his white Oxford shirt. He'd left the first three buttons undone, revealing a smattering of chest hair and what appeared to be a Sanskrit tattoo on his collarbone.

His eyes met hers, and he smiled—the kind of smile that invited a woman to confess her darkest secrets.

"I'm Yari Malek, owner of Sid's."

His slight accent confirmed Erin's suspicion the man was of Persian descent.

"How can we help the police? And before you ask, I'm a United States citizen. I was born here. The accent is from growing up surrounded by my family."

Behind his smile, Erin recognized the edge to his tone. He'd probably had to defend his citizenship to countless people since the 9/11 terrorist attack on Washington, D.C. and New York City. She didn't condone the hatred or the generalization of an entire religion, but she also didn't have time to soothe any bitter feelings Yari Malek might hold.

"We're not here about your citizenship, Mr. Malek." She matched his edge. "I'm sure you're telling the truth." She made a point to take a long, lingering look around the club. "Since you're a reputable businessman."

He grinned, his dark eyes twinkling. "All right. Please, call me Yari. How may I help you?"

"We're here about Bonnie Archer. She's one of your employees."

Malek nodded. "Part-time, evenings. She's due in tonight, actually." His wonderfully shaped, dark eyebrows knitted together. "Is she in some kind of trouble?"

Evidently, Malek didn't watch any more than the first few minutes of the news. "I'm sorry to tell you someone murdered

Bonnie in her home last night."

Malek's attractive face sank into an appropriate shocked expression. His glossy eyes darted between Erin and Beckett. "My God. Do you have any leads?"

"People of interest," Beckett said. "Did you know Bonnie well?"

"As well as anyone else here, I suppose," Malek said. "She was a private girl. Not rude or antisocial, understand. She came in, did her job, and went home."

Sid's might cater to a higher end clientele, but human needs all came down to the same basic things. "Her job ended at dancing?"

Malek's full mouth slanted up, but his tone stayed firm. "We don't charge for sex here. Of course, I can't control what the girls do after hours. But that's their business."

Erin wanted to tell him she didn't care whether he had a side business as long as it didn't affect her case. Instead she asked another question. "How many nights a week did Bonnie work?"

"Two to three," he said. "She went to school as well."

"About how much did she make?"

"Depends on the day," Malek said. "Easily $700 per night on the weekend, less during the week."

"In cash tips?" Erin asked. "I assume you're only paying a few bucks an hour."

"No," Malek said. "I pay my girls ten dollars an hour. We cater to a higher standard of clientele, so I want to provide my customers with more professional girls. I need to pay them well to ensure high standards."

Only in the service industry would ten dollars an hour be

considered decent pay. "So Bonnie could have been bringing home $1400 a week in cash plus, what, another $200 in hourly pay?"

"Sounds about right." Malek nodded. "Why do you ask how much money she made?" He looked at Beckett as though he expected Erin's male counterpart to jump in at any moment.

Beckett said nothing, and Erin decided to change tactics. "I'm trying to learn all I can about her. Did she have any specific admirers? Guys who bothered her?"

Malek walked to the bar and waved off the beautiful hostess, who'd been watching their exchange with wide-eyed interest.

She obediently nodded and hurried out of sight.

Malek reached over the shining wood counter and retrieved a bottle of bourbon. "Since you're on duty, I won't offer you a drink."

His silky voice held a teasing tone, and his dark eyes shined with a look Erin imagined made most women melt.

He grabbed a glass, poured two shots, and then downed them one after the other. "First off, an admirer and a man who bothers the girls are two different things. Admirers come back during the same girl's shift and give great tips. The creeps try to follow them home."

"Did that ever happen to Bonnie?" Beckett asked.

"Not that she told me." Malek sat the glass on the counter with a thud. "I have security to keep an eye on my ladies. I think if anyone had been a problem, I would have heard about it."

"Did you or the other dancers notice bruises on Bonnie?" Beckett asked.

Malek shrugged. "As long as the girls look good on the stage, I don't pay any attention. Several of the ladies are excellent with makeup. Bonnie likely covered any marks. You'd have to ask the other dancers."

"What about admirers?" Erin pressed.

"Bonnie didn't really have anyone specific." Malek looked down at his empty glass, his tone growing soft. "Certainly not because she wasn't beautiful. She had an ethereal quality that made men want to watch from a distance. Almost like she stood on a pedestal. She didn't have to fully disrobe to keep their interest."

"So she was a snob?"

"No!" Malek shook his head. "She just seemed kind of ... too sweet and delicate for this, which draws a certain man. Those men tip nicely, but they are looking for a different experience."

"They want to see a real dancer as opposed to some bump and grinding?" Beckett asked.

"Yes, these men are looking for more mystery than flash. Bonnie showed less skin than the others, but she matched their earnings." His gold ring glinted beneath the yellow bar lights. "Wait, I almost forgot about Tori."

Erin's pen paused. "Tori?"

Malek's soft lips inched into a smile. "An older gentleman who prefers to dress like a woman. He used to come in every week, but there was an issue with Bonnie a couple of months ago."

"You're saying Tori is a cross-dresser?" Erin could hardly grasp the significance of Malek's information. *Jack might have dressed like a woman to avoid detection.*

"A very skilled one. Always elaborately made up, dressed impeccably, with a stylish black wig. A real gentleman. Or lady. I'm not sure of the politically correct term."

"And something happened with Bonnie and Tori?" Erin asked.

"She danced for him once—a lap dance. He must have said something she didn't like, because she grew angry, yelling at him. My security asked him to leave. He never returned, and Bonnie never mentioned him."

"She didn't say what they argued about?"

Malek shrugged. "She only said she couldn't believe the balls on him." He smiled wryly. "Her phrasing, not mine."

"What about friends?" Erin asked. "Did Bonnie ever talk about anyone staying with her? Her boyfriend?"

A muscle in Yari Malek's jaw twitched. He reached again for the bottle of bourbon but didn't pour another glass. "Bonnie never talked about boyfriends, but we all had the impression school kept her too busy. As to your first question, no. She didn't have anyone staying with her that I'm aware of."

"Bonnie was pregnant," Beckett said.

Malek's face darkened. "I wondered."

"Why?" Erin asked. "I don't think she was showing yet."

"She stopped having drinks. She always needed a cocktail before her shift to loosen up. But a few weeks ago, she stopped. And she quit smoking. She said she needed to get healthy, but I sensed she wasn't being honest."

"And you have no idea who the father might be?"

Malek's dark eyes flashed, his chin jutting out. Had she pushed him too far? "I didn't know she had a boyfriend."

Erin glanced at Beckett. The frustration on his face matched her own. Bonnie kept to herself, and no one knew a damned thing about her. The broken record grated, and it wasn't going to help them catch her killer.

"I'll need a list of your employees. Please tell them all to call me, especially if they know anything about Tori." Erin handed him a card and watched him pocket it.

"Why do you need a list?"

"Background checks," Beckett said. "No offense to your establishment, but women in this line of work tend to have a different social circle. We need to make sure everyone checks out."

"I run background checks on all of my girls." His jaw muscles flexed, his tone hinging on unpleasant.

Beckett smiled. "I assure you the police department will be more thorough."

Malek nodded stiffly and then called for the girl who'd greeted them. He told her to make a list of employee names. "But I can't give out personal information."

"Of course not," Erin said. "Make sure you give them my number."

"I'll gather them all tonight and let them know. Most of them are working since it's Thursday. That's when Sid's gets busy."

He sagged against the bar. "I don't understand why this sort of thing happens to good people like Bonnie."

Beckett stared at him for a long time without saying anything, but Erin sensed a question brewing. Beckett didn't disappoint her.

"What about her cousin Sarah? Did Bonnie ever mention her? Or a friend named Jane?"

Malek smiled and poured another drink. "Jane? I don't know anyone by that name. But Sarah's the one person Bonnie talked about. They seemed close."

"I thought so," Beckett said. "What can you tell us about Sarah?"

"She's a student at American University, getting her master's, I believe," Malek said. "Surely, you've informed the family?"

"We have," Erin said, "but Sarah hasn't returned our calls."

"There is some family discord," Malek said.

Erin perked up. So Bonnie confided in this man but not Will Merritt? "Bonnie told you about her family issues?"

"Only briefly," Malek said. "She and Sarah came in shortly after they reunited. Bonnie mentioned it when I gave them drinks on the house."

"Did Bonnie ever mention spending time with a friend who had a young daughter?" Erin asked.

"No," Malek said. "But I told you—"

"You weren't close," Erin finished.

The brunette returned with a list of about twenty people—all women, including the bartenders.

Beckett made a humming noise, looking at Erin. "I'm good here if you are."

"For now." She nodded to Malek. "Don't forget to get the message to the girls."

Erin's mouth watered at the scent of fresh bread coming from the sandwich shop. The dreary day had stretched into late afternoon, and in the chaos after the phone call, they had skipped lunch.

She checked her watch. "The director at the Adult Learning Center leaves at five. If we want to talk to her about Bonnie's interaction with the staff and students, we need to hurry."

Beckett stopped near the sub shop's door. "Do we at least have time to grab a sandwich?"

Erin's stomach issued a growl worthy of a hungry grizzly. "Absolutely."

While their sandwiches were being made, Erin made a few phone calls and then joined Beckett at the table.

"So Sarah's at AU. I called in a favor and got her roommate's name from the registrar. Fowler found the address. It's about six blocks away from the university. He stopped by, and the roommate said Sarah's been staying at her parents' house the past few days."

"You've got a contact at American University?" Beckett asked.

"My alma mater, and my parents still contribute to the alumni fund. Sometimes you have to wade into the muck to get results."

Beckett chewed slowly, clearly savoring his ham and cheese. "Sarah's lack of response bugs me."

"Yeah, but think about it," Erin said. "Bonnie's parents didn't know they reconciled, so it's safe to say Sarah's didn't either. If she's hunkered down working on her thesis, maybe she didn't hear about it until this morning. And she's trying to find a way to talk to us without alerting her father. Trust me, I know the exact kind of cloth someone like Simon Archer is cut from. The Republican Governors Association wouldn't approve of his niece—and that's high priority for someone like him."

She took a swig of Diet Coke. "You know what bugs me? Everyone talks about Bonnie being this nice, private girl. Her boss at the strip club says she wasn't the sexually promiscuous type. And yet she's filming porn. No one really knew her at all. And now we've got a cross-dresser who pissed Bonnie off in the mix."

"Jack the Ripper's alleged way of escaping," Beckett said. "But cross-dressing isn't that uncommon. Tori may be a coincidence."

Erin rubbed her aching head. "I feel like we've got a bunch of threads and no way to tie them together."

"Things aren't always so neat," Beckett said. "Sometimes you have to keep grabbing at the threads until the right one sticks out."

Chapter Sixteen

Charlie paced, no longer able to stay in his hiding spot. He pointed his finger at Mina. "You shouldn't have called her."

Mina's eyes turned liquid. "The Princess can help us."

"No one can help us, Mina. It's just you and me together like it's always been."

The little girl sniffled. "But I saw her on T.V."

Charlie wanted to bang his head against the wall. Why did he get saddled with the kid again? He felt bad for thinking it. Mina didn't have anyone else. "Just because you saw her on T.V. doesn't mean she can help us."

Mina's cherub lips trembled. "Then what do we do? I don't want it to happen again!"

"Be quiet," he hissed. "There's nothing we can do but lay low and hope it's over soon." He didn't believe that. But he wouldn't scare Mina.

He mustered his silly smile, the one that always made her laugh. "Close your eyes and rest now, little girl."

Chapter Seventeen

The sky remained the color of steel, but at least, the mist stopped by the time they arrived in the Edgewood neighborhood of northeast D.C. Nestled between Rhode Island Avenue and Michigan Avenue, Edgewood was yet another area struck by gentrification. Many of the 1900s row houses had already been renovated, and young professionals gave the area a hip, up-and-coming vibe. New shops and restaurants had popped up since the last time Erin came out here on one of her first sex crimes cases.

A woman had caught her live-in boyfriend molesting her six-year-old daughter. Erin sat with the woman while she described what she'd witnessed, allowing her then-partner to ask all of the questions. After they left the woman's house, Erin had to pull over to throw up. Brad talked her out of transferring to another department.

"It's a stepping stone to homicide," he'd said. "The big leagues. Isn't that where you want to be?"

At the time, she'd said yes, of course. The big leagues meant the opportunity for big cases and making a real difference. And to finally prove to her sister and father becoming a cop meant something. Just because she didn't make the nightly news or a lot of money didn't mean she couldn't be proud of her job.

Thinking about the slaughter of Bonnie Archer's body, Erin wasn't so sure.

She parked her black Impala at the far end of the Adult Learning Center lot. The new model car had been a present to herself for her birthday, and she didn't want door dings in the first six months of owning it.

Beckett stepped out and looked around. "Decent neighborhood," he said. "I like the old row houses in this city. So many different ones, like home. All with stories to tell."

"They are pretty cool." She and Brad considered buying in one of the older neighborhoods, but she wanted Abby to go to the safest and best schools without being completely sheltered. So they'd ended up in Arlington, investing in a duplex and enrolling Abby in private school.

"A lot of them have original fixtures like clawfoot tubs and crown molding. They also have the shitty wiring and bad heating." She turned her attention to Academy of Hope's three-story brick building.

"It looks like a community center," Beckett commented.

"It was," Erin said. The L-shaped structure had freshly cleaned bricks and a cheerful portico at the entrance. Welcoming and safe. "Two teachers started the academy in the 80s. They worked out of a church. This is their third location, thanks to a big grant."

She led the way to the entrance, glaring at the ugly day. Soon the dying fall colors would give way to more dank and dark days like this one. Gray skies, ice, and snow. Joy.

Inside smelled clean and new along with the distinctly academia scent of printed papers, brewing coffee, and microwaved lunch. A reception desk sat in the middle of the wide hallway.

A woman with a bright smile and dangly skull earrings smiled at them. "Can I help you?"

Erin and Beckett showed their badges. "We're investigating the murder of Bonnie Archer. Is the director available?"

The receptionist's smile disappeared. "I saw it on the news this morning. Who would hurt someone like that?" She tugged at a string on her orange sweater. The Halloween kitty's eye had started to unravel. "Bonnie was so nice."

"You knew her well?" Beckett slouched against the tall counter, unthreatening.

"Not well," she said. "Just in passing. But she stood out. Never in a bad mood, always said hello and goodbye. Always asked about my day. Just a happy person." She blinked, her heavy mascara ghosting against her skin. "I can't understand it."

"We can never truly understand these things," Beckett said. "All we can do is find justice for her." He offered a kind smile. "The director?"

"Yes, of course. Dr. Key's office is down the hall, the first room on the right. We've got an open-door policy."

"Thank you," Beckett said. "Are most of the classrooms upstairs then?"

"Yes." The skull earrings danced. "We use the downstairs for social areas and meetings."

"Social areas?" Erin asked.

"We believe an informal environment, while keeping with a solid academic structure, makes adult students feel more at home. We encourage them to socialize and get to know one another. They're the only ones who can empathize with each other. A lot of students end up having study groups in the downstairs areas."

"Did you ever see Bonnie in any of these groups?" Erin asked.

"Yes," she said. "During the summer."

Erin leaned onto the counter, lowering her voice. "Any chance you could tell me the names of the students in her group?"

Wide eyes answered her. "I'm not allowed for privacy reasons. You'd have to ask the director."

"Thank you," Erin said. "We'll see ourselves to her office."

Erin stopped at the first open office door.

An African-American woman looked up from her computer. Or rather, over her tortoise shell reading glasses. "Hello. Can I help you?"

Erin and Beckett introduced themselves. "We'd like to speak with you about Bonnie Archer."

Dr. Key took off her glasses and rubbed her eyes. "I thought we'd be hearing from you. Stephanie Key."

She looked to be in her mid-forties, a few wrinkles around her eyes. Her glowing ebony skin needed no makeup, and her gray suit made her appear professional yet stylish.

She motioned to the chairs in front of her desk. "Please, sit."

Erin sat and pulled out her notebook. She could barely read her earlier notes. "To confirm, you're the director of the Adult Learning Center, correct?"

Key nodded. "Yes, of both our GED program and our Pathways program, although each one has its own coordinator."

"Pathways is a different program?" Beckett questioned.

"It's for students with a diploma or GED who will be entering the workforce or going on to college. We have readiness programs for each."

"Which Bonnie was interested in, right?" Erin asked, remembering what the Archers told them.

"Yes." Key reached for her desk phone. "Why don't I invite the GED coordinator to talk as well? He would know more about Bonnie than I would."

Erin and Beckett waited while she made the phone call, speaking quietly.

"Thank you." She hung up the phone. "Brian is on his way down. He's in between meetings."

"Do the coordinators also teach?" Erin asked.

"No," she said. "Our coordinators deal with the Department of Education and the local schools. They facilitate teacher training and student tracks. Brian makes it a point to connect with all of his students. I knew Bonnie in passing and by reputation. He's spent time with her." She leaned back in her chair, rubbing the tender skin beneath her eyes. "Please tell me you have an idea of who did this."

"We're working very hard." Beckett sidestepped the question. "What can you tell us about your students?"

Key considered for a moment. "Our GED program is a mixed bag. We have young adults, like Bonnie, who made poor choices in their early lives but are getting back on track. We've also got older adults who want to get their GED as well as foreign-born students."

"What about social class?" Erin asked. "Are most of these people from lower socio-economic backgrounds?"

Key smiled. "You don't have to worry about political correctness, Investigator Prince. Yes, most of the students are poor. Many of them grew up on the streets or ended up there. And our minority students are a larger segment but not by much. We have plenty of white kids too."

A knock on the door stopped Erin from asking her next question. She and Beckett turned to see a tall, sandy-haired man with wonderfully broad shoulders standing in the doorway. He smiled at them, revealing perfect teeth. An all-American poster boy, and the sort she'd never gone for. But looking at his blue eyes, she could see making an exception.

"Brian Reese." He extended his hand. "And this is Vanessa Carrington."

A short woman with spiky hair stood behind him.

"Vanessa is the language arts teacher. Bonnie needed to finish language arts for her GED, and she spent a lot of time with her."

Beckett stood and motioned for the petite teacher to sit.

Red streaked her eyes, and her tawny skin appeared pale. "I keep thinking this isn't happening." Her voice trembled. "It's a nightmare."

Brian Reese wedged into the small space between Key's desk and her bookshelves. "How can we help you?"

Erin cleared her throat. "Tell us about Bonnie's time here. Was she a good student?"

"Oh yes," Vanessa said. "She flew through her math course, but she had some issues with reading and writing. She worked hard, and she always had a good attitude. One of those people who brightened a room." Vanessa played with a loose button on her sleeve, twisting it tightly enough to pop off.

"She wanted to enter the Pathways program once she earned her GED," Brian said. "She was set to finish this spring and, assuming she passed the GED test, would enter Pathways in the fall."

"Did you spend much time with her?" Erin asked.

Brian crossed his arms, making his biceps bulge, and furrowed his brow. "Not a lot. When a student enters the program, they work with me to get their course schedule figured out. And then if they have any issues, they can always come to me. Since Bonnie started, I only saw her in passing until she stopped in to talk about Pathways a few weeks ago. She was excited about it, and I was excited for her."

Beautiful and young, Bonnie clearly knew how to attract men, at least when being paid for it. Brian Reese was flat-out hot. He didn't look the sort who would need any help getting a girl, and Erin didn't know too many women who wouldn't have been attracted to him. "So your relationship with the students is from afar, essentially. Unless a question or problem arises."

"Exactly," Brian said.

"When did you last see Bonnie?"

"I've been away at a conference," he said. "I actually flew home late last night, so I haven't seen her—or any of the students—for nearly a week. But we hadn't spoken much since we discussed Pathways. Just exchanges in the hall."

Erin caught Beckett's eye. Nice of Reese to offer his alibi.

"We'll need to confirm you being out of town." Beckett said the words casually.

Brian cocked his head. "Really?"

"Anyone with any contact with Bonnie is a person of interest," Beckett said. "We've got to rule out everyone we possibly can."

"Of course." He crossed one ankle in front of the other, unfazed. "What do you need?"

"Do you still have your boarding pass?" Beckett asked.

"I probably do. I crashed as soon as I got home and then rushed to work. I might have the parking receipt too."

Convenient. "Those would be great. We can send a uniform to pick them up later."

"Anything I can do to help?" He caught Erin's gaze and smiled at her, his blue eyes bright.

Erin turned her attention to Vanessa. "You knew her best among the staff?"

"Yes."

"What was she like? Did she have any issues with anyone?"

"Sweet. Smart. Caring." Vanessa wiped her constantly watering eyes. "I told you she brightened the room. We all liked her."

"Did you or anyone else ever notice her being bruised or injured in anyway?" Beckett asked. "Anything that might have prompted you to ask her if she needed help?"

All three staff members shook their heads.

Erin suspected Bonnie kept her bruises hidden. "She participated in a study group this summer?"

"A math group," Vanessa said. "Math came easily to her, and she wanted to help other students. She spent a couple of hours a few times every week."

"So she interacted with a lot of students." Beckett looked at Key with the expression of a boy caught digging into the cookie jar. "I don't suppose we could have a list of your enrolled GED students?"

"Absolutely not without a warrant, as I'm sure you expected," Director Key said.

They had no probable cause for a warrant. Not yet, anyway. "Are there any students she spent more time with than others? Any she might have hung out with outside of class?"

Vanessa thought a minute before answering. "I don't know for sure, but my gut says no."

"Why?" Erin leaned forward. "I thought she was a social butterfly."

Vanessa pulled a tissue out of the pocket of her baggy sweater. "I'm not using the right terminology. She came to learn, and while she was nice, she didn't spend her time talking and getting to know people." Vanessa shook her head. I got the distinct impression she wanted to keep her private life private."

"How so?" Beckett pressed. "Can you give us an example?"

Vanessa thought about it for a minute. "Before class and during breaks, most students chatter about something other than school. Bonnie listened, but she wasn't very talkative."

"Did you ever ask her about friends and family?" Erin kept an eye on Brian Reese. He knew the students and likely counseled them on some level. He struck her as the kind of man who could easily convince a woman to confide in him. His expression gave nothing away, his gaze on the teacher, seemingly unaware of Erin's observation.

"I did ask whether she had people supporting her at home," Vanessa said. "She told me her parents were supportive and helping her with her homework. And her cousin as well."

And right back to Sarah. They needed to find her soon. A troubling thought brewed in the back of Erin's mind. She stowed it and asked her next question. "What about a boyfriend? Did Bonnie have one?"

All three shook their heads.

"She stayed focused on school," Vanessa said. "She worked part-time, but she mentioned once she didn't have time for anything serious."

That at least backed up Will Merritt's side of the story.

"There was one student," Brian Reese said. "I never thought anything about it, but I saw her leave with him a few times. Walking in the direction of the Metro. I assume they both rode the same line. But they seemed friendly."

"What was his name?"

Brian glanced at Key.

Her face hardened, the fine lines around her mouth deepening. "Reese."

"It's not a privacy violation," he argued. "You're not giving his information out."

She looked at him for several tense seconds before nodding.

"Ricky Stout," Brian said. "Brilliant kid, just twenty-one. Grew up in Anacostia, so you can imagine the things he's seen. He's in the Pathways program."

"Another black male who made it out and won't make it to the news," Key said, a sharp edge creeping into her voice. "He's worked hard to get his life straightened out."

"Is Ricky in class today?" Erin asked.

Key shook her head. "Not until tomorrow night. I'm sorry, but if you want any other information on a student, you'll need a warrant."

Beckett seemed satisfied, but after Key's last comment, Erin wanted to know why the woman remained so protective over one student's privacy when another had been brutally murdered.

Chapter Eighteen

"Sarah's still not answering, so I called her dad. And Simon Archer refused to take my call until I told him Calvin Prince was my father." The disgust in Erin's tone didn't compare with the rush of irritation at the way Simon Archer kissed her ass when his assistant finally put the call through.

She reached for the half-full coffee pot and took a careful whiff. Semi-fresh. Good enough. "You should have heard the guy. 'Ms. Prince, the Republican Governors are so grateful for your father's monetary contributions. He's made a huge difference in our cause.'" She dumped two sugars into the coffee and stirred. "And then I asked him whether he knew his niece had been murdered last night. Tone completely changed."

"Why else did he think you were calling?" Beckett clutched two donuts wrapped in a flimsy napkin.

The corners of Erin's mouth crept up. "I might have forgotten to tell his assistant I was a cop."

Beckett laughed.

It was a lot heartier than she would have expected.

"Well done. What did he say?"

They walked toward Sergeant Clark's office to debrief him. "He'd heard the news. Such a tragedy, but her lifestyle. Blah, blah,

blah. I asked him about Sarah, and he got defensive."

"Did you tell him they were in contact?"

"No. I wanted to wait. I said her name came up as family, and we needed to talk to her. He said the same thing as his brother: 'the girls haven't spoken in years.' He claims Sarah is staying at their house, hunkering down on her master's thesis. He saw her this morning. Like I thought—Sarah's probably trying to find the chance to call without raising her parent's suspicion. Simon didn't make any effort to hide his disapproval of his niece."

"Did he offer the information about Sarah willingly?"

Erin took a drink of the coffee and scowled. The first chance she got, she would purchase a Keurig along with a couple of months' worth of coffee pods. "He told me his daughter's whereabouts were none of my business."

Simon Archer dripped venom during their conversation. But his constant name-dropping of Erin's father royally pissed her off.

"So I told him I knew what it was like to be close to your parents, and that this whole thing reminded me I needed to catch up with my father today. He took the hint." She wished she could have been in Archer's office to see the look on his face. "Did you get anything back on Ricky Stout?"

"A sealed juvenile record. Not surprising. Last known address was a shelter, two years ago. Still, it's worth swinging by."

Sergeant Clark's door stood open, and he motioned them inside. "Please tell me you've got something. Bonnie's parents have already called me twice today."

Beckett ran through what they had so far, which amounted to a pile of questions and no answers. Clark rocked in his chair to the point Erin worried it would break and dump him on the floor.

"I still think we could be looking for a female killer hung up on the idea of Jack the Ripper being a woman," Erin said.

Clark rubbed the muscles in his shoulder. "Beckett, what do you think?"

Nerves tightened Erin's stomach. Would Beckett make her look like a fool?

"I'm not completely against it," he finally said. "I think we've got to follow the leads we have, and other than the papers, we don't have anything leading to a woman—yet. We need to keep our eyes open though."

Erin filled Clark in on the phone call with Simon Archer. "So Sarah is safe. But if she knew about Bonnie's sex videos, she may be in danger. And she's our best link to Bonnie."

"And Ricky Stout, who may only be an acquaintance," Beckett reminded her. "But his is the only name we've got. Any chance we can get a warrant for his contact information?"

"Come on." Clark rocked hard in his chair, the headrest smacking the back wall. "How many years you been a cop? Right now we have no probable cause. And in this environment, no judge is going to be eager to issue a warrant to put another black man in jail without something rock solid. Get a phone number, match it to Bonnie's records. Then maybe."

"There's nothing in the system for him," Beckett said. "He hasn't filed taxes. Every online search came back with the wrong Ricky Stout. He's got class tomorrow night. We should pay the school another visit, hang around."

Erin winced. "You'll have to go without me," she said. "Abby's got a school thing I can't miss." She'd promised her daughter she would attend her concert.

"No problem," Beckett said. "I'll keep you updated."

"The drug clinic sent over the records," Clark continued. "Bonnie was clean. Merritt came in for his DNA swab too."

Erin checked at her watch. "He wasn't supposed to come until six."

Clark shrugged. "He got off early today. Our computer guys checked the security footage from Baker-Allen. Merritt did exactly what he said he did, and there's no evidence of tampering."

Erin hoped her sister hadn't fired Will Merritt. The guilt would eat at Erin until she had to do something, which would be calling their father. Cue a fresh round of battle between her and Lisa.

Clark's chair creaked as he reached for a note on his desk. "What about the strip club owner?"

"Sarah came into the club a few times to see Bonnie, and we've got a warrant for the list of employees. We'll run them through the system, see whether they've got anything interesting in their backgrounds and who their known associates are."

Clark nodded. "Yari Malek's number is listed in Bonnie's cell contacts, but there's only a couple of calls to him. And he's her boss, so not unusual."

"What's the status on her full phone records?" Beckett asked. "We need more than the call log on her phone."

"At least another day. They have the warrant, but the fucking companies are more concerned about a lawsuit over privacy violations than helping out a murder investigation." Clark let the chair snap back straight. "Temple hasn't released Bonnie Archer yet. She's waiting on some additional tests, and she's asked the forensic anthropologist to examine Bonnie as well. Apparently, some of the cuts nicked the bones. Which means her parents are stuck in limbo and frustrated. With some of the shock worn off, they may be able to tell us more. I'd like to know what caused the family divide, because it obviously affected Bonnie's life."

"I'll call Mrs. Archer," Beckett said. "Hopefully, I can talk with her before we speak with Sarah. Do we have anything on the fingerprints from Bonnie's apartment?"

Clark nodded. "Merritt's were found in the bedroom and living room, as we expected. Nowhere near the body. At least two other sets of prints don't match anyone in the system. The lab is still working on the rest of the trace evidence Marie's people collected. And I'm trying to get a rush on the fetal DNA." He leaned back in his chair, suddenly looking far older than just a few days ago. "Any more weird calls?"

"Not yet." Erin hedged, not sure whether she wanted to know the answer to her next question. "Have you read the article on Channel 4's website?"

Clark curled his lips as though the air in the room had gone sour. "That reporter likes her tabloid shit," Clark said. "Nothing she said matters. What matters is what's going on right now. Make something happen."

* * *

Beckett's call to the Archers turned out to be a bust. They wanted answers the police couldn't give, and their limited knowledge of their daughter was increasingly apparent.

A chill raked up Erin's spine. How many years did she have before Abby stopped sharing every minute detail of her day and became a sullen teenager who thought the world—including her mother—was against her? Could Erin navigate those teenage years well enough to keep Abby out of trouble? Would she become a bigger hypocrite and use her family connections if Abby got in trouble?

Her father had done as much with Lisa, and she turned out to be a cold, successful bitch living a shallow existence, feeding off the misery she inflicted on others. Lisa had never been held accountable for any of her behaviors.

Thinking about her sister made Erin remember Lisa's smug words from earlier. Maybe if she sucked it up and read the damned article, she could put it out of her mind.

Bonnie's murder remained on Channel 4's home page. The "Princess" reference stood out in bold beneath the picture of herself, Beckett, and Clark talking on Bonnie's porch. Titles identified the men, Sergeant and Investigator, respectively. Erin's caption read: *new homicide member Erin Prince—known as "the Princess" among the ranks—is the daughter of Washington power-elite Calvin Prince.*

Red danced in her vision. Forget about the Princess dig. How about the misogyny? What the hell century did they live in?

"It's bullshit." Fowler leaned against her desk, offering her Hershey's Miniatures this time.

Erin took three and steamed. "Some asshole uniform who thinks he should be a homicide cop talked to that reporter who always wears a skirt barely covering her ass. It's the closest he'll get to the real investigation."

The fact Erin couldn't defend herself or speak out against the reporter burned the hell out of her. Freedom of speech didn't exist for everyone. "It's not just the nickname. Did you read the caption? They might as well have said I was a secretary! I didn't realize we'd jumped back in time."

Fowler shook out more chocolate into her outstretched hand. "They're going with the angle that sells. It's just a way to get Calvin Prince's name in the article and get more hits. Don't you know anything about metadata?"

She sucked down the last chocolate. "This is why women still fight to be equal. Because of the ones like that reporter who rely on their *assets* more than brains."

"Fuck her. Focus on the victim. This job isn't about accolades. It's about bringing in scum-sucking criminals before someone else gets hurt. So do your job, Princess." Fowler winked at her and sauntered off.

Her phone vibrated, and a blocked number flashed on the screen. Erin's insides twisted into a painful knot. "Erin Prince, Homicide."

Soft, rapid breathing filtered over the line. "Is this the Princess?"

Erin snapped her fingers, signaling to Beckett. He wheeled his chair over, and she moved the phone from her ear so he could hear. She didn't want the little girl to hear office sounds and hang up.

"Hi, sweetheart. I'm glad you called again. Will you tell me your name?"

A couple seconds of silence and then, "Mina."

"Mina. That's so pretty. Do you need help, Mina?"

"It's going to happen again if you don't stop it." Mina's voice trembled with tears.

Erin's stomach bottomed out. She struggled to keep her tone even and not barrage the girl. Mina couldn't be more than five or six. She might clam up if Erin started badgering her. "What's going to happen again?"

Mina didn't answer right away, and Erin worried she'd hung up.

Then the child sniffled. "Me and Charlie are in trouble. That's why I called again, even though he said not to."

"Who's Charlie?"

"He's the boy who takes care of me. But that's not what I'm tryin' to tell you!" Childlike impatience mixed in with Mina's fear.

"I'm sorry."

Beckett slid a note across her desk. *Give your desk number. Can trace call.*

"Mina, can you do me a favor?" Erin asked. "This is my cell phone, and it's about to die. I really want to hear what you have to say. Can you call this number?" She recited her direct line.

Mina spoke as though she didn't hear it. "We're so scared," the little girl whispered. "Poor Bonnie."

Erin's heart stopped. "Who are you scared of?"

"Bonnie was nice to us." Mina's words shook with the effort not to cry.

Her desperate voice made Erin think of her own little girl sitting safely at home with Brad. The sudden urge to take her daughter into her arms nearly overwhelmed her. "Mina, is the person you're afraid of named Jane?"

"I can't tell you. But it's going to happen again." Mina's bell-like voice made the words sound more ominous. "Bye."

The call ended. Erin threw the phone across her desk and knocked a plastic holder full of pens onto the floor. "Beckett, we've got to find Mina."

Chapter Nineteen

Frantic calls were placed to child services. No Mina in the system. To NCMEC—no Mina listed as missing. No Mina associated with any active cases or known criminals. A search for Charlie came up with three kids in the system but only one older than ten. His foster parents' address was listed in Rock Creek Park, and they denied knowing anyone named Mina or Bonnie Archer. Juvenile arrest records pulled up half a dozen Charlies. Tomorrow, Erin and Beckett would start tracking them down.

She took two aspirin and turned to Beckett, who tossed back his umpteenth cup of coffee. "You get anything from Bonnie's parents?"

"They don't know anyone named Mina or Charlie. Nor Jane for that matter."

After talking to the Archers yet again, Beckett looked as sick as she felt. Bags bloomed beneath his eyes. His narrow face seemed longer, his cheeks hollowed out. His five o-clock shadow only made him look haggard.

"Bonnie never mentioned any children to them."

Erin watched the digital clock switch to 9:00 p.m. She didn't want to add up the hours she'd worked today. "Did you tell them about the pregnancy?"

He shook his head. "I'll leave that to the M.E. Coward's way out, but I didn't want to tell them over the phone."

"Can't blame you." The Archers' pain was about to multiply astronomically. Erin selfishly thanked God she didn't have to witness it, but she considered that a small respite compared to the heavy load on her conscience. Mina had called Erin for help twice. If she was the next victim, Erin was to blame.

Erin closed her eyes, replaying the words over. What had she missed?

Her desk phone rang.

She dived for it. "Erin Prince, Homicide."

Instead of Mina's little voice, the officer manning the front entrance coughed like he was trying to hack up a load of phlegm and then said, "Sarah Archer is here."

* * *

Sarah Archer waited in the same interview room Will Merritt sat in last night, in the chair closet to the window. Her knees stayed drawn tightly into her chest, her strawberry blonde hair spanning across her reed-thin legs. Her small feet rested in front of her on the chair, her lithe body somehow drawn into an impossibly tight position. Erin hadn't been flexible before she had a child, let alone after. Sarah's thin arms kept her legs at her chest. She'd chewed her fingernails to the quick. Her pale, youthful skin radiated even with minimal makeup.

A small surge of jealousy nagged Erin. As a child, she was the chubby kid in the corner with the wavy brown hair who didn't quite fit in. Her last name was the only reason many kids socialized with her. Eventually, she'd grown out of her chubby duckling phase, but she'd never quite shed the mental state, especially when she perpetually carried an extra ten pounds no matter how much effort she put into losing them.

"Hi Sarah," Erin said. "I'm Investigator Erin Prince, and this is my partner, Investigator Beckett."

"Hi." Sarah's soft voice shook as she somehow drew herself into a tighter ball. Rocking back and forth, she could have been a small child afraid of her mother's scolding.

"I'm very sorry about your cousin," Erin said. "Thank you so much for coming in to talk with us."

Tears welled from Sarah's closed eyes and seeped onto her cheeks. "I can't believe it. Poor Bonnie."

Sarah's teary eyes focused on Erin. They were two different colors: one brown and one startlingly blue. Not exactly a rare phenomenon, but still unsettling.

Erin turned one of the free chairs around so she faced Sarah. "Why didn't you return my calls?"

"I've been at my parents." Sarah played with the gold watch on her left hand, turning it in fast circles. "Working on my thesis. I shut off my phone. I heard about Bonnie this morning. The horrible things they said about her ..."

"Because of Bonnie's drug history?" Beckett asked.

"Apparently, she must have been asking for it." She made a disgusted noise. "My parents are judgmental, and they don't forget." She wiped her eyes. "When I tracked her down a few months ago, I was amazed at how hard she worked to stay sober and get on her feet. Anyway, I couldn't listen to them, so I left for the day. When I got home, my father told me you'd called him."

"Your parents aren't aware the two of you reconciled?"

"They are now." Her soft voice took on a hardened edge. "I'm not concerned about their feelings anymore. I only kept it from them for Bonnie's sake. Her parents would have been upset."

"Can you tell us about the family falling out?"

Sarah focused on her slender hands, obviously debating on whether or not to betray her family's trust. When she looked up again, those strange eyes gleamed with determination.

"The summer she was eight and I was six, Bonnie was sexually abused by a family friend of my parents. They didn't want to believe the truth, but Bonnie's parents did. They took her away and got her counseling, but I guess it didn't work. By the time she turned fourteen, she was having sex and doing drugs. She hated herself." Sarah wiped away new tears. "And then she got raped. It took her a long time to get straightened out, but she did. This is so unfair!"

Erin handed the girl a tissue and gave her a moment. No wonder Bonnie's parents remained bitter. If Brad allowed something like that to happen and then didn't believe her daughter, she'd never forgive him.

Sarah's slender body curled tighter, her hands locked around her knees and her bleary eyes focused somewhere to the right of Erin. She loosened her grip to chew on a fingernail, still not making eye contact.

Erin's grip tightened on the box of tissues. "Sarah, were you abused by your parent's friend, too?"

Sarah's contrasting eyes locked with Erin's, her posture rigid. "No, of course not. Why would you ask that?"

Because I know how to spot a victim of sexual abuse.

Sarah perched on the chair with all her muscles tensed, ready to bolt.

"It's a logical question. Your father's friend abused Bonnie, and the two of you spent a lot of time together. It makes sense he would move on to you once Bonnie was removed from the picture."

Sarah's hair whipped back and forth. "My parents didn't allow that to happen. I was never alone with him after that." A muscle in her cheek twitched. "Which tells me deep down they knew Bonnie was telling the truth. My father's reputation was just more important."

"And your parents are still friends with Bonnie's abuser?" Beckett flipped through his notes and jotted something down.

"He moved away a long time ago, but it didn't matter, because they never believed her. I think it made them look bad, so they couldn't accept it. You know?"

Yes. Erin witnessed it more times than she wanted to think about during her brief tenure as a sex crimes investigator. Many women didn't want to believe a husband or boyfriend could be capable of hurting their child. Some flat out refused. Add that to the high-profile life Simon Archer lead, and everything made twisted sense. "You have a name?"

She shook her head. "They never told me. Bonnie didn't like to talk about it."

"But you were six when all of this happened?" Erin asked, watching the girl's strange eyes. The different colors reflected light in subtly different ways, and the effect was fascinating. "So I assume you grew up hearing your parents' version?"

"Yes, when they would talk about it, which wasn't often. Aunt Carmen told me the truth a long time ago."

"So you had some contact with your aunt and uncle?" Erin asked.

"Just with Carmen, back in high school. I knew I wasn't getting the whole story, and I wanted to know why Bonnie disappeared out of my life. Carmen told me, and she told me about all of Bonnie's problems. I felt so terrible." She snatched another tissue out of the box on the table. "My parents and I had it out. I got grounded for speaking with her. I finally realized what sort of person my father is." Her delicate face took on the sharp expression of an eagle hunting for prey. "He doesn't care about anyone but himself. And his reputation."

Erin said the same thing to her own father years ago. Their fight had been something of a wake-up call to him. "I'm sorry. I know this is tough for you. Did you ever notice Bonnie being bruised or injured?"

"A couple of times." Sarah touched her bicep. "Around here. She said she took self-defense classes. I thought that was a good thing. A way for her to feel like she had control over her life and safety." Her voice hitched.

Erin studied the girl.

Sarah fidgeted with Erin's silence. "Did she lie? Do you think someone else gave her those bruises?"

She seemed so fragile, so desperate to believe she hadn't missed some crucial sign of her cousin's impending danger. But if they were so close, did she really not know about the sex videos? "We have reason to believe Bonnie sold amateur porn videos online, and her bruising came from those sessions."

Sarah sat back against the chair. "Bonnie would have told me."

"Why?" Beckett pressed. "Would you have tried to talk her out of it?"

"I ... I don't know. But I can't see Bonnie doing something like that. She said didn't like sex. She was still dealing with a lot of self-worth issues."

"But you knew she worked as a stripper. The owner of Sid's mentioned you came in with Bonnie a few times," Beckett said.

Sarah twisted the tissue into a ropelike strand. "She liked working there. She said her boss treated her well. Better than the other girls. But Bonnie wasn't like them."

"How do you mean?" Erin asked.

"It's not what you're thinking," Sarah said. "I'm not saying those women are bad for stripping and Bonnie was good. I'm saying Bonnie was special. She had this sort of contagious lightness about her. I think people wanted to be around her because of it. Does that make sense?"

"Yes." Beckett scratched his chin. "Did Bonnie have any issues with Sid's clientele?"

"The cross-dresser," Sarah said immediately. "I don't remember his name."

"Tori?" Erin supplied.

"Yes. He asked Bonnie to dance one night, and something happened. She wouldn't say what, but she told me she got him kicked out." Sarah's disconcerting eyes narrowed. "She got so upset about him. She wouldn't tell me what he said, just that he was a hypocrite."

"Did she ever mention him again?"

Sarah shook her head. "She said she wanted to forget about

him."

"Did you know about Will Merritt?" Erin asked.

Fresh moisture built in Sarah's eyes. "I think he's in love with her. But she didn't want to be tied down. And he accepted it. But I think he would have waited for her."

At least Erin's female instincts weren't completely off. "I hate to ask this, but would you mind allowing us to fingerprint you? There are two sets of prints in Bonnie's house we can't identify. If one set is yours, ruling them out would be a huge help."

"Of course," Sarah said. "I've been at my parents since Wednesday, so I'm not sure whether that will help."

"Fingerprints can stick around for a long time," Erin said. "She offered a conspiratorial smile. "So you've been holed up at your parents in Chevy Chase? No trips into the city?"

Sarah shook her head. "I wish. My thesis is killing me." She flinched. "Bad choice of words."

"It's all right," Erin said. "Can you give us the names of any of Bonnie's other friends or classmates?"

"She didn't mention any of them. I got the impression she kept to herself."

"What about Brian Reese, one of the school counselors?"

Sarah nodded. "She talked to him about their college program. She was excited about it." Her voice caught as she realized the sad finality of her cousin's dream.

"And nothing else about Brian, maybe about him being inappropriate?"

"No," Sarah said. "Why?"

"We need to get a clear picture of her life. Think back over the last few months. Did Bonnie mention having issues with anyone?"

"No ... well, no not really."

"What is it?" Erin prodded. "Even if it seems trivial, it's important."

"She talked about a boy at school who asked her out." Sarah smiled. "She called him a boy because he was only twenty-one. She wasn't interested. I think it took him a while to get the hint."

Erin's pulse kicked into her throat. Out of the corner of her eye, she saw Beckett sit up a little straighter. "Did she tell you his name?"

"No. She said he was black, though. I remember because we talked about how my dad would be scandalized if I ever dated a black man. He still lives in the dark ages." She banded her arms over her narrow chest.

Ricky Stout? A possibility, but dozens of black males attended the Adult Learning Center. Still, the age matched. "Anyone else? No other female friends?"

"She didn't have many friends. Bonnie had trust issues. The only women she talked about were the ones she worked with at Sid's." Her face twisted into sorrow. "I wish I hadn't waited so long to find her again. And now she's gone." Sarah ducked her head and cried.

Erin's throat swelled, and she reached for the girl's fragile hand while Beckett offered a tissue. But her mind galloped ahead. *Jack might have disguised himself as a woman. Bonnie had a cross-dresser at the club.*

"When did you last see Bonnie?" Beckett asked.

"A week ago," Sarah said. "We'd planned to get together a few days ago, but I cancelled because of my stupid paper." Her head dropped against her thin knees. "Maybe I could have helped her."

"I'm sure that's not the case," Erin said gently. "How did Bonnie seem the last time you spoke?"

"Fine," Sarah said. "She understood why I couldn't make it because she was busy with school too. Everything was going so well in her life. I just can't believe this happened." She drew in a long, shuddering breath, her striking eyes unsettling. "The news said she was cut up."

"I'm sorry." The words seemed so flat, so worthless. As if they could somehow soften the girl's grief. If Bonnie had told anyone about the pregnancy, it would have been Sarah. But the parents hadn't been informed. Then again, Bonnie was a legal adult, and Sarah had been hard to track down. They might not have a chance to talk to her again. "Did you know Bonnie was pregnant?"

Beckett's head jerked toward Erin.

Sarah's hands went to her mouth. "Oh my God, no." Fresh tears rolled down her cheeks, and she rocked again.

"I'm sorry to be the one to tell you." Erin felt like a broken record. "I thought maybe she confided in you."

More teary-eyed headshaking. "She still had a hard time trusting people after what happened when she was a kid."

"I hate to ask this," Beckett said, giving Erin a dark look, "but her parents don't know. The medical examiner will inform them tomorrow."

"I won't say anything, I promise."

"Thank you." He looked at Erin once more, like a father silently chastising a kid.

"By chance, did you ever go into Bonnie's attic?" Beckett asked abruptly.

"The attic?" Sarah's creamy skin turned ashen. "The news said that's where it happened."

Erin shot him a look, wishing he had been more subtle with Sarah. The girl twitched like a cracked piece of glass ready to shatter.

"I'm just asking because we'll need to eliminate fingerprints up there as well."

"I helped her put the air conditioner away a few weeks ago," Sarah said.

"Did you see anything strange up there?" He asked.

Her eyebrows came together, mouth bowed. "Like what? Junk?"

"Anything you thought looked odd?"

Another shake of the head. Exhaustion crept onto Sarah's face, her skin decidedly more pale than when she first sat down.

"We just have a couple more questions," Erin said. "Have you heard of a little girl named Mina or a boy named Charlie?"

Sarah's feet came down off the chair, her boots clacking onto the floor. She cocked her head. "Mina? Charlie? I don't know any kids."

"What about Bonnie? Did she ever mention either one of them or mention a friend having a little girl?"

"Maybe one of the other dancers at the club? But Bonnie didn't socialize with those girls."

"What about Jane?" Erin asked. "Did Bonnie ever mention anyone by that name?"

Sarah rubbed her temples hard enough her fingers left white marks on her fair skin. "No, I don't think so."

"And Bonnie never mentioned this possible cross-dresser

again?" Beckett asked, his eyes bright.

"No, that I would remember. Bonnie felt bad, but we joked about the poor thing. Bonnie wanted to give him some style tips. I don't know whether she ever did."

"What about Jack the Ripper?" Beckett's blunt question surprised Erin. "Did Bonnie have any interest in him, maybe as a research topic for school?"

"Jack the Ripper?" Sarah repeated the words slowly as though she didn't understand. "I have no idea. She never mentioned anything like that, but I'm starting to think she didn't tell me a lot of things."

Beckett nodded, his gaze never leaving Sarah's face. "Can you tell us where you were yesterday afternoon and evening?"

"My parents'," Sarah said. "I told you—working on my thesis."

"Right," he said. "Were you there by yourself?"

Creases lined Sarah's brow. "My mother stayed in all day, and the cleaning lady came some time during the evening. You'd have to ask Mother when. I was locked away in my room."

"We'll be sure to ask her." The undercurrent in Beckett's tone bordered on condescension.

Sarah's eyes grew large and her mouth slack. "Surely, you're not trying to ask me for an alibi?"

"It's procedure." Beckett tucked his notebook into the pocket of his slacks. "We need to cross you off the list."

"Thank you for coming in," Erin said. "If you remember anything else, call me." She handed Sarah a card. "And we may need to talk again. I don't want to come in between you and your parents, so will it be possible to arrange a meeting if we need to?"

"I think so," Sarah said. "As long as I have a little notice."

Erin and Beckett walked her to the main entrance and watched as the officer buzzed her out.

"You shouldn't have mentioned the pregnancy." Beckett didn't waste any time.

"Why not? Sarah's the one Bonnie would have told." A weariness unlike Erin had ever experienced settled into her bones.

"Because Bonnie's parents haven't been told. And how do we know she's not going to run back and tell?"

"She said she wouldn't."

"That doesn't mean she won't."

Too tired to argue and afraid she would pass out if she kept standing, Erin started for the squad room. "So how does Sarah not see the bed and video equipment in the attic?"

"Bonnie probably piled junk on it. Or maybe she hadn't gotten into the porn yet. Sarah did say that was a few weeks ago. But my guess is she knew about the amateur porn. She tried too hard to act like she didn't when you asked."

"We had a cool September," Erin said. "Brad opened our windows the second week." She didn't say anything more, her thoughts cluttered.

"But," Beckett prompted, "you don't think Sarah's being entirely truthful either, do you?"

Erin's body suddenly ached as though she'd just finished a marathon. She'd never participated in one, but she imagined the level of fatigue surging through her had to be similar. "I think the chances of Sarah being sexually abused by the same man who hurt Bonnie are high, even if the parents put a stop to it once Bonnie came forward. Her body language is indicative of an abuse victim.

She's extremely protective of herself. Not defensive, but ... guarded."

"Why didn't you push her on the issue?"

"Because you can't go at a sex victim like a bulldog," Erin said. "And her being abused may not be pertinent to the case, especially since the guy's long gone. It's part of what shaped her life and personality—including her general distrust." She unlocked her bottom drawer and retrieved her purse. "If our juvie Charlies turn out to be a bust, then what?"

"We talk to every one of the dancers at Sid's about Mina and Charlie," Beckett said. "And we keep looking for Tori. Maybe one of them can tell us his real name. Then we go back to the school. Keep hammering. Those are the places Bonnie spent her life. We also check into Sarah's background. See if she's been in trouble or in treatment for anything. Simon Archer might have handled his daughter's abuse differently."

Erin sagged against the wall. "I need to sleep. Start over fresh in the morning. If I can sleep. Between bad dreams and waiting for the next phone call, I doubt I will."

Beckett walked to his desk and retrieved his coat. "We should warn the other dancers at Sid's. If the killer targeted Bonnie because she danced and then rejected him, one of them could be the next target."

The unspoken possibility hung between them. Erin crossed her arms over her waist against the sudden rush of chills. "I'll see you tomorrow. I'm going home to my daughter."

* * *

Sarah Archer sat in her red convertible watching the rain trickle down the window. Her heart hurt for Bonnie. Why hadn't her cousin told her about the pregnancy? She thought they knew everything about each other.

But maybe you never really knew anyone. You only knew what the person wanted you to see. Bonnie's secrets hurt Sarah almost as much as her death.

She turned the ignition and let the engine idle. She didn't want to go back to her parents' house and listen to them insult Bonnie anymore. They had no right. Her father never answered for his silence, just like his friend never answered for his despicable acts.

And yet Bonnie apparently answered for hers.

Sarah wiped her face and put the car in gear. She'd done everything she could to help her cousin. It hadn't been good enough.

Chapter Twenty

A bby slept like a log, completely oblivious when Erin squeezed in next to her. Her butt hung off the side of the twin bed, but she didn't care. She buried her face into Abby's tangled hair and wrapped her arm around her daughter's slim waist. She sensed Erin's presence, snuggling into her with a satisfied sigh that brought tears to Erin's eyes. How had Abby gotten this big so quickly? It seemed like just yesterday she brought her tiny baby girl home from the hospital to the first apartment she and Brad shared. He'd been Abby's father figure from the start. Her worthless sperm donor had disappeared soon after Erin told him about her pregnancy.

Erin didn't care as long as she had her daughter. She pulled Abby closer and tried not to think about the fear in Mina's voice or the agony in Carmen Archer's.

Brad peeked around the open door. "I thought I heard you come in."

She could have stayed with Abby all night, but she also needed to sleep. The bed wasn't big enough for both of them. She kissed her daughter's soft cheek and carefully peeled herself away.

She met Brad in the hallway. "This has been a day from hell. The little girl called again. Her name is Mina, and so far, we can't find her anywhere."

Brad dragged his hands through his already messy blond hair. "Maybe it's a crank. Someone who saw the article and is putting their kid up to it."

Erin couldn't remember all the uniforms on scene last night. "Maybe. Could be the asshole unnamed source who told the reporter my nickname was Princess. Just trying to mess with me. But why? I don't have a beef with any of them."

"They might have one with you though," Brad said. "People are assholes in general. Speaking of, Dad called."

She rolled her eyes and shuffled toward her room. A hot shower sounded like heaven but so did passing out in her clothes. "Stop. He's not an asshole to you."

"He's not exactly a loving guy."

"He could be worse. What did he want?"

"You," he said. "He said Lisa and you had a spat at the office."

"That bitch." She shoved open the door to her room and flopped onto the bed. Decision made. "The guy who found Bonnie is a lobbyist for Baker-Allen. We needed his DNA and had follow-up questions. Lisa showed up and did her thing."

"Then she told Dad a different story," Brad finished. "Boy, there's a shock."

Erin set the alarm on her phone and plugged it in. "Did he sound pissed?"

"No, actually. He heard about the case and said if you need anything more, come straight to him. He'll get anything on Merritt you need."

"In other words," Erin spoke into the pillow, her eyelids already sagging, "don't make a scene. Keep things behind closed doors."

"Exactly." Brad didn't quite manage to hide his bitterness. "That's the same thing he said to me when I came out to him."

"I'm sorry," she said. "But he's better. You guys are better now."

"Thanks to you." Brad dragged the quilt out from underneath her and threw it on her hips. "Get some sleep."

"These next few days are going to be busy," she said. "You're able to help with Abby? Or do I need to ask Mrs. Bakas?"

Ellen Bakas, their next door neighbor, was a widow whose grandchildren lived three hours away. She doted on Abby, and Abby adored her—along with the rich Greek desserts she kept in stock. Erin usually didn't mind leaving her at Mrs. Bakas's house, but she didn't want to leave Abby with anyone else, not with the phone calls.

"I've got it. Just solve your case."

She slurred something about how badly life would suck without him, but exhaustion prevented her from making any sense. Her last thought was she'd have to do something special for him as soon as she solved this case.

Chapter Twenty-One

I no longer have control over my own mind. The demon has insinuated himself in every crevice, using the skill taught to me by my father for his dark deeds. He laughs with glee at the letters in the newspaper, for we did not send them. Unless I have forgotten doing so, which may be the truth. Voices war inside my head, and I know I'm going mad. My memories fade in and out. The demon enjoys the blood. My only solace is ridding our city of another dirty slag.

—JTR
30 September, 1888

I like their pain—an unexpected part of this little adventure. At first, killing them was a means to a necessary end. But every time I jam my knife into their flesh, through tissue and muscle and into precious organs and arteries, I feel a rush unlike anything I've ever experienced. Better than any anti-anxiety drug, recreational or off the street. Gloriously fucking addictive. I might keep doing this after I've taken care of the second traitorous bitch.

She let me in, of course. How could she refuse?

I watch her fat ass bounce as she walks ahead of me to the living room. Her robe doesn't flatter her plushy shape. Her thighs rub together when she walks, like two big marshmallows fused together. At this point in her life, with her pot belly and jug thighs, men don't notice her. At least men who aren't just as fat and gross as she is. That's probably why she suddenly became a lesbian. Women usually forgive because they understand the bullshit double standard females have to live with.

I let her talk for a minute, rattling about something I don't give a shit about, and then I make my move. The fat woman's eyes bulge when I punch her in the stomach, like a fat-ass doughboy getting the stuffing knocked out of him, and his eyes are the first orifice his innards can squeeze out of. Her eyes don't pop out, but I would have laughed if they did. Maybe I would've stuffed them into her big, fat mouth.

She doubles over, sausage-fingers clutching her middle. I hit her again, this time in the left temple. She drops to her knees, squealing like a baby pig taken off its mama's teat.

"What are you doing?"

She doesn't sound so smart any more. She sounds like a desperate woman who knows her time is up.

I kick her in the head, sending her overfed body flat to the floor. Her skull damn near smacks the fireplace.

I straddle her, my ass sinking into her thighs. "Tying up loose ends."

The knife takes a lot longer to sink through her extra layers of skin and into her stomach. I should have kept the cleaver instead of sticking it in Bonnie's well-used pussy. I shove as hard as I can, half-expecting to see yellow fat escaping from the wound. She screams something I can't understand. Or maybe I'm not listening to the words. I am caught up in the feeling of her body collapsing on itself, of the sight of the blood spurting, and of the guttural fear in her voice.

"What's it like to know you're about to die?" I ask. "Are you scared? Do you think you'll go to hell?"

She screams so loudly I hope the neighbors don't hear. I should be cautious and cut her throat completely, but that takes all the fun out of it. And that's not what Jack did, anyway.

She twists and jerks, trying to fight me off. I dig my knees into her sides, making sure to jam them up under her ribs, and hit her in the face again. Shock and being out of shape has fucked her chances of winning. I grip the knife with both hands and shove it deeper, jerking it toward her chest.

Her rolls bounce like a swollen Jell-O mold. This time, her eyes really do pop, at least to an extent. Red streaks burst across the left one as it hemorrhages from stress and pain. Glorious.

Blood gurgles from her wounds and then her mouth. I must have nicked something important. Anatomy isn't my strong suit, but I know the basics.

She keeps bouncing, making me bounce. My work becomes uneven and not as accurate as I hope. Her eyes roll back in her head. If I don't end it now, she'll pass out. And I want to have the final decision.

I lean over and grab one of the decorative throw pillows off her ugly couch. Her rolling eyes refocus, and she raises her stumpy arms in a final attempt to fight me off. I smack them away and press the pillow over her face, putting all of my upper body weight on it.

"This is what you get for being a tattle-tale."

Chapter Twenty-Two

Three damned days and nothing. No more calls from Mina and absolutely zero leads on anything. The paper found crumpled in Bonnie's attic didn't have a single print—bolstering Erin's belief the killer deliberately left it. Erin and Beckett, with help from Fowler—who quickly volunteered for the task—had talked to every stripper at Sid's. All liked Bonnie, and all expressed shock and grief.

All of the dancers described Tori as an older man with great makeup skills and nice clothes. He usually wore a dark, loose-fitting dress and a black wig cut in a stylish bob. He didn't keep an account or tab with the club and always paid with cash. Bonnie's disagreement with him surprised her coworkers, who considered Tori a perfect gentleman who happened to like wearing ladies clothes. Bonnie refused to discuss Tori, and her coworkers dropped the subject. No one knew his real name, or any Jane, Mina, or Charlie who might have been associated with Bonnie Archer.

Subsequent searches at neighboring bars and strip clubs for Tori came up empty with the exception of The Point. The low-key gay bar on the waterfront was a known favorite of the LGBT community, and several bartenders remembered Tori frequenting the establishment within the last two months, although he hadn't been seen in a couple of weeks. All cash transactions and no decent images on the security footage meant yet another dead end.

Bonnie's phone records proved useless. Calls to her work, to her parents, to Sarah and Will Merritt and to her school, as well as several calls to an unlisted number, probably a throwaway phone. Another dead end.

Brian Reese's alibi checked out as expected. Ricky Stout skipped his night class. A trip to the shelter listed as his last address yielded exactly nothing. No one knew where he'd gone. The director was on vacation and was the only person who worked at the shelter when Ricky would have been living there. Erin left her card.

The Charlies with juvenile records went nowhere. The computer people had yet to hit on Bonnie's porn videos—another job Fowler volunteered to help with until he needed to search for rape porn.

This world is full of sick fucks. Erin pulled up another site. The amount of pay-per-view porn sites on the dark web astounded her. New ones seemed to pop up overnight, and Erin couldn't get in without giving her credit card information.

11:00 p.m. and she holed up in her room, half under the covers, watching the stuff of nightmares. Women tied up and screaming, begging for mercy. Fake and usually poorly acted, but cold sweat still soaked Erin's nightshirt, and the memories still rushed back.

She hadn't screamed. She let him do it because she thought fighting back would get her killed. Abby couldn't grow up without her mother.

Rape crisis counseling helped her move on, at least to an

extent. But she struggled with trusting men, with trusting her own judgment.

The thought made Bonnie Archer hard to feel sorry for. But then Erin remembered the cleaver sticking out of the girl's destroyed body, and she pulled up another video.

Her ringing phone gave her a respite from the latest filth.

"It's Sergeant Clark."

Erin froze at the grave tenor of his voice. "It's another body, right? It's not Mina, is it?"

"Not a kid, thank God."

"Is it a boy? Mina talked about Charlie taking care of her."

"It's a middle-aged female in Takoma Park." Worry colored Clark's baritone. "But Mitchell says it's the same killer."

Clark rattled off an address as Erin fumbled for paper and pen. "Get over there ASAP. Beckett will meet you."

* * *

Dawn hadn't yet reached the horizon when Erin parked her car in front of the restored craftsman home in Takoma Park. Although she'd moved as quickly as possible, she still limped woefully behind. After waking her snoring brother and getting his assurance Abby would be taken care of for the day, she'd rushed to the car, still trying to wrap her mind around the sergeant's words.

Not Mina or Charlie. Not another struggling young woman in a challenging neighborhood but nearly her polar opposite: a forty-something college professor in a middle class suburb.

Takoma Park was trendy, fun, and loaded with security-cautious people who could afford to install alarm systems. People who noticed someone strange on their street and had no problem calling the police. So why would someone who so obviously planned his attacks risk coming to a place like Takoma Park? Did he need to up the thrill factor?

At least it's not a kid.

Erin shut her car door, and gooseflesh immediately covered her arms despite her fleece jacket. The last week had brought nothing but gray skies and a dampness intent on leaching warmth from the skin. Death lingered everywhere: prickly brown grass, often swampy with rainwater; fall leaves that had been a brilliant red and gold had turned putrid and crisp; perennials reduced to a tangle of stems. Erin would welcome an early snow just to cover the decay.

Headlights shined in her eyes. Erin shielded her face and then waited for Beckett to park his Prius behind her car. He unfolded his long form and emerged in khakis and a snug fleece jacket, looking fresher and more put together than Erin. She'd tugged on what she hoped were clean jeans and a long sleeved shirt, and she was pretty sure her socks didn't match.

"I just got here," she said by way of greeting. "I suppose you've heard the basics. This victim has nothing in common with Bonnie."

"Sometimes the common denominator is the random selection." Beckett followed her up the walk. They stood side by side at the base of the wide steps, both taking in the home.

"No sign of breaking and entering." Erin studied the rectangular porch. She loved the house at first sight and took a brief moment to appreciate it. Like many of the revitalized homes in the area, the house looked as though it weathered the decades, soaked in the history of the city, and came out stronger. "So our victim knew the guy, just like Bonnie?"

"My gut says a preliminary yes. And who called in the body at this hour?" Beckett glanced around. "This isn't exactly a night owl sort of neighborhood."

"That's one of the most interesting parts." Sergeant Clark emerged from the shadows of the porch.

Erin jumped at the sound of his voice and hoped the men didn't notice.

"The 9-1-1 call came from an untraceable number, probably another damned pay-as-you-go. We're searching the property to see if the caller tossed it."

"So the murderer called it in?" Erin hoped her voice sounded steady.

"Possibly, but not until about forty-five minutes ago. Mitchell puts preliminary time of death at, at least, eight hours ago. But the killer might have come back, admiring his work and all." Clark shuddered. "You need to talk to Mitchell. We've got another message, but there's more to this one."

Erin hesitated on the wide front porch. The house's blazing lights did nothing to shed the sensation of walking through the devil's doorway. Her knees buckled, sweat beaded across her hairline. Her chest tightened.

Beckett stood somewhere behind her, patiently waiting. Did he sense it too? Did he feel the weird, baking humidity seeming to crawl out of the house?

Terror washed over Erin, but she had to get going. Another butchered woman waited for Erin and Beckett to stop the killing. Erin willed her feet to move forward.

The sharp, pungent odor of decay assaulted Erin and Beckett as soon as they entered the welcoming entryway. She covered her nose and tried to breathe through her mouth. Dan Mitchell and his assistant knelt in the large living room, positioned on either side of the body. Wide columns separated the living room from the entryway, and Erin couldn't help but think she'd crossed into the threshold of hell when she saw the dead woman.

Virginia Walton lay spread-eagle in front of the fireplace, her pink robe and nightgown hiked up to her knees. Thankfully, it appeared the killer hadn't stuck anything up her vagina.

Fuzzy slippers covered her feet. "No blood on the slippers," Erin heard herself saying. "So he got her down to the floor before he … started."

Her gaze went to the mahogany fireplace mantle. Scrawled in dark blood were the words *snitch* and *1888 Hanbury Street*. Beneath the address, the initials *JTR*.

"The second Ripper victim." Erin forced the words out.

Copious amounts of blood saturated the carpet. Erin dug her toes into her shoes in an effort not to sway. Her breathing sounded ragged and fast. Beside her, Beckett sucked in a breath as ragged as hers. The noise somehow steadied Erin enough to take stock of what lay in front of her.

Virginia Walton's left arm lay across her generous left breast, which had been sliced open to reveal yellow fatty tissue. Her legs were drawn up with her feet resting on the carpet, the knees turned outward. It made Erin think of being stuck in the stirrups in the gynecologist's office. Swollen and purple, the woman stared blankly at the fireplace. Blood crusted along the right side of her face and neck. Part of the right earlobe was missing.

180

"Did you find the earlobe?"

"Not yet," Mitchell said softly.

Long, purplish, ropey strands extended from the vicious cuts to the abdomen.

He filleted her. Like the fish her father caught during one of the family vacations to the lake. Erin remembered standing at the doorway of the little building where the men went to cut the fish. The smell made her sick, but the way the helpless fish flopped while her father dragged the knife through it made her and Brad run screaming to their mother. Their older sister laughed.

That hateful laughter echoed through Erin's head as she edged closer. "Those are her intestines." Erin sounded as though she spoke into some kind of bell jar.

Dan Mitchell swiveled around on his toes and then pointed to Virginia's pelvic region.

Copious amounts of blood prevented Erin from figuring out what Mitchell wanted her to see.

"He tried to cut her uterus out too. And her bladder. He either tired out or didn't have a good enough knife. Or maybe he lost the nerve."

Mitchell sounded like he might cry, or maybe, Erin just assumed the possibility given his Droopy-Dog face.

"Jack the Ripper cut off part of the right ear." Beckett said.

"Catherine Eddows," Erin said. "The fourth victim. Jack sliced her whole body up. Severe facial lacerations and part of her ear was missing. He destroyed her labia. This," she pointed to Virginia Walton's body, "isn't as bad as that."

"He's inspired," Beckett said. "But he's trying to be original at the same time."

"Obviously, you have the cleaver that killed Bonnie Archer," Mitchell said. "These cuts were done by a long blade, at least six inches. Incredibly sharp to do all of this. But he still left something in her vaginal area."

Sweat blistered on Erin's face as Mitchell handed her a clear evidence bag containing a piece of college-ruled notebook paper covered with blood and bodily fluid. She could only make out a few words, once again written in modern black ink.

I no longer have control
Voices war
The demon blood.

—JTR

Tendrils of the same evil energy from Bonnie's crime scene ghosted around Erin with the strength of an iron fist. If an act of cruelty left an imprint, surely this must be it. "I've spent the last few days digging into Ripper lore. I can't find any letters matching any of the passages we've seen so far—not even the ones known to be fake."

She handed the bag to Beckett with more force than intended as though the crux of evil rested in the handwriting itself. Erin hated the way the fear seeped into her voice. But the world seemed to be spiraling out of control, and she had no clue how to stop the bleeding. Literally.

Beckett cleared his throat. "She appears to have been smothered. Do you agree?"

Mitchell glanced down at the woman's purple, swollen face.

"Definitely. And then cutting started, based on the blood flow."

Erin asked the question she wasn't sure she wanted an answer to. "How similar to the second Ripper victim is this?"

"Very close." Clark glared across the expanse, shaking his head. "The Ripper did worse things to Annie Chapman—the victim found at Hanbury Street—but we can't deny the similarities."

"I don't understand it," Erin said. "Our killer is inspired by the Ripper murders, but he's not exactly copycatting them. Especially with these notes. So what's the killer's obsession about?"

And what about Jane—or Jill, as the lore called her? Erin didn't say the name out loud, but it rested on the tip of her tongue, waiting for the right moment. What better role model for a killer than a woman who escaped justice—and history—for butchering at least five prostitutes?

"I don't think it's all about Jack." Clark motioned for them to follow him back to the entryway. He lowered his voice. "We have to keep this information contained. Aside from us, Mitchell's the only one who's seen the body and the message. If the press gets wind we have two women killed by a nut job paying homage to Jack the Ripper, all hell will break loose. That doesn't help us catch him. The Ripper stuff is all window dressing, same with the notes. Distractions."

Beckett clearly agreed, his head bobbing up and down, his face passive and thoughtful as usual. "So we know why Bonnie is a whore. Why is the professor a snitch? Was she in the attic?"

"Surely not, or he would have killed her then. But there's got to be a link between the two women. He chose them for specific reasons." Clark looked down at his phone, his crooked index finger scrolling over the screen. "I need to notify next of kin."

He pointed to the fireplace where several pictures of a thirty-something woman and a gap-toothed little girl held court. "I'm assuming that's her daughter. We found her contact information in the professor's cell. It lay on the dining room table with her purse. Wallet and credits cards still there."

"Is the daughter local?" Erin's heart beat a little bit faster. "If she's got a child, maybe that's Mina. Maybe she was too scared."

Clark's brow furrowed, his graying eyebrows knitting together. "Not sure, but I'll find out. Although I can't imagine a daughter orchestrating something like this for her own mother."

"That doesn't have to be it," Erin said. "Maybe the daughter had a drug problem, and that's the connection to Bonnie. An old friend from the past asks for help, and Bonnie agrees. The dealer tracks her down to Bonnie's place, and then Bonnie gets it. Same thing happens here." Reaching, but they needed to put this gruesome picture together before yet another woman died.

Beckett crossed his arms, looking between Erin and the sergeant. "I wouldn't rule it out. But this seems way too bloody for something like that. You've worked a couple of drug homicides," he said to Erin. "Doesn't this feel like the opposite end of the spectrum?"

He meant to be conversational, simply tossing a theory back and forth the way partners do. But Erin's skin still heated with embarrassment. Why couldn't he back her up in front of Clark? "I guess."

"The number is a South Carolina area code," Clark said. "So if she is in town, she's visiting. I'm going outside to make the call." He shook his head, looking disgusted. "It's not right, but this murder is going to make the news. Possibly national. A prominent, white college professor literally slaughtered in her home. That'll be the sickeningly sweet icing on the press's shit cake. Her family can't find out that way." He took one last, long look toward the dead woman. "Figure this out before things get worse."

Beckett strode back over to Mitchell.

Erin took her time, trying to gather her emotions. She forced the steaming indignation into the same reservoir she always did and focused on the issue at hand. "So we are sure she was killed at least eight hours ago?"

Mitchell nodded. "She's in pretty good rigor."

"So somewhere around eight or nine p.m. last night." Erin spoke before her partner could. "That's when he attacked and smothered her. But could the killer have come back and mutilated her and then made the call?" She directed her question to the death investigator still cataloguing the injuries.

Beckett answered before Mitchell had the chance. "No way. The 9-1-1 call came in less than an hour ago. She would have been in at least partial rigor then. And the blood flow would be completely different, correct?"

Mitchell nodded. "Absolutely. I'm not saying your killer didn't make the call. But the mutilation happened shortly after death." He pointed to the walls and then the ceiling. "No arterial spurt. It just drained out of her like a sink drain after you take the stopper out. All this damage occurred right after her heart stopped beating."

Erin flushed at her foolish mistake. "Okay, so let's work the scene. When's the crime scene crew due to arrive?"

"They're at least twenty minutes out," Mitchell said. "Some

kid found a guy in a dumpster. The body's a few days old, and the scene is a mess. Marie's been there all day. I woke her up."

"You couldn't call another crew?" Erin asked.

"Marie worked Bonnie's murder," Beckett spoke up. "It's better if she works this one. She has an idea of what to look for. And using her will help keep information contained." He knelt down to look closer at the victim. "Is that bruising on her face from the suffocation?"

Mitchell took a closer look, slipping on a pair of glasses that made his Droopy eyes enormous. "He punched her in the face before she died. She's discolored from suffocation and the effects that followed."

He touched Virginia Walton's forehead, which had a strange blue circle of blood in the center. "But this almost looks like lividity. Just the initial stages."

Erin tried to figure out the size of the blood pool. "If the killer turned her over, wouldn't it be obvious?"

Dan pointed a gloved finger to the center of the enormous bloodstain. "At first, I thought the circumference was smaller than Bonnie Archer's because the carpet soaked up the blood. But there are no arterial spurts since Virginia died before he started cutting. And you can see she simply bled out." He touched the soft flesh of Virginia's outstretched arms. "This looks like possible lividity here too." His eyes danced like he'd won the jackpot. "Can you help me turn her over?"

A body in rigor is literally dead weight, and Virginia Walton had ample flesh on her frame. Mitchell and Beckett took several minutes to carefully turn her, both men's faces red and sweating with the effort.

Time stilled. The whoosh of blood roared in Erin's ears to the point of being painful. Her lips moved, but no sound came out of her mouth.

Beckett appeared to be rendered mute as well. Huffing, he stared down at the dead woman's back as though he didn't quite believe what he was seeing.

"Holy hell," Mitchell said. "Does that mean what I think it means?"

The killer had signed Virginia's ample back, slicing into her flesh with the flourish of someone who clearly enjoyed the task.

Jane the Ripper.

Chapter Twenty-Three

"The killer *is* a woman." Erin whispered, unable to speak any louder.

Beckett stared back at her, white-faced. "If a woman did this ... if a woman stuck a cleaver in Bonnie's vagina ..."

Erin's patience snapped. "Look, I know I don't have your experience. But I have instincts, and every single one of them tells me we are dealing with a woman. Women are vindictive, cruel creatures when they're scorned. Add in a little bit of insanity and obsession, and you've got the perfect recipe. She signed her fucking name in this woman's skin!"

"But why?" Beckett countered. "Common sense—not to mention crime statistics—indicates the killer is a man. Why wave the truth around like a red flag?"

"She wants credit. She's proud of what she's done. The media will love her."

Beckett rubbed his face until the skin turned red. "All right, fine. Virginia Walton is over fifty. She's not pregnant. She's not a prostitute or drug addict. She has zero in common with Bonnie Archer. You're still quite a ways from the Ripper's preference."

"You know it's possible," Erin said. "You've seen what a woman is capable of."

"Don't tell me what I know."

Beckett's sharp tone surprised her.

"I know people are capable of terrible, terrible things. People can masquerade as anything. Women can be the most vicious creatures on earth. And the most resourceful." He closed his eyes. "But this. Physically ... how?"

"She incapacitates first," Mitchell said. "Both Bonnie and Professor Walton were beaten first. If the killer—if she—planned ahead and had the right tools, it's plausible."

"But why the name Jane?" Beckett asked. "The lore calls her Jill the Ripper—Jack and Jill. So why hasn't she used that name?"

"Maybe her real name is Jane. Considering the way she's cutting people up, it's not high on my list of things to ask her."

"Don't forget the cross-dresser at the strip club," Beckett said. "Jack supposedly dressed like a woman. It's just another piece of the lore this killer's choosing to emulate."

"A cross-dresser who seems to have disappeared. And Bonnie's the only dancer at Sid's who reported any issues with him. I don't think he's the killer." Why the hell was Beckett so against the killer being a woman? The questions boiled inside her, but she fought them back. Dressing him down in front of Dan would be unprofessional and rude.

Erin followed the trail of dark crimson dots on the hardwood floor leading to the dining room. "She wasn't as careful this time. Maybe Jane ran out of time." She crossed through the two mahogany pillars separating the living room and dining room, stopping at the pool of blood next to the antique dining room table. "She stood right here."

The mess on the table nearly gave Erin hives. Essays on dreams and their impact on everyday life had been stacked neatly next to several textbooks and an agenda. Professor Walton still operated in the old school world. Most people used their phone or computer calendars to plan their lives. More red caught her eye. One of the papers had a series of drips on the inside panel, its contents scattered over the table.

"Damn," Beckett said. "I hoped we'd catch a bloody fingerprint."

He seemed resigned, but she noticed his trembling fingers.

Her blue latex gloves shining beneath the modern chandelier light, Erin carefully thumbed through the papers. "Oh shit."

"What?" Beckett had started leafing through the planner.

"Virginia Walton is a counselor at the Adult Learning Center."

"So there's our connection to Bonnie Archer," Beckett said. "But if Virginia knew Bonnie, why didn't she come forward after her murder?"

Frustration built into a scream from somewhere deep in Erin's gut. Every time she thought she found a crack in this case, another unanswered question snapped it shut. "But so much for asking her now."

Chapter Twenty-Four

The fetid air clawed at Erin's throat, and her stomach heaved. She stepped out on the porch to breathe in some fresh air.

"Investigator Prince!" The redhead's shrill voice cut over the din of birds greeting the dismal morning.

Crap! She had forgotten the press vultures had arrived shortly after the crime scene crew. Erin nearly flipped her off, but throwing fresh meat on the lawn would have caused less of a ruckus. The last thing she needed was the reporter who kept calling her "The Princess" asking questions while she felt sicker than a dog. She couldn't let the press know the crime scene had overwhelmed her or Red would have a field day with it.

"I heard the victim has multiple stab wounds. Is this related to Bonnie Archer's murder?"

Erin stepped off the porch, wincing as the digital cameras started clicking away. "No comment." She'd pretend she had come out to check on the status of the search for the throwaway phone.

She dropped to a squat and twisted to look beneath the porch. A scrollwork border kept critters from burrowing underneath, and no way could someone squeeze the phone through one of the intricate loops.

"If it's not related to Bonnie, then why are you here?"

Red wasn't ready to give up.

"Because I happened to be on rotation." Erin pushed through the dead rhododendrons and scanned the foundation.

"Isn't that a lot of pressure for an inexperienced homicide investigator?"

Erin's gaze snapped toward the redhead.

A lackey held an umbrella over the reporter's head to protect her perfect hair.

"No comment." Erin stood and strode toward one of the uniforms searching near the backyard.

"What does your father think of you going into homicide? Surely he would rather you do something safer."

Erin changed direction and closed the distance between her and Red. She lowered her voice. "Listen. These murders aren't about me or my family name. Do the victims some justice, will you?"

After checking with the uniform, she stalked back into the house. In the entryway, she placed a call to Metro. She needed the moment to settle before facing the crime scene again.

She rejoined Beckett. "I talked to Fowler. He cross-referenced the numbers on Bonnie's phone with the 9-1-1 caller's. Not a match. And he lives near American University, so he's heading in to interview the staff."

Beckett watched Marie gather trace from the dining room. "Still worth checking."

Erin scowled.

Beckett gave her a sharp glance. "Something wrong? Beyond the obvious nightmare of a morning?"

"Just that asshole reporter. Nothing major."

"I think asshole is a requirement on a fledgling reporter's résumé," Beckett said without humor. "Mitchell's getting her ready for transport."

"Jane." Sickness built in Erin's throat. "How could one woman do this to another."

"Let me ask you something," Beckett said. "Why are you so sure it's a woman? We could still be looking at a smoke screen, a damned good one."

Erin tried to frame her answer in a reasonable and mature way instead of losing her cool the way she had earlier. "It's Mina. I keep hearing the sheer terror in her voice and the way she said *her*. Like she was afraid of that person, not worried about her."

"Possibly," Beckett said. "Or maybe your memory is tricking you. It happens to all of us." Beckett raised his hands in either defeat or frustration. "But for the record, I'm confused as hell. And you could well be right."

"I think you just don't want this to be a woman."

He looked up at the somber sky. "Do you?"

"I want to stop her before she kills again."

The drizzle picked up as they walked to their cars. The reporters—with Red front and center—called out more questions. Erin and Beckett ignored them.

Erin's phone pinged with a text. "Sergeant Clark says the daughter's still in South Carolina. She teaches and can be alibied. So that wipes the theory."

"At least we can throw it out quickly."

Across the street, a woman in a blue robe watched them and waved at Erin.

"Have we talked to any of the neighbors yet?"

"Not yet," Beckett said. "Most are just waking up."

Erin crossed the street with Beckett on her heels. "Let's see what she wants."

The short, stocky woman met them on the steps. Her hair still stuck up from sleeping, and the intoxicating aroma of coffee wafted from her. "Your medical examiner's van is here. Did someone murder Virginia?"

"I'm afraid we can't give you details," Erin said. "But she is deceased."

The woman sagged as though she'd been hit. Erin guessed her to be about the professor's age, although Virginia Walton's swollen face made comparison impossible. "I had a feeling she was in trouble."

Beckett shifted beside Erin, leaning against the handrail. "How so?"

"I don't know her well," the neighbor clarified. "But we talk, coming and going. Sometimes we have coffee together."

"What did Virginia tell you?" Erin asked.

"She's been through a lot the past couple of years." The woman played with the edge of her robe tie. "Finally coming out and then trying to navigate that lifestyle as a middle-aged woman."

"Virginia Walton was a lesbian?" Erin asked.

"Yes," the woman said. "And I didn't care, mind you. I'm not one to judge. Live and let live, I say. But the transition was hard. That's why she came here from South Carolina. Guess she taught at a small Christian college there. You can imagine their reaction."

"Right." Erin remembered the whisper-mongering among her parents' friends after Brad came out—though most of them already suspected. Apparently, in their conservative circle, daring to own one's sexuality was a greater crime than the actual preference. "Did she have issues with her colleagues at American University?"

"She never mentioned any. And I'm not saying her murder had anything to do with sexuality. She's had a tough time of it. Maybe she latched on to someone she shouldn't have."

"Did you see anyone unusual around last night?" Beckett asked.

"No, but I went to bed early," the woman's voice shook. "I normally don't."

"Did you notice any visitors?" Erin asked. "Maybe a girlfriend?"

The woman nodded. "The dark-haired girl. Small thing and half Virginia's age. Of course, they may not have been involved."

Erin clung to a neutral expression. "How often did this girl come around?"

"I only saw her a few times a couple of weeks ago." The neighbor glanced around them to look at Virginia Walton's violated home. "But ever since she showed up, Virginia had become really edgy. Nervous. She didn't like my noticing the girl, and I thought maybe she was a student at AU. That's probably some sort of violation."

"Quite possibly," Erin said. "Did Virginia mention the girl's name?"

"No, I'm sorry."

Erin chewed her bottom lip, hoping for some kind of signal as to how he wanted to proceed. She pulled her phone with Bonnie's picture out of her bag. "Is this her?"

The neighbor retrieved a pair of reading glasses from her robe pocket and pulled the phone closer to her face. "It could be. She looks small like this girl. Same hair. But I never saw her face very clearly. I just can't be sure."

"Thank you," Erin said as Beckett stowed the phone. "You've been a huge help. Our sergeant is going to come by in a while, and he'll ask you more questions." She handed her a card. "Please call me if you think of anything else."

"Of course." The neighbor's face suddenly fell. "God, Virginia is really dead. You don't think about something like that happening here."

"We believe it's an isolated incident," Beckett said. "But do take extra precautions."

"We need to check with the bartenders at The Point," Erin said as she and Beckett jogged through the drizzle to their respective cars. "It's high end and a private gay bar in a safe area of the city, which might be the perfect spot for someone relatively new to the local scene. Virginia might have checked it out."

Beckett ducked his head against the rain. "I want to get my hands on Bonnie's laptop. The killer stole it because he was on there."

"You mean Jane," Erin said.

"I mean the person who wants us to believe it's Jane."

Erin stopped near her driver's door. "I'm trying to be polite, but I'm tired and cranky, so I'm probably going to sound like an asshole. Why are you so against this killer being a woman?"

Beckett's face smoothed into a plastic-looking, fake expression. "I'm not against it. I'm trying to look at the entire picture. Tunnel vision in an investigation causes major mistakes. I learned that the hard way. And we might be looking at a man in

196

cross-dress. Don't forget Tori."

He hadn't shared the entire truth, but Erin doubted she'd get anything more from him. "As for the missing videos, they might answer a lot of questions. But Bonnie wasn't a student at AU, so if the professor got involved with her, she didn't break school rules."

"What about societal rules?" Beckett asked. "We're in a liberal zone, but how would people react if she were dating a girl half her age?"

"No clue," Erin said. "What if Bonnie and Virginia were seeing each other, and Bonnie told Virginia about making the porn? Jane finds out and gets pissed. If Tori's our killer, what's his motive? Although plenty of men who cross-dress still identify as straight males, so I suppose he might have had a thing for Bonnie and gotten jealous." She shook her head. "But why call the professor a snitch? Bonnie's videos aren't illegal. Unless Virginia planned to tell Bonnie's parents. But if she cared for Bonnie, that doesn't make sense either."

Worry lines carved their way across Beckett's forehead. He ducked his chin against the cold, his eyes flickering between the slate-colored sky and Virginia's body being wheeled out of the house. "To make someone suffer the way these two women did takes an enormous amount of anger, not to mention psychotic tendencies. Whoever did this enjoys inflicting pain on people he— or she—believes wronged them."

Erin remembered the malevolent atmosphere at both crime scenes and shivered. "Absolutely."

Beckett put his back to the activity across the street and looked down at her, the stress of the morning clear in his eyes. "I don't think we have a clue what any of this is about. We've been on the wrong track the entire time, and I have no idea how to find the right one."

His words struck Erin like a fist digging into her solar plexus. In the few days they worked together, she quickly learned to count on Beckett's quiet confidence. She blinked as cold rain sheeted from the swollen sky. Beckett's confession seeped into her bones and festered like a forgotten piece of food stuck in the back of the refrigerator. Her wet lips worked to say something inspiring, but everything sounded desperate and stale.

Rain plinked in her eye, snapping her out of it. "Let's start talking to the rest of the neighbors before the reporters beat us to it."

Chapter Twenty-Five

Most of the neighbors had been interviewed by mid-morning. They claimed Virginia Walton kept to herself, and none had more to contribute. No one else noticed any visitors, but the area struck Erin as sterile and segregated. Most of the neighbors knew little about each other and preferred it that way.

"Where are we at on trace?" Erin stood near the heating vent in the dining room, willing to put up with the stench of the house in exchange for warmth. Her fingers throbbed from cold.

Marie grumbled something unintelligible. She sat on the floor, surrounded by white boxes. "This woman did not like technology. Boxes and boxes of printed records. She's got papers from students going back to her college in South Carolina. She brought it all with her! It's going to take days to catalogue. Beyond the mess of paper, we're finding the usual mishmash of hair and fiber. No fingerprints so far, and I'm not expecting to find any belonging to the killer. He's too smart. Wait, she." Marie peered over the stack she'd marked for evidence. "You think it's a woman?"

"Both crime scenes have been signed with a woman's name," Erin said. "We don't have hard proof yet, but it's a definite possibility."

Marie shuddered. "I can't imagine one woman doing this to another."

"Neither can I," Erin said. Her phone vibrated in her pocket, and Sarah Archer's number flashed on the screen. "Hello?"

"Investigator Prince."

Sarah's shrill voice made Erin's ear ring.

"I just saw the news. Is it true? Is Professor Walton dead?"

"I'm afraid so," Erin said. "How do you know her?"

"She's my thesis advisor." A choking sob came over the phone. "She knew Bonnie, too. My God, who's doing this?"

Erin waved at Marie and headed outside to find Beckett, fresh chills rushing through her "We're going to find out, Sarah." Rain plinked in Erin's eye as she waved to Beckett to get in the car. "Stay put. My partner and I are coming to talk to you."

* * *

The drive to Chevy Chase took nearly an hour. Erin drove with the radio turned off, still trying to come up with something to put Beckett's mind—and hers—at ease. But she had nothing. The investigation fell on its heels from the start, and they had done nothing but spin in circles. Virginia Walton's murder might have widened the playing field but only to multiply the sense of confusion.

A woman both Bonnie and Virginia trusted executed those brutal killings. Intellectually, Erin accepted women were capable of despicable things. Women killed lovers and children, and women abused and tortured. Women killed multiple people. Her emotional side couldn't make sense of any of it.

Sarah Archer had connections to both of these women. She'd likely been sexually abused around the same time as Bonnie. She might be hiding something, but Erin couldn't see meek Sarah as a killer, especially when Virginia Walton probably had at least fifty pounds on her.

Erin tried to navigate the giant jigsaw puzzle of evidence. The murders weren't about obsession or ritual but punishments inspired by the exploits of Jack the Ripper. Could the mutilation simply be a smoke screen or a taunt because the killer believed she couldn't be caught?

And was Sarah the next victim—or something far worse?

* * *

"Carmen Archer claims she had no idea Sarah and Bonnie reconnected." Beckett said as soon as he rolled out of his tiny car. "I called on my way here. She didn't sound too happy about it, either."

"Did she talk to you about the sexual abuse?" Erin asked.

"No, but she backed up Sarah's time frame on the family fallout, and she admitted she did speak to Sarah several years ago. Asked me not to mention it to her husband."

"Well, I can't blame the Archers if Sarah's version is true. Anyone who rapes a kid deserves to have his dick cut off, at the least. As far as I'm concerned, their lives should be an automatic forfeit."

Beckett jerked his head, staring up at the house.

Erin worried she'd gone too far. "I'm speaking from a parent's perspective. We can't toss all the pedophiles into the abyss. But I'd like to."

"It would be wonderful if justice could be that black and white," Beckett said. "Speaking of pedophiles and all things scum of the earth, you need to let me ask Lucy for help. She might even be able to do it without her NCMEC resources. She's got a friend who can basically track anything online."

"Legally?" Erin asked.

Beckett shrugged. "I don't ask those questions. They've been able to help me catch some extremely bad people. And I trust them."

Erin wanted nothing more than to cut corners. Their case was one of many, and the computer guys had to prioritize. "Sergeant Clark won't like it. I don't want to piss him off on my first major case. And you shouldn't, either."

"Think about it. Lucy could give us the break we need." Beckett stared at the house—a big Greek revival with cultivated flowerbeds already prepared for the oncoming winter. "Nice digs."

"Definitely," Erin said. "McLean, Virginia, is the top dog when it comes to money and snobbery, but Chevy Chase doesn't lag too far behind."

"Isn't McLean where you grew up?"

"Yep. As for the Archer family dispute, some grudges never go away, especially when a kid's involved. They just get stronger."

"Like you and your sister," Beckett said.

Erin shot him a look. "That's more than a grudge. And not something I want to talk about."

"My bad," he said. "I'd like to ask Sarah about the messages left."

"You mean the killer calling Bonnie a whore and the professor a snitch?"

He nodded. "She's family, and it's going to be hard for her, but right now, she's the only person connected to both of them. We have to push her this time."

Erin chewed on her lip. "But she has an alibi for Bonnie's murder. Her mother confirmed it, and the housekeeper remembered Sarah's car being in the driveway, because she'd blocked the girl in." She leaned against the car. "And you said you had a hard time seeing a woman kill Virginia because of her size. Do you believe Sarah is physically strong enough?"

"If she incapacitated her, then possibly." Beckett worried his lower lip. "But Sarah's afraid of her own shadow. I honestly can't see her having the presence of mind to commit either murder. But she knows more than she's telling us—even if she doesn't realize it." He stroked his mustache. "As for the Ripper being a woman, I accept we've got to consider it, although I think Tori the cross-dresser is more likely. You think the medical examiner will have any luck expediting the DNA on Bonnie's baby? That could help narrow things down."

"I hope so," Erin said and pushed upright off the car. "Our killer may simply be a jealous ex, and Will Merritt lied to us about the nature of his and Bonnie's relationship. Even if he's not a suspect, he may still be involved somehow."

She and Beckett walked toward the door.

He nodded. "Definitely possible. But in that scenario, Sarah's out of the equation, and there's no connection to Virginia Walton. Which makes no sense."

Erin rang the doorbell. "Sometimes the connection is in the randomness of it."

Beckett grinned down at her. "At least we're communicating."

Erin recognized the woman who answered the door. Not her face but the sort of person she was. Her polished skin gleamed like heirloom china, and the woman's most likely graying hair was dyed a shining blonde to match her daughter's. She dressed like Erin's mother and most of the Princes' conservative friends: expensive, tailored tweed slacks complimented by a cream cable-knit sweater. The only pieces of jewelry the woman displayed were pearl earrings and a beautiful diamond wedding set. Her stylish house slippers appeared made for snow but probably resulted in soaked feet. They looked great with her outfit.

Old wealth and proud of it, ready with a subtle insult but unlikely to be outright rude.

"Can I help you?" Her soft voice seemed to match her outfit, and Erin became acutely aware of her own faded jeans and unruly hair.

"Investigators Erin Prince and Todd Beckett. We're here to talk to Sarah about Bonnie's murder."

"And a new development," Beckett added.

The woman's skillfully applied blush dimmed. Her careful smile diminished enough for her mouth to sag and age her at least a decade. "Professor Walton. Sarah is devastated."

"I'm sure," Erin said. "We do need to speak with her. Your name is Melinda, right?"

"Melinda Archer." The woman's dark eyes narrowed, and she leaned forward to get a better look at Erin. "You're Calvin Prince's daughter. You spoke with my husband yesterday."

"Yes."

Melinda's voice immediately warmed. "We attended his

Republican rallies for the last presidential election. He was a wonderful speaker. And if I can be painfully honest, far more appealing than Romney. I told your father he should run for office. He got a kick out of it. And of course, your father has been a wonderful contributor to the Republican Governors."

Erin plastered a smile on her face. Her older sister had been telling her father to go into politics for years. Erin could only imagine how Lisa would worm her way into the White House. "I'm sure he did get a kick out of it. May we come in?"

"Of course, dear." Melinda stepped aside, beckoning them into a large, tiled entryway. "My husband is at work, but I'll get Sarah."

Her slippers slapped against the floor as she led them into a posh living room. "Please make yourselves comfortable. I'll be right back with her."

"Well," Beckett said as soon as the woman shuffled away, "the Prince name reigns again." He nudged her. "See what I did there?"

Erin shot him a look.

"What I find fascinating," Beckett said, "is how her attitude completely changed when she realized who you were."

"Welcome to my world," Erin said. "Here's where things get really smarmy—I'm going to try to use it to our advantage."

Erin preferred to stay in the large foyer, but Melinda Archer insisted they take tea in the next room. Erin and Beckett both refused the drink and asked again to see Sarah. Melinda stroked the ribbing on her sweater, her mouth drooping into a deep frown.

She must have missed her last Botox appointment because her lips had slipped to her chin.

"Sarah's a good girl. She's under a lot of stress."

Erin crossed her legs and then thought better of it when she realized her socks, in fact, didn't match. She planted her feet on the floor. "Mrs. Archer, why do you say that? Sarah's not in any trouble."

"Of course not." Melinda's voice pitched high and then back to conspiratorially low. "It's Bonnie, to be honest. Sarah reconnected with that girl out of guilt. And I don't want her dragged into whatever her cousin got into, especially while Sarah's trying to finish her thesis."

"Someone slaughtered your niece like an animal," Erin said. "Worse, actually. Hunters kill the animal first."

Melinda quivered, looking at Beckett as if he might intervene. Erin didn't give him the chance. "Please get Sarah for us."

Manicured nails tugged at the expensive pearls, and Melinda's eyes narrowed as they searched Erin again, traveling over her too-casual clothes, lingering over her slightly ragged fingernails and the extra roll of belly flesh that made itself known whenever Erin slouched.

She straightened and returned Melinda's appraisal.

"We have contributed heavily to your father's many fundraisers." Melinda's cool voice hit Erin's nerves with the force of a burning match. "You might treat me with respect."

"I'm trying to solve two homicides." Erin's gut twisted, a hundred insults yearning to be released. "Please don't make me ask you to get Sarah again."

Chapter Twenty-Six

Wearing yoga pants and a loose-fitting man's shirt, Sarah sat with her legs crossed, elbows on her knees, chin in her hands. Her mismatched eyes stared at them in disbelief. "I don't understand what's happening." Her voice sounded rough and deeper from the hours of crying.

"I'm sorry to do this, but we need to ask you some questions." Erin tried to be gentle. Melinda had disappeared, probably to call her husband. "What do you know about Bonnie and Virginia Walton's relationship?"

"I didn't know they had one," Sarah said. "I told Bonnie a long time ago my professor volunteered at her school, and that she was a psychologist. I thought Bonnie should talk to her. She still had anger issues and needed to figure out her future. Professor Walton is—was—a great listener. But Bonnie didn't like the idea. We never discussed it again." Sarah stilled, and then her hands flew to her mouth. "Oh my God. I told Bonnie about Professor Walton. Is this my fault?"

"Of course it's not your fault," Beckett said. "We're not sure why they were both chosen. "When did you give her Professor Walton's name?"

"A few months ago," Sarah said. "Bonnie mentioned calling

207

her to learn more about the college program, but she never said anything more."

"Do you think she would have told you if they started spending time together?" Erin asked.

Sarah rubbed her temples, shaking her head back and forth. "I wouldn't expect the professor to. And I thought Bonnie was pretty open with me, but I guess not."

"Sarah," Beckett said, "we have to ask you a couple of questions you're not going to like. They involve information from the crime scene."

Sarah blanched. "I don't want to look at pictures. I can't."

"You don't have to," Beckett said. "But the killer left a message."

Sarah seemed to steel herself. "All right. Go ahead."

Beckett glanced at Erin. "Please keep this between us. The killer carved *whore* on a beam in Bonnie's attic and *snitch* on the professor's fireplace mantle. Does that mean anything at all to you?"

Sarah seemed to shrink, her thin frame getting lost in the loose shirt until the collar reached her nose. "Bonnie wasn't a whore. She worked at the strip club, but she never slept with any of those guys."

"The killer might have considered stripping just as damning as prostituting. But calling the professor a snitch doesn't make sense if she didn't know Bonnie well," Beckett said. "I assume you knew Professor Walton was a lesbian?"

"She didn't keep it a secret."

"What about Bonnie?" Beckett asked. "Did Bonnie date women too?"

Sarah's head slid up the way a turtle emerges from its shell. "I—she never said anything about it. She didn't want to get serious with Will Merritt. But she never said anything about an interest in women. Is that what you think went on?"

Erin hated having to be evasive with her questions. Family deserved any details they wanted, but the investigation was too delicate, with too many gaping holes, and Sarah was a suspect.

"It's hard for me to imagine Bonnie letting someone else in. She didn't trust many people." Sarah looked over her shoulder toward the doorway. "You can thank my father for that."

"That's tough to forgive," Erin said.

"I haven't forgiven him." Sarah's tone flattened. "They're my parents, and I love them. They've given me every opportunity in the world, paying for school and my apartment and anything I need. All I have to worry about are my classes. But everything about my world has to be approved by them, because Dad's an important man. It's exhausting. What happened to Bonnie—he played a part. And never took responsibility. It's so typical of him and everyone I grew up with." She stopped, flustered. "Does that make sense?"

It made perfect sense to Erin. With the exception of Bonnie's abuse, Sarah could have been describing Erin's own upbringing. Money and privilege brought numerous opportunities but came with a different set of rules. Once she broke free and started living on her own, Erin managed to shed most of her bitterness toward her father. But Sarah had yet to forgive.

Erin imagined the young woman as a confused child, those strange eyes probably more noticeable, wondering what happened to the cousin she loved. A little girl stuck in a world dominated by public perception and selfishness. "Perfect sense."

"I guess you would understand," Sarah said. "I heard my father talking about your family. What do they think about you being a cop?"

Erin sucked at poker, but she made the effort to keep her expression neutral. "It's complicated."

"I understand." Sarah twisted her watch around her slim wrist. "After all the things they said about Bonnie's murder being her fault because of her circumstances, I wonder what they'll say when I tell them the same person killed Professor Walton."

"Please keep that information to yourself," Erin said. "We have very little to go on, and if it gets out, people will panic."

"I won't," Sarah said. "I wish I had something more for you."

"Did you ever go to the professor's house?" Beckett asked.

"Once," Sarah said. "I was kind of a wreck about my thesis—I had to trash most of the first draft. She told me to stop by."

"What's your thesis on?" Erin asked.

Sarah withdrew back into the safety of her shirt collar. "Well, this is actually my second thesis. Professor Walton said the first one was too personal and not nearly analytical enough. It read like a memoir. So I had to start all over again."

"It's a quantitative study and analysis on recovered memories of childhood sexual abuse and how victims individually react."

"You're a psychology major?" Erin remembered the ulcer-inducing months spent writing her own thesis.

"Yes. I've been working on it for so long, and I'm about ready to give Professor Walton the final draft." She wiped a tear off her cheek. "Of course, that doesn't matter."

Erin leaned back in the chair. "I'm sure the University will assign you a new advisor right away. Did Bonnie's experiences give you the idea for the thesis?"

"In part," Sarah said. "I've known other people who have been sexually abused. No two of them react the same way. That's the heart of my research. Why do some victims live relatively normal lives and heal while others derail like Bonnie?" Sarah's voice gained momentum as she spoke about a topic she clearly felt passionate about. She lowered the shirt yet again and leaned forward, hands on her slim thighs. "And why do some become perpetual victims? Do you know 17.7 million American women have been victims of rape or attempted sexual assault? And then there are the unreported rapes. The Justice Department says over eighty percent of rapes on college campuses aren't reported. Women are too scared, and not coming forward allows another woman to be victimized. We have to do something as a society to stop this. Instead of getting better with my generation, it's getting worse. The same with child sexual abuse."

Erin's head buzzed as though she'd been dropped into a pressurized chamber. Tension pounded against her skull. Her brain seemed stuffy. She wanted to run from the room and out into the fresh air, but she couldn't look away from Sarah's bright, contrasting eyes.

The girl stared back, face flushed. "I'm sorry. I got carried away."

Erin's lungs burned like she hadn't taken a breath in several minutes. "You're passionate about it. I'm sure your thesis is great."

"It seems so trivial now." She retreated back against the cushions, emotions depleted. "Who would do this to them?"

"What can you tell us about Professor Walton's experience at the Adult Literacy Center?" Beckett asked. "Did she ever talk about anyone there? Maybe someone she had an issue with? One of her students?"

Sarah ran her fingers through her long ponytail, examining the strands she'd pulled out. "Well, she had an argument with one of the African American students at the Adult Learning Center. Professor Walton seemed upset by their altercation. She thought a lot of him. Anyway, he had an issue with a class. She tried to talk to him, and he got in her face. Called her a dyke and a bunch of other names."

"What did they discuss?" Erin asked.

"She wouldn't have betrayed student confidence."

"Did she report him or tell any of the staff?"

"She didn't want to get him in trouble. She thought her not reporting him might help his attitude."

"Do you remember his name?"

"Ricky," Sarah said. "I don't know the last name."

Erin shot Beckett a look of satisfaction, but he remained focused on Sarah.

"Why did the professor tell you about this?" His normally gentle voice held the ghost of an edge.

"Because I just happened to talk to her shortly after," Sarah said. "I called her with a question on my thesis, and I could tell she was upset."

"So you and Professor Walton were close enough for her to confide in you?"

"I think it was more of a timing thing," Sarah said. "She needed to talk to someone."

Erin glanced at her partner. In the short time she'd known him, his face had never been so vibrant. Like a dog about to take back its favorite chew toy.

He didn't take his eyes off Sarah and asked the next question. "Sarah, we're certain Bonnie made amateur porn—likely rape scenarios—as a way to earn extra cash. You're sure she didn't tell you?"

Sarah set her jaw and crossed her arms, her defiance betraying her. "She wouldn't have done that after what she went through." Her ponytail bounced as she shook her head. "No way."

"We have strong evidence she did," Beckett said. "And she may have confided in Professor Walton."

"It's possible the videos led to her murder," Erin said. "Virginia's too. We're still putting things together, but Bonnie may have involved the wrong person. I'm not sure how Virginia fits in yet, but you visited Bonnie at home plenty of times. Even if you didn't know about the movies, it looks like you could have."

Sarah's mismatched eyes popped open, her pupils dilating. "You're saying I might be in danger?"

"We have to consider it a possibility," Erin said. "You need to be cautious the next several days. Keep staying here with your parents. Make sure your security system is on at all times. And if anything strange happens, call 9-1-1 immediately."

Sarah covered her mouth with her slender fingers. "I can't believe this is happening. You have to be wrong."

"I hope we are, for your sake." Erin stood to leave and asked the question she'd been dreading. "Sarah, we need to ask where you were last night."

"You're not serious." Sarah's hands slipped down to rest in her lap, her body slouching.

"I'm afraid so," Erin said. "You're the main connection

between these two women. Eliminating you as a suspect is crucial."

Sarah blew out a shaky breath. "I was here. I never go anywhere anymore."

"And your mother can verify this?"

Sarah nodded.

"Any other staff?" Beckett asked.

"I honestly don't know," Sarah said. "But I park in the driveway because my father's cars take up all three stalls in the garage. So my car was here."

Heels snapped across the tile floors, and Melinda Archer swept in, her arms going around her daughter's shoulders. "I can confirm my daughter remained home all evening, Investigator Prince. Considering her a suspect is insulting. Sarah's devastated, and she's exhausted from all of this."

Erin ignored the woman and gently touched Sarah's knee. "Please call me anytime. Even if you just need to talk. We'll show ourselves out."

Beckett closed the front door behind them. "Why didn't Virginia Walton call us after Bonnie's murder? If Virginia's the snitch, then it's a safe bet Bonnie did talk to her. Or the killer thinks so anyway."

"I'm more focused on Ricky Stout." Erin felt energized as they walked down the stone path. "He knew them both. He's got a juvenile record. It's still not enough for a warrant, but maybe we can get the director at the ALC to talk."

Beckett's eyebrows raised. "Do you think that's likely?"

"Director Key's first priority is protecting her students and the program, which I get," Erin said. "But it's time for her to start talking." She zipped up her coat against the wind. At this rate, she would never be truly warm again. "We need to swing by The Point. By the time we get there, it'll be late enough for a full staff to be on hand. Hopefully, someone recognizes Virginia Walton."

"Sarah's hiding something," Beckett said. "Don't tell me you didn't notice how defensive she got about Bonnie's amateur porn. She knew about it and won't admit it. What's the point of lying about it?"

"I noticed," Erin said. "But look, I come from this type of environment. To someone like Simon Archer, those videos are scandalous. Sarah's got to protect his name, so the less she tells us, the better. She's grieving, and she's torn between helping her cousin and dealing with her parents. I get it."

"I'm sure you do."

Erin halted, craning her neck to look up at him. "What's that supposed to mean?"

"Her parents are judgmental, narcissistic jerks," Beckett said. "She comes from the same type of background as you, right? You said you understood her mother's kind."

"My parents aren't like hers," Erin said. "My father is a good man, even if he's got screwed up priorities. But he's not cruel enough to say things like Melinda did about her own niece. Calling an eight-year-old a liar about being molested? How could a person do that to a child? Aren't the adults supposed to protect them? And let's not forget Sarah was likely molested too."

Beckett jammed his hands in his pockets. "Sometimes people don't want to face the hard stuff. Especially when they're younger. We want to believe what's easy and convenient."

Erin stood her ground. "And a child becomes a victim over and over again."

"I'm not saying it's right," he said. "And you're missing the point."

"Exactly what is the point?" Her nerves had worn down to a fragile thread.

"You aren't looking at Sarah objectively. You automatically sided with her because her mother pissed you off, because you recognize her mother as the sort of person you've grown up loathing and rebelling against. You think the killer is a woman. Who's the one woman in both Bonnie's and Virginia's lives?"

The pressure returned to Erin's head. "We'll double-check with the neighbors, but Sarah's alibied for both. And she's got zero on her record. We have no physical evidence to tie her to either murder at this point. Marie's team is still looking for trace, and Sarah's fingerprints and hair can probably be explained in both cases."

Beckett held up his hands. "I'm not saying Sarah's our killer. Her dishonesty is hurting the investigation. And if you really think the killer is a woman, Sarah needs to be on the suspect list."

Nothing about Sarah Archer indicated she could be the killer other than her simple connection to both women. But Beckett had a point. Until they'd exhausted every possibility, she should suspect anyone and everyone at this point. "We'll check with the cab companies and the private car services then. If one of them has a record of picking Sarah up here on the night of either murder, then I'd consider her a real suspect."

"I'm not trying to insult you," Beckett said. "I've been doing this job a long time, and the one thing I've taken away is to always ask myself why a person says and does the things they do. The answer I've come up with is that most people—myself included—

see the world behind a veil of their own past experiences. The trick is learning to take off the veil. It's taken me a long time and a lot of mistakes to figure out how to do it."

"I see." The air shuddered from her lungs. Erin hated the anger welling inside of her, hated the voice in her head shouting out all of her insecurities. "And I'm too inexperienced to possibly be able to figure this out. Right?"

Beckett either didn't notice her anger or didn't understand. Or didn't care. "That's not what I said. You need to try to be more objective. Some people are really good actors. Some people can hide things from the best detectives. Sarah isn't telling us everything. I'm not sure what it is yet, but I promise you she's keeping something from us."

"Is that what you thought when Lucy almost died because you didn't figure out the truth in time?" A low blow, childish and unnecessary.

Beckett sucked in a hard breath. "My previous work has got nothing to do with my perception of this case. And I'm not discussing it."

"Of course not," Erin said. "You wouldn't want to appear infallible."

He pulled his car keys out of his pocket. "You just proved my point. You can't look past your perceptions." In two long strides he reached his little Prius. "I'll meet you at the Adult Learning Center. Don't worry about leading me there. This car has a guidance system."

* * *

Sarah rested her head against the closed door. Erin Prince seemed nice. Caring. Easy to talk to. Beckett acted like he expected something horrible to happen at any moment. But she liked them.

"Did you tell them everything?"

Sarah turned to stare at her mother standing in the hallway like a well-dressed eel. Always slithering around, listening. "I told them what I know."

"Did you tell them about what happened when you were little? With," her lips twisted as though she'd tasted something awful, "your cousin?"

Sarah's nerves thinned and stretched, a rope ready to snap. "They know enough."

"I would hope you thought about your father. We took care of the situation a long time ago. Her parents obviously didn't."

There it was, Melinda's haughty, holier-than-thou attitude. The woman truly believed she could fix something as horrible as what happened during Sarah and Bonnie's childhoods. Just sweep it all away with some threats and cash.

Sarah desperately wished Bonnie were here. The past few months had gone by too quickly. The cousin she'd looked up to as a little girl experienced so much pain, and yet her positive outlook on life inspired Sarah to be better. But Bonnie was dead, and Sarah had only her parents again.

Her palm stung. She realized her fingernails dug into it. "I have to get back to my paper."

Chapter Twenty-Seven

Erin hadn't gone two miles when Clark called for them both to get back to the CID. Virginia Walton's daughter had apparently jumped in the car at the crack of dawn this morning and would be at the station shortly. Erin told him what Sarah said about Ricky Stout. "You think it's enough for the judge to issue a warrant for his personal information?"

"We can sure as hell try. Two vicious murders in three days. All depends on the judge. I'll do everything I can."

As she threaded through traffic, Erin worked to calm down. She and Beckett were both tired and stressed. They hadn't worked together long enough, and their contrasting backgrounds meant they saw the world differently. She owed Beckett an apology for the jab about Lucy's life. He'd done nothing but his job since he arrived. He certainly hadn't been unfair or belittled her.

"Damn." His little wind-up car wasn't in the CID's lot. She wanted to get the apology over with and move forward. Hopefully, he wasn't lost. GPS had its merits, but in an old city like DC, it tended to muck people up, especially with the construction.

"Princess!" Fowler called out as soon as she entered the squad room. "Lovely morning, isn't it?"

She growled a response.

Fowler grunted in return. "Yeah, well, I don't have much to give you. Professor Walton's colleagues at American University had little to offer other than the professor kept to herself and she certainly wasn't discriminated against for her sexuality." Fowler made a face resembling a shrew. "The dean wanted to be very clear his former employee's civil rights weren't violated. As a fairly new hire and an adjunct professor, Walton wasn't around enough to form any bonds with any of her AU peers."

"Great. Yet another victim no one really knew. Today keeps getting better."

"It's about to get worse," Fowler said. "The victim's daughter is waiting for you in Interview Room A."

* * *

"My mom was a good lady." Rylan Walton clutched a nearly empty packet of tissues. Her caramel-colored skin was sallow and raw beneath her eyes, probably from rubbing at the tears. A lock of her thick, curly brown hair escaped the messy knot on the top of her head. She tucked it behind her ear and breathed in fast, asthmatic beats. "She didn't deserve this."

"Of course she didn't." Selfish relief flowed through Erin when she found out Sergeant Clark had already told Rylan the necessary details of her mother's murder. She wasn't naive enough to believe a family member shouldn't hear the gruesome details if she truly wanted to hear them, as long as the information didn't jeopardize the investigation. But many of the bereaved only thought they wanted to know exactly how their loved one died. Getting what they asked for often broke them, and sometimes a cop needed to omit things. Erin didn't trust herself to make the right decision. "Thank you for coming in so quickly."

Erin checked her watch and then her phone. Beckett still hadn't arrived.

Rylan wadded up several tissues in a white-knuckle grip. She stared across the table at Erin, the pain in her lovely eyes searing. "What are we waiting for?"

"My partner."

Rylan rubbed one of the tissues across her eyes, further irritating her already raw-looking eyelids. "I Googled you."

"Excuse me?"

"When Sergeant Clark called and told me what happened, he said to ask for you if he wasn't here when I arrived. I wanted to know who I would be talking to. Your dad is a big-time defense contractor, right? He contributes to a lot of conservative causes. Another article mentioned you being a cop."

"Oh, I see." Erin struggled for a better response. Sometimes she hated the Internet.

"So you grew up rich, white, and conservative." Rylan's tone wasn't accusatory but matter-of-fact.

"I suppose that's a good way to summarize it," Erin said. Where the hell was Beckett?

"Normally, I'd try not to judge, because I know what it's like when people have pre-conceived notions about you," Rylan said. "But I grew up half black in the South, and my momma is gay. So I've spent plenty of my life dealing with prejudice from people with your kind of background."

"I'm sorry." Erin sounded like a broken record, but what else could she say?

"Don't be. And don't let it affect how you help my mother."

Erin got the woman's point. "Of course not. Your mother's life choices aren't my business and have no bearing on how I work the case. I want to catch the person who did this."

"That's all I wanted to hear." Rylan's watery eyes drifted toward the clock. Erin wasn't going to make the woman wait any longer. One more thing to apologize to Beckett for.

"Let's get started without my partner." Erin said. "Tell me about your mother's decision to move here from South Carolina. Why did she leave?"

"She needed a change after she and my dad split," Rylan said. "They'd been living as strangers for years. Mom got the courage to come out as a lesbian. I always found it funny it took her so long because she married my African-American father in a state where that's barely accepted. Back when they got together, it sure wasn't. But coming to terms with her sexuality and then coming out to her family and friends took my mother a long time." Pride filled her voice. "My mother went through a lot and never gave up."

"How did people in her life take it?" Erin asked.

"Some were surprised. My father had known for a long time. Instinct, I guess. Some of her friends and family shunned her. Some said okay."

"Your parents had an amicable split?"

The lock of hair flowed loose again. Rylan twisted it around her index finger. "Yes. No attorneys. Just a mediator."

"What about after your mother arrived here?" Erin asked. "Was she happy? Did she have friends? Anyone special?"

"At first it was tough," Rylan said. "She basically started from scratch. And she was lonely. But everyone accepted her. She never talked about any issues like that. She kept herself really busy."

"Did she date anyone?"

Rylan shook her head. "I don't think so. No one she mentioned, anyway." She steepled her hands together, pressing the tips of her fingers to her mouth. Her eyelids fluttered in an effort to stave off fresh tears. "I just can't believe she's gone. It's not real."

Helplessness descended over Erin. She had no words of comfort to offer that didn't sound trite. How could she pretend to understand what Rylan felt?

"Can you tell me about her work with the Adult Learning Center? Her colleagues at the university didn't seem to know much about her outside of their work environment."

"She loved working at the ALC." Rylan tried to smile. "She said it was more fulfilling because those students were so desperate to better their lives. A lot of the ones at AU were privileged snobs who didn't want to work as hard as they needed to."

The current state of the union.

"A lot of the students at the ALC are at-risk," Rylan continued. "They didn't finish high school. Some are being forced to go because of their parents or are court mandated. Others are adults trying to get on their feet, but they've got a lot of baggage keeping them down. My mom loved being able to help them."

How many lives had Virginia Walton touched in her short time in the city? The harsh truth of the world pressed down on Erin. Society needed more people like Virginia Walton. Yet she had been savagely murdered, and how many scumbags still walked the streets? "Did your mom ever mention anyone specific at the Adult Learning Center? Anyone she had an issue with?"

"She talked about a lot of different students," Rylan said. "But she never made it sound like she was scared of them."

Rylan hiccupped, a sob mixed in, and pulled a fresh tissue out of her crushed packet. "Please tell me how this happened. Was she targeted because she was gay? Is that why he ... cut her up?"

"We don't think so," Erin said. "But we're still gathering evidence. Did your mother ever mention a woman named Bonnie Archer?"

Rylan's eyes opened wide and then narrowed, the freckles on her nose disappearing into her creased skin. "She told me someone stabbed the poor girl to death. My mother knew her in passing; Bonnie went to the ALC." Her wet eyes flashed. "That happened three days ago. You think the same person killed my mother?"

Rylan's heartbreak and despair turned to rage, the fury darkening her bloodshot eyes and reddening her cheeks. The woman's slender hands came down hard on the table, her athletic body lurching across at Erin. "My mother is dead because you can't do your job?"

"We're working on it." Erin tried to hold her ground.

The anger rolling off Rylan filled the small room. She had a few inches on Erin and several pounds of lean muscle.

"It's a complicated case, and we don't have a lot to go on."

"Three days." Gut-wrenching despair colored Rylan's tone. "And you didn't protect my mother?"

"Your mother wasn't on our radar as a possible target." Erin tried to sound gentle and not defensive. "A killer like this one usually targets similar victims. But we have new information that makes us believe Bonnie and your mother were targeted for a specific reason."

"What information? What reason?"

Rylan deserved answers, and she might physically take them if Erin didn't tell her something soon. "I'm not at liberty to say. It's an active investigation."

"And it's my mother at the morgue!" Rylan stood up, fast as a bullet. More hair escaped the knot and haloed around her face as she shouted. "Not at liberty my ass. You don't have a clue who's doing this. You're just giving me face time and hoping I'll tell you something that will help because you don't know your ass from a hole in the ground."

"I'm sorry," Erin said, fighting to keep her composure. "You're grieving and not thinking clearly. We are doing our best, I promise."

"Your best isn't good enough. You have no idea what I'm going through. Have you ever had a call telling you the most important person in your life was dead? Have you ever had to go into a fucking morgue and identify their body?" Rylan choked out, tears flash flooding her face.

"No, but—"

"But nothing," Rylan spat. "You don't know anything about me. Or my mother. Or Bonnie Archer, evidently."

"Please," Erin said. "Sit back down. I'm sorry I offended you."

"I don't want to sit." Rylan crossed her meaty arms and stared back, daring Erin to argue.

"All right." Erin knew when to pick her battles. "What did your mother tell you about Bonnie Archer?"

"She said she met Bonnie through her cousin Sarah. She liked her. Bonnie had gotten her life on track."

"Did your mother mention Bonnie coming over to her house?"

"Why would she?"

"We're just trying to figure out why someone would want to kill both of them."

"She never said a word about it. And I have no idea why the girl would go to my mom's house." Rylan kept glaring at Erin, the grief in her eyes clouded with judgment and anger.

Erin's skin heated; her stomach danced. How had she gotten off so terribly wrong with the woman? She needed to bring things back on track.

"Your mom did great work with the ALC." Erin tried a new tack. "Did she ever mention a black male named Ricky?"

Rylan's teeth dug into her upper lip. "I don't remember. Why?"

"Sarah Archer said your mom told her about an argument she had with Ricky a couple of weeks ago. It was fairly heated and frightened your mother."

"Oh Christ." Rylan's hands went up, and she paced. "So because a black man from the streets confronts a white professor, he might have killed her? And you're basing that on a rich white girl's interpretation of what my mother said?"

"No." Erin couldn't believe she'd stepped into it again. "I'm trying to get some more information before we go to the ALC."

"Well, let me give it to you," Rylan said. "My mom liked working there better than she did American University. She took the job at AU because of the pay."

"I understand," Erin said.

Rylan barked out a hoarse laugh. "But you don't. My mom grew up in the South. She fell in love with a poor black man who worked his ass off to put food on the table. She knew how easily under-privileged kids could—whatever their color—fall between the cracks and have zero opportunities in life. Those are the kids she wanted to help. But the college kids at American University—like Sarah Archer, like you—the vast majority are rich white kids who don't have a clue about the real world. So excuse me if I don't put much faith in Sarah's recollection of what my mother said. I guarantee you Mom wasn't worried about how to handle that boy."

She gripped the back of the chair with both hands, leaning against it, looking down at Erin as if she'd just scraped her off her shoe. "Is this the best you've got? The best my mother's got?"

"Look." Erin's fine thread of patience snapped. "My job is to go over every piece of information we have. Let me decide what's relevant and what's not. How about that?"

Rylan's head jerked back, curls bobbing in time with her emotions. "Oh, you're going to decide? Like you decided after that girl got cut up? Like you decided while someone slaughtered my mom?" She slammed the chair against the table.

Erin slid her own chair back and stood up. "I understand you're hurting. But you're not helping the situation."

"Neither are you, evidently. Why is my mother dead?"

"That's what I'm trying to find out, so stop fighting with me."

The door swung open, revealing a flustered looking Beckett. "I'm so sorry." Beckett offered his hand to Rylan Walton. "I got delayed, and my partner's still new to working homicide. Let's you and I start over. How about that?"

Erin's mouth fell open. "Are you kidding me?"

Beckett shot her a look. "Sergeant Clark wants to see you anyway."

"I'm leading an interview."

"Not anymore." Beckett wasn't going to budge. He stood there in pressed pants and an ironed shirt, his dumbass mustache twitching. "I'll take it from here."

Erin never wanted to scream at someone so badly in her professional life. The vitriol bubbled on her tongue, but she saw Rylan out of the corner of her eye. Making a scene would accomplish nothing. "Fine. I'll speak to you after you two are finished." She turned her attention back to Rylan, who looked both smug and distraught. "Again, I'm sorry for your loss. We'll find whoever did this."

She shut the door and marched out of the room. Bright spots danced in her vision. What the hell had just happened? Weren't partners supposed to present a united front? Beckett had come in there and treated Erin like a kid caught joyriding with her older brother's car. And Sergeant Clark allowed it?

Fresh anger rolled through her. She stalked around the corner intent on going straight to Clark's office, but her superior waited in the hallway, arms crossed over his big chest.

"What the hell, Prince? What happened in there?"

He'd been watching on the live feed. Had Beckett been as well?

"We never had a chance to establish any kind of confidence," she said.

"You alienated her."

"She alienated herself. She already knew my family background and made a judgment before she even met me."

"Which you then fulfilled." Sergeant Clark shook his head. "You had the right idea but the wrong words. She's grieving. She's probably got a chip on her shoulder about race and God knows what else."

He took off his glasses, cleaned the lenses, and then put them back on. "And the truth is you do come from a different world than most people. You rubbed elbows with the Reagans and the Bushes and other bigwigs. You went to an expensive private school, where you were protected and sheltered from real life."

"Not by choice," Erin said. "And I got out of it as soon as I realized how little I knew about the rest of the world."

"You did," Clark said. "And you don't judge by skin, class, sexual preference or anything else. You're fair. And fierce. I know." He pointed in the direction of the interview room. "That woman doesn't. All she knows is her mother is dead, and you're a Prince. She found some basic shit about your family on the Internet, and she needs someone to lash out at. You didn't handle her with kid gloves and gave her the perfect opportunity."

Erin's hands fisted against her hips. Frustration tickled the back of her eyes. She would not allow angry tears. "I tried to."

"I saw. It's not your fault. It's an experience thing. Think back to when you first started working sex crimes and talked to a victim's mother for the first time. You didn't know what to say, did you?"

"Somewhat," Erin admitted. "But I'm a mom too. Common ground came easily."

"Exactly. Not so easy in homicide—which is a good thing. That's where years on the job come in. The more you do it, the better you get. You learn to read people."

"Like the Wonder Boy in there."

"He's good, and you know it."

"He embarrassed the hell out of me. And where'd he disappear to? Didn't you call him back?"

"He was already halfway to The Point, so I told him to follow up. Turns out one of the bartenders remembered Virginia Walton coming in more than once over the past couple of months. She had a heated conversation with another customer who matches Tori's description two weeks ago—the last night Tori was seen at The Point."

"But the bartender can't definitively ID Tori?"

Clark shook his head. "He never got that close to him, but he's positive the person was either a masculine-looking woman or a man in drag. I'd say that's pretty good odds. Talk to Beckett for the details. As for him embarrassing you, that's your fault. He had to play off what you started with Rylan Walton. It's not personal."

Erin threw up her hands. "So you're saying life and death is a game?"

"Dealing with people is a game," Clark corrected. "The sooner you learn to play, the better off you'll be."

Just like everything else in life. Do the dance, pull the right strings, learn to work the system. God forbid anything ever be as simple as right and wrong. "Tell Beckett I'll meet him at the Adult Literacy Center in Columbia Heights in an hour. I'm going to lunch."

"Before you leave ..." Clark handed her a signed warrant. "We lucked out this morning. The judge is an LGBT supporter. I might have hinted we thought this could be a hate crime. Made me feel a bit scummy, but we got our warrant for Ricky Stout's contact information."

Erin tucked the warrant into her bag. "First good news I've had all day."

Chapter Twenty-Eight

Charlie didn't know what to do anymore. Mina wouldn't stay quiet. She'd always listened to him in the past. But she fixated on that homicide cop as if she could somehow magically save them from the prison they called life.

Anxiety rippled through him in shockwaves. He wished the end would come and save him the fight of trying to be the voice of reason for people who never wanted to listen and didn't give a damn about anyone else.

He thought about running away, escaping into the dark with Mina. But he'd tried that before. They always got caught.

He had no choice. He couldn't go to the police because he shouldn't know the things he did. He couldn't fight because he always lost. He couldn't keep a lid on Mina because she never listened.

Charlie sank into his secret hiding spot and cried silent tears.

Chapter Twenty-Nine

Erin didn't eat. Instead she drove to Columbia Heights and used her Bluetooth audio system to call her brother from the car. The irony of driving a nearly new car with all the bells and whistles wasn't lost on her. She only used her trust fund for important things like a down payment on a house and a reliable vehicle. She justified the Bluetooth as a safety measure.

"Maybe he's right," she told Brad as she navigated the traffic around the National Mall. Tourist season slowed in November, but the traffic never seemed to change. "We grew up with everything. And even though we left the nest and the lifestyle, we still enjoy a few perks, like the cars we drive. And we can't imagine what it's like to be poor or a minority."

"Speak for yourself," Brad said. "I'll give you the poor. But I've been a minority."

"Fine, but the color of skin is something a person can't hide. You lived in the closet for a long time. Yeah, it sucked, but you could walk into a store and buy whatever you wanted without the clerk expecting you to rob the place."

"Walton's daughter is our age. She didn't have to fight for a right to sit at the counter."

"No," Erin said. "But she grew up in South Carolina. She's

got a valid point about racism. And about how I can't relate."

"Who can?" Brad asked. "So Beckett knows how to talk to her. That means he's good enough to fake it, not that he can actually commiserate with her. He's just better at pretending he doesn't have an opinion." Brad snickered. "That's never been your strong suit, anyway."

Erin rolled her eyes. "Whatever. The entire thing made me feel like an asshole."

"'Cause you are," Brad said. "Two women are dead, and you're gettin' all butthurt because your partner taught you a lesson. Quit being a whiner and learn from it."

"Thanks a lot."

His laugh filled the car. "You called me to lift your spirits. That's what I'm doing. You don't get to feel sorry for yourself. You get to bust your ass and stop a sicko, and you get to learn some things in the process. So what if you were humiliated? Welcome to life."

Brad always knew exactly what to say to make her see things clearly. He also excelled in pushing every damn button possible in the process.

"You're a self-righteous asshole."

"But am I right?"

Erin jabbed her finger against the car's touch screen and ended the call. "You won't get me to say the words."

Chapter Thirty

Erin waited for Beckett beneath the portico entrance of the Adult Literacy Center. She chose a heavier coat this morning, but the damp chill still seemed to permeate the fabric and leach warmth from her bones. She always hated this time of year for its drab coloring, but this stretch of gray days felt like some kind of record. She needed to see the sun again.

"I'm sorry," Beckett said as soon as he walked up. "I made you feel terrible, and I didn't intend to. I needed to make Rylan feel like we were on her side. Because we are."

"And because I mucked the interview up so badly."

"You two just didn't gel," he said. "It happens."

"But I don't have enough experience to keep it from happening."

Beckett sighed. "No, not always. Some of it is instinct. And that's honed by repeatedly being in the situation, which also takes a toll on you. So it's a double-edged sword."

Some of Erin's anger ebbed, but the humiliation clung to her system. "You could have handled it differently. At least shamed me in the hall instead of in front of her. Now she won't want to talk to me." A sudden thought bloomed. "Are you trying to be front and center to bask in the glory if we catch this person? Add to your résumé?"

"You don't know anything about my résumé. And I don't care about glory. I care about finding a killer." Beckett brushed past her and took the steps two at a time. He kept his shoulders rigid, his fists jammed into his jacket. "So, the college program has two tracks, right? That's what Dr. Key said."

Erin bit her tongue and followed him. She struggled to keep pace.

"Look, I'm sorry for acting like a brat. I'm afraid Rylan is right. And the reporter. I'm a liability. So I took my frustration out on you. I did it earlier too. I'm sorry."

The bright spots on his cheeks faded, and he slowed down. "Thanks. Did Sergeant Clark tell you I went to The Point?"

Cold wind gusted from the north. Erin zipped her coat up to her chin. "Sounds like Tori, but we've already checked the paper trail from The Point. Nothing."

"I want to go over the security footage again, this time looking for Virginia Walton. She might be easier to spot than someone wearing all black. At least we've got a face to look for." Beckett stopped walking and turned to look down at her. "And for what it's worth, I get the insecurity. Every good cop has it."

"Yeah?"

He nodded. "Erin, ego is the worst thing to have when you're a cop. It keeps you from seeing what's right in front of you. You're doing fine. Stop second-guessing yourself and trust your instincts. You're going to make mistakes. So will I. But we have to keep trying, because these families and the victims deserve justice."

Resolve surged through her. She straightened her shoulders and braced herself for the task ahead. "Then let's go."

The Adult Learning Center seemed like a vastly different place than last week. No smell of lunch, no sounds of brisk work or joking students. Only the cars in the parking lot hinted at life going on as usual.

"Rylan said her mother knew of Bonnie in passing," Erin said quietly. "So maybe they didn't talk."

"Or Virginia didn't tell her daughter. If she knew something, she might have been afraid to share after Bonnie's murder."

Wearing jeans and a button-down shirt and looking like she needed another cup of coffee, Director Key waited for them at the desk. "Carrie—our front desk girl—is sick. We cancelled classes today. Everyone is shocked and heartbroken."

"I take it you knew Professor Walton better than Bonnie Archer?" Beckett's implication didn't go unnoticed by Key.

"Of course we did. We were heartsick for Bonnie as well. But we saw Virginia nearly every day."

"If Virginia is one of the counselors, why didn't she talk with us about Bonnie?" Beckett asked.

"You'll have to ask Brian," Key said. "I'm not sure the two of them knew each other. We have more than one counselor."

"How many of the staff are here?" Erin asked.

"Quite a few. I called them shortly after you called earlier. I wanted everyone to have the chance to speak with you."

She led them down the hall, past her office, and into a large social area much like the common area in a dorm: big couches; a couple of well-loved, comfy-looking chairs; a couple of end tables; a pop machine; and a snack machine. Erin counted seven women and two males, including Brian Reese.

"Small staff."

"Only two aren't here, Carrie and our night front desk assistant," Key said. "We have to run a lean operation despite the grant." She walked over and took the empty chair next to Reese. "As I said, we are all just devastated. The news said the same person who killed Bonnie killed Virginia. Is that possible?"

Erin never understood how the news media managed to weasel into crime scenes and thread information together when every single official had been told to close ranks. Then she pictured the beautiful redhead and her sly smile, and she knew exactly how she had done it.

"It looks like it," Beckett said. "Bonnie's cousin Sarah suggested the two of them discuss some of Bonnie's personal issues."

Reese snapped his fingers. "That's right. I remember Bonnie mentioning that when she came to talk to me about Pathways. She'd already spoken with Virginia."

"Any idea what they discussed?"

Reese shrugged. "The program, Bonnie's options."

Faces of many different colors, all wearing the same desolate expression, stared back at Erin. Most either had watery eyes or sniffled. "Why didn't we hear from Virginia the other day?"

"She had classes at AU the day you spoke with us," Brian said. "She only met with Bonnie a couple of times about classes. She didn't really have anything to contribute. I told her not to worry about it."

Erin instantly rankled, fed up with his innocent expression and blue eyes. "Don't you think we should have made that decision? Virginia may have known something about Bonnie Archer that got her killed."

"Then why didn't she come to you anyway?" Brian seemed unfazed by Erin's ire. "She didn't have to do what I told her to."

His smooth delivery reminded her of all the preppy boys she'd endured growing up. Hounding him in front of the group wouldn't get them anywhere, so she changed tactics. "How many of you knew both Bonnie and Virginia?"

Vanessa, the Language Arts instructor, raised her hand. "I didn't know Virginia as well as the others. We had different schedules."

"Did Bonnie ever mention her?"

"No. We told you Bonnie never shared anything personal."

"What about Virginia?" Erin asked. "I assume you were aware she was gay?"

Heads nodded. "No one cared," said a thin woman whose black boots looked heavier than her.

"Did she mention dating anyone?"

The woman tried to laugh, but it came out a sad sob. "She didn't want to get into a relationship. She didn't have the time for it. She spent her social life here, helping us."

"You two were close?" Beckett asked.

"I teach the computer courses, which meant a lot of nights," she said. "Virginia worked nights, so we chatted."

He looked at Key. "What did Virginia do here?"

"A volunteer counselor, and she assisted with some of the math students who are having difficulties. But she mainly provided counseling in all areas: emotional, mental, career. Virginia was a skilled psychologist with a lot of experience."

"And only volunteered?" Erin asked.

"We didn't have the money to pay her when she first came on.

She'd just come from South Carolina, and she wanted to be involved. She didn't care about the money, and she wouldn't take it when we freed up funds."

"This is going to sound strange," Beckett said. "But did Virginia ever mention counseling an older male student who cross-dressed?"

The entire group stared at him. Key finally spoke up. "No. If she did, that's confidential. We stay out of our students' personal lives."

So not out of the realm of possibility. But Erin didn't think Bonnie's cross-dressing customer had anything to do with either murder. "Were you aware Virginia had an issue with Ricky Stout?"

Key's eyes snapped to hers. "We resolved that."

"So she did report it." The professor must not have followed up with Sarah on the outcome.

"She came to me the next morning." Key leaned forward in her seat, tapping her finger on the armrest. "And let me make this clear, she wasn't concerned for her safety but for Ricky's."

"How so?" Erin asked.

Key hedged.

Erin considered the warrant she had in her bag. She didn't want to bring it out yet. She wanted to get everything she could before she pissed off Key. "I'm not asking you to divulge anything Ricky Stout may have told you. But Virginia Walton is dead, and we're trying to solve her murder."

Key sighed. "Ricky frequented her office. He comes from a terrible home environment—drugs and abuse—and he had no one. I think he became attached to Virginia. She was sort of like a mother figure. He came to her about advice in all sorts of areas, not just school and career."

"Did he ask her about Bonnie Archer?"

"She never mentioned it." Key's jaw set.

If Ricky Stout had ever mentioned Bonnie, Key wasn't going to say a damned word. Erin understood the need to protect her student body. But two people had been murdered.

The thought popped out before she could stop it. "Is it because Ricky is black?"

A couple of people sucked in shocked gasps as though Erin had spoken a forbidden language.

"Excuse me?" The professor said.

"You're protective of Ricky Stout," Erin said. "I realize you have rules to play by. But I think there's more to it. Are you afraid he'll be railroaded because he's a black male with a sealed juvenile record, and the dead women are white? I can't blame you if that's the way you feel. A certain precedent's been set, and race relations are a serious issue in this country. And I'm sorry to be blunt, but I'm trying to solve two brutal homicides, and I'd rather deal with the elephant in the room."

Erin cut a glance at Beckett, expecting him to shut her down. But he watched Key with interest, the vein in his neck pulsing.

Key crossed her legs, her movements lethargic and her face drawn. "Did you have any African Americans at Sidwell Friends School, Investigator Prince? The president's daughters currently attend, but you were there in the late 80s and early 90s, right? Things have come a long way."

Erin didn't react as Beckett's attention switched to her. She directed her answer at him. "Sidwell Friends School is the Harvard of Washington's private schools. A lot of politicians and people with political influence send their kids, the president and vice president included. Chelsea Clinton attended at the same time as me." Erin met the First Daughter a few times. But she didn't dare socialize with her; her father was still fuming about Clinton's election. "To answer your question, yes, there were. But a minority."

"So it's fair to say it's hard for someone like you to have a grasp on the economic divide in this country—race excluded?" Key asked. "Not just in social class and wealth but in education."

"I've been a cop long enough to be well aware of it," Erin said. "And I don't deny every one of those things exists, but I'm not here to debate them. I wouldn't be asking about a black male if he hadn't already been mentioned as knowing both dead women and having an issue with one of them. Race and social class aren't affecting my judgment. Is it affecting yours?"

Key appeared to weigh her options.

She wasn't the only one who had done her research. Key came from a broken family, grew up poor, and earned scholarships to college. Her mission to help other young adults stemmed from her own experience, and the instinct to protect them came naturally.

"You need to tell her," Brian Reese said. "If they don't have a warrant, they'll be back with one."

Key glanced at him and then around at the rest of the group. Vanessa nodded.

Key folded her hands on her lap. "Ricky is my nephew."

Erin watched Beckett out of the corner of her eye. He nodded along with Key's words. He already knew Ricky was her nephew.

"All right then," Erin said. "So you have a personal interest."

"He's a good kid who saw his mother murdered. My sister."

"I'm sorry."

"Ricky was only seven. I'd gone off to college, and his daddy was in prison. My parents couldn't take him because of their health. He went into foster care, and I was never able to get him out."

Key likely hadn't wanted him to get out of juvie. A problem kid would have made her career a hell of a lot more difficult. "So he got into trouble. We'll have a warrant to unseal his juvenile records by tomorrow."

Key's lips thinned. "He was angry. Lashed out at anyone with authority, including teachers. He got physical with more than one, and he dropped out at sixteen. Two years ago, I hired someone to track him down on the streets, and I set about getting him straight. He's been doing well, keeping a job and a place to live."

Erin moved to show her the warrant and ask for Ricky's address, but Beckett spoke up. "How was his mother killed?"

Key looked at Beckett for a long time. "Her boyfriend stabbed her twenty-two times in front of Ricky. He watched her bleed to death while he waited on the police to get there."

A perfect recipe for violence. Erin produced the warrant. "Where does Ricky live?"

* * *

Contact information in hand, Erin marched outside trying to think of a way to diplomatically handle the tension eating at her.

Beckett easily caught up. "Nice work on the race call. You handled that well."

She tried hard to sound rational. "You knew Ricky Stout was her nephew and didn't tell me."

"I wasn't sure," he said. "I did some digging and found out Key's maiden name was Stout. I didn't tell you because I wanted to let the whole thing play out organically. I had no idea about him seeing his mother murdered. But if he saw her stabbed as a kid, this makes a lot more sense."

Erin stopped in the middle of the sidewalk. "How are we supposed to work together if we don't communicate? We're like two roommates who have no interest in getting to know each other."

"You're wrong," Beckett said. "I want to get to know you, and I like working with you. We've just got to fine-tune our routine. Figure out how to share the bathroom." He smiled at his bad joke.

Erin rolled her eyes, snatching her ringing phone out of her pocket. "Hey, Sergeant. What do you have?"

She listened as Clark rattled off numbers. Her heart raced. "Sounds good. We're going to talk to Ricky Stout, and then we'll be in."

"What is it?" Beckett asked as soon as she ended the call.

"We finally got financials back on Bonnie Archer. She'd paid two months ahead on her mortgage, and she had over $100,000 in a savings account. Her parents are coming into the station to discuss the new developments, but I bet they're totally unaware."

Beckett let out a low whistle, staring into the darkening horizon. "Well. That's one hell of a stripper."

"Or an online porn star. Clark's trying to get the overtime approved for the forensic examiners to find her on the web, but we don't have time."

She'd end up regretting it, but every instinct told her there would be more dead women soon. "Get Lucy and her friend on it. Find Bonnie Archer's sex videos. If we get lucky, Ricky Stout will be a star."

Chapter Thirty-One

Of course Ricky Stout wasn't home. He lived in a one-bedroom, second-floor apartment in a crummy building on 12th and U Street, right above the Walgreens. A patrol cop stationed on the corner served as a wary deterrent for neighborhood thugs. The uniform hadn't seen Ricky in a couple of days. He'd called in sick to the tire shop where he worked part-time.

"I think she warned him." Erin and Beckett stopped by Clark's office to give him an update. "Now he's on the run. I put out BOLO, but I wouldn't be surprised if he's holed up at Key's place. I'd like to get into his apartment, but we'll never get the warrant."

"Put more pressure on the DNA lab again," Beckett suggested. "If Bonnie's baby is African-American, we might have enough probable cause."

Erin didn't think so considering the current environment. Everyone worried about further pushing the racial issue, especially judges and law enforcement. Unless a case came wrapped in a red bow, a judge likely wouldn't issue a warrant for Ricky's DNA.

Sergeant Clark handed Erin the printout containing the information the warrant dredged up about Bonnie's financial information. "Here's what's interesting. She made a hundred grand in less than six months. And all of it appears to be monthly transfers from an offshore account."

"Six months? Holy shit," Erin said. "I'm in the wrong line of work."

"No way she made that from selling porn, even if she had a pay-per-view site," Beckett said. "Without the backing of one of the frequented sites, it's word of mouth."

"What if she didn't set up a pay-per-view site?" Erin asked. "What if it's buried deeper? One of those things where the user has to give their life away for access."

"Like the child porn creeps," Clark said. "But rape porn isn't that taboo." He held up his hands at Erin's look. "I'm not saying it's right. But you can find it on any Internet search, half of it by simply searching for rough sex. The buried stuff on the deep web is usually the freak show. Animals, real violence, snuff films. Dark and twisted."

"Which means she could have charged a mint for it," Erin said.

"It makes more sense given this amount of money." Beckett leaned against the wall, ankles crossed, looking completely unconvinced. "And unless you have more specific search information and people with the access to the right things," he cut a look at Erin, "we aren't going to find it."

"Maybe there's another source of income," Erin said. "Will Merritt lives nicely, but he doesn't come from money. I can't see him being her sugar daddy, but Sid's is frequented by all sorts of Capitol Hill types. Who's to say she didn't have someone else on the side? Someone who fell in love with her and wanted to help her."

"But why the offshore deposits?" Beckett asked. "Why not cash?"

"Because he's married and influential," Clark suggested. "Big cash withdrawals raise questions with the wife. He keeps money in an offshore account because if the wife finds out about his philandering, she'll take everything. This way, he's got a safety net. Then Bonnie comes along, and it's the perfect way to help her."

"Or pay her blackmail," Erin said. "We keep talking about her blackmailing one of her sex partners, but what if it's Simon Archer? Her uncle's likely got the means to pay her, and if it ever got out that he covered for a child molester, he'd be ruined."

"But then where does Virginia come in?" Beckett asked. "She and Bonnie are loosely connected by the school and Sarah, but her murder doesn't make sense in either of those scenarios."

"The killer called Virginia Walton a snitch and herself—or himself—the name Jane. Maybe Jane's the jilted wife. Bonnie confides in the professor. Jane takes them both out. Or Simon paid someone to take care of the situation, and you're right about Jane being a smokescreen."

Clark played with a yellow stress ball, squeezing it until his knuckles nearly popped out of their sockets. "Where are you with Sarah Archer's alibi for both murders?"

"Two neighbors remember Sarah's car being there the night of Bonnie's murder and last night," Erin said. "Out of twelve local cab companies, no one has picked anyone up from her parents' home in the last ten days. So far, none of the places providing personal drivers have any record of picking up Sarah, either. One company has picked up Simon at his home multiple times but not within the last week and never Sarah."

"So other than her personal connection with both women, we've got nothing else on Sarah Archer?" Clark asked.

"No," Erin said. "Beckett doesn't think she's telling us everything."

Clark mushed the ball between this thumb and index finger. "What about you?"

Erin shrugged. "I think she's got her head buried in her thesis and doesn't see anything she doesn't want to. We've still got to go back over the security footage from The Point, and I think our time is better spent trying to find Tori and talking to Ricky Stout."

"Probably so," Clark said. "Let her stew unless we get something on the trace evidence side."

The same desperation from this morning flashed across Beckett's face. "Tori might be a legitimate suspect, but he's a ghost at this point. Where does Ricky Stout fit into all of this? And don't forget Mina and Charlie. Who are they to our victims? I still feel like we're chasing our tails, and we've fallen off the map.

Erin didn't want to admit she felt the same way as though she flailed in the dark for something living only in her imagination.

Clark rolled his neck from side to side, wincing as it cracked. "The assistant chief's on his way down to bitch Fowler and me out for the lack of progress in the Ted Moore case. No one wants to talk about which gangbanger killed the guy. Imagine." His deep voice dripped with sarcasm. "And this double homicide. With the Goddamned media in tow."

He turned his angry eyes on Erin. "Speaking of which, you want to tell me why you told that redheaded reporter the same person killed Bonnie and Virginia?"

"What?" Erin's guts lurched. "I didn't say anything to her but 'no comment.'"

Clark pointed at his computer. "The article says you confirmed."

Erin shook her head, but the morning swam back to her. The reporter goading her about her family, angling to use her involvement as the main story. "I said victims. Plural. Oh God, I'm sorry."

"Don't worry about it. I'm sure her panty-chasing source would have told her anyway. But you need to be careful what you say, Prince. These people will twist your words to the very limit of the First Amendment."

The mistake didn't hinder the investigation, but Erin's pride wanted to run away in shame. Stupid rookie mistake.

"The Archers are going to come at you hard," Clark said. "They called me this morning as soon as Channel 4 broke the story, asking why we suddenly have more manpower with a prominent professor as a victim."

"We have more manpower?" Beckett looked around Clark's crowded office. "Is there a turd in your pocket?"

Clark snickered. "Not until the assistant chief's done with me. But apparently that's the line of bullshit the media is peddling."

Erin couldn't join in the humor. She kept picturing the redhead's smug face. She played Erin exactly as she wanted to.

Clark waved his hand in the direction of the door. "So you two better get out of here unless you're interested in bending over for an epic ass douching."

Erin didn't wait and hurried out the door.

Beckett caught up with her in the hallway. "Erin, wait a minute."

She stopped but didn't turn around. She didn't want him to see the tears welling in her eyes.

"You didn't jeopardize the case."

She rubbed her eyes until stars danced in front of them. At least she hadn't had time to put mascara on this morning. "I played right into her hands."

"You did."

"Thanks."

"I'm not going to say it doesn't matter, because it bugs you," Beckett said. "So it matters to you. But you live and learn for next time. That's all you can do."

"You're right." At least she could still fake confidence. "So how do we handle the Archers?"

"We go in soft, understanding. Expect to be yelled at. They're hurting, they want answers, and they see us as the reason they aren't getting any information."

"How do we softly ask them whether they knew Bonnie made amateur porn?"

"We don't unless we absolutely have to. Kid gloves, right?"

This had all the makings of a grand clusterfuck. Erin kept silent as she led the way down the hall to the open interview room.

Carmen Archer sat at the table, staring blankly at the wall, looking drastically different than she had a few nights ago. Locks of her hair clung to her tired face, and gray bags hung under her eyes. Her cheeks drooped, and her mouth sagged. She'd aged a decade in days. Her husband paced the small space in front of the window. He stopped short at Erin's knock, his bright, angry eyes honing in on her.

"We're sorry to keep you waiting," Erin said, taking the seat across from Carmen. "How are you holding up?"

Carmen shook her head.

Neil immediately turned on them. "How are we holding up? You couldn't make any headway on our daughter's murder, but you're adding additional investigators because the bastard killed a more prominent woman? Or is it because some crazy person is copying Jack the Ripper?"

Erin froze, trying to think of the right response. Red must have talked to the right people this time.

"I'm not sure where you heard that, Mr. Archer." Beckett kept his voice soothing and patient. He sat down next to Carmen. "Our unit is stretched thin. We've had some help from our sergeant, but everyone's overloaded. Investigator Prince and I are the only two working the case. As for a Jack the Ripper copycat, we have no such thing."

"That's not what the reporter said." Neil Archer said.

"What reporter?" Erin asked.

"The one from Channel 4 who called an hour ago. She said both women were gutted like the Ripper victims, and the killer left messages referring to the Jack the Ripper murders."

Erin tried to keep her face neutral, but inside her heart galloped. A lot of people had access to Bonnie's crime scene, but Clark managed to keep the professor's on lockdown thanks to the quick thinking of the responding patrol officer. Only a handful of people knew about the messages.

Jane must still be a secret. The press would have raced with the information.

"We can't comment on details," Beckett deflected again. "But I can tell you this isn't a Ripper copycat."

"I think you're lying," Neil said. "At this point, I trust the media more than you."

"Mr. Archer, we've told you everything we can. That's why we wanted to talk to you today. We have more information to share, which means more questions to ask."

Nothing shook Beckett, Erin grudgingly admitted. Either that, or he managed to hide it well.

"Why haven't you formed a task force then?" Neil demanded. "Two women are dead. What's it going to take?"

More murders. But Erin didn't dare voice the idea, and no answer would satisfy Neil. "Would you like to sit down? The things we're about to ask you aren't going to be easy to talk about."

"I prefer to stand," Neil snapped. "And before you say a word, we know Bonnie and Sarah had starting talking. She called us and apologized. Carmen talked to her."

"What did she say?" Erin rested her hands on the table, giving Carmen what she hoped looked like a kind smile but felt more like an exhausted grimace.

"She said she found Bonnie because she missed her." Carmen sounded hoarse. "They kept it from her parents. She knew we would have understood as long as Bonnie stayed away from Simon."

Neil grunted, eyebrows slashing into one solid line at the mention of his brother's name.

"You wouldn't have approved?" Beckett remained standing as well, leaning against the wall, hands in his pockets. "Even though Sarah wasn't the reason for your family falling out?"

"She's a reminder," Neil said. "She told you about Bonnie's sexual abuse. But my brother accusing her of lying really screwed

252

her up. She believed she did something wrong! Therapy helped for a while—until puberty turned everything upside down. She started hanging around the wrong people. She was raped. Then she got addicted to pain killers. All to deal with the self-loathing my brother caused."

"Did Simon molest Bonnie?" Erin asked quietly. The vast majority of children were molested by family members or close family friends. Sarah had said a family friend, but she might not have been told the entire truth. Little kids lied to protect their parents all the time, no matter how horrifically the adults made them suffer.

"No." Neil clenched his hands like he wanted to throttle her. "And I'm not giving you a name. It's in the past, and Bonnie's dead. The bastard got away with it because my stupid brother, the big-shot attorney, is an asshole. Bonnie had obvious physical signs of being molested, but we had no DNA, no hair, nothing. Just an eight-year-old's word against a powerful man."

Erin didn't comment on the slip. "If you didn't report it, then how do you know DNA evidence couldn't be recovered?"

"He made sure it didn't exist."

Erin wanted to argue a search warrant would have garnered an extensive search of wherever Bonnie said the abuse took place and that DNA could hide in places people never think of. But instead, she said, "Bonnie was old enough to understand what happened and who did it. Why didn't you give her the opportunity to tell the police?"

Neil's mouth puckered, the bags beneath his eyes making his face appear swollen. "Because my brother said he would act as defense attorney, and he would make our lives—including

Bonnie's—hell. She'd always had an active imagination. She entertained everyone with wild stories. He even had home movies of her and Sarah doing plays. And these weren't typical kid plays. They always had bad things happening, always had conflict. Bonnie didn't want to have to talk about it. She didn't want to have to fight her uncle. She wanted it to go away." His voice cracked. "Simon coached Sarah. She stood right in their living room and primly told us that Bonnie told her daddy did it, and she made up the story so the abuse would stop."

"Sarah was six years old. They taught her how to lie," Carmen said. "She told us she needed years of therapy to deal with it all. Sarah became nearly as much of a victim as Bonnie."

Erin worked to keep the harsh accusation out of her voice. This was her specialty, the experience she could bring to the table to match Beckett's homicide knowledge. "Do you seriously believe Sarah needed years of therapy just for being coached to lie as a six-year-old?"

Carmen's pale cheeks turned red. "I don't know."

"You realize this same person likely abused Sarah as well, either during the time of Bonnie's abuse or after? Especially since the abuser had access to her."

Tears welled in Carmen's eyes. "We tried to talk to Simon and Melinda, but they were so livid and made so many threats. We had to put Bonnie first."

"So you decided Bonnie would be better off by cutting ties with the family and going to therapy?" Erin held no judgment. She'd like to think she would have made the man pay if Abby had been a victim, but she'd seen too many families go through absolute hell during the trial phase. And she knew full well how powerful money and influence could be.

Neil jerked his head up and down. Tears welled in his eyes. "When she started doing drugs, I blamed myself. I never could stand up to Simon."

"Sarah believes the man who abused Bonnie left town sometime after you found out."

"He left town shortly after, though Simon never believed Bonnie told the truth." Carmen rubbed her already bloodshot eyes. "I don't understand why we're going over this. It has nothing to do with Bonnie's death."

"We're trying to gather as much information about Bonnie as we can," Erin said. "You're sure he's no longer living in the area?"

"Positive." Neil Archer spoke with finality.

Erin's nerves rippled with desperation. "I promise you the information will stay with us," she tried again. "We need to know Bonnie's state of mind in the last few months, and with Sarah back in her life, it's possible they discussed the abuse. Don't you think Bonnie finding out Sarah took her place would have been devastating to Bonnie? She may have tried to contact him, looking for closure."

"She didn't." Neil's hard gaze landed on Beckett. "I'm not answering any more questions about it. You said you had a suspect?"

How could he be so sure? He'd said the man was an important figure—did he remain in the public eye? Or had Neil Archer made it his life's mission to keep tabs on the man he more than likely allowed to continue molesting other little girls? In Erin's mind, that sad truth hurt the most. Neil should have stood up to his brother to prevent future victims.

Beckett took over. "Did Bonnie ever mention a man named Ricky?"

Both parents shook their heads. "I don't remember a Ricky."

"You knew about her study group at the ALC this past summer, right?"

A tiny glow of pride in Carmen's eyes. "I did. She loved helping others. Was Ricky in her group?"

Shaking his head, Beckett directed his question to Carmen. "We'd hoped you might be able to tell us more about him."

"She never mentioned him," Carmen said. "And she told us everything as part of her therapy."

Erin glanced at Beckett. He scratched his chin and then the back of his neck. Letting them wait for a minute. Or working up to the anger he expected to receive?

"What is it?" Neil demanded. "We have a right to know about our daughter's case."

"Mr. Archer," Beckett started, "please understand we have to keep some details private because the investigation is still open. But we can tell you your daughter had over $100,000 in a savings account. Is that something you set up for her?"

Neil Archer blinked. "That's not possible," Neil said. "We helped her out occasionally, but we couldn't do much. She had a grant for school, but there's no way. You must be mistaken."

"I'm afraid we're not," Beckett said. "Which means Bonnie did something you didn't know about to earn quite a bit of money. And it likely got her killed."

"Not drugs," Carmen said, as if drugs were the only real evil Bonnie could have wandered into. "She was clean."

"Yes," Erin said. "But she could have been dealing. Bonnie

256

never worked at Daniel's. She worked at Sid's Gentleman's Club near the Capitol as an exotic dancer." Erin couldn't bring herself to say stripper. It seemed like a cruel taunt to the already shocked couple.

"No." Neil's fist shook the table. "You're lying."

Carmen's eyes darted to her husband's and then to the table, her hands clasped as though in prayer.

"I'm afraid we're not," Beckett said. "We've confirmed it with both establishments as well as her boyfriend. We also found evidence she filmed in the attic." He cleared his throat. "Of a sexual nature. And our crime scene experts believe a wireless transmitter was taken. You also confirmed Bonnie had a laptop. That's missing as well."

Neil's face bloomed red. "Are you saying our daughter made porn?"

"We don't know anything for sure," Beckett said. "We're telling you the facts as we know them."

"I don't understand." Carmen Archer appeared unfazed by the attic revelation. "Sarah told us she introduced Bonnie to Virginia Walton. We already knew Bonnie had spoken with her about Pathways. If Bonnie was killed because of this money or something bad she got herself into, then why would the same person kill the psychologist?"

"We think Bonnie may have confided in Professor Walton." Erin wasn't at all sure of this, but she had to give them something. "Carmen, how long did you know Bonnie worked at the gentleman's club?"

Carmen paled further. "I didn't."

"I watched your reaction," Erin said gently. "You weren't

surprised."

Carmen said nothing, not quite looking at her husband, who stared at her as though he'd never seen her before.

"I'm not trying to cause friction," Erin said. "And I don't judge Bonnie. But she told you about Sid's. What else did she tell you?"

"Nothing," Carmen said.

"You knew she took her clothes off?" Neil turned on his wife.

"I heard her on the phone a few weeks ago." Carmen looked her husband straight in the eye, her body braced for an argument. "I confronted her, and she explained she made more money there. She said the men never touched her. And her drug tests came back clean. She begged me not to tell you. She knew you would be angry, and you'd want to give her money." She finally turned back to Erin. "In 2008, when the market crashed, we lost a good chunk of Neil's retirement. Things are tight. Bonnie didn't want us helping her."

Neil shook his head, eyes wet. "You should have told me."

"I promised her I wouldn't. She didn't want you to be disappointed. She wanted to make it on her own."

"Did she tell you anything else?" Erin asked. "Did she say anything about filming or selling videos online? Or mention anyone she might have been working with?"

"No," Carmen said firmly. "She didn't."

Erin sighed.

"I would tell you," Carmen insisted. "I want her killer found!"

"Of course," Beckett said. "What about a Jane?"

Another no. "We told you she didn't have a lot of friends."

Neil Archer paced again. "So you still don't know anything

beyond accusing my daughter of using her body to make money?"

The break in his tone told Erin he knew his wife spoke the truth.

"We have one strong lead we are following up on and a couple of other possibilities," she said. "This case will be solved."

"We need the name of Bonnie's abuser." Beckett swung the conversation back to where they'd started. "I'm not convinced she earned $100,000 making amateur movies of any sort. She may have been blackmailing him, and he decided to take care of her."

"It wasn't him. He's in California," Neil said flatly.

Erin didn't believe him, and Beckett's skeptical expression said he didn't either. Bonnie's pig of an abuser probably had nothing to do with her death. She had eyes on a bigger prize. If Sarah had been abused and told Bonnie, the older cousin might have decided to target the man responsible for their abuser going free, especially if the abuser couldn't be located.

"What about your brother, Simon?" Erin watched Neil's slouched form turn rigid at the mention of his brother's name. "Do you think he'd have the financial means to pay Bonnie that kind of money?"

Neil's teeth clacked together. "You'd have to ask him."

She and Beckett promised to keep the Archers updated, but neither parent looked confident.

"What if all three blackmailed Simon, or Bonnie's abuser, or both?" Erin said as soon as the couple left. "I don't think they had anything to do with Bonnie's murder, but they lied when they said Bonnie's abuser lives in California."

"I thought the same thing," Beckett said. "Let's see if Clark can get a warrant for their financial information."

"No chance in hell," Erin said. "They're the grieving parents, and we've got nothing but gut instinct. The judge will rage on about invasion of privacy."

Sergeant Clark stormed out of his office. "I called Channel 4. They confirmed they have a story. Of course, the vultures won't reveal their sources." His hard gaze travelled around the sea of cubicles and straining ears. "But I will find out who did it. And their ass will be on a silver platter on my fucking desk."

"Can you get them to sit on it for a day or so?" Beckett asked. "Promise them some kind of exclusive, an interview with one of us."

Clark shook his head. "I tried. They're running it on the nine o'clock news."

Chapter Thirty-two

They watched the news from the small break room at the CID. The three of them plus Fowler and the assistant chief, a surly woman who always looked as though she'd been sucking on sour lemons, surrounded the twenty-two-inch television like it might sprout unicorns. Clark passed the time answering his phone and fielding mini-crises, while Beckett made guy-centric small talk with Fowler. Who the hell cared about the Wizard's chances for a good season?

Erin's stomach soured. She wished she'd grabbed the Tums out of the medicine cabinet this morning. Someone here likely had a pack, but she'd have to leave her post, and as soon as she did, the news would go from a top story about a skirmish in Afghanistan to the D.C. murders.

The silver-haired lead anchor, his pancake makeup as firm as his voice, announced the top local story: "The Princess and the Ripper."

Erin froze. The men's eyes shifted to her, but she didn't acknowledge them. Blood pulsed through her so fast her forehead throbbed.

Red—real name Camille Torrence, no doubt a stage name—stood somberly in front of the yellow tape at Virginia Walton's home. Savvy camerawork framed the scene perfectly, capturing just to the outer edge of the lot, where the naked trees and morose sky provided an appropriate backdrop. Torrence's bright blue coat stood out as the only splash of color, sucking in the viewer's focus.

"Is a modern day Jack the Ripper terrorizing Washington, D.C.?" Torrence spoke with importance but also with the gossipy air of a friend desperate to deliver the juicy goods. "And is a rookie homicide investigator, known as the Princess, capable of catching him before he kills again?"

Erin's grip on her plastic water bottle tightened until water spouted out.

Torrence blew through the description of both murders, barely acknowledging the women's names, and then moved on to the messages, describing those in detail. She didn't mention the killer being a woman, so Jane remained secure—but for how long?

The rest of Torrence's four-minute story focused on Erin, detailing her time as a sex crimes investigator and her move to homicide while subtly hinting her family name played into her promotion.

"Prior to the Ripper case, Prince worked just two homicides. Concerned citizens are demanding to know why she's the lead investigator on such a volatile case."

Cut to a shot of Beckett and Erin standing by their cars, Beckett confessing his fear and confusion about the case. But the shot and seeds of doubt already planted by Torrence made it look like he'd chastised Erin.

"We can only hope the police are able to work together to find this killer before yet another innocent woman is brutally murdered."

Back to the lead anchor, who lamented the tragic killing and the politics of police work, indicating Calvin Prince must have lined someone's pockets for Erin to have such a major role. She'd heard enough. She hit the OFF button and slammed down the remote before turning to face the gathering peanut gallery—other investigators, two of the uniforms at the scene that night, and more who had no other reason to be there. Shift change, she realized. Nice excuse.

"Who leaked the information about the murders?" Her hoarse voice cracked in the effort to hold back tears. She would not cry in front of these people.

"They don't have all the information," Clark looked sideways at the uniforms. "You people are supposed to be out on the street, not here. Beat it."

He waited until the crowd cleared, leaving only Beckett, Fowler, himself, the glowering assistant chief, and Erin. "It could be any number of people," Clark said. "Only those of us in this room plus Mitchell know about the name. But the crime scene people, the uniforms, someone from the M.E.'s office—they have the access to the other information. Trying to find out who leaked it is a waste of time and resources."

"Neither of which you have, Investigator Prince." Assistant Chief O'Rourke's husky voice came down like a gavel. "With this information out, your reputation is at stake. At the very least."

"I earned my promotion." Erin kept her voice even.

"Right now, that doesn't matter," O'Rourke said. "Perception is what matters to the people who decide whether or not you have a job. After this, if another woman dies, you'll be first in line for the fallout. The chief and the mayor will see you as a public relations threat to the department."

"Are you kidding me?" Erin said. "No offense, ma'am, but you of all people know how difficult it still is for a woman in this job."

"That's why I'm giving you this warning. The whispers about your family connections, however unfounded they may be, are now public. Am I to understand you've postulated this killer may be a woman inspired by the theory that Jack the Ripper was a female?"

Erin's jaw throbbed from clenching. "I think it's a possibility we have to consider. The name 'Jane the Ripper' has been signed at both scenes."

"Which could all be a distraction," O'Rourke said. "Do you have any women on the suspect list? A female who had issues with both Bonnie Archer and Virginia Walton?"

"The only woman connected to both of them is Sarah Archer, Bonnie's cousin," Erin said. "She's devastated, and she has alibis for both murders."

"She's also the daughter of a prominent member of the Republican Governors Association," O'Rourke said. "But we do have another suspect—a male suspect, correct?"

"Ricky Stout, a student at the literacy school. And a cross-dressing male at the strip club where Bonnie worked." Erin struggled to remain respectful of the assistant chief. Politics played front and center in nearly every homicide investigation in D.C., and Erin didn't envy her superior's job. But tiptoeing around Simon as a suspect infuriated her. "We also believe he may have had contact with Virginia Walton at another club, but we don't have any tangible proof. Simon Archer is a potential suspect. Bonnie may have been blackmailing him." She set her jaw and waited for the backlash.

"About that," Fowler cut in. "I've been going over the Moore case, looking for something I missed. And I found it—the Republican Governors Association. Moore's been donating to them for the past five years, which is really interesting since he's a registered Democrat and publicly endorsed their last presidential candidate. I talked to their media liaison this afternoon, and she told me Simon Archer procured the donations." He glanced at Erin and raised a graying eyebrow. "Guess the two of them go all the way back to their days as undergrads. But I can't find any correspondence between Simon and Ted Moore—no emails, no paper trail other than the donations to the Association. Simon hasn't returned my call."

"Are you finished?" O'Rourke's lips barely moved.

"Nope." Fowler popped a Hershey into his mouth, clearly enjoying making the suit wait. "Ted Moore moved to California the same year Bonnie Archer was molested. And he returned six months ago, around the same time she started receiving big deposits into her account. And get this—his documentary on the local gangs aired three weeks before Bonnie received her first big deposit."

Erin's pulse hammered against her chest. "Neil claimed Bonnie's abuser moved to California, and he seemed confident he couldn't have killed her. Being dead's a pretty good alibi."

Fowler grunted. "Moore donated to the Governors Association because Simon had something on him."

"We need to take a closer look at Simon Archer." Adrenaline pumped through Erin. "If Bonnie blackmailed Moore, she likely blackmailed her uncle as well. Especially if she reconnected with Sarah and found out she'd been abused too. Simon decided he needed to wipe his entire past clean. You think he had Moore killed?"

"Nah," Fowler said. "His murder reeks of a gang hit. One of the big gangs in Anacostia is known to castrate, and he mentioned them several times in his documentary. But with him dead, Bonnie loses her blackmail income. That could be the catalyst for going after Simon—or she upped his dues."

"Did Sarah Archer admit to sexual abuse?" O'Rourke's sharp voice interrupted their exchange.

Erin braced for the argument. "No, but it makes sense, and my gut tells me—"

"Your gut isn't good enough." O'Rourke's nostrils flared like she'd inhaled something rotten. "What about Ricky Stout? Is there a possibility he's the cross-dresser?"

"The cross-dresser's a middle-aged white male," Erin said. "Ricky is a twenty-one-year-old African American."

"Then see if he knows anything about the cross-dresser," O'Rourke said. "Don't do a damn thing with Simon Archer unless you get tangible proof Bonnie blackmailed him. I'm not getting into a political mess unless I absolutely have to. And drop this Jane the Ripper business unless we have something absolutely concrete. If the name breaks to the press, we will never get a handle on it. Do you understand?"

"Yes, ma'am." Erin willed her tears to hold off a few minutes longer.

O'Rourke's cheeks hollowed further, mouth practically disappearing. "Life's not fair, Prince. This sucks for you, and it sucks for the department. But it sucks for those women more. Find this guy, and prove that reporter wrong."

She nodded at Clark and shot a nasty look at Fowler. "If you talk to Simon Archer about this, don't treat him like a person of interest. Be subtle. And if the press hears we're looking into him, I'll shove that entire bag of chocolates up your skinny ass." Her heels clacked down the hall.

"Erin, I'm sorry," Beckett said. "This whole thing is bullshit. But you have to try to put it behind you and keep your head in the game."

She rounded on him, unleashing all the nastiness she had to hold back with O'Rourke. "It's funny. You're the one coming out like a rose in all this. Almost like you're being painted as the hero riding in to save the day. Mr. Bigshot serial killer hunter."

Beckett's mustache stretched out like a caterpillar trying to cross the road. "What are you implying?"

"You're the one to gain by feeding this bitch information. A uniform doesn't get anywhere except a chance to get in her pants."

"That's plenty of motivation for a lot of guys," Fowler said. "Look, you're angry and embarrassed. Everyone gets it. But no one in this room believes Torrence."

Erin still glared at Beckett. "How do I know?"

"Because I'm your partner," Beckett said. "And I've had my name in the papers enough to last a lifetime. But if you want to waste time and energy, go ahead. I'm not going to beg you to believe me."

"And I'm not going to beg anyone for the chance to prove myself. You said yourself I grew up in a house like Sarah Archer's. You think I didn't hear the resentment? Believe me, I'd rather have grown up poor than the way I did."

Beckett laughed. "Why? Because having money and influence

are such bad things? Having parents who actually want good things for you are so bad? My father's a drunk who looked the other way while my brother suffered terrible abuse. He's never accepted his role in what happened with Mary Weston. Your dad might have put unfair pressure on you, but so what? At least he taught you about real life. I had to learn on my own. So don't tell me about how bad you had it growing up. All of your anger about the Prince name is giving the reporter power."

Erin's chest ached. "I didn't want the Prince privilege. I left it as soon as I could."

"Then stop letting it control you." Beckett brushed by her. "I've got paperwork to do. But feel free to check my cell records. I haven't talked to any reporters."

Shame prickled on the back of Erin's neck and spread to her cheeks. Her throat swelled.

"Hey." Fowler awkwardly patted her shoulder. "Everyone's stressed about this case. And we all have a common goal. Forget about the rest of the bullshit, and do the job. And I've got a full bag of chocolate if you need it." He headed for the break room door. "I'll be wasting my time trying to get people to turn on a gangbanger if you need me."

Erin and Clark stood silently. She didn't look him in the eye and focused on the wall.

"Fowler's right," Clark said. "And for what it's worth, I've got faith in you. But if you don't have any in yourself, you'll never survive in this job."

Erin waited until his footsteps faded away and then rushed to the ladies' room. Tears came fast and furiously, her throat going raw from trying to be quiet. Embarrassment washed over her in hot waves. Beckett hadn't talked to the reporter. The men were right about her being her own worst enemy. Erin had been that way for as long as she could remember. What used to manifest as self-consciousness about her weight and looks and the ability to appeal to the opposite sex had matured into an adult complex about whether or not everyone she cared about saw her as a failure.

The change started in high school when she got the guts to follow Brad to a party full of people outside of their social circle. For the first time, Erin realized how different her life had been from everyone else's. And how everyone looked at her differently because of her last name. Once she became aware, she noticed it more and more until she felt completely excluded. Then she rebelled, as her father liked to say. She didn't go to Georgetown like the other Princes. She didn't major in business. She did everything people expected her not to do and loved it. Maturity and motherhood soothed much of the anxiety over what people thought of her.

At least, she thought it had. But she'd slipped right back to that stupid party, standing alone against the wall while the girls from the public high school, whose fathers had relatively normal jobs, whispered about whether or not she'd rat them out to the police.

Over twenty years ago, and the emotions from that night still wielded power over her. The humiliation and the frantic desire to crawl inside her skin and hide from their stares, to escape—she relived them all in the ladies' room until her head ached.

She had to let those sensory memories all go before they destroyed her.

Crying jag over, she ventured to the mirror to see how bad she looked. Her thick waves hung limply from running in and out of the rain all day. She should let her hair grow long enough for a real ponytail instead of a stubby turd-tail attached to the back of her neck. But she didn't have the patience.

At least her complexion, however pale, remained acceptable. A few wrinkles around her eyes to match the sandbags from lack of sleep. "Ugh. Pull up your panties, and go apologize."

Only Beckett remained in the squad room. He stood up when she entered.

She held up her hand. "Let me go first because I suck at this. I'm an asshole, and I'm sorry." Simple, but not enough. "I had no basis to accuse you of talking to the press. You've treated me as an equal, and you've never given me real reason to be offended or intimidated. And you're right—all of that's in my own head." She forced a tired smile. "My brother likes to tell me my brain is my own worst enemy. I'm working on that. Anyway, I'm sorry."

He stuck his hands in his pockets, the corners of his mustache twitching. "Thank you. I accept."

Erin breathed a sigh of relief. "This seems to be a pattern with us. We need to shake up our routine."

Beckett tried to smile, but he didn't quite manage it. "So Lucy's friend found one of Bonnie's videos."

"How?" Erin perked up, but the gray pallor of Beckett's face didn't offer much hope.

"Sheer luck. Most of these sites are paid via Bitcoin, and getting a subpoena for any of their financial records is nearly impossible since the vast majority of the transactions are overseas. Lucy and her team have been after a specific child porn site they think is using a server in the Ukraine. It's a miserable endeavor without much hope of success, but she's bullheaded. Anyway, a video with Bonnie showed up."

"On a child porn site?"

He nodded. "Remember, she looked younger than her actual age. But the oldest comment on this video is four years old."

"She would have been twenty-two. Still, that's a stretch."

"Not for the guys who only want teenagers," he said with disgust. "This site caters to a variety of scumbag preferences. Grouped by age and sex of the kid. Bonnie's video was in a special section: girls who enjoyed being molested as a child and want to be further dominated."

Erin wasn't quite sure she understood what he said. "Is that what the site says?"

"Oh no, they don't consider themselves molesters," Beckett said. "The specific wording is 'Peter and Patty: children who were loved by adults and never want to grow up.'"

"I think I'm going to be sick."

Beckett pointed to the bottle of antacid on his desk. "I was."

"How bad is the video?"

"As bad as you'd expect. She's dressed like a little girl and acts like she's being raped. Real tears, bleeding—from her genitals and in the mouth from being hit—begging for them to stop."

"So not fake?" Anxiety exploded like a bomb in her chest. Her abdominal muscles tightened, her legs flexing with the reflex to run. She would have to watch the video.

"It's possible." Beckett reached for the antacid and took another swig. "Most of the rape porn videos are people living out extremely sick fantasies. But some are questionable. Bonnie used at this time. She likely got involved with all sorts of people willing to use her."

"Can Lucy's people get anything from the video, like an I.D. on the prick raping her?"

"He's covered up. All black, right down to his mask and gloves. The only piece of anatomy we see is his penis. It's not white. Could be black, could be any other ethnicity. Impossible to tell."

Erin still tried to wrap her mind around Bonnie's torment. "So whether the video is real or not, she's been doing this for a while. And she had to be all sorts of fucked up in terms of self-worth."

"It's one of the saddest things I've seen," he said. "But apparently not all that shocking to Lucy's people. Kids who are sexually abused and don't have any real support system have a hell of a hard time getting healthy. That's how so many kids end up running away and being taken into sex trafficking. Deep down, a lot of them believe they deserve it."

"But Bonnie did get help," Erin's voice bordered on desperation. "Her parents got her therapy."

"So they say." Beckett put the cap back on the antacid, his face twisted like he could throw up at any second. "But a therapist is required to report sexual abuse of a minor. I went back to the year Bonnie was eight and all the way up to her turning eighteen. No reports."

Tension clotted in Erin's neck and shoulders. Why the hell couldn't they get one solid answer to some part of this mess? "Neil Archer is so angry at himself and his brother, and it's obvious he loved his daughter. I can't believe he didn't get her therapy."

"Maybe he did. But whoever did it chose not to report it," Beckett said. "Maybe Simon Archer paid the therapist to be quiet."

Erin rubbed her temples, wishing away the dull ache. "If

Simon's not involved in the murders, he still deserves to be trussed up and hung out like a turkey. But if Bonnie's been doing amateur videos that long, maybe she really did make $100,000, and we're off on the blackmail angle."

"No," Beckett said. "I dug into her financials. Most of these amateur porn sites are paid via Bitcoin. Bonnie's went into the same account as the offshore deposits, but the Bitcoins are infrequent and amount to a few hundred bucks a month."

"Simon Archer has an alibi for the night of Bonnie's murder. Fowler confirmed Simon Archer attended a fundraiser. But he still could have paid someone to kill her, figuring that would still be cheaper than Bonnie continuing to blackmail him."

Beckett balanced his hip on the corner of his desk. "Bonnie and Virginia's murders are about more than money."

"Maybe that's what the killer wants us to think," Erin said. "He throws in the Ripper stuff to keep us confused."

"I suppose."

Erin motioned for the bottle of antacid. "I don't believe it either. But I'm too tired to come up with anything else right now."

Chapter Thirty-Three

Erin dragged out of bed before the sun came up. Beckett emailed her the video of Bonnie last night, but she put off watching it, hoping for one night without nightmares. Her mind barely gave her the opportunity. Scenario after scenario went through her head in a vain attempt to try to piece things together. Everything leading to Bonnie's murderer fell apart when she tried to tie the professor to it. Some crucial piece eluded her.

When the sky turned silver, she threw off the covers and cued up the video.

Beckett's description hadn't done it justice. Either Bonnie Archer possessed exceptional acting skills, or she was raped again as an adult. Or—and this option broke Erin's heart—Bonnie agreed to make the video. But her physical and emotional pain resonated throughout the entire video.

Simon Archer needed to take responsibility for Bonnie's miserable life. What would Erin's father say if he knew the truth?

He would cut off any funding for anything associated with Simon Archer, even if it meant no longer supporting an association he believed in. He wouldn't want the Prince named tied to a scandal. And he possessed a moral compass—he just didn't always apply it to business.

5:30 a.m. Her father would be up, probably finishing up his morning treadmill routine. The truth would stop at her father. Necessary steps would be taken. An excuse would be made to cut the funding. Bonnie's name would never be mentioned. And Simon Archer would feel the sting.

* * *

Erin's stomach bottomed out when she drove into the CID's small parking lot. News vans from every local outlet, including CNN, had staked out a spot in the miniscule space. As rabid as the hungry gulls flying over the Potomac, searching for any morsel they could find, the pack descended, moving as a single unit toward Erin's car. Anxiety plugged her throat, sweat dampened the roots of her hair. The taste in her mouth reminded her of the time she'd taken Lisa up on her dare to eat dirty sand.

Torrence appeared at her car window, shouting questions. Erin's panic flashed to anger. She shoved her door open and stepped out, badge and bag clutched in her opposite hand. She and Torrence locked eyes, the redhead's bright and the set of her mouth smug.

"Investigator Prince," she shouted. "What can you tell us about the new Jack the Ripper?"

"No comment." Erin shouldered her way through the small throng. Voices blended together, flashes made Erin's eyes burn.

The vitriolic band of squawking media closed ranks in an attempt to entice panic and something newsworthy.

Back the hell up. Cornering me is only going to blacklist you.

Erin bit back what she really wanted to say and barked the

standard "no comment" as she squared her shoulders and stalked through the mass, who parted just enough to keep her from completely losing her mind.

By the time she buzzed into the building, her damp curls stuck to her face, and she had sweat all over. She dragged a hand through her messy hair as the back of her neck grew hot and a tingling sensation slid down her spin. Erin spun around expecting to see Torrence bulldozing her way into the lobby.

"Sarah, what are you doing here?"

The tall blonde uncurled her long legs and stood. Her fair skin had gone stark white, and purple circles beneath her eyes highlighted their contrasting colors. "I saw the news. I wanted to talk to you."

"The news doesn't have accurate information," Erin said. "Whoever's feeding them tidbits isn't privy to the real details." *And God help the bastard if I find out who he is.*

"So Bonnie and Professor Walton weren't killed by a Jack the Ripper freak?"

Her hopeful expression reminded Erin of a small child's who still believed sweet talk could earn a treat.

"I'm not at liberty to discuss those details."

"You told me they were cut up." Sarah wrung her hands so her knuckles popped. "And before, you asked me about Jack the Ripper and told me about the messages left. Jack the Ripper killed whores. This killer called Bonnie a whore—"

Erin put a hand on the girl's trembling arm. Sarah towered over her—she had to have at least six inches on Erin's short frame. "This Ripper stuff is probably all bunk. The press bought into it, but we haven't. We're not going to panic and start making mistakes. We have several suspects. I promise you we'll find the person who killed Bonnie and Virginia."

"Please find out who killed my cousin and Professor Walton," Sarah said. "And don't let them kill me."

"I don't think that will happen," Erin said, "but it's a good idea to be vigilant for a while. You're still staying at your parents'?"

"My father insists," Sarah scowled. "He claims it's for my safety, but it's all about control with him. He's made me completely dependent—he'll only pay for school and allow access to my trust fund if I behave the way he thinks I should." Her strange eyes flashed. "I envied Bonnie's freedom. We were polar opposites, but she leveled me out. She understood my life better than anyone. I don't know how I'm going to go on without her. I tried so hard to understand, but I finally accepted you can't always understand a broken mind." Sarah's chest heaved, her eyes watering. She reached into her leather bag and retrieved a delicate handkerchief with three intricate monogrammed letters.

Erin gently touched the lacey hem. "Ah, the hanky with your initials. My Grandma Prince used to make those. She believed they helped separate us from the lower income groups."

Sarah dabbed her eyes with the white cloth. "Sounds like she and my father would get along."

"She was something else," Erin said. "Thankfully, my dad's ego isn't nearly as large. His snobbery is a lot more subtle." She tried to smile but faltered when she saw a fresh wave of tears in Sarah's eyes.

"You're lucky," Sarah said. "My father still believes status is everything, and it's our duty to maintain the gap between social and economic classes. I think that's why he hated Bonnie so much.

She threatened his perfectly controlled family picture."

Erin hated to push when Sarah appeared to barely be holding herself together, but getting Sarah to give them Ted Moore's name might break the investigation wide open. "Sarah, I need to ask you something."

"Okay." Sarah wiped her eyes.

"Child molesters aren't capable of stopping." Erin spoke as gently as she could, making sure to give Sarah personal space. "Whoever did this to Bonnie would have needed a replacement. Are you sure there's nothing else you want to tell me?"

Sarah's eyes briefly closed, and then the mismatched pupils stared daggers at Erin. "I wasn't molested. I told you that already." Her tone hardened, clipped, and bordered on arrogant. "Why can't you let it go?"

"Because I've worked with many victims of sexual abuse." Erin lowered her voice to a whisper. "And the person who hurt Bonnie and you is still out there. Do you think he could be the one who killed her?"

"I got no idea." Sarah narrowed her eyes, arms tight around her waist, hands in her armpits, her narrow hip cocked.

Her sudden aggression seemed like a major twist, but many abuse victims used anger as a defense mechanism.

Erin stepped back, hoping the additional space would help Sarah relax. "Do you happen to remember Ted Moore? Your father's old friend?"

Sarah's aggressive stance stiffened. The vein in her neck pulsed. She shook her head. "Is there a back exit to this place? The reporters weren't here before."

Erin motioned for the desk sergeant. "Let me have a uniform

escort you. Is your car out front?"

"Took the metro," Sarah said. "I had some stuff to do on campus, so I left my car there. Station a couple of blocks away from here. Easy walk."

Erin's fingers flexed to reach out for the girl, but Sarah responded with antagonism.

"I promise you I'll find the person responsible for killing your cousin and Virginia."

Sarah shrugged, completely closed off.

Failure swarmed over Erin as she watched the girl shuffle behind the uniformed officer to the back exit. So much for a good start to the day.

* * *

The morning briefing had already started when Erin slipped into the room. "Sorry I'm late. Sarah Archer was waiting in the lobby. She didn't admit to being molested, but I think we're on the right track with Ted Moore." She took a chocolate donut out of the box on Fowler's desk and filled the group in on her conversation.

"I got nothing from Moore's financials." Fowler licked pink frosting off his fingers. "And we haven't found anything to link him to an offshore account yet. We need a warrant for Simon Archer's financials."

Clark barked a laugh. "On circumstantial evidence? I'm not shaking that tree. Not without something in black and white."

"But everything points to Simon having Bonnie and Virginia taken out," Erin said. "Sarah and Bonnie's reconciliation is a threat to him. Simon learns all he can about Bonnie from his daughter.

Then he sets things up like dominoes and hires someone to make them fall. Meanwhile, he's got Sarah sequestered at his place to make sure she stays quiet if she does suspect. Virginia is collateral damage because Bonnie confided in her."

"What happened to your Jane theory?" Beckett asked. "If you're suspecting Simon Archer, where does Jane come in?"

The one snag she couldn't eliminate. The idea of Jane the Ripper, combined with the messages, had seemed gruesomely romantic. And completely random. "Maybe Simon hired a woman to kill Bonnie and Virginia because he thought they'd trust her? Or Jane's a ruse like you've said from the start."

"I'll also have Marie check to see if Simon Archer's prints are in any system," Clark said. "He's a public official, so it's possible but a long shot. If we get a hit, we'll compare them to the ones at both crime scenes. Prince, we can't go after a man like Simon Archer without a mountain of evidence to back us up. We've got to have something more tangible than his relationship with Ted Moore—and there's no proof beyond Moore's donation. A good defense attorney could say Sarah tried to get revenge on her dad for allowing Bonnie's abuser to go free."

The chocolatey-goodness of her cake donut suddenly tasted like sawdust. Erin knew the game, and Clark had a point. But she hated it. "What about Virginia Walton?"

"Her autopsy was unremarkable. She suffered as Mitchell theorized, but the killer carved the name on her back after she died." He used a black marker to scribble on the white board hanging in the middle of the squad room and slashed a black line to create a column for Bonnie and a column for Virginia. Beneath, he listed the known elements of each woman's life, underlining the overlap.

"We're getting the security video from The Point today. We'll start with the night the bartender mentioned, but we might have to go out farther. We're all going to have to take turns going cross-eyed looking for Virginia Walton on bad security video. And thanks to Beckett's breakthrough"—Clark's derisive tone made it clear he knew damn well how Beckett had ascertained the sex video of Bonnie—"we know Bonnie Archer made the amateur stuff for a long time. Our forensic guys have already combed through Virginia's computer and found nothing that suggests a connection to the online sex world. Her files consisted mostly of school-related information. Prince, what about that box you guys found in Virginia's bedroom?"

"We skimmed through it at the scene," Erin said. "More school stuff, dated back several months. Nothing we can use. Temple didn't get any trace from the autopsy?"

"Temple recovered a few hairs and fibers we're going to test, but that's going to be like pissing in the wind," Clark said. "Beckett, you said you had something good for us."

Beckett nodded, looking slightly more rested than he had last night. He still hadn't shaved, and the scruff didn't make him look anything but unkempt. "Guess who called me this morning?"

Erin reached for a Styrofoam cup for coffee. "Who?"

"Stephanie Key. She's on her way with Ricky Stout and their lawyer. Apparently, Ricky has something to tell us."

* * *

Ricky Stout's lawyer was a thin, bald man with a groomed beard.

His trench coat hung loosely on his small frame, and his briefcase looked heavier than he did. While an officer led the group back to the interview room, he made an announcement in a voice loud enough for the entire department to hear.

"I'd like to make it clear I'm a member of the NAACP. I won't stand for this police department railroading another innocent black male for the murders of two white women." His orator's voice and sharp eyes begged for a pulpit to use for his own agenda, and he had sauntered into the offices with the explicit instruction he and his client would only speak to Calvin Prince's daughter.

In the past few years, Attorney James R. Thomas had made a name for himself, taking on mostly African-American clients and structuring many of their defenses around racial bias. Only two had made it to trial. He walked away with a victory and a hunger for more. Ricky Stout represented more headlines for the attorney, especially with a Prince painted as the villain.

"You should go in with me."

Erin, Beckett, and Clark stood on the other side of the two-way window watching the trio wait impatiently.

"I mucked up the interview with Rylan Walton, and I didn't consider race as an issue."

Thomas paced in the room, glaring at the window, hands on his narrow hips. "He's looking for a fight."

"He wants to talk to you," Beckett said. "Ricky came on his own. We have nothing to hold him on. If I go in, I'll piss off the attorney, and things will go downhill from there."

"Go in there with confidence and compassion," Clark said. "Be his friend, and follow your instincts."

"If it goes south, I'll come in," Beckett said. "But it won't."

Erin wished she hadn't chosen to wear a threadbare tank top underneath her sweater. She wasn't about to show off her damp and doughy body. "All right. Let's see what Ricky Stout has to say."

"It's about time." Thomas had shed his overcoat to reveal a silk shirt and sleek trousers. Soft in all the wrong places, his body resembled a pre-pubescent girl's. "We're here voluntarily, and the first thing you do is keep us waiting."

"I'm so sorry." Erin took her seat across from Stephanie Key and Ricky Stout. "Thank you for coming in."

"My client," Thomas sat down, tiny bits of white froth at the corners of his mouth, "is a young, black male working to better his life. I won't have him being treated like a street thug because he's poor."

Ricky Stout groaned.

While Thomas could only be called homely, Ricky existed at the opposite end of the spectrum. The man was beautiful. His blue fitted shirt accentuated the width of his shoulders and was lovely against his glossy skin. High cheekbones, brooding eyes, and sculpted lips completed the picture. He smiled shyly at Erin.

She smiled back. "We have absolutely no reason to do that." She offered her hand. "I'm Investigator Erin Prince."

Ricky took her hand in a gentle, firm grip, his warm hand much larger than her own. "Nice to meet you."

His politeness changed her tactics. "Ricky, your lawyer said you wanted to tell us something. Do you mind if I ask a few questions first?"

"No, ma'am."

"Erin, please. Ma'am makes me feel as old as I am." She winked at him.

He tried to smile back, but the worry lines dug into his dark skin. "I can't believe this happened to Bonnie and Ms. Walton."

"It's awful." Erin matched his quiet tone. "Can you tell me how you knew them?"

"I met Bonnie at the ALC. We had a reading class together. She struggled with that. I suck at math. We helped each other out."

"That's nice. I suck at math too. So you two spent a lot of time together outside of school?"

"Why is that relevant?" Thomas piped up.

Erin raised an eyebrow at him. Surely he wasn't that stupid.

"James, it's fine," Key said. "I don't think Investigator Prince is out to get Ricky."

"Thank you. Ricky?"

"Some, I guess. We walked to the Metro together. She took a different train than me. But sometimes we got coffee and worked on homework."

"You're graduating this year as well?" Erin asked.

"As long as I pass the test." He tapped his fingers on the table. "I don't take tests too well."

"He's working really hard," Key said. "He can do it."

"Of course he can," Erin said. "Hard work always pays off. And good for you. I can't imagine going back to school as an adult." Although with Abby in fourth grade, Erin had begun to realize being a parent essentially meant going through school all over again.

Thomas made a sharp sound. "I'm sure there are a lot of things about Ricky's life you can't imagine, Investigator *Prince*."

Heat rose in her cheeks, but she kept everything else where it belonged. She kept her attention on Ricky. "And what about

Virginia Walton? I'm sure your aunt told you we heard about the disagreement you had with her."

"Aww." Ricky dragged his hands over his face. "I'm a dumbass. I got pissed off and ran my mouth like a fool."

"Did she think you threatened her?"

"No! I called her nasty names. I didn't mean it. I just took it out on her."

"What did you take out on her?"

"My grade. I didn't want to take responsibility for it, and she called me on my attitude. But I apologized."

"Good for you." Erin continued to play the friend, although it wasn't hard with Ricky. "Back to Bonnie for a minute. Her cousin said you asked Bonnie out, and she turned you down."

He drew his shoulders in. "Yeah."

"Did that upset you?"

"Prince," Thomas warned.

"I'm not asking anything out of context," Erin snapped. "Ricky is an adult and a smart kid. Why don't you let him use his common sense?"

Thomas wanted to come over the table at Erin. Key stewed, and Ricky grinned.

"At first. I liked her a lot. But she had issues." His smile faded, sadness in his eyes.

"Bonnie had a hard life," Erin said. "Things that happen to us when we're kids can really mess us up. Some people rebound better than others."

Ricky picked at an imaginary thread on his shirt, eyes everywhere but Erin's. His nerves rolled off him like sound waves.

"Ricky," Erin asked softly. "What did you come here to tell

me?"

Ricky didn't respond right away. Erin waited. He trusted her. He liked her. She sensed that as much as she sensed his tension. But his eyes shined with fear.

"Ricky, go ahead." Key placed a hand on his arm. "You didn't do anything wrong. And they're going to find your fingerprints. Let's be honest."

"Stephanie!" Thomas rose from his chair. Key clamped her other hand on his wrist. "Sit. I brought you here in case something happened. This is what he came to say. He's going to explain the situation and be done with this."

Erin had to remember to breathe. "How many times were you in Bonnie's house?"

"Once." Ricky studied his nails, sucking in his right cheek to the point it looked painful. "I didn't want to do it."

Erin's eyes flickered to the camera mounted in the corner, making sure the red light blinked. "What didn't you want to do?"

"Did you find the camera and all the other stuff?" Ricky said the words in a fast breath as though he'd decided to get it over with.

"We did." Erin said. *Conversational. Don't get excited. Don't scare him off.* "But we haven't been able to find any videos. Would you happen to know where they are?"

"Online."

Erin laughed, trying to break the tension "Can you narrow it down just a bit, Ricky?"

"I don't know the names of the sites." His face twisted as though he'd taken a bite of a bad apple. "That shit is disgusting. And they're like one giant machine. Click on one, and you're in the matrix."

"You mean you click on a video, and you go to something different? Like they're layered on top of each other?"

Ricky nodded.

"I know exactly what you mean." Erin made a face to match Ricky's. "In the past few days, I've watched so much offensive porn. And I don't mean rough sex or fetishes. I mean extremely violent. And you described them perfectly. Layers and layers. We can't hope to get through them all."

"Yeah," Ricky whispered. "Violent."

"Ricky, did Bonnie tell you she made rape porn?"

A single tear ran down his cheek. "I told her she was better than that. The porn's one thing, but she didn't need the money. She did it for kicks. She called it her therapy."

The backs of Erin's eyes watered. "Did you ever watch one of the videos?"

"Only part of one she showed me." He looked at his aunt, who nodded and took his hand. "I *do* need the money. So when Bonnie told me she sold amateur porn online, and she wanted to do it with a black man, I thought about it. I liked her, and maybe doing it would make her like me. She offered me a grand."

"For one video?"

"I need to get my car fixed," Ricky said defensively. "And it's not illegal."

"Of course not," Erin said. "But you didn't do it?"

"Not after I realized what she wanted me to do. I've seen rough sex ones, and I've seen the ones that are supposed to be rape but are obviously fake. This stuff was on a whole other level. Violent. Degrading. He made her bleed from both ends, and she did it willingly." He shook his head trying to get the image to go away, more tears falling. "She wanted me to do that to her, and I couldn't. Not for any amount of money."

"You're a good guy." Erin wished she could take Ricky's pain away. And she said a silent thank you for her decision to call her father. Someone needed to be held accountable. "So we'll find your fingerprints in the attic?"

"Just one time. She had the laptop up there. She wanted me to see the set up and watch the video."

"I'm sure you're trying to get his juvenile records unsealed," Thomas said. "And if you succeed, you'll match the prints. We're getting ahead of you."

"I tried to help her," Ricky said, his throat sounding tight with emotion. "She was nice. Smart. And she got off the streets and got clean just like me. But she said she needed to do it. It made her feel."

"Made her feel what?" Erin asked.

"Feel," Ricky said. "She said doing those videos made her feel."

"Clearly, Bonnie had issues no one knew about," Key said. "Ricky has been struggling with whether or not to come forward. He didn't want to become involved, and we didn't know whether what he knew had any merit. But after Virginia's murder, we knew he had to."

My ass. You wanted to keep him quiet and out of it. And from the looks of it, keeping quiet was killing Ricky.

"Thank you, Ricky," she said. "You mentioned Bonnie not needing the money from the videos?"

Ricky wiped his eyes with the back of his hand. "She had settlement money from something that happened a long time ago."

Erin glanced at the two-way mirror, half expecting Beckett to meet her gaze. "Did she say what?"

"No, just that she was set up because the settlement obligations hadn't been met yet. He still owed her another $150,000."

"He who?"

Ricky shrugged. "She didn't tell me anything else."

"Do you have any idea who else was involved in her side business?"

Thomas glared at her, motioning for Ricky to stay silent. "He told you what he came to say."

"Two women are dead." Erin looked the attorney in the eyes for the first time. "And this man you're so afraid we're going to railroad is obviously grieving for his friend. He wants to help. Don't you want justice for these women? Or does it not matter because they aren't black?"

"Of course it matters."

"Then stop interrupting me. I'm not asking anything your client shouldn't answer. Am I, Ricky? Because if you want to invoke counsel you have the right. But you're not here as a suspect."

"I don't need him." Ricky rolled his eyes at Thomas. "My aunt wanted him here. But he doesn't care about me as a person. He's got his own agenda."

"Ricky." The lawyer adjusted his silk tie. "That's simply not true."

"Then let me answer the questions. I want this to be over with. Just Bonnie and another man, Ms. Prince. And it wasn't even her side business. He did all that sort of thing. Plus had sex with her."

"Did she tell you anything about him? The smallest thing might help us."

"She knew him from her time on the streets. He wore a mask in the video."

"What color was his ..." Erin's cheeks burned, "skin?"

"Brown. Didn't look like a brother to me though. Maybe an Arab."

Key elbowed him. "Middle Easterner is the correct term."

"Sorry. But that's what he looked like. And sounded like. So did the woman behind the camera, although her accent wasn't as noticeable. Her voice sounded real husky—not like a smoker's but throaty. Sexy—until I saw the rest of the video. She seemed to be the one giving the orders." Ricky shivered, sinking lower in his seat. "She got off on Bonnie's pain. I thought I might get sick listening to it. I couldn't finish watching."

Adrenaline raced through Erin with such force she nearly jumped out of the chair. "Did the man have any tattoos?"

"Here." Ricky's long fingers traced his collarbone. "Fancy lettering in a different language."

Sanskrit.

Chapter Thirty-Four

"Yari Fucking Malek." Erin burst into the room, slamming the door into the wall. "That dirty sonofabitch. Ten to one the DNA test says he's the father of Bonnie's baby."

Beckett dropped his phone into his breast pocket. "I just got off the phone with the manager at Sid's. Malek left work the night before last and told the manager he'd see him in the morning. But he hasn't come back into work, and he's not answering his phone."

"How much you want to bet he plucked Bonnie off the street when she was strung out and desperate for a fix? He feeds her habit. They get close. He figures out she's been abused and sees his opportunity. I wouldn't be surprised if he passed her around."

"What about the woman behind the camera?" Clark asked. "You have any idea who that might be?"

"His hostess," Beckett said. "Remember her?"

The beautiful, raven-haired woman who greeted Erin and Beckett at Sid's the day after Bonnie's murder had left Erin's radar as soon as they walked out of the club. But she remembered the young woman's voice. Ricky described it perfectly. "Shit. She's in on this with him. You think she could be Jane?"

291

"I've got no idea." Beckett held up a list of names Erin recognized as the employees from the strip club. "Aleta Gilani. Nothing came up on her initial background check, and she cooperated when we questioned the employees."

"Do we have a home address?" Erin asked.

"No, but she might have been living with Malek. Or using a different name or staying with a relative." Beckett leaned against the wall. "But what's the motive for murder? Filming the porn isn't illegal unless they used underage girls."

"I wouldn't doubt it," Erin said. "If Bonnie talks, she opens up the door for their entire operation to be discovered. It could be a lot bigger than we realize. And don't forget about Simon. He could have found out about Bonnie's extracurriculars and orchestrated the entire thing. We need to question Malek and Aleta." Erin turned to Clark. "Can we get a warrant for Malek's house?"

"Not a chance," Clark said. "We don't have proof he's on video. We can't corroborate Ricky's story."

"Beckett and I both saw the tattoo," Erin said. "It's not enough probable cause?"

"With nothing to link him to the professor. No way." Clark crossed his arms. "You need something more. Go back to Sid's, and see if you can get any of the girls to tell you anything. Bonnie's probably not the only one he did this to."

"What about Malek? He could be planning to skip town if he hasn't already."

"I'll send a uniform to check his house. You guys see if you can get something more to back Ricky up, and then we'll bring him in."

Erin dug her keys out of her pocket. "I'll drive."

* * *

Apparently, men liked to watch strippers over their lunch break. A pulsating bass blared as three blonde women in pink thongs danced for an appreciative group of suited-up men.

With the exception of his slicked-back hair, the manager resembled a watered-down version of Malek. He maintained he still hadn't heard from him. He didn't see why they needed to question the girls.

"Because one of their colleagues was murdered." Beckett's surly tone carried over the music. "We have more questions."

The manager led them to the dressing rooms, where several dancers milled about in various stages of undress and makeup. None seemed particularly happy to see the cops, and no one had any information.

"Where's Aleta Gilani?" Erin asked. "The hostess with the black hair and green eyes?"

The manager's square face went carefully blank. "Vacation."

"Until when?"

"Two weeks."

"Nice vacation," Erin said. "Could I get her home address? We have a couple of things we need to clear up with her."

His cold, dark gaze bore into Erin, a muscle in his cheek flexing. "Ask Yari."

Erin smiled. "Thank you so much for your help." She handed him her card.

He threw it in the trash behind the bar.

She and Beckett reconvened in the sub shop next door—a good dose of salt and carbs to help clear her head. "We need to bring Malek in. That guy's going to call him."

"You think he's lying about not knowing where he's at?" Beckett took a large bite out of his flatbread sandwich.

"Do we have a reason to think he's not?"

"No. But the cruiser is sitting on the house. Malek's car is still in the driveway. If he takes off, we'll know."

Erin let out a huff of air. Beckett was right, except they could be watching an empty house; Malek already had plenty of time to escape.

"We need to keep following the money," Beckett continued. "Simon Archer's the most likely candidate. If Malek is Bonnie's business partner and pimp, then he's probably getting a cut. Same goes for Aleta, although she might be higher up in the stable."

The stable. Erin still hated the term. Most sex traffickers had one, however. And most pimps used a seasoned girl, already broken down and completely dependent, to control the newer ones. "So if Bonnie decides she's had enough and wants to get away from Yari, he loses his cut of the blackmail money. Bonnie talks to Virginia Walton about what she should do. Yari and Aleta take them out and concoct this Jane the Ripper thing to confuse us."

Erin had been so sure the killer had been a woman obsessed with Jane the Ripper. Her lack of homicide experience diluted her ability to be objective. She slumped in the seat. "Well, shit. I guess I had that one wrong, didn't I?"

"Don't be so sure," Beckett said. "You've got good instincts, and I've learned not to discount those. What about Sarah? What are your instincts telling you?"

Erin picked at her bread and mulled over his question. "At first it bugged me that Bonnie likely started blackmailing her uncle around the same time her cousin came back into her life. But after talking to her earlier, I don't think Sarah knew about the money."

"Why?" Beckett said. "Sarah hates her dad for what he did to Bonnie. She might have encouraged the blackmail. Watching him twist would be wonderful revenge."

"Yeah, but ..." Erin wished her partner had seen the frightened young woman in the lobby this morning. "Sarah's very fragile. She's been sheltered in the arms of money and wealth, and if she was sexually abused, she had to keep quiet about it, even if she got help. She's the family embarrassment for someone like Simon Archer. He's kept her completely dependent to control her and protect his reputation. Bonnie probably already felt partially responsible for Sarah's abuse, and she may have felt like Sarah knowing about the blackmail would have caused Sarah more stress. So she kept some things to herself. You have to understand wealth and status in a city like D.C can be absolutely all-powerful."

Beckett wadded up his sandwich wrapper, his eyes boring into her.

The scrutiny made Erin want to burst. "But you were right about my empathizing with her because I come from a similar world. That's also why I understand her. She's not experienced like Bonnie. Bonnie knew people like Simon play by a different set of rules, and she knew where to attack—his wallet."

Erin's phone vibrated in her pocket. She read the text and

almost knocked her soda off the table. Another blocked number, but the message sounded anything but childlike.

> I know what Yari Malek did. Meet me at Sal's on the Waterfront in thirty minutes.

Beckett tossed his napkin into the trash. "You know where that is?"

Erin choked down the rest of her sandwich. "No, but my car will."

Chapter Thirty-Five

Washington, D.C.'s historic Southwest Waterfront ran the gamut in demographics. Many of the renovated buildings dated back to the city's first years, while others were trendy and new, seizing on the prime real estate offered by the Potomac. Unfortunately, Sal's belonged under the former.

The dive bar wasn't actually on the waterfront but a block off of it in an alley that had probably once had a great view of the river before the expensive restaurant on the corner broke ground.

The stench of old leather, decades of smoke, and greasy food nearly overwhelmed Erin. She blinked, trying to adjust to the light and figure out who she'd come to meet.

"There." Beckett pointed to the beautiful, dark haired woman waving at them from a corner booth.

Beckett slid into the booth first, and Erin sat down across from Aleta Giliani, wincing as a crack in the leather cut into her thigh. "Why did you text from a blocked number?"

Aleta smoothed her luxurious hair, her gaze unwavering. "You can't be too careful these days."

"Thanks for saving us the headache of finding you. We've got a lot of things to discuss."

"I thought so. You've discovered what Yari and I did with

Bonnie?"

"Sounds like you were in control and had a grudge against Bonnie," Erin said. "But why kill Virginia Walton?"

Aleta shook her head. "I didn't kill anyone. Yari might have, but I'm as much of a victim as Bonnie."

"Except you're alive," Beckett said.

Erin leaned forward. She could be on Aleta's side. "Tell us what you know."

"Bonnie was all sorts of screwed up," Aleta said. "She was molested as a little girl and then date raped as a teenager. Drugs put her on the street, and Yari found her. He convinced her he could give her a better life if she worked with him. A bed, three meals a day. No more tricks. All under her control. She fell for it."

Like so many other discarded girls before her.

Aleta's ruby lips twisted into a bitter smile. "Yari is a master manipulator. He knew how to play Bonnie. He became her friend, her only ally. He kept her loaded on pills. By the time I came into the picture, she'd gotten clean, but making those videos had become her newest addiction."

"Yari asked you to join?"

"He wanted someone else behind the camera, and he wanted another female. He offered me a lot of money." She shrugged. "I like sex, and I like pain. As long as Bonnie consented—which she did—I had no issues."

"How did Bonnie get into making the videos?" Beckett asked.

This time, malice darkened her grin. "I told you, Yari's a manipulative prick. And he likes to brag. One night we both got high, and he told me Bonnie made movies long before she realized it. In those days, he tricked her out to a higher class of perv, all in the guise of helping him out for the money he spent on her. When she found out about the videos, she left him and got clean."

"Then why did she go back to him?"

"Because he made her believe he was the only one who really knew her. By then, he had other girls, but he convinced her she was still his favorite."

"And then she became a willing participant?" Erin asked.

"I think she hated herself so much she did it as some kind of punishment." Aleta took a sip of the dark liquid sitting in front of her. "She never talked much to me about it. But she wanted to quit. The last time I saw her at the club, she told me she planned to tell Yari she was done with him.

"Why?"

"I figured it had to do with her rich boyfriend. She liked him."

Erin slowly digested the information. The case began to piece together like a patchwork quilt. "How is Virginia Walton involved in all of this? And what about Tori?"

"I have no idea about the teacher. Tori, the cross-dresser? You think he had something to do with this? He barely knew Bonnie."

"They had an issue one night," Erin said. "He never returned to Sid's."

Aleta waved her hand as though swatting a fly. "He's a pervert who invited her back to his place. She gave him a lap dance, and he asked her to come back and do a snuff film. Told her he'd wear a special black cape and a costume. She told him to fuck off and made security run him off."

"How do you know this?" Beckett asked.

"Yari told me." She laughed. "So I guess I should take it with a grain of salt, right?"

"What about the blackmail?" Erin asked. "Were you and Malek in on it?"

Aleta's dark eyes narrowed. "I wasn't. My family takes care of me. You'd have to ask Yari, but it wouldn't surprise me. The only thing he likes more than sex is money."

"Who's Jane? And Mina and Charlie?" Erin asked.

Aleta took another long sip of her drink, her eyes not meeting Erin's. "I don't know those names."

"Where's Malek?' Beckett asked.

"No idea. I haven't seen him since my last shift four days ago. I'm going back to my family and working in the family business." Aleta's hand trembled. "I don't want to end up like Bonnie."

Erin tried one last question. "Did you ever meet Simon Archer?"

"Bonnie's uncle, the Republican?" Aleta cocked her head. "She mentioned him once. She called him a hypocritical bastard. But no, I never met him." Her eyes seemed jet black, either devoid of emotion or expertly matching any real feelings.

"I'm going to call a uniform to take you to the office for an official statement," Erin said. "While you're there, consider telling the entire truth. Otherwise, you're going to be spending the next twenty-four hours in a holding cell."

* * *

Erin jumped onto 695, bypassing the traffic choking up the roads around the National Mall.

Beckett hissed as she cut in front of a box truck, its horn blaring. "That was a ballsy bluff. We don't have enough to hold her. She came forward willingly."

"I can't tell if she's keeping information back or not. Let Clark have a go at her. No one can spot a liar like him."

"I wish Bonnie's phone records showed direct calls to Virginia Walton. That's the kind of evidence prosecutors like." Beckett's fingers dug into the leather.

"But the records show quite a few calls to the school, most of them at night," Erin said. "There's no way to track where the call ended up. And the neighbor saw someone at Virginia's house who matched Bonnie's description shortly before her murder. But why the hell didn't Virginia call us after Bonnie's murder?"

Beckett straightened out in the seat, his right leg jerking like he might have been slamming his foot on an imaginary brake. "If Malek did this, he did it to punish Bonnie. And Virginia is collateral damage. He might have scared her into silence and then decided leaving her alive was too risky. Same goes for Simon Archer pulling the strings. Fear trumps loyalty most of the time."

Erin's fingers ached from her tight grip on the wheel, but she couldn't relax. "You don't sound too convinced."

"It makes sense except for the Ripper and Jane angles. And who are Mina and Charlie to him?"

"Aleta's daughter and another family member who helps take care of Mina." The answer hit Erin like a metal fist. "That's why she didn't want to tell us she knew the names. She said she's going back to work with her family. Aleta's young, but she's old enough to have a small child. Either the rest of the girls at Sid's weren't aware of her or were too scared to tell us."

Erin wrenched the wheel through traffic, her foot feeling like lead. "You were right all along."

Beckett huffed and clung to his seatbelt. "What about Tori?"

"Hell if I know." Erin honked her horn at a Porsche that cut her off. "Wild card, I guess."

"Coincidence." Beckett sounded unconvinced.

Erin gunned it and took the exit onto 16th Street. "I thought there were no coincidences?"

Beckett offered her a wry smile. "I guess there's a first time for everything."

Chapter Thirty-Six

While Columbia Heights' gentrification centered on bringing in bars and new condos, 16th Street Heights' residents enjoyed grand homes in a peaceful environment. Some actually had decent-sized backyards—a rare commodity in D.C.

"There's a bit of everything in this area," Erin explained. "It's pretty diverse, with a lot of younger families starting to move in. You'll see more affluent houses on one street and standard, low-middle class on the next." She put Malek in the upper-middle-class section since his house sat in the corner lot on Georgia Avenue. While many of the homes boasted bright, cheerful colors, Malek's was a simple white with green shutters. Nice, but not remarkable. She made an illegal U-turn and pulled up behind the unmarked car stationed a few houses down from Malek's.

"What are we talking in terms of housing here?" Beckett asked as he shut the door.

"Probably close to $500,000 for a single family home." Erin said. "But I'm sure Malek brings that in from the strip club alone."

Armed with coffee and energy bars and listening to droning talk radio, the officers in the unmarked car greeted Erin with jovial smiles. The driver could have doubled as a bodybuilder. He had no neck to speak of, and his hands could have crushed melons.

He gave her a gap-toothed grin. "Hey, it's the Princess. You find the Ripper yet?"

His patrol partner, a man half his size with bat ears, chortled with glee.

Erin twisted up inside, wishing she could jam her Taser into meathead's neck. He probably wouldn't feel it. "Yeah," she shot back. "He's in that house you're supposed to be watching. So you better not have screwed up."

Meathead—whose uniform read Simmons—curled his thick upper lip. "We're not the ones screwing up. No one's come out since we got here this morning. No one's gone into it. Place is a dead end, Princess."

She smiled sweetly. "Kind of like your job, huh?" Erin sauntered away before he could think fast enough to retort. "Sit tight," she called over her shoulder. "We're going to check things out."

Swollen clouds moved in from the east, ready to eclipse the already weak sun. The air smelled like rain, the wind bitingly damp again. She and Beckett casually walked toward Malek's house.

"Jesus, Princess. You're not going to make any allies with that attitude."

Erin glanced over her shoulder. Meathead watched with a scowl. "A guy like that will never be my ally no matter what I do."

"You should have asked him where he bought his steroids," Beckett said. "Or offered him the name of a good dermatologist."

She started laughing. "I'll remember that for next time."

They jogged across the street, Beckett's strides almost twice as long as hers. "Looks like a quiet neighborhood."

"Most people are probably at work." Erin pointed to the older model black Jaguar sitting in Malek's driveway. "Except our guy. This is his only registered vehicle?"

"According to the DMV. And I doubt he's got something unregistered. No reason to draw any unnecessary attention." Beckett strolled around the Jaguar, shielding his eyes to peer in the windows. The big muscle in his neck flexed. "Describe Bonnie's laptop again."

"Black, eleven-inch." Gooseflesh rose on Erin's skin. "She had a sticker of Wonder Woman on the logo."

"I think I found it."

Erin mirrored his stance, peering into the car. The tan interior appeared impeccable. No straw wrappers or crayons stuck in the cup holders. A few items littered the back seat: an umbrella, an ice scraper, and flashy red gym shoes. And a black laptop with a Wonder Woman sticker over the logo.

"Shit." Erin's adrenal glands kicked into overdrive. A swarm of bees hatched in her stomach. Her mouth dried to parchment. She took the safety off her gun as they crossed the front of the house to the porch steps. No curtains moving in the window. No sudden shouts or slamming of doors. The street seemed eerily silent.

She eased up to the porch, waiting until Beckett took a defensive position to her left before ringing the doorbell. No answer came.

"He might have rented a car," Beckett said. "We can check with the rental car companies."

"We don't have a warrant."

"You couldn't make a case to persuade them?"

She didn't bother to hide her surprise. Maybe Beckett wasn't so straight-laced after all. "I don't know how your department in Philadelphia handled things, but Metro P.D. is all about procedure. You cover your ass because the next person up the food chain will leave you out to dry. And then your case is screwed."

"Good to know," he said. "And we'll get a warrant for his credit card information too."

"We don't have time." Erin's pulse beat at her temple. "If he's running, then his manager probably told him we came around again. And who knows whether Aleta's trustworthy. She might have found a way to warn Malek."

Beckett walked around the side of the house, his open coat billowing in his wake like a 1920s gangster. Erin followed, grimacing against the gusting, cold wind and trying to watch the windows for any glimpse of their quarry. Malek was one of the lucky people in the city with a backyard larger than a postage stamp. His outdoor patio looked closed up for winter, the chairs neatly stacked and the grill covered.

A bang made both of them nearly jump out of their shoes. Erin drew her gun and whipped around so fast her ankle popped. Instead of Malek bearing down on them, a utility door swung open in the wind.

Erin breathed fast, trying to catch her breath. "It must not have been latched."

Beckett moved forward first. Erin's blood pressure spiked, her hands numb with excitement. She gripped her gun tighter, hoping her clammy hands didn't make her reckless.

"Yari Malek," Beckett called. "Investigators Prince and Beckett. We need to talk to you."

A horn blared a few streets over. Mist fell. No sound came

from the shed.

"Either it's empty, or he's getting ready to ambush us." Erin stood on tiptoes to whisper to Beckett. The sight of his artery pulsing with adrenaline only made hers ratchet up a level.

Made of cheap pressed wood, the shed had no windows. They'd have to use the front door to find out the shed's contents.

"Stay back," Beckett whispered. "Let me go first."

She opened her mouth to argue they should go together.

"You've got a child. I don't."

He edged forward, his hand closing around the latch of the door swinging steadily in the wind. Beckett eased the door in front of him, using it as a shield until he stepped to the other side of the door frame and could peek inside. "He's not in here."

Erin couldn't relax yet, but she moved to stand with Beckett as he pushed the door back open.

Home maintenance necessitates filled the shed. Various tools, a push mower, and a weed wacker, weed killer, grass seed. And a nasty smell reminiscent of the bags of rotting leaves Brad left in the yard for a week before finally taking them out to the curb.

Beckett pulled a pair of wool gloves out of his pocket. "Do you have any?"

She shook her head, and he handed her one of his.

"Try to use one hand."

They stepped inside, careful to make sure the door remained open. The shed wasn't much bigger than Abby's bedroom, and Malek kept it neat and orderly, organized to the point of compulsion. The sight of the two discarded black yard bags made Erin's skin crawl.

"Might be rotting yard clippings," she said. "That stuff gets putrid, especially if it's wet."

Beckett opened the first bag.

The smell hit Erin like a train, slipping into her throat and making her gag.

Beckett held the bag open. "That doesn't look like yard clippings to me."

He hooked the finger of his gloved hand around the collar of the men's dark blue dress shirt and carefully pulled it out of the bag. Dried blood covered nearly the entire front of the shirt, patches of it so thick they still appeared to be congealing.

The awful smell stole Erin's breath.

"Call Clark," Beckett said. "I think we've got enough for a warrant."

"And probable cause to go into the house right now," Erin said. "You up for it?"

She let Beckett do the honors of breaking a windowpane in the back door. He fished his hand inside, and the door unlocked with a click. Beckett slowly pushed it open, once again announcing their entry.

They stepped into a small but immaculate kitchen. Erin sniffed. "Bleach. Faint, but it's there."

"Why would he wear the bloody clothes into his house?" Beckett asked. "He's got the means to clean off outside." He eased through the door into the next room. Like most houses this age, this one didn't have an open floor plan. Moving from room to room meant checking doorways, their weapons ready. First the dining room, then the living room.

"Nothing personal," Beckett whispered as they slipped through the house. "No family photos, nothing that ties him here.

He doesn't want to implicate anyone else. Or leave a trail."

They reached a home office that appeared to have been ransacked.

"Jesus Christ."

Erin halted next to Beckett and stared at the dried blood coating the hardwood floor. A torn piece of college-ruled notebook paper had been placed in the middle of the pool, presumably after the blood started to dry because the words scrawled below the picture were still legible.

> *The female wasps crawl through the streets like rats, strewing their filth behind them! No remorse for the lives they ruin. Only the drink appeals to them. I will take as many as I can before the demon eats me whole. He kept a kidney tonight. I do not know what will become of it, only that I am descending further into hell for which there is no escape.*
>
> *—JTR*
> *30 September, 1888*

"Is that a kidney?" Erin stared at the shriveled human organ acting as a paperweight.

"Looks like it."

Streaked through the blood was the familiar signature: *Jane the Ripper.*

Chapter Thirty-Seven

Within an hour, cops and crime scene technicians descended like locusts onto Yari Malek's property. The malodorous yard bag contained his dress shirt and pants, a pair of shoes and socks, and blood in various stages of drying, which coated nearly everything.

"Egotistical fucker embroidered his initials on his shirt." Erin huddled in the front yard with Beckett and Clark to bring him up to speed. "And then he didn't make sure he'd locked the shed door. It's like he wanted to get caught."

She shivered. "We found the rest of the missing equipment from Bonnie's attic in the trunk of his car. Including the digital camera. But the memory's been cleared."

"That bugs me." Beckett's rounded shoulders, drawn up to his ears to stave off some of the rain, made him resemble a hunchback. "Malek's careless with everything else, but he erases the memory?"

"Maybe he figured having a recording of him killing her would make his sentence worse," Erin said. "But D.C. doesn't have the death penalty. Double homicide means life without parole."

"Again, it makes no sense." The more bits and pieces they uncovered, the worse the situation smelled—literally.

"So whose kidney is that?" Beckett's chin disappeared into the turned up collar of his jacket. Windburn stained his cheeks. "Did you get anything out of Aleta?"

Clark shook his head. "Not much more than what she told you. Insists she doesn't know Jane, Mina, or Charlie, and she has no clue where Malek would run. She maintains she's never had contact with Simon Archer. But guess what? Gilani's not her real name. She doesn't come up in the system."

Erin rubbed her temples. "So it's possible she did this and then called to throw us off her trail. At this point, I feel like we're getting further from the answer instead of closer."

Clark stared into the gathering crowd of media. "I want to believe this is a man we're dealing with because then we've got a real suspect in Yari Malek. We're going to get into his computer. Maybe we'll get a break and see he liked the Ripper, and this is all an elaborate distraction. In the meantime, she's cooling her heels in a cell. But she called a lawyer. Unless we get her real name and find something to hold her on, she'll be out by tonight."

The fine mist had turned into heavier drips. The flimsy hood on Erin's jacket barely covered the top of her head, leaving her forehead and face exposed. Her hair stuck to her cheeks, her lips were frozen, and her canvas tennis shoes had soaked through the toes. She cast a bitter glance at the squawking media already preening across the street. Torrence and her crew showed up minutes after the crime scene crew. Her lackey held a different umbrella this time, a giant yellow one matching Torrence's coat. Erin wanted to run across the street and smack her upside the head with the yellow monstrosity. Instead, she huddled closer to Beckett, whose umbrella barely covered one person. She had to crane her neck to make eye contact with Clark, resulting in cold rain dribbling down her neck.

Beckett worried his lower lip, his plain face pale. "Malek runs, but he leaves everything behind, including his computer that probably has evidence on it? All his expensive, monogrammed clothes? Jewelry? His car I can see, but he just left with the shirt on his back? The damn case has practically been handed to us, which is exactly why this all smells like bullshit."

Erin's phone vibrated; the caller ID read *Brad*. She sent it to voicemail. "Meathead and his fanboy showed up around seven a.m. this morning, and Malek had already gone. That's a minimum eight hours' head start for Malek—or his killer."

"So we'll track Malek's credit cards," Beckett said, "Put out a BOLO. Go back to Sid's and hammer at his manager. I bet he's got an entire stable of girls on the side who have nothing to do with the strip club and everything to do with the sex trade. We need a list of those. And we need to find a way to get Simon Archer's financial records."

Clark blew on his hands, flexing his wet fingers. "Keep dreaming. Not happening unless everything leads to him and is giftwrapped with a big, fat bow. We've got two options: Malek's the killer, and he used Jane as a distraction so he could skip town, or he's dead, and the killer planted all this stuff. Number one suspect is Aleta Gilani, who apparently goes by a fake name 'cause she doesn't exist in any system. Her sending us here is just another mind game."

Erin's phone rang again with Brad's number. She stepped away from the two men and punched the green button. "I sent you to voicemail because I'm busy, so this better be an emergency."

"Mommy!"

Her daughter's terrified cries sliced through Erin like shrapnel. "Mommy!"

Erin's throat swelled, and tears burst in her eyes at the sound of her daughter's distress. "Abby, what's wrong?" Erin dug her keys out of her pocket, vaguely aware of Beckett and Clark's worried stares.

"S-s-s-something's wrong with Uncle Brad. He's lying in the hallway, and he won't get up. Mommy, he's so cold!"

In that moment, time stopped. Her surroundings faded into a gray mist. The cold rain pricked her face like glass shards and mingled with her tears.

From far away, as if he were talking through a tunnel full of cotton candy, Beckett asked whether she was okay. Her chest felt like someone had forced her into a corset and was in rush to cinch it tight. She couldn't catch her breath.

Her eyes stung as bursts of light hit her from all sides, and she screamed her throat raw telling Abby to call 9-1-1 before her life went black.

Chapter Thirty-Eight

The next hours came in flashes: a mad rush to her home where the ambulance sat, its emergency lights off; Abby in Mrs. Bakas's arms, sobbing uncontrollably, her blue eyes wet and filled with pain; Mrs. Bakas gripping Erin's arm and telling her not to go inside.

The paramedics took off the blood pressure cuff. Erin recognized the taller one from years on patrol. He silently stuck his stethoscope down into his uniform and shook his head.

Erin saw her brother—her anchor in this world—crumpled in a heap, his hands already going stiff in the beginning of rigor. A woman's ear-splitting keening drilled into Erin's eardrums and pierced whatever sense of control she had left.

She was the one screaming.

* * *

An undiagnosed brain aneurysm had ruptured—a tragic and fairly common occurrence, according to Judy Temple. Dan Mitchell took Brad to the Consolidated Forensics Lab, and Judy Temple came in on her day off to rush the autopsy.

With Abby at a friend's, Brad had been completely alone.

"Did he know what happened?" Erin sat in Judy's office that night. "Did he know he was alone and dying? If I had been there, could I have called the paramedics in time?"

Temple handed Erin a tissue. The normally harsh lines of her face smoothed into an almost motherly expression. "He might have had a terrible headache, some severe neck pain. But it was a very large rupture. Once it happened, it was all over quickly. You couldn't have saved him."

"But he wouldn't have died alone." Erin had gone numb as if a powerful force had ripped her from her body and imprisoned her in purgatory.

Temple's cool hand folded over Erin's. "You should go home and be with your daughter and the rest of your family. You can make the arrangements together in the morning. There's no rush."

A bitter laugh scraped through her raw throat. "God, the arrangements. I can't wait to sit down as a family and do that."

Her parents had arrived at the CFL while Temple conducted the autopsy. Both of them appeared as numb as Erin felt. When Temple came into the small room designated for family counseling, she quietly told them the cause of death. Calvin and Helen Prince cried in each other's arms, asking God for guidance. They left together, and Erin promised to handle things that night. Except she had no idea what those things were.

"Who's driving you home?"

She blinked, looking at Temple but not actually seeing her.

"Erin." Temple rarely used her first name. She spoke slowly, enunciating each syllable. "Your car isn't here. You rode in with Dan, and your parents have left. Do I need to call someone?"

"I'll take her home." Todd Beckett's voice snapped Erin out

of her trance.

He stood in the doorway of Temple's office, his coat soaked and his hair plastered to his head. "I'm sorry it took so long to get here. Clark wanted me to stay at Malek's house until the crime scene crew finished." Beckett took a hesitant step forward to touch her shoulder. "Erin, I am so sorry."

She stood up on legs as wobbly as a newborn calf's. Nausea rolled up from her stomach and into her throat, but she had emptied her stomach hours ago. She licked her chapped lips, and rubbed her throbbing head so hard the skin on her temples burned.

"Do you have a headache?" Temple stood as well, touching the space above Erin's ears.

"I'm fine. Dehydrated." Was that stone cold voice hers?

"Do you frequently get headaches?"

"I'm working the most stressful case of my career," Erin said. "I get headaches."

Temple pursed her lips, her hands going to her broad hips. "I'm not one to tap dance around things. Headaches are one of the few ways aneurysms can be caught. A person's been suffering, she goes in for a checkup, and hopefully the doctor sees it. Or she's there for something else going on, and it's a lucky catch. My point is"—she paused, peering at Erin as though trying to figure out exactly how much more she could handle for today—"sometimes, these things can be hereditary."

Erin swayed, grabbing onto the back of the chair. "What are you saying?"

"It's probably nothing, but you should look into your family history. Most physicians believe two deaths from aneurysms in a family warrants a closer look. And if there's someone within a few

316

generations with the diagnosis, then you and anyone else in that direct bloodline should be checked out."

Erin simply couldn't take another shred of life-changing news. She wasn't sure she could put one foot in front of the other long enough to make it to Beckett's car. "Thank you for what you did tonight, Dr. Temple." She pulled on her still damp coat and zipped it up, turning her attention to her partner. "Let's go, please."

* * *

Beckett eased to a stop in front of Mrs. Bakas's house. The neighbor insisted she and Abby stay with her for at least the night. Erin hadn't put up a fight. She stared down the block at her own dark home. How could she live there without him?

She hadn't been able to find the energy to speak since leaving the CFL. The lights of Washington flew by like a dream, the monument shining above all the rest. She watched the blinking light at the top until Beckett's monotone GPS told him to turn, putting the city in the rearview mirror. Her brain slogged, unable to form a clear thought beyond the paralyzing sorrow leaking into every part of her body. Memories of Carmen and Neil Archer flashed and then Rylan Walton. Only days ago, Erin wondered how she would cope if she were in their positions.

"Erin?"

She continued to watch the house she shared with her twin. Had shared, she corrected herself. Only the night itself seemed darker than the empty house. Brad always left the porch light on for her.

Brad was dead.

The pain came in a jolt, crushing her lungs. She pressed her hands against her mouth to hide the sobs, but they persevered. Tears soaked her cheeks and fingers. Her airway ceased to work, the pressure on her chest so strong she could have been drowning. She could only manage nonsensical sounds. A coherent thought refused to come. Her back smacked against the back of the seat, her body rocking in time to the anguish.

"Erin!" A warm hand gripped her shoulder, holding her in place. "Breathe."

She clawed at her throat.

Beckett grabbed her wrists in his other hand. "Listen to my voice. Erin, you need to calm down. Your daughter needs you. Abby needs you."

Slowly, the debilitating panic subsided enough for Erin to see Abby in her mind's eye. Her sweet, broken little girl who walked in after an afternoon out with a friend and found her beloved uncle dead. "Abby."

"Yes, Abby." Beckett let go of her wrists, but kept his hand on her shoulder.

"What is she going to do?" Erin's throat stung with the effort of speaking. "How can I help her through this?"

"Kids are resilient," Beckett said. "More than most adults. And you'll help her because you love her. All you can do is be there for her and allow her to grieve."

"But I don't know how to be me without Brad." And that was the heartbreaking truth. From birth, their lives were intertwined; one could not do without the other. She trusted Brad more than anyone. He and Abby were the center of her world, and now half of it had vanished. How was she supposed to be strong enough to handle losing Brad, much less strong enough to help her daughter?

"You'll figure it out because you have to," Beckett said.

She faced him for the first time since leaving the CFL. "Thank you."

Beckett drew a long breath. "I'm sorry there's nothing I can do or say to make it any better. There's no making a person feel better in this situation. I'm here if you need me. And Lucy too. She's still a licensed social worker. If Abby needs to talk to someone, call me. Lucy has plenty of connections."

Erin nodded. "The case—"

"Forget about it," he said. "If you want updates in the next few days, text me. But focus on your daughter."

She didn't know what to say, and she couldn't have spoken over the lump in her throat. So she squeezed his arm and exited the little car.

Chapter Thirty-Nine

Hundreds of people attended the funeral. Erin recognized less than half of them, and most didn't know Brad. Mostly her father's colleagues and friends came to pay their respects. Lisa had enough heart to keep her usual insults to herself. She used the wake as an opportunity to mingle and schmooze, but Erin didn't care as long as she wasn't talking trash about Brad. Beckett came, along with Fowler and Clark.

True to his word, Beckett kept her updated, but things had stalled. In addition to Virginia Walton's blood, the medical examiner found traces of Bonnie's on the clothes Yari Malek stashed in his shed. Erin couldn't imagine Virginia allowing him into the house if he wore the same clothes he'd killed Bonnie in, but the medical examiner was confident the clothing contained both victims' blood.

Malek had vanished and hadn't used his credit cards. Aleta's lawyer sprung her, and she'd gone off the grid. Beckett and Fowler convinced one of the older girls to give up Aleta's real name. "Aleta Gionese. Charged with prostitution, drug trafficking, and possession five years ago. Couldn't get the drug trafficking to stick, she served a few months for possession," Beckett confided. "Not a single blip on the radar after her release. No credit cards, no driver's license, no utility bills."

"Gionese." Something in Erin's exhausted brain sparked. "Why does that name sound familiar?"

"Because it's been tossed around in the investigation of the drug cartels," Beckett said. "The FBI believes someone named Gionese is a major carrier for the Mexican cartel working its way up here. We don't know if Aleta is affiliated in any way, but since she managed to get one of the best defense attorneys in town within a couple of hours after we detained her, I'm thinking there's a good chance."

"But if she's from that world, she's been exposed to killing," Erin said. "The cartels don't leave witnesses, and they always leave a message."

The good news kept coming. Bonnie's computer contained over fifty amateur sex videos starring herself, Aleta, and Malek in violent rape fantasies that turned Beckett green when he described them. In one particular video, Aleta beat the hell out of Bonnie, calling her a whore in both English and Arabic, threatening to kill her if she didn't behave. Beckett believed the video wasn't scripted. But Malek and Aleta weren't the only movie stars in Bonnie's world. Reese, from the Adult Literacy Center, took his turn at violence as well. His financials showed Yari Malek extorted Reese for more than $25,000—a damned good motive in any cop's book. So Reese, and his intact kidney, had been left to sweat it out in a holding cell while the forensics crew combed his apartment. Beckett seemed particularly excited about the scratches on Reese's arms, claiming they could be defense wounds, but Erin felt only numbness.

"We found Virginia on the security footage from The Point,"

Beckett whispered as Erin tried to eat something. "There's about ten blurry seconds of her talking to a tall person in black who may or may not be Tori, but there's nothing to trace. And he didn't leave any sort of paper trail from The Point, either."

Judy Temple came to pay her respects and quietly reminded Erin to look into her family history. Erin didn't tell her she didn't need to. In a crying jag the day after Brad's death, her mother talked about an aunt who died from an aneurysm around the same age as Brad. Erin stowed the information away to deal with later. All of her energy went into caring for her daughter.

Abby kept asking why this happened. In her young mind, life was still supposed to be black and white. There should have been a logical explanation for everything; telling her bad things happen didn't cut it. And trying to explain something went wrong in Brad's brain only scared her.

"Could that happen to you or me?" She asked, her big blue eyes loaded with tears. "I don't want you to die."

Thinking about Judy Temple's warning turned Erin cold inside. But she lied to her child and promised her she wouldn't die.

"Mother of the Year," Erin whispered as she poured another shot of tequila. When the wake at her parents' house finally ended, she crossed the acre yard for the Princes' posh guesthouse. Abby wanted to sleep with her grandmother, and Helen had been such a wreck she thought it would be good for both of them.

So Erin had the night to herself. She celebrated by doing shots of tequila, the first drink she and Brad ever got drunk on. Brad threw up, and Erin teased him for being a lightweight. He didn't touch the stuff for two years.

The guesthouse sat tucked away on the eastern end of the

Princes' property, bordered by a thatch of evergreen woods thick with wildlife. The builders had the foresight to put in a large bay window on the eastern wall, complete with a cushy window seat. Erin curled up on the seat, a new tequila shot in one hand and a lime in the other. She leaned her head against the cool glass. Over the past few days, some of the heavy cloud cover dissipated, allowing a few stars and the quarter moon to be visible. In the meager moonlight, the woods seemed dark and much deeper than they actually were. Erin wished a deer or maybe a raccoon would come out. Anything to draw her attention away from the parasitic sense of loss.

Brad wouldn't want her to be like this. In fact, he would be ragging on her day and night. But this was a contingency no one prepared for, and she had yet to figure out how to navigate life with such a gaping wound.

The doorbell chimed, and she nearly dropped the shot. Midnight had come and gone. Her parents had gone to bed and hopefully fallen asleep. But maybe Abby had a nightmare, and someone had come to fetch Erin.

Erin left the shot and the sticky lime on the kitchen counter and hurried to the door, not bothering to check before she opened it. The last person she expected to see stared back at her.

"Lisa." Erin didn't have the energy for this. Her half-sister had gone home two hours ago, citing an early morning.

Lisa played with the collar of her designer coat. The stress of the day had melted off most of her makeup, and the circles under her eyes betrayed the truth: an overworked woman in her mid-forties. "I wanted to talk to you."

Erin debated. She couldn't handle a fight with Lisa. Not

tonight. But she saw no sign of animosity in her sister's liquid brown eyes.

"I won't stay long," Lisa said. "Not even long enough to take off my coat. Dad's going to be out of the office for the next few days, so I've got to pick up the slack."

Calvin Prince had taken his son's death extremely hard. Although he'd grudgingly accepted Brad's sexuality, they were never close. Calvin now wore the regret like a crushing suit of armor.

"Is this about the company?" In their wills, Erin and Brad had left their trusts to each other, with stipulations made for Abby. Neither of them had shares in the company, so she didn't see what Lisa would need to talk to her about.

"No, it's about you. About us. Brad." Lisa bit her lip, her mouth twisting in a way that told Erin she didn't want to say whatever she stewed over. "About fixing things between us."

Erin's knees weakened. Her stomach growled. Was she about to pass out? "Listen, I really appreciate you coming to make amends. And that's something we can discuss but not tonight. I'm just beat."

Lisa's cheeks flushed, the vein in her forehead pulsing the way it always did when she got angry. She took a deep breath and nodded. "Fair enough. Can we talk in a few days?"

"I'll call you, I promise." Erin intended to fulfill her promise. Lisa had swallowed a lot of pride tonight. Erin headed back to take her last shot before passing out.

Her phone flashed with a text. Beckett. Her stomach dropped out as she read.

Found Yari Malek.

Chapter Forty

"You didn't have to come." Beckett stood at the edge of the Potomac watching Dan Mitchell and his assistant negotiate a bloated corpse into a body bag.

Erin waved him off. She never welcomed death, but she welcomed the distraction. Her stomach, however, didn't appreciate the gas station coffee she sucked down to thwart the effects of the tequila. She popped in a breath mint. "Hell of a place for a body dump. If we're sure that's what this is."

Yari Malek floated to the surface underneath Arlington Memorial Bridge, mere feet from the backside of the Lincoln Memorial. Erin gazed up the hill at the monument. From this angle, it could have been a beautiful stone building surrounded by ornate pillars. Lincoln's impressive statue sat on the other side of the wall, overlooking the Reflecting Pool, meaning the backside of the monument wasn't a spot most tourists ventured. But it could be seen from Ohio Drive, which ran between the grounds and the river. At 3:00 a.m., moderate traffic still lumbered across the bridge overhead, and a car came by the scene every few minutes, the driver's mouth gaping.

"We're sure it's a body dump," Mitchell said. "I can't tell how long he's been in the water exactly, but my best guess is a few days.

She slashed his throat and then went for his abdomen. She probably stabbed him a couple of times and then forced him outside. It's hard to tell thanks to decomposition, but I'm betting his kidney is missing. Oh, she carved her initial on his forehead too—after his heart stopped."

"Jesus Christ." Erin halted a few feet from the unzipped bag. The smell hit her in the face like a hammer. Her stomach roiled against it, and she gagged, the liquor and crappy coffee threatening to make a second appearance. Mitchell tossed her a tube of Vicks. She swiped a generous amount beneath her nose and edged forward.

With skin blue and swollen to the point of bursting in places, Malek was virtually unrecognizable. Fish had chewed out his eyes and part of his nose. But the crimson *J* in his forehead couldn't be missed.

"Why not the whole name?" Erin asked.

"No time is my guess." Beckett walked beneath the bridge, the structure partially hidden by the tall, reedy weeds browned from the cold weather. "I'm assuming it's night, so traffic was slow. But her time was still limited, so she stopped with the *J*. Then she shoved him in the water."

"Did she weigh him down with something?"

"Looks like it," Beckett said. "There's a rope tied to one of his ankles. It came loose from whatever she used, and he floated up."

"Pure luck, at least for us." Mitchell arranged the corpse's swollen hands over its chest. "Otherwise, she would be off the hook for this murder. We would have never found him."

Erin turned away from the putrid face of what had once been Yari Malek and tried not to think about Brad in his casket. He might have been peacefully asleep, except he was still and silent and horrifically stiff. She cleared her throat and ignored her stinging eyes. "Where are we with Brian Reese?"

"Fowler broke him down an hour ago," Beckett said. "He claims that after Bonnie's murder, he and Malek had words."

"Reese thought Malek killed her?"

"Malek thought Reese killed her," Beckett corrected. "Reese just wanted to get out of paying Malek any more money, because Bonnie was dead. Malek said that didn't matter; he still had the proof to ruin Reese's career. They apparently fought—a convenient excuse for the scratches on his arm. He swears that happened two days before Malek disappeared, and he left him alive."

"Of course he does."

The Potomac's current rippled, and small waves quietly broke on the shore.

"What about Aleta?"

"Says he doesn't know her. We can't prove he's lying; she wasn't in the video he made nor can we pick up her voice behind the camera. And we still haven't found her. The Gionese family lawyer claims she's no relation. No one believes him."

"So did Reese pay Bonnie too?"

"He says no. We can't find any record of it so far."

"But Virginia Walton found out about them, right? He threatened her into silence."

Beckett shrugged. "Reese says no. We're searching Virginia's computers at school and work for any correspondence about it. I'd feel good about him as the killer if Sarah hadn't come by the station earlier in the day. Someone left this in her mailbox." He handed

Erin a piece of white notebook paper carefully stored in a clear plastic bag. "She found it after we brought Reese in. He probably had it delivered, but the timing bothers me."

A lump grew in Erin's throat as she read the letter, all the noise from the road sounding as though coming through a vacuum.

Dear Princess,

I keep on hearing you might be the one to catch me, but you won't manage it. I don't like whores and tattletales, and I won't quit until things are right again.

Great fun the last job was. I gave the lady time to fight, and she flopped like a dying pig. How can you catch me now when you don't even know where to look? I saved some things from the last job, and now they're so crusty I can't hope to use them. Too much red, but I like it so much. Maybe next time I'll cut the lady's eyes out. Good luck with your nightmares.

Jane the Ripper

P.S. Mina thinks you're a real princess. I know it's all a lie.

Erin thrust the letter back at Beckett. She didn't have the

strength to be upset about being made a fool of yet again. The killer's brazenness terrified her.

"So she didn't care if someone found Malek's body," Erin said. "She wanted me to know she's still out there. This was delivered to Sarah's parents' house?"

"No," Beckett said, his eyes roaming the letter again. "Her rental. Her roommate came home and found it stuck in the door, addressed to you in care of Sarah Archer. Her roommate told her she saw a dark-haired woman walking about a block away from their rental before she got home and discovered the letter, but they live in an area heavily populated with college students. It could have been anyone walking. Sarah and the roommate are terrified."

"Of course, their rental doesn't have any security cameras." Erin stared at the black water, half-wishing the river would rise up and swallow her. "If Reese isn't our guy, then it's got to be Aleta. She's a Gionese and knows what she's doing. She told us she liked pain. Where are Sarah and her roommate?"

"Roommate's staying with her boyfriend. Sarah's safe at her parents'. I told her to stay there and make sure the doors were locked and all the security armed."

Beckett rolled his neck, looking up at the murky sky. "I think we can take Tori off our list. He's a coincidence. My gut tells me Simon Archer discovered Aleta's involvement with Bonnie and hired her to do his dirty work. Jane the Ripper is a ploy."

Erin didn't respond. Some twisted part of her felt disappointed at Jane not being real. What a story to tell. *Christ, I'm losing it.*

"Aleta's probably not a legal citizen, but her daughter is, assuming she was born here—and if we're right about Mina being

Aleta's daughter, Simon Archer could have threatened to have Aleta deported," Beckett said. "Mina would stay here. She did whatever she had to do to save her daughter. Including killing three people. You're a mother. How far would you go?"

"I'd kill for Abby," Erin said without hesitation. "But I have options. There are people I could go to for help. My father …"

"If Aleta is really another one of Malek's victims, she's been brainwashed and broken down," Beckett said. "She didn't have someone like your father to go to. Simon Archer might have seemed like the devil to her. Then again, if she is related to the Gionese affiliated with the cartel, Simon Archer might have signed his own death warrant."

Erin's stomach growled, the tequila reminding her that her last meal had been this morning. "She lied and managed to disappear as soon as her lawyer got her cut loose. How brainwashed can she be? How do we know she's not the master manipulator she made Yari out to be? She completely played us."

Mitchell zipped up the body bag, and Beckett turned to Erin. "To be honest, I feel like I'm drowning in a big pool of shitty theories that don't quite add up."

Her phone vibrated in her pocket. She answered without bothering to look at the ID, hoping Abby hadn't awoken to a nightmare and found out her mother wasn't there. "Prince."

"Princess!"

The high-pitched, childish cry paralyzed Erin. "Mina, what's wrong?"

"Jane's going to hurt us!"

"Mina, where are you?" Erin waved frantically at Beckett.

The little girl answered with a scream. Then silence.

Chapter Forty-One

For the second time in two weeks, Erin knocked on Neil and Carmen Archer's door. After Mina's frantic call, she and Beckett decided to split up. Fowler joined Beckett at the strip club to try to force something out of the dancers and manager, while Erin talked to the Archers.

Her patience long gone, she steeled herself against the confrontation. Neil Archer wasn't going to like what she had to say, but a child's life was at stake. She no longer had any empathy for Bonnie's parents. They failed the girl time and again in her life, and they continued to fail her in death.

Neil wrenched the door opened and glared at her with hollowed eyes reminiscent of a war veteran unable to speak of the things he witnessed. "What do you want at this hour?"

"The truth." She shouldered her way past him and into the foyer. "Get Carmen, because you're both going to tell me everything I need to know."

"Investigator Prince." Neil Archer's voice thinned to the consistency of a razor blade. "I don't know what kind of show you're trying to run, but we aren't the bad guys. Our daughter is a victim, and you've done nothing to find out who killed her."

"Listen to me." She slammed the front door and then stood

on tiptoes to get in his face. He probably caught a whiff of the tequila from hours ago, but she'd gone past the point of caring. "Your daughter is dead, and you're not helping us find out who killed her. I buried my twin brother less than twenty-four hours ago, and all I want to do is crawl into bed and stay there. But I'm trying to find a killer before someone else dies. So let's start with Ted Moore."

Neil Archer jerked, stepping back as if she'd planted her fist in his chest—a scenario that wasn't out of the question at this point. "Ted Moore is dead."

"No shit," Erin snapped. "But I've got a little girl calling me claiming someone is going to get hurt again, and we just dredged our only suspect out of the Potomac. So it's time for you to come clean about who abused Bonnie."

"Investigator." Carmen Archer descended the stairs like a withered ghost, tightening her fuzzy robe. "I'm sorry to hear about your brother. But there's simply no way Bonnie's abuse has anything to do with this."

"I think your brother is the key to this whole thing, and it all goes back to Bonnie being molested."

"Simon?" Neil Archer stood motionless as an old tree stump and just as oblivious. "I don't understand."

"Bonnie blackmailed someone in the last six months for a lot of money, and she told Sarah more cash would be coming." Erin didn't have time to worry about the Archer's feelings. "The most logical person is the man who molested her—or the uncle who helped cover it up. Ted Moore's return to the area and the timing of his documentary gels with the deposit. But Ted Moore's dead, and the only other person with something major to lose is your brother. Bonnie likely blackmailed them both."

"What does Professor Walton's murder have to do with it?" Neil asked.

"Bonnie confided in her." Presenting the theory as fact was the only chance she had of getting Neil to talk. "Virginia was killed because of what she knew."

Neil tugged at his graying hair. "My brother's a bastard, but he wouldn't kill anyone."

"We think he hired a woman Bonnie knew to kill her. And anyone who can lead us to Simon is in danger." Erin turned her attention to Carmen, who stood on the bottom step, wringing her hands. "This killer is vicious and signing her name as Jane the Ripper, and a little girl named Mina is calling me begging for help. She says Jane is going to do it again, and you people are all I've got. Give me something to throw at Simon Archer other than your accusation he covered up the molestation. Give me more details. Help me find your daughter's killer!"

"Ted Moore molested Bonnie." Carmen hushed her husband when he rounded on her. "Enough, Neil. You think it's not going to come out? They're saying Bonnie made violent sex videos! That will become public knowledge. The least we can do for her memory is to help people understand why she had such low self-esteem."

Neil emitted a string of unintelligible pleas.

Erin stepped between the couple, focusing all of her attention on Carmen. "Keep talking."

"Ted and Simon went to college together. When the girls were little, Ted hadn't made a name for himself yet. Simon let him stay with them when Ted ran out of money. Simon and Melinda had a function, and Ted volunteered to watch the girls. Bonnie said

Sarah was already asleep when he came into the bed." She clawed at her head, tangling her already unkempt hair. "He raped my eight-year-old daughter and then told her she would ruin her uncle's life if she told. He did it again a few days later. I noticed something changed in Bonnie, and she finally told me. We confronted Ted and Simon. Ted Moore is a great actor, and Simon wanted to believe him. He said Bonnie was a manipulative child who just wanted attention."

Carmen's broken tone turned bitter. "Sarah was so delicate, and people were drawn to her, especially with those beautiful, strange eyes. Bonnie got jealous sometimes. But for Simon to say Bonnie made something like this up? The doctor confirmed she'd been molested. She was ... injured."

"But Ted Moore's semen was already gone." As a mother, Erin couldn't imagine any set of circumstances or any threat big enough to keep her from cutting off Moore's balls. No way in hell would she have kept silent.

Carmen nodded. "Simon said Neil must have abused our daughter, and we coached Bonnie to say otherwise. He threatened to call the police and have Neil investigated. And he assured us he would make our lives—Bonnie's life—miserable. We were too scared to do the right thing."

Judging them accomplished nothing, and the little voice in her head debated on whether or not the security of her family name would have played a part in her decision. Beckett and Clark were right. No matter how far she ran from the Prince legacy, she would always view life through that veil of experience.

"How long did Ted Moore stay in town?"

"At least a couple of months," Neil said. "I saw him once, in the grocery store. Shopping with Sarah like nothing had ever happened." He slammed his right fist into the opposite palm. "I will never forget the look on his face. He grinned like a sly fox, patting the top of Sarah's head. His way of letting me know he'd gotten away with it."

The sick feeling swept over Erin with the force of a hurricane. How could these two not have considered the obvious? "What did Sarah do that day?"

"She wouldn't look at me," Neil said. "Stared at the floor the entire time. And yes, we knew Moore had likely abused Sarah too. But we had to take care of Bonnie first."

"How did you find out Moore went to California?"

Neil's chin jutted out, his narrowed eyes glossed over from the memory. "I got drunk and showed up at Simon's a couple of days later. He told me he'd banished Moore the day before. That Moore moved to California. I hired someone to find out whether it was true. Once he confirmed it, we tried to go on with our lives."

"He used the word *banished*?" The truth hit Erin like hives festering just beneath her skin.

"Yeah. They had some kind of argument, I guess."

"You said you got Bonnie therapy, but therapists are required to report sexual abuse. There is none on record for Bonnie."

Neil shuffled his feet. "All I ever wanted to do was protect my daughter. I failed her by leaving her at my brother's. Risking her going into the foster system because my brother made my wife and me look like the ones who did something wrong terrified me."

"So you didn't get her therapy?" This family created their own brand of cancer by allowing their daughter to be victimized long after the sexual abuse stopped.

"We did," Carmen said. "Someone Melinda recommended. A friend of Simon's. He agreed to keep things quiet and focus on Bonnie's mental health."

"Jesus Christ." Erin threw her hands in the air, but she envisioned taking them both by the hair and knocking their skulls together.

"We tried to talk to Melinda and Simon, and they wouldn't hear of it. I begged Melinda to keep Sarah away from Ted Moore." Carmen's voice broke. "I don't know if she did. When I saw Sarah years later and she talked about therapy, I worried Melinda didn't listen."

"Did you ask who her therapist was?"

Carmen's eyes closed. "The same one Bonnie went to."

Erin should have walked away. But the venom rolled through her. A parent's job was to protect the child, even if the price required self-sacrifice. "Congratulations. You failed your daughter and your niece. And those failures may have gotten Bonnie killed." If she stayed one more minute, Erin would end up saying something guaranteed to earn a suspension. And Mina still needed her. Erin turned to leave, but Neil Archer seized her elbow.

Spit bubbled in the corners of his mouth. His hair jacked up in all directions. "Don't you think we know that? I've lived with the guilt for years. I watched Bonnie go through hell time and again, and I couldn't do anything because she didn't trust me. She didn't think I would fix it because I never made things right with Ted Moore. He never had to answer for what he did." Something feral flashed in his eyes. A satisfied smile tugged at his frothing mouth. "But I guess he finally did, didn't he?"

Cold, stinging air rushed through Erin's esophagus. She

yanked free of Neil's bony grasp and moved toward the door, never taking her eyes off him. "I'm going to ask you two one more time— do the names Jane, Charlie, or Mina mean anything to you? Do any of those names have a connection with Sarah?"

Still breathing hard and looking like something straight off the crazy train, Neil shook his head.

But Carmen made a sound of recognition as something clicked into place. "Sarah's middle name is Jane. Her maternal grandmother's name."

Erin left them standing in the doorway crying and holding each other. Her call to Sarah Archer's cell went unanswered as expected. No one picked up at the Archers' Chevy Chase home. Beckett's phone went to voicemail. Erin left a message with the new information and told Beckett where to meet her. "I'm stopping at Virginia's first. I need to check something."

Chapter Forty-Two

Virginia Walton's home in Takoma Park had been cleaned by a crime scene crew, but the aura of violent death still hung in the air like a cloying perfume. Violence like that left a black mark, a dark energy felt by all who crossed its path.

The dark energy clung to Erin as she eased through the house. She had no reason to be quiet, but silence seemed like the right thing. The jagged circle had been cut out of the carpet where Virginia's blood soaked through to the subfloor. The wood had been cleaned, but the stain gleamed in Erin's flashlight beam.

She wished Rylan hadn't canceled the power and prayed she didn't take the box from her mother's bedroom. The night of the murder, she and Beckett didn't think much of it. Just a regular cardboard storage box marked as *old thesis drafts and works in progress*—Marie called the woman a paper pack rat. The dates marked with a sharpie on the box were several months old. Likely not pertinent to the investigation. Had that decision changed everything?

Sarah Archer's words played on repeat in Erin's mind as she moved with quiet reverence down the hall. *My second thesis ... the first one was too emotional and personal ... like a memoir.*

Questions raced through Erin's mind. What about the Dear

Princess letter? And what about the letter Sarah received earlier?

Had Sarah really been ballsy—or disturbed—enough to hand deliver a letter she'd written? And why?

Because she could. You didn't see what was right in front of you.

Sarah practically waved it in Erin's face the other day at the CID. The two of them had even discussed her embroidered initials on the handkerchief: *SJA*.

Sarah knew Erin would empathize with her upbringing and the terror of being cut off from the money.

The bedroom still held a faint whiff of Virginia's flowery perfume, and it looked exactly the same. Rylan must not have been able to bring herself to go through her mother's things yet. Erin didn't blame her. She hadn't been inside Brad's room yet. Mrs. Bakas had brought out his clothes for Erin to choose from for the burial. She blinked against the sting in her eyes and called up the memory of Mina's terrified voice to stave off the threat of crushing despair. She shined her beam into the corner and exhaled hard when she saw the box still sitting in the corner.

Heart racing, she knelt down and balanced the flashlight between her ear and shoulder. Dust rose from the papers, making Erin sneeze. She sliced her fingers on the edges of the paper three times before she reached the middle of the pile and caught the name Sarah Jane Archer.

Her original thesis discussed unreported sexual abuse in children and the longstanding ramifications. Erin licked her thumb and tried not to let her disgust mess up her focus. She could easily see why the paper had been rejected. The tone was more conversational than academic, and instead of any real evidence, many of Sarah's theories were only conjecture.

And it did read like a memoir, with names omitted. But the text made it clear Ted Moore molested Sarah, possibly before he touched Bonnie.

Things picked up on page five. Sarah theorized violence in women throughout history could have been the result of sexual abuse and the rejection from loved ones. *Women had been forced to live lies,* Sarah wrote, *and in some of them rose a violent need to lash out.* This time, she cited evidence.

The next four pages laid out the theory Jack the Ripper was a woman. A woman Sarah referred to as *Jane.*

* * *

Beckett answered his phone this time. He swore when Erin told him what she'd read.

"She took the metro to the station the other day. Which means if she walked to the metro then, she could have done it the night of Bonnie and Virginia's murders. Her mother and the housekeeper wouldn't have noticed, especially if Sarah was supposed to be locked in her room and working on her thesis. I missed it." Erin clenched the wheel until her hands throbbed. Sarah had practically given her the truth giftwrapped with a big, red bow.

"Don't beat yourself up," Beckett said. "You'd been dealing with the press, and we'd already eliminated her as a suspect."

"I'm on my way to Chevy Chase." The faintest tinge of pink decorated the eastern horizon. "I should be there before six, but traffic's picking up. Let's hope Simon Archer is still alive. And Aleta and Mina and Charlie."

"We just walked out of Sid's." Beckett's rapid breaths sounded like he might have been running.

"Please tell me you're in Fowler's car. He always uses the department ones. You need a siren."

"I can do that. Fowler!"

"You're still at least twenty minutes out." Erin jammed her foot on the accelerator and ran a yellow light. "I'll be there in five."

"Don't go in by yourself," Beckett said. "If Sarah's the one behind this, she's extremely dangerous."

How had Erin missed all of the signs? Sarah might be an incredible actress, but she thought back to Beckett's words. Had she ignored the obvious because she allowed her and Sarah's similar backgrounds to influence her?

A terrible thought skidded through Erin's racing mind. What if Mina was actually Sarah's child? What if she'd been kept hidden for some strange reason? But why? Unless Ted Moore fathered the child, which made no sense. Simon's? A product of incest? Simon might have kicked Ted Moore out of their lives, but how long had he looked the other way? Or did he have some kind of twisted thing for his adult daughter, and that's why she kept Mina hidden?

But what about Charlie? The boy who took care of Mina. An older brother? No, too dark. If Sarah had children she kept hidden, the more likely reason was those kids didn't look good for Simon's conservative agenda.

"Erin? Do you hear me?"

She took a sharp left into the Archers' stately neighborhood. "Hurry."

* * *

The Archers' small mansion seemed as lifeless as Virginia's modest home. A red convertible sat in the driveway. Sarah's car? Headlights off, Erin blocked it in and tried to summon patience.

She had to be wrong. But it all made sense.

Sarah and Bonnie reconnected after Ted Moore came back into town. That had to be the catalyst. Sarah probably apologized and told her cousin what she'd gone through. They bonded again and hatched the blackmail scheme.

Why would Sarah snap on her cousin?

The answer came to Erin like a zing from a live wire. The amateur rape videos. Had Sarah snapped over the violence Bonnie perpetrated?

Virginia Walton was the snitch because she could have pulled out the original thesis and started talking.

Yari Malek was the filth responsible for turning Bonnie into a whore. Aleta—if she hadn't been killed—was another enabler.

Erin watched the house, bouncing in her seat and tapping her uneven fingernails against the steering wheel. Where the hell were Beckett and Fowler?

A call came through her Bluetooth, flashing onto the car's touchscreen as unknown. Erin's eyes never left the Archers' home. "Mina?"

The dark drapes in the house's front bay window parted. "I see you, Princess. Do you want to come play?"

Adrenaline flushed through her system until Erin's throat nearly closed. She should stall the girl and wait for Beckett, but the child could be attacked at any moment. Erin took the safety off her gun and exited the car. "Of course I want to play. I've been trying to find you for weeks."

The little girl giggled. "I know. I like games."

"Me too." Erin moved slowly up the walk, trying to see inside the small opening in the drapes. They fell closed, and Erin dropped to a crouch. Jane's weapon of choice appeared to be a knife, but Erin didn't know whether the Archer's kept a gun in the house.

The click of a lock escaped into the stillness.

Erin's gaze shot to the front door slowly opening into a mouth of darkness. "Mina? Is that you? Come out to me, sweetheart."

Pale feet appeared first. Erin tried to draw a breath, but her lungs fought against her. Never moving from her crouch, she slipped the gun out of its holster at her waist, keeping the weapon low. "Mina, are you coming out to play with me?"

Sarah Archer moved into the open doorway. Shadows obscured her face as she stepped onto the granite entry clutching a large knife dripping with blood. Her blonde hair stuck up in the back and tangled around her face. Dark streaks marred her ghostly white nightshirt.

"Princess." The excited, childlike voice of Mina singsonged from Sarah's lips.

Erin went cold and still inside, but her entire body convulsed.

"I told Jane not to do it. But she never listens to me."

Chapter Forty-Three

"**M**ina." Erin's mind stayed blank. Had she jumped into another dimension? "Sweetheart, can you come closer? I can't see you very well." The pieces clicked together. *I had called Sarah from my personal cell. That's how Mina got the number.*

Sarah cocked her head, revealing clumps of blood on her neck. "Okay."

Slowly, she padded forward on tiptoes, the unmistakable gait of a whimsical child. The movement triggered a motion sensor, and artificial light suddenly bathed the front of the house. Sarah froze. Her eyes popped wide, and her mouth curled up like a toddler getting ready to wail. She jerked the knife into a defensive stance. In her other hand, she held an old, beat-up, leather-bound book.

"Mina, shut up." Her new voice was a tenor and decidedly masculine. Her expression shifted from a scared little girl to a surly teenager. "You're going to get us all in trouble."

Erin's knees throbbed, but she didn't dare stand up. "Charlie?"

Sarah's narrowed eyes met Erin's. Her lips curled in cocky, adolescent defiance. "Go away. I've got the situation under

344

control." Her—*his*—voice cracked at the last word.

Her brain screamed this could not be real, but it very much was.

Charlie edged closer, knife still hiked up, face twisted.

Erin noticed more blood—Simon's or Melinda's? Or both? "Charlie, I don't want to piss you off, but I'm too old to be kneeling like this."

Charlie curled up his nose like he'd just noticed a steaming pile of dog shit. "You are old. You're what, like thirty-four?"

Erin mustered a smile. "Nice compliment. Thirty-eight and feeling every minute. Is it cool if I stand?"

He waved the knife, making blood fly. "Throw that gun behind you, and it's cool."

Erin obeyed, tossing the Sig Saur behind her into the soft yard. Hopefully, she hadn't thrown it so far she couldn't get to it if she dived fast enough. And the Taser rested inside her jacket, heavy and secure against her ribs. Her knees throbbed, and she made a show of shaking her legs out. "Thanks. So what's going on here?"

"I told you I got it under control." He cocked his hip, and his face twisted into a cocky, adolescent grin that turned Erin's stomach.

"That was you at the CID the other day," she said. "After I asked Sarah about being molested, she changed. I thought Sarah had just reverted to a self-defense mechanism, but you took over to protect her, didn't you?"

"No shit, Sherlock." Charlie rolled his eyes. "And I am the self-defense mechanism. That's my job." He tapped his chest with his fist.

Erin held up her hands and tried to believe she really faced an angry teenage boy. "Dude, okay. But you've got blood all over you. Are you hurt?"

"Not me." He noticed the nightgown and made a face. "She keeps fucking everything up. We just want to live our lives."

"Jane?"

Charlie's eyes narrowed. "What do you know about Jane?"

"She's signing her name at the crime scene," Erin said. "She's doing some bad shit, Charlie."

"I know!" The voice cracked again.

Ridiculously, Erin pictured Brad at that age. Every week, he seemed taller and his voice different. Erin got stuck with the acne, and Brad had taken her to a makeup artist to learn how to cover it up without caking the concealer on.

"We had her under control for a long time, and then Sarah went looking for Bonnie. Brought all that shit back up again."

Erin didn't know a lot about multiple personalities, but its' proponents believed horrific childhood sexual abuse to be the root cause. A child's fragile mind split into various parts to cope with the abuse. "At least Ted Moore is dead."

Charlie's cheeks flamed. "How did you know about him?"

"I figured it out." Erin lowered her voice, trying to sound friendly. No big deal. Two friends talking. "Did Jane kill him too?"

"Bonnie thought money would hurt him more."

"Bonnie knew about Jane and you and Mina?" Erin hoped no more people lived in Sarah's head.

"She didn't believe we were real." Charlie gazed at the knife handle. "When Sarah first told Bonnie, she still had control. That's what therapy was about—integrating us. We all worked together. Sarah didn't have blackouts. Most of the time, we stayed quiet.

And then Bonnie happened. And she didn't believe us!"

"That made you all mad?"

Charlie watched the blood dripping off the knife. "It made Sarah mad—and Jane, but Jane's always mad. Jane started being louder, and Sarah couldn't stay in one piece. I tried to speak up, but no one listens to me. Mina's the only one I can help."

The protector. Charlie cared about Sarah and Mina. Maybe Erin could use that to her advantage. "So what happened?"

"Sarah decided to prove it to Bonnie. She let Jane come out, and Bonnie recorded it on her stupid computer. She freaked out, but I don't think she believed it. But then everything went wrong. Jane kept coming out more and more. Sarah broke down. Me and Mina tried to hide." Charlie suddenly glared the knife. "Fuck!" The voice cracked again, going from a burgeoning baritone to a high tenor.

The sun continued to creep up in the east. Neighbors had to be starting their day. One of them would look outside and call the police.

Beckett would be here any minute.

Erin edged back a step. How far had she thrown the gun? "So why did she kill Bonnie?"

Charlie's heels rocked back, legs taut as if prepared to charge. "Sarah told Bonnie she was thinking about going back to therapy. Sarah knew Jane had taken over more and more, because she lost big chunks of time. And then she caught that Arab raping Bonnie. Except Bonnie liked it! She wanted him to do it! And then she told Bonnie about Simon, about what she saw him do ..."

"What did Bonnie see Simon do?" At least Erin had been right about the trigger to Bonnie's murder. The rest of the stuff she had yet to truly process.

"I tried to keep Mina from seeing it. But Sarah walked in and heard Bonnie screaming from upstairs." Charlie's head whipped back and forth, his free hand smacking against his temple. "We thought she was dying. That fucking Arab had her pinned down and did it to her from behind. She bled, too. We screamed at him to stop hurting her, but Bonnie said she needed him to do it. What the hell?"

"Bonnie was all kinds of messed up," Erin said. "Because of what happened to her and Sarah when they were kids. Sarah split apart, and she had you to help her. Bonnie didn't have anyone. What did Simon do? Did he abuse the girls too?"

Charlie's head dropped, and his shoulders shook. But Erin quickly recognized the laughter. She took another step back, edging closer to the gun. Sarah's head shot up. Charlie had vanished, and in his place, a feral cat appeared, her contrasting eyes gleaming with hate.

She pointed the dripping knife at Erin and spoke in a raw voice. "You shouldn't have come."

The British accent sent chills down Erin's spine. "Hello, Jane."

Chapter Forty-Four

A smile as taunting as the knife she wielded sliced through the air. "Erin Prince. I'm so glad to get the chance to meet you."

"You're quite a difficult person to track down."

"That's how I like it."

"I love your accent. It's British, right?"

Another chilling smile. "Right."

"So," Erin's trembling voice betrayed her fear. "Are you going to tell me what Simon did?"

Jane's lips twisted until her delicate looking face seemed savage. "He's a hypocritical bastard. He let a child rapist go free, even though he knew his own daughter had been a victim."

"He wanted to protect his reputation." Erin tried to slow her breathing, preserve her energy.

"And his hobby," Jane snapped. "Daddy dearest always played dress up with Sarah and Bonnie when they were little. No big deal—good fathers do that sort of thing, right?"

Mouth tasting like she'd eaten wet sand, Erin nodded.

"But I guess he liked it. Because he kept doing it after Sarah grew up. And then he started going out and pretending to be a woman. Mister high and mighty morals was a cross-dresser who

349

liked to go to strip clubs."

Nervous sweat stung Erin's eyes. "That's why Bonnie got so upset with Tori when she gave him a lap dance. She recognized her uncle."

"Aren't you clever?" Jane's accent dripped with sarcasm. "Bonnie didn't tell Sarah at first. Not until we realized Bonnie was a whore who needed to be punished. Then she told us about Simon, like that would somehow make me not want to tear out her guts!" Jane held up the knife, watching as the blood dripped onto the wet grass. "I made Simon put on his favorite dress before I killed him."

Fear made Erin's throat swell nearly shut. She had to keep talking. "Are you Jack the Ripper?"

Jane threw back her head and laughed. "You dumb bitch. You think I'm reincarnated or I time travelled?" She held up the book. "Abberline was right about the Ripper. Let me tell you my favorite passage. I know it by heart." Jane tilted her head back, the words coming out as melodic as a lullaby.

"A child saw me this morning on my way to the post and hid in the safety of her mother's skirts. Lesions eat the flesh on my face now. My limbs work slower. Soon I will no longer be able to wield the blade. But a wasp has asked for my assistance in ridding her putrid body of the child she created in sin. She may be my last. I will make her my greatest.

—9 November 1888"

"What is that book?" Erin asked, hoping to buy time.

"My ancestor's diary," Jane said. "Two greats down the line.

A midwife. A noble woman trying to rid the world of the filth around her. Lost to history—until now." She examined the knife, delicately tracing the blade with her finger and pressing her lips to the blood-covered skin. "I can't believe you're so surprised. Women kill all the time."

Erin's knees knocked together. She had no idea if Jane told the truth about the book or made up her own history. Both options made her bladder weak. "So you decided to emulate her?"

Jane shrugged. "I took her name because she's a hero. And Bonnie deserved to pay." Her face twisted, her focus still on the knife. "The things she did ..."

"What about Virginia Walton?" Erin prayed she could continue to buy time.

Jane sneered. "She called Sarah after the murder. She said Bonnie told her about us, but the professor didn't believe it. She didn't want to go to the police without talking to Sarah first." She held the knife up again, gazing at it as though she'd found a talisman. "I had to take care of her. But I couldn't take all the credit. The real Jane inspired me."

"The letters were a nice touch." Erin tasted blood and tried not to allow her fear to overwhelm her. "If I hadn't remembered Sarah's initials, I wouldn't have suspected her. Did she call the police when she realized what you did to Virginia?"

"Charlie's dumb ass did that," Jane's mouth curled up. "Always meddling." The glare of the security lights made her eyes black as a demon's. "And Sarah is weak. She's always been weak. I'm strong, and I take my strength from the heroine who scared the hell out of London in 1888. Gutting all those whores with such skill. No fear of anything. That's the way I want to live."

351

Erin didn't dare take her eyes off Jane. She visualized the yard behind her. The gun had to be close. "I think we'd all like to be able to live that way. Most of us don't have the guts to try."

"I'm not a fool," Jane's accent thickened, the menace still coloring her tone. "There are things I would have done differently."

"You killed Yari Malek. Where's Aleta Gilani?" The alcohol she'd consumed earlier might come up, but she had to act. "Nice of you to make sure you got both Bonnie's and Virginia's blood on his clothes."

"Wasn't it? I stole the same shirt he wore the night I caught him fucking Bonnie." Jane spit out the words, her pretty face twisted into pure evil. "That little Arab bitch got away. I'll find her." Jane's head was down, her eyes on the bloody knife, her hand white from her tight grip. "Ted Moore didn't. He came first. When I realized he was back in town, I had to act. He was alive when I cut off his dick and stuffed it into his mouth."

Erin gathered all her courage and took a quick step back.

Jane's gaze flashed up, a predator suddenly aware its prey was trying to escape. She slashed the bleeding knife upward, her long legs closing the distance between them before Erin could do anything more than raise her arms as a shield.

She screamed as the blade sliced through the tender flesh on the backside of her forearm.

Jane's fist slammed into Erin's stomach. She staggered back, feeling her insides knot into one painful mass. Jane screamed a war cry, raising the knife again. Erin dropped to her knees, the concrete tearing her jeans and her skin, and rolled for her gun. Her fingers raked through the muddy grass for the weapon, her knees and feet slipping in the struggle. Blood from her arm streaked over the dead lawn.

"Bitch!" Jane jammed the knife into Erin's calf.

She bit her tongue as the pain shot through her leg, every nerve ending on fire. But she kept digging forward.

Jane yanked the knife out, the burning sensation far worse than the attack. And then a strong foot slammed into the back of Erin's knee, snapping the joint in the wrong direction. Pain worse than childbirth tore through Erin, and she screamed into the wet earth, tasting the days of rain and lawn chemicals. Jane kept pressure on her knee, but Erin squirmed like a fish tossed out of water until she got her hand beneath her and inside her jacket. The gun was still too far away.

Erin's fingers closed around the Taser. She sucked in raw gasps of air, nauseated from the pain and the chemical taste on her tongue. Jane's athletic legs and youth kept Erin pinned. Jane liked to see her victims suffer. She would want to see Erin's face when she died. Going silent and forcing Jane to turn her over was her only chance. She forced her body to go limp.

A hand clawed at her shoulders. Erin allowed Jane to flip her over onto her back. She blinked against the bright yard lights, staring up at the twisted, bloody visage of the devil.

Her nightgown more bloody red than white, Sarah as Jane planted her feet on either side of Erin's hips. She spit on Erin's cheek.

A siren wailed. Nearby, maybe down the street, tires squealed. Erin blocked out the pain and made a final appeal. "Jane, let me talk to Sarah. We can help all of you to heal."

Jane laughed again, a hoarse, nightmarish sound certain to

haunt Erin's dreams.

"You can't heal a broken mind, Investigator." She kicked Erin hard in the stomach and then squatted over her as though about to take a piss. "I heard about your brother. Such a tragedy for your family." She grazed the knife down Erin's cheek, leaving a trail of Erin's own blood, and then down to her neck where her life force raced. "At least you'll get to join him a lot sooner than you expected."

Jane adjusted her grip on the knife, the blue eye cold as glacier ice and the brown gleaming like a cat ready to pounce.

"Stop!" Beckett shouted from somewhere behind them.

Jane's angry eyes shot up, and Erin pulled the Taser out of her coat and shot it straight into the girl's chest.

Jane wiggled like a beached seal. The knife fell. Erin grabbed it and threw it as hard as she could. She managed to roll onto her side as the other woman fell face first into the grass, her lean body still flopping.

Erin tried to get to her feet, but her injured leg didn't have the strength. Beckett's cold hands closed around her wrist, and he hauled her up.

His voice trembling, Fowler recited the Miranda rights as he cuffed a now still Sarah.

Erin dug her fingers into Beckett's shoulder in an effort to stand on her own.

"Ouch," he said.

"Don't tell me about ouch!" She shot back. "That crazy woman stabbed me twice."

Beckett leaned down to look at her leg.

Her soaked jeans and the hot pain told Erin the wound cut

deep.

"The paramedics are on their way, but you need to sit down so we can wrap that thing. You don't mess around with leg wounds."

She didn't argue, allowing him to help her over to the driveway. He took off his sweatshirt and used the arms to tie off her leg. "Why didn't you wait for me?"

"I intended to, but Mina called me."

Beckett's head swiveled from side to side. "Where is she?"

Erin stared at the young woman sitting up in the grass. Covered in blood, Sarah cried in pain, completely in a daze. Then, they locked eyes.

"Investigator Prince?" Sarah's normal voice broke through her sobs. "What's happened to me?"

Numb and cold to her core, Erin turned back to Beckett. "Right there, Todd. She's right there."

Chapter Forty-Five

"You're not serious." Beckett's legs jumped like he wanted to come out of his chair.

Erin sat beside him in the U.S. Attorney's office, but she stayed quiet. John Marsh, the U.S. Attorney assigned to Sarah Archer's case, liked to have the spotlight, and he didn't appreciate being questioned. Beckett would learn in time.

Marsh folded his hands over his immaculate cherry desk. His thick black hair was slicked back with a product that made him look more stylish than smarmy. In his mid-forties, the guy had a face for the cameras and the personality of a fetid asshole. He also had a reputation for never prosecuting a case he couldn't win.

"Investigator Beckett." Marsh spoke in a disinterested tone. "In the last six weeks, two different psychiatrists from leading mental health programs—including a psychiatrist from Johns Hopkins who's been extremely vocal about the legitimacy of DID over the last decade—have interviewed Sarah Archer and her various personalities."

DID—dissociative identity disorder—was the updated terminology for multiple personality disorder. The semantics didn't matter to Erin. She witnessed multiple personas sharing a body. Most nights she relived it time and time again in her nightmares.

"And this psychiatrist agrees that Sarah Archer is very likely the real deal." Marsh finished with the same firm tone he used at the end of his closing arguments.

Erin rolled her eyes and resisted the urge to remind him there were no cameras in the room. "Each personality is strikingly different, right down to body language, accent, and inflection. Sarah's original psychiatrist who diagnosed her with DID provided recordings of their early sessions. Every personality acted the same as they do now, down to the smallest details. If Sarah faked all of this, she would have slipped up somewhere."

Beckett rocked back in his chair. "You do realize this diagnosis is so overused by defense attorneys it's cliché?"

Marsh's face reddened, and a thick strand of his carefully styled hair cowlicked to his glistening forehead. "I have some experience in the courtroom, Beckett. But I have to make my decision based on the evidence presented and the diagnosis of people a lot smarter than I am."

"And they're absolutely certain she didn't fake the entire thing?"

Marsh took off his designer glasses and made a show of cleaning them with a green cloth from his top desk drawer. "Nothing is certain in this world, Beckett. What I can tell you is after listening to the experts and watching the video recovered from Yari Malek's safe deposit box, Sarah is a very sick girl. She believes she has multiple personalities, and there's nothing to indicate she had any awareness of what went on—including the moment she sliced her father's throat."

Bonnie must have realized the danger from her cousin. A few

days before her death, she mailed Yari Malek a flash drive containing the video of Sarah's personalities. He'd put the drive in a safe deposit box and kept his mouth shut. For the past six weeks, Beckett and Erin had kept an eye on the unidentified females coming into the morgue, but so far, it appeared Jane had been telling the truth. Malek likely sent Aleta away to safety—but she hadn't been sure she could trust him, so she'd provided Erin and Beckett with her side of the story before slipping away with her family. The FBI believed Aleta's uncle to be one of the top men in the D.C. mob. Erin wished them luck proving it.

Simon Archer's corpse had been found wearing a black dress and wig, his throat sliced so deeply his neck had been nearly severed. Melinda admitted he'd been cross-dressing for years. She had no idea he'd accidentally propositioned his estranged niece at Sid's.

From her hospital bed, her scarred face far from healed, Melinda Archer told how she and Simon quietly enrolled a teenage Sarah in the care of a therapist after weeks of bizarre episodes. The therapist treated her for DID and, by the time Sarah started her freshman year of college, pronounced her personalities integrated—meaning they were aware of each other and able to function with Sarah in complete control. But in the weeks leading up to Bonnie's murder, Melinda noticed her daughter slipping into old patterns. She lost hours of time. She talked in strange voices and became more and more withdrawn. The video Bonnie recorded of her cousin a few days before her murder also worked in Sarah's favor. At the time, Sarah claimed she still had control and allowed the personalities to speak, but in the video, she appeared to fight for control, and Jane screamed Sarah would destroy them all. In short, the girl appeared to be coming unhinged.

The night of Bonnie's murder, Sarah broke the lock on her bedroom window and snuck out. She walked the half-mile to the nearest Metro station and rode it to Columbia Heights. Melinda didn't want to believe it could be true, but after Virginia Walton's murder, she had her home security footage pulled. She saw Sarah both nights, sneaking out. Melinda had the video destroyed. She told Erin this in a deadpan tone, likely well-beyond guilt. Melinda Archer's desperation to protect her child cost lives—and Melinda's spirit.

"And don't forget the diary," Marsh said.

The diary, in Erin's opinion, had to be the grand jewel of the evidence. Melinda Archer confirmed the story Jane told Erin that night. The diary was a family heirloom and semi-dirty secret. An antiquities expert declared the diary to be at least 100 years old. Erin didn't know if its authenticity as the Ripper's journal would ever be proven, but the aged letter tucked into the back of the diary proved that in December 1888, from her presumed death bed, Jane Blackwood took responsibility for the Ripper killings. The midwife had contracted what sounded like syphilis and blamed her husband for sleeping with the London prostitutes. She'd shipped her young son to America to live with his uncle and sent the diary, along with the letter. Historical records in London's old Whitechapel area did confirm a Jane Blackwood's birth in 1864, but death records had yet to be found.

Every one of the passages found at the crime scenes were diary entries from Jane Blackwood's leather journal—entries which also described the Ripper killings in great detail.

Her mother claimed Sarah had been fascinated with the family history from a young age and copied the letters as a way of coping with her psychological issues. If experts declared the diary to be a legitimate record of the Ripper murders, the historical significance would be staggering.

"But Investigator Prince's testimony helped me make my final decision." He looked pointedly at Erin, expecting her endorsement.

Erin didn't want to argue with Beckett. "You don't understand. I don't either. I just know what I saw. And there's no way it wasn't real."

Beckett shook his head and held up his hands. "This is the wrong decision."

"What if she did fake it?" Erin asked. "Then she faked it as a teenager, faked it through treatment. Faked it with everyone for years. And even if that's true, wouldn't she have to be extremely mentally disturbed?"

"Plenty of people on death row are mentally disturbed," Beckett said. "But they can still stand trial. You don't think Sarah was in her right mind when she handed me the letter she wrote and told me the killer sent it?"

Marsh's mouth tightened. "The psychiatrist believes that is another symptom of her illness. And we've all agreed Sarah Archer is unable to stand trial." Marsh spoke with finality. "There's no reason to put Melinda through anything more than what she's already experienced."

"And Simon looking the other way about his niece and daughter being molested remains a secret," Beckett snapped.

Marsh's eyes glittered. "That has nothing to do with the

360

decision."

A lie. Melinda still had connections. Marsh had political aspirations. The combinations led to a decision to commit Sarah to the continuing care program at McLean Hospital in Massachusetts. A team of psychiatrists would continue to grill and evaluate her progress. If at any time they believed the decision to be false, charges could still be brought. Erin expected as much, but she and Beckett weren't aware of the official decision until today. Bonnie's parents and Rylan Walton had filed suit against the District this morning, naming both Erin and Beckett as potential witnesses.

"Let me tell you what would happen if we decided to take her to trial," Marsh said. "After graphically detailing her sexual abuse, a defense attorney would put Sarah on the stand, and those personalities would emerge. The jury would see what Investigator Prince saw that night. More than likely, she's found not guilty by reason of insanity. And then where do you think she goes? A psychiatric hospital. The decision we've made skips the waste of tax dollars and my time."

"What if she's found guilty?" Beckett demanded.

Marsh waived him off. "Wouldn't happen."

Beckett stood and started for the door. "You're making a mistake that's going to come back to haunt you. Someday, she'll be out."

"I realize you've worked some extremely unusual cases, Investigator," Marsh said. "Perhaps your experience is diluting your judgment."

"And Melinda Archer's deep pockets are affecting yours." Beckett stalked out.

Erin moved to follow, her knee burning. Her stab wounds had mostly healed, although she still endured the sting of healing nerves in her calf, and the knee Sarah knocked out of place throbbed for no reason at times. One day, she'd start the physical therapy the doctor recommended.

"Investigator Prince."

She turned and regarded Marsh in silence, waiting for him to finish so she could catch up with Beckett.

Marsh sat in his big leather chair the way a king might preside over his court. "You agree Sarah belongs in a psychiatric facility?"

Erin hated going against her partner. He was a good man, a good cop, and a good friend. But he hadn't witnessed it. "Yes."

Beckett waited for her in the expansive lobby. He jammed his hands in his pockets and said nothing as they walked into the winter cold. January had arrived with a vengeance, dropping nearly a foot of snow over the city.

"You didn't see her." Erin spoke once they'd escaped to the relative warmth of the Impala. "You didn't see the way these people crawled out of her. Like she was possessed.

"A mental institution is her only chance to get normal again. It's likely she'll never be released. You know that, right?" Erin shouldn't care about Sarah. But every time she thought about the way Sarah cried when she realized her father died at her own hands, Erin agonized over not figuring it all out sooner. If she and Beckett had gone through Virginia's papers earlier instead of shunting them aside, then maybe Sarah wouldn't have had to live with having killed her father.

"Tell that to her aunt and uncle and to Rylan Walton."

In addition to the suit against the city, Neil and Carmen, along with Rylan, filed a wrongful death suit against Sarah and Melinda Archer. It likely wouldn't make it to court, but their tell-all book would make more money than Simon's estate could ever pay them.

"At least the Malek family won't be joining the suit," Beckett said. "Since the bastard tricked out little girls for years."

Additional investigation into Malek's computer and financial records showed Bonnie Archer wasn't the first child he'd plucked off the streets. DNA results showed Yari Malek to be the father of Bonnie's baby and probably other girls as well. Erin delivered the news to Will Merritt, and she couldn't tell whether sorrow or relief fueled his tears.

"You were right all along," Beckett said. "I didn't want to believe the killer was a woman—I didn't want to fight that sort of evil again."

Erin took little solace from his compliment. "You were right, too. I wasn't able to be objective with Sarah because I saw myself in her life. If I had, maybe Malek and Simon could have been saved. Even if they were scum."

A wry smile crept over Beckett's face. "Fair enough. But you had no clue how many people called Sarah's head home."

"So you do believe she's a true case of dissociative identity?"

"I don't know," Beckett said. "But a mental institution doesn't seem like justice for all of the people she killed. She'll never have to answer for those murders."

"What about Melinda? She should be charged with obstruction of justice at the least. And she's partially responsible for Virginia, Yari, and Simon's deaths. Everything she did to protect her child was wrong. If she'd done the right thing as soon as she suspected Sarah had come apart again, they might still be alive."

Beckett's dark eyes shot to hers, an emotion in them she couldn't quite place.

"For some people, right and wrong are both shades of gray."

Erin laughed and started the car. "I'm pretty sure that's a line from a movie."

"No, it isn't." Beckett turned up the heat on his side and held his hand over the vent.

"Pretty sure it is."

"You should come to dinner tonight. Lucy would love to see Abby."

In the weeks since Brad's death, Erin and Abby had taken Lucy Kendall's advice and had started seeing a grief counselor. And Lucy and Beckett had slowly become a part of their lives. Abby thought Lucy was the most beautiful, fascinating creature on earth. And Lucy seemed to love her as well. Erin just liked seeing her daughter smile again.

"We will, but it will be closer to six," Erin said. "I've got a stop to make."

Chapter Forty-Six

Erin hadn't been to her brother's grave since his headstone had been placed. Her mother wanted an ornate huge granite stone with Brad's face carved in it. Erin argued against it, knowing it wasn't what Brad would want. To her shock, Lisa took Erin's side, and Calvin followed. So Brad's black granite stone was simple and beautiful, with a short epitaph: *Beloved son, brother, and uncle.*

Erin used her gloved hand to clean off the freezing snow and then stood with her shoulders rounded against the north wind.

"I finally went to the doctor." Her voice sounded small against the cold gusts. "I guess we're still two peas out of the same pod. The neurologist found a tiny aneurysm. She compared it to the scans Judy Temple took of yours and said mine is a lot smaller. It's not ready to be operated on yet, but she thinks it will be in a few months. So I've got to go back for checkups. And when it's ready, I guess I'm getting some of my head shaved."

Erin still couldn't grasp that she had a ticking bomb in her brain, ready to explode without warning. The diagnosis was still too fresh, too close to the loss of Brad—too unreal. And she didn't feel any different.

Erin laughed, the cold air making her breathless. "Guess who

365

went with me to both appointments? Lisa. She even held my hand when the doctor told me." Getting to know her sister wasn't as comforting as the companionship of her twin, but Erin appreciated their time together. "I haven't told Mom and Dad. But I will."

She banded her arms across her bulky down winter coat. "I miss you every fucking day, Brad. But you wouldn't want me to sit around feeling sorry for myself, so I'm trying to move on. For Abby. That's why I'm having the surgery. I've got to be there for my daughter." Her voice cracked like a teenager's. "And I miss the shit out of you, but I don't want to die. Not yet."

The wind gusted again, dusk rolled in from the west, and Erin decided to call it a day. Besides, her friends expected her for supper.

As she trudged through the foot of snow on the way back to the car, she thought about the different ways the mind could break and how people dealt with it. Bonnie Archer's broke, and she punished the body she hated. Sarah's broke, and she split into parts to cope. Brad didn't have the chance to fix his.

"But I do," Erin whispered. "I guess you can heal a broken mind after all."

She stopped in the middle of a snowdrift. The cold cascaded into her boots, and the ice shot up her spine like nails. She heard Sarah Archer's soft voice in her head from the day they met at the station—*I finally accepted you can't always understand a broken mind.* Erin's memory then flashed to Jane sneering down at her, ready to plunge the knife into her stomach, and replayed the feral woman's words—*You can't heal a broken mind, Investigator.*

Erin stood still until the cold pierced her heavy coat and her legs like blocks of ice.

What if Sarah Archer had known what she was doing all along?

Chapter Forty-Seven

My Dear Brother,

The end comes for me. My waking hours are fewer and fewer, and much of my time is spent in a state of madness. Visions of things which are not present, a rage I have no hope of stowing, and such pain I am ready for death.

Before I depart this world and answer for my sins, I must leave the truth for the child I sent with you to America. I know you care for him as your own, and I pray he brings you peace over the death of your precious son. With God's grace, this diary will find you in the capital of America. Many of the accounts are of the mundane sort, the daily activities I now long for. But within the pages is a truth I must pass on to my son.

Dearest child, know that I sent you away for your own safety. The despicable French disease

367

given to me by your wayward father progressed far more rapidly than I expected. Lesions, fever, loss of body weight, and fatigue I accepted. But the mental decline placed you in mortal danger. That I could not allow. And so I gave you to your uncle. I pray someday you will understand my choice.

Know this, my son. The Great Evil is a scourge on good society. It will destroy your life and the lives of everyone around you. Beware the female wasps offering their bodies for a pittance. They spread disease and death and despair. Is it any wonder I tried to cleanse the city?

Mary Ann Nicols. Annie Chapman. Elizabeth Stride. Catharine Eddowes. And lovely Mary Kelly, blessed with a child she happily discarded. By the blade of my father's surgical knives, those five will spread their filth to no other man.

I am weak, and the demon in my brain is stronger. It will not be long.

Remember always, your mother loved you enough to give you a new life.

After I am gone, do what you will with this

*truth. My only concern is that you know what
I tried to do for your well-being.*

*All my love,
Your mother,*

*Jane Blackwood
—JTR*

Mina liked the hospital because their private room looked out over a great big snow-covered yard with lots of bird feeders and colorful winter birds making tracks over the snow.

* * *

Charlie liked the hospital in Massachusetts because their mother said it was affiliated with Harvard, and that's where he dreamed of going to school. Maybe if Sarah had gone to college out of state like he wanted, they wouldn't be here watching a bunch of birds fight for food in the snow.

* * *

Jane hated being in hospital. She hated the view, she hated the staff, and she hated all of them. But she always had, ever since Sarah split apart. Because they were weak and stupid and couldn't take care of themselves. Jane spent their childhood fighting for them, only to have Sarah go to that fat, big-haired doctor and learn how to "integrate." If the bitch hadn't taught Sarah control, they wouldn't be in this mess. Jane would have been in charge a long time ago. But she'd been labeled the fucking bad girl, the psychopath who wanted to be like Jack the Ripper. Like Jack the Ripper was a woman. That had to be the dumbest theory of all the dumb theories about the madman.

* * *

Sitting quietly in the cozy chair overlooking the picturesque winter scene, Sarah Archer commanded the voices in her head to be silent.

And then she smiled.

about the author

Stacy Green is the author of the Lucy Kendall thriller series and the Delta Crossroads mystery trilogy. All Good Deeds (Lucy Kendall #1) won a bronze medal for mystery and thriller at the 2015 IPPY Awards. Tin God (Delta Crossroads #1) was runner-up for best mystery/thriller at the 2013 Kindle Book Awards. Her next novel is Lovely Boys (The Katy Madison Series).

Stacy has a love of thrillers and crime fiction, and she is always looking for the next dark and twisted novel to enjoy. She started her career in journalism before becoming a stay at home mother and rediscovering her love of writing.

She lives in Iowa with her husband and daughter and their three spoiled fur babies.

www.stacygreenauthor.com

OTHER TITLES FROM
VESUVIAN BOOKS

Hell has a new master

BLACKWELL

Alexandrea Weis with Lucas Astor

Via Tapas Media 9.13.16
In print and ebook 1.17.17

Hell has a new master

BLACKWELL

By Alexandrea Weis with Lucas Astor

In the late 1800s, handsome, wealthy New Englander, Magnus Blackwell, is the envy of all.

When Magnus meets Jacob O'Conner—a Harvard student from the working class—an unlikely friendship is forged. But their close bond is soon challenged by a captivating woman; a woman Magnus wants, but Jacob gets.

Devastated, Magnus seeks solace in a trip to New Orleans. After a chance meeting with Oscar Wilde, he becomes immersed in a world of depravity and brutality, inevitably becoming the inspiration for Dorian Gray. Armed with the forbidden magic of voodoo, he sets his sights on winning back the woman Jacob stole from him.

Amid the trappings of Victorian society, two men, bent on revenge, will lay the foundation for a curse that will forever alter their destinies.

SOUTHERN GOTHIC

A NOVEL

DALE WILEY

In print and ebook January 2017

SOUTHERN GOTHIC
A NOVEL

By Daley Wiley

Aspiring author Meredith Harper owns the hottest bookstore in Savannah.

Michael Black is her favorite writer—long thought dead—until he mysteriously approaches Meredith with a new manuscript, and a most unusual offer. Meredith can keep the manuscript to herself, or publish it under her own name.

Her decision results in a bestseller, but the novel contains a coded secret; one that will put her on trial for murder and in hiding from "the blood stalker," proving too late that making a deal with the devil comes at a heavy price.

Made in the USA
Middletown, DE
21 September 2016